For

from Brennan's

friend

May.   Mick   1991.

The
Campbell
Companion

The Campbell Companion

The best of Patrick Campbell
Edited and introduced by Ulick O'Connor

PAVILION
MICHAEL JOSEPH

First published in Great Britain in 1987 by
Pavilion Books Limited
196 Shaftesbury Avenue, London WC2H 8JL
in association with Michael Joseph Limited
27 Wrights Lane, Kensington, London W8 5TZ

British Cataloguing in Publication Data
Campbell, Patrick, *1913–1980*
The Campbell Companion.
I. Title   II. O'Connor, Ulick
823'.914   F   PR6013.L43

ISBN 1–85145–147–1

Printed and bound in Great Britain by
Billings & Sons Limited, Worcester

Acknowledgements
I would like to thank Lady Glenavy for giving me permission to
compile this collection.
I would also like to express my gratitude to A. T. Cross
Limited for their help while I was working on this book.
Among those who generously helped me with their recollec-
tions in writing this memoir were Brian Inglis, Jennifer
Johnston, Ned Sherrin, Francis Stuart, Eamonn Andrews,
Monk Gibbon, John Kelly (St. John's College, Oxford), The
Daily Telegraph Library, Tony Lennon (*Irish Times*), Sir Dennis
Hamilton, John Lovesey (*Sunday Times*), Geraldine Fitzgerald,
the late Michael MacLiammoir.

Contents

Patrick Campbell – a biographical memoir

One of the remarkable things about Patrick Campbell is how someone who had, on his own admission, read so few of the English classics, was able to write in a manner which would allow him to rank with modern day masters of the humorous essay, authors such as James Thurber and Stephen Leacock.

Someone once asked him how he had made his living for twenty-five years by writing and yet didn't seem to know the first thing about literature. He had no explanation other than to reaffirm that not only had he never read a word of Thackeray, Carlyle, Donne or Thomas Hardy, but even a rudimentary account of a plot of any of Shakespeare's plays was beyond him, nor could he even state with certainty whether it was Keats or Shelley who had written the 'Ode to a Skylark'. As a boy Paddy had read, on his mother's recommendation, *Candida* ('Shaw's all right') in between motor-cycling magazines and the adventures of Buffalo Bill, and found the play as good as a detective story; in later years he would delight in Tolstoy and Proust, but he had none of the passion for the classics one would have expected in a writer. The only clue he would give as to how he had become such a widely recognized writer was that his mother didn't believe in pushing people on the principle that 'it will be all right in the end' and that in this rather negative way he had stumbled on his proper vocation.

The fact is, however, that one reason why Patrick Campbell became a writer was that he was born into a culture which has produced more masters of the English language per head of the population than any community in the English-speaking world, among them Goldsmith, Sheridan, Shaw, Wilde, Yeats, Synge and Samuel Beckett. His native city of Dublin is the only one which has produced three Nobel Prize winners for literature. In the Anglo-Irish world where Patrick grew up there was a special feeling for language, imagery and wit, derived from the fact that it straddled two cultures, which provided a natural kindling for anyone wishing to embark on a literary career. When one considers that Patrick Campbell's father, later a brilliant civil servant and banker, was a frustrated writer whose early work had been admired by D.H. Lawrence and Middleton Murry, and that his mother was a distinguished painter, it is not surprising that their elder son should have turned out to be what Shaw claimed himself to be – 'a born writer'.

Patrick Campbell's grandfather's grandfather was probably a policeman in the little Ulster village of Glenavy. This wasn't a subject much discussed by the first Lord Glenavy, James Campbell, who was Paddy's grandfather and somewhat of a snob. James Campbell had been a contemporary at Trinity College, Dublin, of Oscar Wilde and Edward Carson, who later became leader of the Unionist Party and Lord Justice of Appeal. Campbell had backed Carson in the Ulster revolt against Home Rule and, as Solicitor General, had prosecuted the leaders of the rebellion in Dublin in 1916, securing death sentences for ninety of the rebels. In fact, he had done all the right things to have ended up as he did, Lord Chancellor of Ireland, just before the English pulled out of Southern Ireland in 1921.

Not a particularly good pedigree, one would have thought, for a man hoping to make his mark in a new State born (after a particularly ferocious guerilla war) out of that rebellion of 1916. But James Campbell, who was a man of particularly nimble mind, performed a neat side step into the new Irish Senate where he was immediately made Chairman. He brought to this position a sense of fair play and administrative skill that earned him much respect from both sides in Irish politics and which played not an insignificant part in stabilizing the country in the first years of the new State.

The last Irish Lord Chancellor was a man of noted good looks and patrician appearance. He kept a Dublin mansion with an enormous staff, and, during the last years of his life, spent quite a lot of time and money on the gambling tables at Monte Carlo. When he died in 1928 the poet W.B. Yeats (who was also a member of the Senate) wrote to his son:

> Lord Glenavy was the best Chairman I have ever come across and as Chairman of the Senate he impressed upon that body a dignity that should outlast our time. Handsome, watchful, vigorous, dominating, courteous, he seemed like some figure from a historical painting . . .

His son Gordon (Paddy's father) was educated at Charterhouse and then entered Woolwich Royal Military Academy where he became a second lieutenant in the Royal Engineers and an expert in explosives. His Fabian views not being particularly acceptable in the mess, he was encouraged to leave after five years' service, and was called to the Bar at Gray's Inn in 1911.

In 1912 Gordon married a Dublin painter, Beatrice Elvery, who had studied at the Slade, was a Royal Hibernian Academician, a sculptress, a stained-glass worker, and a pupil of Orpen who had done a well-known painting of her entitled 'An Irish Beauty'. According to Paddy's brother, Michael, 'the groom excepted, the Campbells did not appear at the wedding perhaps because "the bride was in trade" or perhaps because she was an "artist" and had drawn models in the nude'. (The Elverys owned a chain of sports shops in Dublin.) Gordon and Beatrice decided to set up house in London where Gordon entered chambers and set up practice as a barrister.

Their house, 9, Selwood Terrace, off the Fulham Road, was to become a meeting place for writers and painters. Their close friends included D.H. Lawrence, Katherine Mansfield, Middleton Murry, Mark Gertler, Dorothy Brett and Dora Carrington. Gordon was very far from being a dry-as-dust barrister interested only in untying briefs. He had a ranging mind and, encouraged by Lawrence, wrote a novel which, Lawrence reported to him, Middleton Murry and Katherine Mansfield 'were wildly enthusiastic about'. Lawrence even went so far on one occasion as to announce that Gordon was 'the only man in England to whom I can say so much', but warned him against 'ecstasy and exaltation' and 'falling into the trap of understanding the artist's position without being prepared to sacrifice the world'.

9

Gordon's conversation, a mixture of fantasy and mockery, so intrigued Lawrence and Murry that they christened it 'Campbelling', recognizing it as a specifically Irish exercise which they were unable to imitate. He seems for a while to have exercised an almost messianic power over some of them. A letter written to Gordon by Middleton Murry after they had gone on a hiking trip in 1913 and Gordon had read his novel to Murry suggests a personality of a magnetic and compelling kind:

> It took me all that time to make up my mind that you had failed me. Besides my love for you grew quietly and in secret. I never knew that it was there until it snapped at about eight o'clock of the night last Saturday week if you would know. It took two years. I can't get rid of it in a day. . . . We might have pulled off some great thing together; but you were divided, perhaps I was divided too. Perhaps we came together too late.

Gordon's wife Beatrice (known to her friends as Beattie) had become close to Katherine Mansfield. Katherine, who shared Beattie's reservations about Lawrence's character, told her that she thought Lawrence was 'a black creature and an anarchist who saw everything as really phallic from fountain pens downwards', while Beattie thought he had been reduced to a 'gentle bearded shadow' by Frieda, his German wife.

Though sometimes they sat at home darning socks while their husbands were away, the two young women had individual artistic careers of their own. Beattie continued her painting career begun in Dublin while Katherine was constantly working at short stories or a novel. Dora Carrington induced both of them to take part in a famous matinée at the Chelsea Palace Theatre in aid of Miss Lena Ashwell's concert for the Front which included sketches about Rossetti and Whistler and ended up with a finale in praise of Augustus John. Katherine and Beattie were members of a chorus that included Jack Buchanan, Violet Lorraine and Ellen Terry. They slouched on, took poses about the stage like Augustus' drawings, and sang:

John, John, how he's got on,
He owes it, he knows it, to me.
Brass ear-rings I wear and I don't do my hair,
And my feet are as bare as can be.
When I walk down the street, the people I meet

All stare at the things I've got on.
When Battersea-Parking, you'll hear folks remarking
There goes an Augustus John.

Though Lawrence wanted Gordon and Murry to involve themselves in 'an Isle of the Blest', which he called Rananin and for which he had written a constitution, Gordon decided not to lend his organizational ability and capital to the scheme, but instead to join the Ministry for Munitions. He was to become Assistant Controller of this department from 1915 to 1918. That he made an important contribution to the war effort is evident from a letter written in 1917 by Winston Churchill to Gordon's father, Lord Glenavy:

> I have been much struck by the knowledge and ability which your son has displayed in the extremely intricate and trouble-some labour business we have had to transact.

After the war Gordon was faced with a decision which was to have a profound influence on his life. Would he stay in London and continue his career as a civil servant, perhaps writing on the side and keeping up his contact with that remarkable literary circle, or would he return to Ireland?

Things had changed radically in his own country. A new independent State had been set up in the southern part of Ireland. What seemed significant was that Gordon's father had decided to row in with the new regime. After making enquiries about the opportunities available, Gordon found himself offered the post of Secretary of the Department of Industry and Commerce in Dublin. He and Beattie returned home in the autumn of 1922 bringing with them their two children, Brigid, born in 1914, and Patrick, born in 1913. (It is an indication of how the parents had felt about keeping up their links with their native country, that Beattie should have returned to Dublin for the birth of both Paddy and Biddy (as they were later to be called) so that the children could be born in Ireland.)

They took a fine house, Clonard, in its own grounds at Terenure near the city and began what was virtually a new life for both of them. The first few months there were not auspicious. A civil war had broken out, the counter revolution was in progress and those who were part of the new administration were in constant danger of attack from anti-Free State forces. As the residence of a senior civil servant, Gordon's house was a target and, predictably, one night a group of guerillas arrived and politely asked the family and servants to vacate the premises while they set fire to it. Beattie argued with them in her own persuasive way, and succeeded in saving not only most of the valuables in the house before it was set on fire (Paddy recalled that 'she had five of the men working for her, running in and out with armfuls of books, pictures and ornaments') but, much to the children's delight, salvaged their Christmas presents as well. It turned out the next day that little damage had been done to Clonard and they were able to return there after a week or two living in grandfather Glenavy's mansion in Milltown.

Life in the twenties in Dublin could be exciting for a privileged class and before the revolution the Campbells had been part of such a class. Now it seemed that under the new regime not much had changed. Levées were still held by the Governor General in the Vice-Regal Lodge formerly occupied by the Lord Lieutenant. As a former garrison capital Dublin, apart from being the only city in Western Europe (with the exception of St Petersburg) designed throughout in a classical idiom, still retained the opportunities for leisure which had been available to the ruling clique. There were thirteen golf clubs within fifteen minutes of the centre of the city, four racecourses and a vast park for riding in and playing polo. At the Fitzwilliam Lawn Tennis Club Championships (it is the second oldest club in existence) the best players in the world were to be seen. Gordon's brother, Cecil, who was a Wimbledon finalist, was one of the stars there, and had beaten Jean Borotra in the Davis Cup competition. Cecil was a financial adviser to the Egyptian government and was a larger-than-life figure who used to stride onto the tennis court dressed in a full-length, tailor-made, lambswool white coat which he would carelessly toss to the ball boys before serving a few loose balls across the net.

The Dublin Horse Show, one of the leading shows in the world, continued as usual except that Ireland was now represented by a team from the equitation school of the new Irish army. In 1924 world-famous athletes, along with 'worthies' such as Augustus John, Compton Mackenzie, Ranjitsinhji, G.K. Chesterton and Edwin Lutyens, gathered for the Tailteann

Games, an attempt to revive an ancient Celtic gathering in the manner of the Olympic Games.

In those days before expense-account eating there was no proliferation of restaurants; but those which were available could rank with the best in Europe. The Dolphin, Jammets, the Red Bank, had the sort of service and style that could only have been generated in a colonial atmosphere like that of the pre-First War period.

At the Abbey Theatre you could see the new playwrights, Lennox Robinson, Sean O'Casey and T.C. Murray, as well as plays by Lady Gregory and J.M. Synge. Abbey actors such as F.J. McCormick, Barry Fitzgerald and Maire O'Neill were already beginning to acquire a world reputation. At the Gate Theatre, Hilton Edwards and Michael MacLiammoir were creating an ensemble which featured avant-garde plays from the continent, and advanced techniques of lighting and production.

Yeats himself was now a senator and was a public figure in the city. George Russell, the poet, was editing the *Irish Statesman* while young writers like Frank O'Connor, Liam O'Flaherty and Sean O'Faolain were making an impact outside Ireland.

In sport the atmosphere of the times seemed to affect the standard of excellence. In 1926 Ireland beat England, Scotland and France at rugby for the first time with the best back line they had ever had and with forwards led by the legendary 'Jammy' Clinch, while at the Los Angeles Olympics a tiny Irish team won two gold medals, in the hurdles and the hammer.

With their special gift for social intercourse, Gordon and Beattie's new house, Rockbrook, which stood in its own grounds on the edge of the Dublin foothills, soon became a centre for writers, artists, actors, athletes and talkers. Among the people who came there between the wars were Orson Welles, Denis Johnston, Samuel Beckett, Thornton Wilder, John Middleton Murry, Marcel Marceau, J.B. Priestley, John O'Hara, Michael MacLiammoir, Hilton Edwards, Frank O'Connor, Geraldine Fitzgerald, Elizabeth Bowen, Feliks Topolski, Constance Spry, Peggy Ashcroft, Erskine Childers, Cornelia Otis Skinner, Larry Adler, Henry Williamson, A.P. Herbert, Siobhan McKenna and Joseph Hone.

Denis Johnston, the playwright, remembered that while the

talk was brilliant, the replies one got at Rockbrook could be unpredictable. One night he went up to Samuel Beckett and asked him for a lift home, remarking that they lived near one another. Sam replied simply 'No' (Johnston added in an aside to the writer, 'And he's been saying "No" in his plays ever since'). Johnston had a theory that there was almost an unwritten rule at Rockbrook that one or other of the guests would be broken on the wheel of conversation before the night was out. This stopped him from going there very often. On the other hand, his daughter Jennifer Johnston, the novelist, revelled in the cut and thrust of the talk. 'I admit that you had to be tough to be able to take it but it was fun,' she explains, 'and my mother [Shelagh Richards, the Abbey actress] just loved it. Those who couldn't take the rows never came back. And Paddy was definitely one of the "rowers" – make no mistake about that.'

Gordon's talk had broadened from the old days in Selwood Terrace in London. He would make conversational leaps from Schopenhauer and Nietzsche, to a discussion about the winner at Leopardstown racecourse that afternoon, to the latest play at the Abbey or Gate, all the time informing his talk with sardonic and derisive comment.

To hear Gordon in full flight for the first time could be an alarming experience. No one was exempt from the lash of his tongue. Friends, relations, institutions, religions were attacked with such indiscriminate savagery that it took a while before one realized that this was just 'Campbelling' and learned to take it in one's stride.

One of the beguiling features of his brilliant tirades was that he seemed to take as much delight in attacks against himself as in those he delivered against others, provided they were couched in sufficiently amusing terms. He related to me once with gusto how because of his chairmanship of both the Turf Board (which manufactures peat as a source of fuel in Ireland) and the tailoring firm Burtons, Oliver St John Gogarty had christened him 'Lord Sackcloth and Ashes'. Another day when I met him on the tram (he liked public transport as he had a free pass as a Director of the Great Southern Railway) he couldn't wait to tell me how he had been ambushed by some tiny urchins, as he drove his car through the local village on the way to the tram terminus, saying

' "Dere's Dord Dundavy, t'row de mud." And they do.'

Beattie used to gather her own coterie around her at Rock-brook soirées and they sometimes competed with Gordon's group. If any of them dared to make a direct intrusion such as 'I wonder what his Lordship thinks', Gordon was quite capable of replying over his shoulder, 'Why don't you do that in the garden? Your own garden, I mean.'

Paddy has recalled the quality of his mother's talk and the rivalry between her and his father:

She held passionate opinions about everyone and everything and particularly about everyone. She would find vitality and imagination – to her the most desirable characteristics – in people that I thought were dull, until she assured me that they weren't. And then the Lord, surfacing briefly from his detective story, would intervene to say that he would rather talk to the lavatory attendant at Harcourt Street Station than to the person in question. Sometimes people that I liked were dismissed by my mother as 'rather rubbishy', or by the Lord as 'maniacal ego-maniacs'. . . .

Bad Irish art would be dismissed by my mother with the inevitable 'But what else would you expect from the tenement Catholic mind?' My father only half in jest used to deliver great rolling denunciations based upon 'the bottomless squalor of Roman Catholic superstition', and conclude with a string of Hail Mary's in the genteel accents of a Dublin civil servant . . . You certainly had to keep your wits about you in our house. But all in all, it was the most stimulating of atmospheres in which to grow.

In summer the talking sessions would be held outdoors with picnics up the mountains organized by Oliver Gogarty and the Swedish Consul who would supply smorgasbord and schnapps. Then there was tennis, golf and swimming and holidays in Parknasilla with the Bernard Shaws. Between 1929 and 1930 Gordon's government work to publicize the vast new hydro-electric scheme on the river Shannon frequently took him to the United States where he would be escorted through cities by motor cycles and police sirens, in between reciting Yeats to beautiful women.

Paddy was nine when his parents returned to Ireland. At first he attempted to fit in, without much success, with the other Irish boys at Crawley's school in Stephen's Green, Dublin. His school fellows weren't too impressed with his English accent and indeed to add to this he had a fearful stammer. But his skill at games and his gift of being extremely funny made up for any deficiencies and by the time he went to Castle Park prep school he was already in the mould of a young Protestant Dublin gentleman with a penchant for repartee and a good eye for ball games.

Though his father wanted him to go to his own school, Charterhouse, Paddy opted for Rossall in Lancashire, because he had heard there was a cupboard there that Castle Park boys carved their names on.

It wasn't a good choice. The place terrified him from the beginning – 'a low-built tangle of redbrick buildings with a grey sea behind it'. It reminded Gordon of 'a workhouse' the day he handed Paddy over to the headmaster. Paddy, however, distinguished himself at games there. He got house colours for rugby, cricket and hockey and also made his mark in the school plays. But it is clear that he hated his public school. Afterwards he could never remember the face of a single friend he had made there. Perhaps the names of his school fellows, with their ring of northern commercial czardom – Barraclough, Thorpe, Furness – struck a strange note for him; and the slaughtered plains in between the great industrial towns that they passed through, on their way to and from school matches, seemed like a stricken hell to him after the elegance of hill and sea that surrounded his native city. 'Gigantic factories belching fire and smoke, and wizened grimy bow-legged people scurrying about them like ants' is his remembered image of the world that he believed surrounded the school he had chosen for himself. Rossall would become a blur in his mind afterwards.

After Rossall he was offered a choice between Trinity College, Dublin, Oxford University or Cambridge University. Oxford seemed the obvious place to go because Paddy's uncle, the Hon. Sir Cecil Campbell, could arrange a place for him there.

At Pembroke College, Oxford, he made even fewer friends than at school and came down after two years of indifferent work without even gaining the half blue for golf that he could almost certainly have been awarded had he remained on. His incapacity for making and keeping friends, both at school and college, demonstrated a curious aspect of Paddy's character. It could be thought of as selfishness — or in another context, shyness or loneliness. A more likely explanation would seem to be that outside his family circle he could find himself somewhat at sea. It was a completely self-contained household. Everything there, from the talk to the sporting activities, was custom made.

Though Gordon was the South of Ireland golf champion and Paddy was a scratch golfer with one of the longest drives in Ireland (they used to say in Portmarnock Golf Club that when Campbell was driving off the first tee you were in danger not only on the first green but on the second tee as well), nevertheless they 'invented' their own golf course at Clonard which they played with a variety of instruments, finishing up with a chip through the open front door. They also had their own version of croquet and tennis.

There was even a special Campbell argot to be brought into play if certain visitors showed signs of becoming over familiar, and intruding on the family sanctuary. Phrases like 'it fruddles', 'et le loopage', 'Kurdistan oblique', thrown out casually in conversation, helped to convey an atmosphere of a secret world in which only the initiated were allowed to partake.

It was easy to believe that the world came to Rockbrook and not the other way about. One evening Paddy had come home to find Beattie bent over the piano in desperate concentration while a huge black man sang behind her. It was Paul Robeson. Another evening Chavchadze had played there. Paddy would never forget how one night Michael MacLiammoir had left the room and come back clothed in a white sheet with a chiffon scarf around his head to give a remarkable impersonation (complete with wooden leg) of Sarah Bernhardt who had, when he was a boy actor, once kissed him.

From time to time the marvellous Campbell parties would be disrupted by the eccentric, and occasionally shocking, exploits of 'Haggie', Gordon's unpredictable sister, the Hon. Violet Lilian Campbell. She was in her fifties, six feet tall and gauntly beautiful. Driven by her chauffeur, Lawless, who wore grey livery and a peaked cap, it was said that she used to pull up at expensive shops in Grafton Street and persuade harassed shop girls to hand over large amounts of perfume, champagne and expensive clothes, to be charged to Gordon's account.

In between trying to cope with Haggie's 'coups' (as she called them) Gordon had to try to sort out her marital affairs, for married once already, she had fallen for the leading comedian in the Dublin Gaiety Theatre pantomime, Jimmy O'Dea, and arranged a white wedding. The only notice she had given to her intended spouse had been her presence in the stage box every night throughout his run. Haggie was to add colour to the Campbell scene for many years to come, the culmination of her 'coups' being a libel action against Paddy's younger brother, Michael, in which she claimed (correctly) that he had used her as a character in a novel. Haggie sued for thirty thousand pounds but after being talked out of her claim by the family solicitor, and otherwise mollified, went into retirement in the far west of Ireland, where, surviving on a remittance, she refrained from 'coups' and outlived both Gordon and Beattie.

The family environment at both Rockbrook and Clonard exercised a powerful influence on Paddy. It wasn't until comparatively late in life (perhaps after his father's death) that he managed more or less to shake off the aura of this remarkable household.

The problem now was what to do with him after his failure at Oxford. The Foreign Office seemed a possibility with Gordon's connections, so Paddy set out for Munich to learn German after spending a period in Paris acquiring some acquaintanceship with the French language. He was to spend two years on and off in Germany before deciding that the political situation was not helping his chance of promotion in Siemens-Shukert, where Gordon had been able to place him on the strength of his own connections with the firm which had built the hydroelectric scheme on the Shannon. Back in Dublin it was again a round of racing, theatre, golf, the Dolphin, the Hibernian Buttery, hunt balls, endless luncheons and massive dinners in the extremely cheap (by standards elsewhere) but excellent restaurants.

Paddy slipped into his true profession almost by chance. In desperation Gordon had asked the editor of the *Irish Times*, Robert Maire Smyllie (known as Bertie), to try his son out as a reporter. This was the discovery of Paddy's life, the only job that required, in his own words, 'no degrees, no diplomas, no training and no specialized knowledge of any kind'. He felt in fact that journalism might have been designed especially for his benefit.

The *Irish Times*, when Paddy joined it, was an unusual newspaper. It had been the organ of the Anglo-Irish establishment. It was about, under its new editor, Bertie Smyllie, to become one of the outstanding newspapers in the English-speaking world. Paddy's essay on Smyllie in this book catches his character better than anything else can, so not too much need be said about him here. Smyllie was an inspired eccentric who should have belonged to an eighteenth-century Dublin where bucks, rogues and gamblers dominated the city scene, or else should have been a notable among the writers of the literary renaissance with Yeats, Russell and Synge. He was far too shy and modest to have chosen the latter company but he brought to newspaper work a love of prose, not always found among editors of daily newspapers.

Under Smyllie's tuition Paddy learnt to write so that every sentence had a balance of its own, so that no word or syllable was too long or too short to break its flow. Smyllie watched over him like a goldsmith with an apprentice.

The semicolon, Mr Campbell, is the prerogative of the senior practitioner. It requires exceedingly delicate handling. You're showering the shuddering things all over the place. Desist.

On the basis that Paddy had no education whatsoever but a rudimentary taste, Smyllie treated him to literary conversations conducted over the partition dividing the indoor cabins which the *Irish Times* editorial staff liked to call their offices.

Mr Campbell, sir.

Yes, Mr Smyllie, sir?

I've just stepped in something horrible.

I'm sorry to hear that, Mr Smyllie, sir.

It has risen over the top of my boot. 'He made me try harder to do something properly than anyone before or since.' It breaks my jaw to read it, Mr Campbell. It fragments my mind. Should we make it, 'He made me try harder to do something properly than anyone before or since had or has done to try to make me try harder to do something properly.'? Does this emendation do anything for the greater illumination of our minds? It does not. A sentence must flow as smoothly as milk from the Great Tit of the Shuddering Sacred Cow of Cahirciveen. Milk it, Mr Campbell, sir. Milk it.

During his first months on the *Irish Times*, Paddy worked as a reporter. Then he became a film critic. After that he found himself literary editor. Later he became a parliamentary correspondent which required being in the Dail (Irish parliament) eight hours a day and then rushing back to the paper to do his report for the following day. In between he did an occasional column for that section of the paper known as 'An Irishman's Diary' which was under the control of Smyllie. That was the way at the *Irish Times*. You covered everything, even those interminable Rotary lunches with their inevitable charlotte russes. If you survived you could be given your head and allowed to write as you wished. It wasn't long before it became clear that in Patrick Campbell, the *Irish Times* had discovered a new writer with a gift for prose and an eye for seeing behind everyday events aspects that could render them very funny indeed.

Gordon and Beattie were delighted at his success. Both of them were imaginative people who had decided to live in a regulated world rather than in the casual bohemian one of the artist. He as a writer–intellectual and she as a painter had turned their backs on the creative life. She continued to paint, and became an artist of distinction, but never acquired the reputation she might have deserved. Gordon wrote a play or two but ended up reading detective novels in his old age and writing appalling TV scripts which he firmly believed were tailor-made for Charlie Drake. Despite their choice of a conventional lifestyle neither of his parents had pushed Paddy into a profession or business life. They allowed the bohemian side of him to flourish. Thus, when he gravitated towards the world they had abandoned – they did not oppose him. Through the sort of journalism he was working at, it was clear he could develop into a writer of merit – and this was enough to please his parents.

His growing reputation as a journalist did not change Paddy's way of life. He played golf, went to race meetings, attended hunt balls. In fact, he continued to lead the life of the squireen while attending to the needs of a fiercely demanding profession. Only someone with unusual reserves and physical stamina could have stood it. It is noticeable, though, that he did not frequent Dublin's literary bars: the Bailey and Davy Byrne's (associated with Joyce, Gogarty and Beckett), the Palace (its notoriety established by an ecstatic piece from Cyril Connolly in *Horizon* magazine), or even the Pearl Bar in Fleet Street where a number of *Irish Times* journalists drank.

No, for Paddy it was the fashionable watering places of the horsey set: the Hibernian Buttery, a delightful cocktail bar with tartan banquettes, topped by large mirrors; the Shelbourne bar; the Horseshoe bar at the Phoenix Park Racecourse – these were where he went for relaxation between bouts in the newspaper world. Perhaps it was because he felt a sense of protection amongst his own class that Paddy chose this escape during his leisure hours. He had his own small circle in which he could play whatever role he wished without being pushed into a protective pose.

His friend Geraldine Fitzgerald, who later became a very well-known film actress and who had known Paddy since she was two, recalls:

There were four of us, a little closed corporation. Paddy and his sister Biddy, myself and my brother David. We would arrive at parties, hunt balls, country house weekends, thinking how wonderful we were and not caring whether people thought we were as wonderful as we believed or not. We felt we had everything in our group that really counted and we certainly had one of the funniest people who ever lived – Paddy – who had been a stand-up comic since he was a child: even then he could make groups of grown-ups, as well as his own age group, dissolve into helpless laughter with his wit.

Paddy was doing so well now he decided that the fact that Lord Beaverbrook and his grandfather had been friends might help to get him onto the *Daily Express* in London. Smyllie was understandably miffed at one of his fledglings flying the nest, but calmed down in the end and gave Paddy leave of absence accompanied by a somewhat ambiguous farewell – 'I hope it keeps fine for you.'

By August 1939, having virtually received his walking papers from the Beaver, he was writing to Gordon asking him for another hundred pounds out of his legacy. In a friend's cottage in Sunningdale enjoying breakfast in the sun on September 3rd he heard the voice of Neville Chamberlain on the radio telling the nation that Britain was at war with Germany. Paddy drove to Holyhead a few hours later and was in Dun Laoghaire the next morning.

The outbreak of war was to involve Paddy in what was for him an appallingly difficult decision. A number of people of his background and class in Ireland were joining the British forces. It was necessary to join up somewhere. Paddy decided to join the Irish Navy.

Afterwards this whole period was one about which he was to be very sensitive. But Paddy's decision must be seen against the background of the time. A number of Southern Irish Protestants did see it as their duty to join the Irish armed forces rather than the British ones. Ireland, after all, was now their country and though it had adopted a neutral status during the war there was a serious danger of an invasion which would have to be resisted with whatever force was available. There was no question of the loyalty of their class to Britain. That was firmly established. But they now had another country to which they owed loyalty as well. Brian Inglis, who came from much the same background as Paddy and who joined the R.A.F. in 1939 (he had a very distinguished flying career), put the whole matter clearly when he wrote:

> Those of us whose homes were in Southern Ireland occasionally speculated on what we would do if Churchill ordered that, say, the Treaty Ports must be reoccupied. My own feeling was that it would be impossible to stay on in the R.A.F. . . . The moment for decision appeared imminent only once, when I was doing my elementary flying training in Salisbury, Southern Rhodesia. A garbled radio message started a rumour in the camp that Ireland had been invaded by the English; and the two of us who were Irish on the course conferred on what we ought to do. It did not enter our heads that we should try to escape; but both of us felt that in the circumstances we could not continue on the course even if the camp commander encouraged us to. We had decided to present ourselves for,

presumably, internment when the rumour was killed by a revised transmission of the message.

If Paddy had joined the Irish Army it would have been different. He would no doubt, given his commanding looks, education and physical fitness, have had an early commission, and maybe would have risen to an impressive rank before the end of the war. But he could never rise above the rank of petty officer in the Irish Marine Service because he was unable to pass the Yachtmaster's Certificate in Trigonometry, while ironically the only acceptable alternative was a certificate from the British Board of Trade – when he applied for it he was indignantly refused.

As a non-commissioned officer his duties were largely those of inspecting ships coming into Irish harbours. He was to use the experience for his more hilarious articles later on, which often would of course ignore some of the dangers and rigours he went through in the Irish Marine Service from 1941–1944. Afterwards, referring to his war service he would say:

In fact, I don't want to talk about the war at all. It's an uncomfortable feeling to say the least to have missed a fearful experience that millions of other people endured and some failed to survive, including my sister.

It is notable that Gordon did not make any protest about Patrick's service in the Irish Marine Service. It is probable that he even encouraged it. After all he himself had come back to Ireland in its hour of need in 1922. It would have been only logical for him to feel that Paddy's first duty was to the country of which he was a citizen.

In 1944 the Allied forces landed in Normandy. This event decided Paddy to apply for his discharge from port control as he felt that since the danger of invasion was past, his country would no longer regard the presence of Petty Officer Campbell in its naval service as absolutely essential.

He begged Smyllie to take him back on the staff at the *Irish Times*, on the grounds that port control was driving him mad.

Mr Campbell.

Yes, sir.

You're a sod.

Yes, Mr Smyllie, sir.

You'd better come and do something about the Diary, it's a shower of lapidary crap.

Eventually, Paddy got a room to himself and began to write that daily diary through which he would carve out the form which would stamp his prose for the next forty years. 'What I wanted', he wrote in his autobiography, 'was to find a situation with a beginning, a middle and an end – almost a short story – with myself right in the middle of it – so that it was seldom indeed that I could get meat in a story given to me by someone else.' The Irishman's Diary shaped that pattern.

Paddy eased himself out of the *Irish Times*. He had begun to write occasional articles for the *Sunday Dispatch* in addition to his Irishman's Diary. To his surprise he was often paid as much for a single Sunday article in the London paper as he was for a whole week in the *Irish Times*. Smyllie wasn't at all pleased with this syphoning off of energy from where he considered it should be applied – the columns of the paper he edited.

It's fouling the nest, Mr Campbell, it's fouling the nest, Mr Campbell. The *Sunday Dispatch* is a shuddering awful newspaper. The thought of a member of the *Irish Times* working for it pollutes my mind.

Paddy insisted he needed the money and he told Smyllie that he knew the *Irish Times* could not pay him any more. The temptation was too much. He wrote to Bertie Smyllie to tell him that he was leaving. The letter was answered by someone from the front office accepting the resignation and asking for a cheque for a year's salary in lieu of notice, which Paddy felt was Smyllie's way of letting him know what he thought of him. There was a coolness between the two of them after that which Paddy regretted because he always saw Smyllie as his 'onlie begetter'. By the time Paddy felt it would be all right to approach the old boy he found he had left it too late as Smyllie had acquired terminal cancer and they never met before he died.

Paddy came to London in 1946 and for the next ten years enjoyed himself more than he ever had before. His *Dispatch* column kept him in funds and also in the public eye. He then began to write for *Lilliput* magazine where he found a special niche with the extended humorous essay which was to provide an outlet for some of his best writing. He played golf at

Sunningdale, drank in Fleet Street bars, lived it up in the night clubs and quickly became a man about town, in what was the centre of the English-speaking world at the time.

But all the time he was developing his craft. Those humorous essays in *Lilliput* he perhaps never excelled. In 1954 when *Patrick Campbell's Omnibus* appeared containing a selection of his writing it was manifestly clear that here was a new talent in the literary world whose work would survive the ephemeral nature of a magazine or newspaper article and which could be read and re-read with pleasure.

Leonard Russell, of the *Sunday Times*, referred to the work as that 'of an artist' who has an artist's ability to extract something new from the familiar or the hackneyed, while H.E. Bates, the novelist and short story writer, interestingly describes the collection as 'short stories' not essays and adds that having laughed his way through the book he wished 'that literature had more Patrick Campbells'.

Like other essayists, such as Thurber, Stephen Leacock, A. J. Liebling and S.J. Perelman, with whom he was now compared, Paddy's spur was humour. But it was humour based on the Irish gift of storytelling – an episode swiftly shaped into a tale with a beginning, middle and end, told in a club or a bar, perhaps, or even at a street corner, the last line delivered as the teller caught his bus, or leaped into a taxi. These *contes* provided the spice for a Campbell story, which he would then proceed to elaborate with his own brand of fantasy. He depended very much on a strong opening. Here, with swift, deft pen strokes, an atmosphere would be evoked which would set the mood of the tale.

Take the beginning of 'The Dicking Bird'. There is not a superfluous word, nor one chosen which will not set the reader's mind in the direction the author wants it to go:

I'd gone down to this place to write an article about their hunt, and passed a tiring afternoon showing enthusiasm in the back of a small car driven by Mrs Milligan, wife of the Master. In the back of the car with me were two sodden dogs, a shovel and an old man called Casey, smelling strongly of ferrets.

Next the implacable hostility of the horsey set to any imaginative activity is established:

That night was even worse. The Milligans, who'd been in

charge of the hunt for two hundred years, produced endless cuttings from local newspapers about the Ballybrackens finding in Flynn's Bottom, and killing in Kelly's Drain, and seemed surprised when I didn't write it all down.

'You've got a note-book, haven't you?' said the Master, a short but powerfully built man with a quick temper, and a stiffness in intellect that made him unapproachable by anything save the simplest of words.

I made the mistake, then, of trying to tell them that I was just going for atmosphere. 'Sort of background and personality stuff,' I said.

This was received with surprise by the Milligans and by their guests – half a dozen hard-faced men and women in tweed suits and canary waistcoats.

I heard someone called Captain Fawcus say, 'How's your background and personality, Mildred?' – and Mildred replying, 'Just atmospheric, Jack.'

But how to set the philistine world against the world of the arts? Difficult enough to achieve in the remote feudal backwater of the Milligan menage, one would imagine. Campbell solves the problem by introducing an ancient German photographer who had followed him down the country to photograph him for a Chicago newspaper:

I pushed back my chair, and at that moment a figure walked into the breakfast-room carrying three cameras, a collapsible tripod, a collection of lamps, and a black velvet muffler round his neck. He stopped inside the door, bowed, clicked his heels, and said, 'Goot morning! Schraub!'

We looked at him with our mouths open. He wore a beret with a pimple on top, a black suit, and sandals.

He raised his hand. 'Do not disturb,' he said. 'I look for my lord editor. I am Schraub. I make picture of all great Irish authors for Chicago paper.'

Roderick Milligan, the Master, rose to his feet.

'What,' he said, simply, 'is that?'

'Just a minute,' I said. 'I think he wants to take a photograph of me. He's working for an American paper.'

Roderick turned his head very slowly. He seemed to be having trouble with the muscles of his neck.

'Why, then,' he said, 'is he here?'

Schraub suddenly dumped all his paraphernalia on the sideboard.

'Not to say more!' he cried. 'Am seeing my writing man!'

He bustled forward. He caught me by the hand.

'So glad to meet,' he beamed. 'I am hearing you are here in your so beautiful house. I fly back Chicago tonight. Now I make picture.' He wrung my hand several times.

One of Campbell's special gifts, having reached a climax, is that of being able to bring a piece swiftly to a close. The majority of them descend to earth in a hundred words or so. 'The Dicking Bird' ends with the hunting party postponing their afternoon's shooting to do a parody of the photographer and his subject, while Paddy is forced to look on, almost in the same fashion as Dubedat reverses the roles of doctor and artist, in Shaw's *The Doctor's Dilemma*.

'Bar Sinister on an Old School Tie' begins innocently enough with a chance meeting with an old school acquaintance in Paris, whom Paddy rather forces himself on for an evening's fun. They find themselves in a Montmartre night club. Arthur Spencer-Watt ('Watto') and Paddy are watching a naked black dancer, when the whole tale turns brilliantly on its head.

'*Bon soir, Zigzig,*' said Arthur Spencer-Watt, '*comment ça va?*'

I supported Zigzig with difficulty. She had one arm round my neck. 'Here,' I said to Watto, 'can't we get this tulip a chair?'

A surprising thing happened then. Watto suddenly went rigid. '*What* did you say?' he snapped.

'I said – "Can't we get her a chair?"'

'No,' said Watto, abruptly. 'Tulip. You called her a tulip. By God, I remember you now!' He turned excitedly to Miss Salter.

'This is the clot,' said Watto, 'who rubbed a dead rat in my hair!'

He sat back. He shook his head wonderingly. 'I didn't know who the hell you were,' he said. 'Couldn't remember you from Adam. But I've got it now, all right. You're Campbell. You used to call the maids in the dining-hall "Tulips". You, and Dixon and that frightful footballing Thorpe.' Very gently, Watto licked his upper lip. 'This,' he said, almost to himself, 'this is just the way I'd like it to be.'

How Paddy is made to pay the penalty is told with the usual deft Campbell finish (150 words) which the reader can savour for himself in this collection.

There is sometimes a surrealist quality in a Campbell story like a Bunuel film or a Dali painting. Bunuel would have liked the idea of an elderly oriental student explaining 'The Flying Dutchman' to an Irishman in Munich Opera House amid a torrent of oriental hisses and misplaced consonants which is the theme of 'Three Years at the Opera'. Dali would surely appreciate the opening to 'The Animal Farm' in which the real momentarily seems to merge with the unreal:

'This is it, all right,' I said to the taximan, and leant against the door. I fell into a foaming sea of dogs. There seemed to be hundreds of them, leaping, barking and snarling in the darkness.

I was going to spring out through the door again, when my hostess appeared. Trousers, of course.

'Down, Roger!' she cried – 'Stop it, Ursula!' Then I saw there were only two dogs – fat, low, white dogs, gleaming like young pigs.

To be taken seriously as a writer was encouraging to Paddy and from the early Fifties, a cult of a sort grew up around him.

In 1949 he paid a three-week visit to Dublin, not as a journalist but as an international class golfer to play in the Amateur Championship which was being held that year in Portmarnock Golf Club. It is often forgotten how good a golfer he was. At Portmarnock (where he was a member) he played off a handicap of plus two.

To his surprise he kept winning successive rounds, even beating the much fancied Billy O'Sullivan, the Irish champion who was expected to reach the final. Paddy's problem was that if he won in the morning match he would have to play another eighteen holes in the afternoon. After he had beaten Billy O'Sullivan in the quarter final he decided things had gone far enough and he got sloshed before going out in the afternoon to play the able Scottish golfer Kenneth Thom, in a game which, if he won, would have qualified him for the finals. To Paddy's horror he started to win the first few holes, despite his somewhat blurred vision. Things got better (or worse) after a while, however, and he was never quite sure afterwards just how many holes Thom finally won by.

By 1947 Patrick's first marriage with Sylvia Lee (whom he had married in 1941) had been dissolved and he married Cherry Monro, the daughter of Major Charles Monro of the Indian Army. To some extent from now on he would live a domestic life, especially after his daughter Bridget was born in 1948. Paddy turned out to be a doting father, and would get much hilarious copy from the encounters of the child kind, whose personalities he seemed to have a surprising sympathy with, and understanding of.

As well as writing for the *Dispatch* and *Lilliput*, Paddy worked on film scripts with Frank Lauder and Sydney Gilliat at Pinewood Studios. The scripts were seldom used but the money was good and he was never afraid of hard work as long as it was on the typewriter. This life had its disadvantages nevertheless. One of them was that it was hard to keep up an output as a humorous essayist, write film scripts and at the same time attend to your family. By 1958 Paddy was feeling the pinch financially and his second marriage was coming to an end, which provoked occasional bouts of depressing self-examination. Jennifer Johnston remembers that it was about this time that Paddy's younger brother Michael began to make a reputation as a novelist. 'There was a tendency then in some Dublin circles to hail Michael as the artist and to look on Paddy as the jokey kind and Paddy wasn't at all pleased with it.' This of course was just an ephemeral judgement, as Paddy had mastered his branch of the literary craft whereas Michael at this time could not be said to have mastered his. But it didn't help Paddy's inherent (if healthy) reservations about his writing talent to have this sort of thing bandied about.

A chance came to lift Paddy out of his despondency when Brian Inglis, who by this time was editing the *Spectator*, offered him a chance to write a series of pieces for the magazine. The first appeared on the 2nd August 1958, and the last one on the 3rd March 1961. Though he was paid the usual miserly *Spectator* rates (£20 a piece) the series was an immediate success and helped to reestablish his reputation as a real writer who could use comic escapades as an outlet for a creative talent.

Though these articles did help to remind people how well he could write, by 1961 Paddy was not at all well off. Then one day his brother Michael (who had, by this time, published two successful novels), mentioned an agent called Irene Josephy who could do wonders for him. By a coincidence, Paddy met Irene Josephy a few days later in El Vino's and after a conversation agreed to phone her.

She caught his confidence immediately. 'I liked very much her tentative method of laying a new project before me. On the telephone she would say "I was talking to someone the other day at lunch – rather a nice man really – and he was wondering if perhaps we might be able to do a little something for him. Of course I told him we were terribly busy, but we just might be able to find time to fit him in. . ." '

This resulted in several new commissions for trade journals and several articles for *Punch* and the *Sunday Express*. Then one day Irene Josephy produced what Paddy, at this stage of his career, would have wanted most, a column in the *Sunday Times*. In a week it was all fixed and he would write his humorous column once a week for the paper over the next sixteen years.

A paper as prestigious as the *Sunday Times* was an admirable shop window for him. On the leader page his column had to compete with formidable writing to catch the reader's eye. But this it did. His prose style was analysed in sixth forms. It began to be recognized that here was a writer, a master of the essay form, who could produce fifty-two pieces a year – a journalist with something else besides. A writer on *The Times* summed his gift up admirably:

Campbell could toss up a trifle of experience and keep it in the air with great dexterity for minutes before letting it spin away into fantasy.

Sir Denis Hamilton, his first editor on the *Sunday Times*, remembers how professional Paddy was:

To keep up his column as he did was one of the most outstanding feats of journalism I ever came across. I never recall a bad column.

Nevertheless, the day after he had sent his column to the paper Paddy was always in a panic. He was never free from the fear that it would be returned to him. It was this insecurity that was at the base of his standard of excellence – he never got to think of himself as too good for the job.

As a freelance contributor he didn't often come into the editorial offices. Once, at a party, shortly after he joined the *Sunday Times*, Paddy said to the person next to him,

What do you do?

I happen to be Editor.

Denis Hamilton remembers that Paddy went round in a flap saying, 'That Editor looks like a chap who wouldn't stand any nonsense', before he was finally reassured that he hadn't damaged his prospects on the paper.

Godfrey Smith remembers how they never thought of their witty colleague as a member of the peerage:

'My lords, ladies and gentlemen,' boomed the red-coated toastmaster at one *Sunday Times* staff lunch. We looked around in surprise. Lord Thomson was of course in the chair, but what other lords were there among us? We had forgotten – as the toastmaster could not – that Paddy in private life was the third Lord Glenavy, scion of a professional Irish Protestant family.

In January 1962 something happened which was to have a major influence on the next fifteen years of his life. He became a television star – one of the best known in Britain.

How could someone with a speech impediment have become a brilliantly successful public entertainer? The answer was that instead of trying to conceal his stammer he capitalized on it. Ned Sherrin, the producer of his first show, recalls:

Paddy used his stutter to his advantage: as the face creased more and more the audience would hang on his words. He was so in control of his stammer you didn't feel you were watching a technique.

In fact, television helped him as a storyteller. It magnified a defect he was able to use so well. Don't forget you could tell a long story with that twitching face that you couldn't recount as well if you were talking normally.

Godfrey Smith has spotted another aspect of the Campbell

stutter. 'It gave him time,' he observed, 'to hone his marvellous retorts.'

It wasn't just the stutter of course. It was his marvellous gift of storytelling as well. But then he had always wanted to be an entertainer, ever since, as a little boy, he had seen his father put on a sad face and say something that would set the table in a roar.

Another valuable characteristic for chat shows had been acquired at the family table, a low tolerance threshold for bores. 'If he decided he didn't like someone he would go in and ferret out the reason for his dislike,' Sherrin recalls.

Paddy told Robert Robinson once on BBC 2, when he was asked if there was anything he wished to prohibit, 'Only the grinding tedium of someone talking off the top of his head.'

It was Kenneth Tynan who introduced him at lunch at the Cafe Royal to Ned Sherrin who, after the success of 'That was the Week that Was', was putting together a new show called 'Not so Much a Programme More a Way of Life'. 'I thought', recalled Paddy, 'that Ned seemed to be watching me closely. I don't know why. Then, suddenly it occurred to me. I thought, 'He wants me to p-p-perform.' Well, I like making people laugh, it gives me a lot of pleasure and to be paid for it as well! So I said, "Yes".'

The *Daily Mail* noted the effect Paddy made on his first appearance:

Millions watched in squirming discomfort that first night as the kindly-faced bald-headed man with eagle eyes blinked his way through his long halting blockages before the dams finally burst and the words came tumbling out.

Sherrin was emphatic about the first night, 'It was an immediate success. Unanimous rave notices.'

Paddy appeared along with two others in that programme, Harvey Orkin and Dennis Norden. They had separate nights. Paddy's was Saturday. It was the most popular of the three. Later he graduated to 'Call my Bluff' with Frank Muir and continued to call Muir's bluff until shortly before his death in 1980. In December 1970 he was guest star on Eamon Andrews' television show 'This Is Your Life'.

Audiences never tired of him. If things were slowing up he

could be relied on to liven up the programme, just as the clown in the circus takes over when the acts aren't pacing themselves as well as they might. On one occasion he pounced on Bernard Levin for using the word 'cretin' about Sir Alec Douglas Home, arguing that 'cretin' was a medical term with physical connotations and therefore an inappropriate word to attribute to the Prime Minister. A shindig ensued but after the programme was over and Paddy had gone home the Press refused to let the matter die. One journalist asked him whether it was true that he had refused to appear on television with Bernard, and Paddy replied that it wasn't. It was simply that Mr Levin was an excitable young man who talked hysterically, but he would appear with him at any time in the future if Levin had obviously learnt the error of his ways.

From now on his life was changed. He had to get used to people recognizing him in the street, the half-shrug of the shoulders to the companion and then two people turning to inspect him; head waiters recognizing him in restaurants, newspaper sellers in the streets, taxi drivers talking to him as if they had known him all their lives.

One day when he came back to his car, which he had parked too long outside a shop, the policeman who was standing on duty said benevolently, touching his helmet, 'Shall we say, Mr Campbell, it is not so much a parking offence, more a way of getting into trouble if we do it again.'

Desmond Zwar, writing in the *Daily Mail* had this to say:

Patrick Campbell has done for stuttering, what the Lords have done for abortion and homosexuals. He has made it a discussable subject.

Articles were commissioned on 'The Stammerer as Hero' and one TV critic wrote of the shameful 'commercialization' of Patrick Campbell's stammer. There was even conjecture that the stammer won so much attention for him that it might not be genuine. Desmond Zwar rallied to Paddy's defence:

Oh, but it is. I was on the phone to him getting directions to his part of Belgravia when the velvety voice went off the air. I interrupted the awkward silence to see if he was still about. He was. He was stranded in mid-stream with the word 'street', it kept him bogged.

'The "STR" in a word is the worst one for me,' he said 'it beats me every time.'

Of course it could be said that Paddy had been in training for such combat all his life in Clonard and Rockbrook. Lashing out at Bernard Levin when he put a foot wrong was exactly the tactics his mother would have employed in a similar situation if she believed that somebody was talking out of place. How often has the present writer seen her leap in and furiously put an offender straight, looking pleasantly satisfied afterwards once the fault was purged and her anger appeased. Paddy must have been aware of the source of a large part of his television technique:

> My mother's passion for life, for art, for the exercise of the imagination was so strong that she was incapable of listening for more than a few minutes to self aggrandizement or to what she believed to be second-hand opinions. She would not stop herself leaping on the offenders and putting them straight with a fury which she regretted afterwards only if they were so small minded as to take offence.

Paddy's father was less impulsive than Beattie but his sharp wit was feared even in Dublin's formidable conversational circles. Between the pair of them they provided an admirable milieu for someone who would later become famous as a chat show guest.

In the meantime, two very important events in his life occurred. In May 1963 his father died. This was a major blow to Paddy. His father had exercized a profound influence on him. He had never forced his son along a pre-ordained way of making a living and seemed content when Paddy's talents as a writer and journalist had blossomed. Clearly, Gordon had wanted to be a writer himself. But his own father had not been tolerant, and prevented him from following his particular bent. That Gordon should have allowed Paddy the freedom he did is a measure of his magnanimity, especially since he knew his son had formed his style on the surrealistically witty household he grew up in. All this was a token of his generosity and a real affection for his son and heir. There was a bond between the two of them of an unspoken kind which resulted in Paddy never referring to his father on usual familial terms, but only as 'Lordship'. ('It sounds a terribly good idea, Lordship: Thank you very much indeed,' is how he had received his father's plan to enter him in the Diplomatic Service.) His father, on the other hand, was in the habit of referring to Paddy's friends by prefacing the definite article to their first names so that they came out as 'The Arthur', 'The David' etc.

Though Gordon was constantly prophesying financial doom for the family, nevertheless he understood his son much better than one would have expected and made considerable sums of money over to him sometime before his death, saying with a certain amount of insight to the writer Francis Stuart, 'Patrick is the sort of person who can't live well without money.' It was no wonder that Paddy once wrote:

> Through the mist and uncertainty surrounding my future, I could always see one small abiding light in the certainty that the Lord, in the person of my father, would provide.

While back for the funeral at Rockall, the house in Sandycove, where his father had died, he recognized for the first time the full impact of what had happened and what it would mean to him:

> Alone in the sittingroom, I sat in the Lord's chair by the window, looking out at Dublin Bay. His race glasses – I think they'd belonged to his father – were on a stool beside the chair. I picked them up and tried to focus on a small collier steaming out of the Liffey past the Poolbeg Lighthouse, but the image was blurred.
>
> Suddenly I got into a state of desperation. Everything was slipping away. The feeling that I'd known nothing about his business life became unbearable. It was idle, ungrateful, unforgivable. And now all the memories of him were becoming shadowy and confused. I had to arrange them, file them away, before it was too late.
>
> I got up and went out of the house, through the front garden and to the sea road and down to the rocks at the Forty Foot, a roughly concreted enclosure that had been a bathing place for Gentlemen Only for many years. The Lord had sometimes bathed here before breakfast in the very early morning, loving the feeling of solitude, the sun coming up over the Hill of Howth and the clean, new sea . . .
>
> I went through the pockets of my father's clothes, the shapeless grey tweed suits, the corduroy gardening trousers,

the white bawneen pair from Galway as stiff and cylindrical as ever. I was glad not to find my own turned suit. But there was no trace of the car keys. All the pockets were completely empty, a strange neatness in a casually untidy man. He must have cleared them out himself, perhaps one afternoon when the pain had driven him to bed, and he guessed what was coming.

I opened the two top drawers of his dressing-table. One of them was empty. The other contained a couple of pipe cleaners, a device for sharpening razor blades and a member's badge for Leopardstown race course.

There was nothing else. No personal jewellery, no passport, no letters, no keepsakes, no photographs – no mementos of any kind. Perhaps he never needed the things by which other people set such store. Perhaps because he was a truly great man.

For a while after Gordon's death he was inconsolable. One friend whom he had met while working on films at Ealing Studios was Vivienne Knight, who was an associate producer. They collaborated on a number of film and TV scripts, starting in 1955 when she invited him to work on the script of *Lucky Jim* which she was producing with Charles Crichton as director. Vivienne, an attractive and witty girl with a high sense of achievement, was exactly right for Paddy. She understood him better than anyone could so far and was able to cope with his black moods when the manic jester in him would go into depressive decline. Having worked together for over ten years they married in 1966, just as Paddy was reaching the height of his fame as a public figure.

In 1968 they left England to live in the South of France where Vivienne had acquired (and restored) half an old farmhouse near Grasse. It was there that they worked together on Paddy's first full-length humorous book, *Rough Husbandry*, and his autobiography, *My Life and Easy Times*.

Paddy had fallen in love with life in France and, in spite of his northern colouring, he was a sun-lover. He had a theory that all humanity sprang from the Mediterranean and that he had at last found his true habitat.

They both enjoyed having well-chosen guests to stay, as many as thirty-eight in five consecutive months during 1973.

One question was, could his *Sunday Times* column survive being written outside England? Paddy did come back to London once a month for 'Call my Bluff'. This would help keep him in touch. But his material would largely have to come from life in the South of France and it is a tribute to his talent as a writer that he was able to entertain readers weekly from 1968, the year he went to live there, to April 1978 when he ceased writing on a weekly basis for the *Sunday Times*. It was agreed that he would become an occasional contributor from then on. Alas, this never happened. His weekly column had been a part of his life; the terror on the Wednesday as the deadline for his copy loomed up, the retreat down a sort of tunnel to his study, the excruciating concentration until a satisfactory 800 words (or more) were on paper, and then the joy and relief as it was sent express to London. Even after years of 'this sort of thing – and several million words' he was unable to free himself from the anxiety of 'never really knowing what it was going to be about until I started, and certainly continuing in total ignorance of what the end would be until I got to it'.

Now he worked on a book about life in the South of France which would be unfinished at his death. Having been persuaded that boules was a good game, he had a piste constructed in the garden of the house. As soon as he discovered that boules was not, as he had maintained, a game for children, he set about becoming (as he could do with all ball games) something of an expert even by native standards. Very occasionally he played golf with John Langley, a former Walker Cup captain on the Biot course, but his swing was uneasy and his enthusiasm uncertain despite the attraction of girl caddies in mini-skirts.

Later John suggested playing the course with a 5 iron only and this attenuated game seemed to satisfy both of them as by now the pair had golfer's back. There was the problem too, because of his television profile, of hearty British tourists on the streets of Cannes. To be slapped on the back by a stranger with 'Good Old Pat' was hardly an event to make his day. Even worse were those who stopped him with 'Now don't tell me – I'll get your name in a minute,' followed by 'Aren't you the one on TV with the stammer?'

Paddy's stock reply was 'I am Dame Edith Evans.'

But Paddy's smiling, sardonic self-confidence sometimes concealed a deep depression. It was the manic aspect of a personality which could direct itself to the manifest doings of humankind and perceive something of an intensely funny sort in circumstances where no one but he would have noted it. Francis Stuart, the novelist, observed Paddy in one of his elated moods as they were driving back along the Louth coast after a race meeting in 1935:

We stopped and looked out at the sea. Then Paddy looked at the sky and the rich green fields below. Then he said something as banal as 'Isn't it a beautiful country to live in'. But I knew by the way he said it that he had had an insight into what was around, in a way that was not at all conveyed by the words. He was in wonderful humour all night afterwards and then next day was as low as one could ever imagine him to be.

This writer saw the depressive side of Paddy the afternoon of his mother's funeral. He insisted on driving into Dublin to buy shuttlecocks in Elverys, his mother's family sports firm. I reminded him that the shop would be closed on Saturday afternoon. But he had his reasons for going as I found out. On the nine-mile drive into the city, he poured out his hatred of Dublin and of people he had known in a way that was almost frightening. It certainly wasn't rational. When he found, as I had told him it would be, that the shop was closed, he just drove home in silence.

In 1972, after a visit to America and Mexico, he developed a high fever for which no immediate cause could be diagnosed. While in hospital in Grasse tests showed that he had had a heart attack some years before without being aware of it. Casting his mind back he was able to recall that while working on clearing a stream in his garden at Bourne End in Buckinghamshire he had suffered extremely severe chest pains and he concluded that that was probably the occasion on which he had had the heart attack.

After a period in University College Hospital in London he recovered sufficiently to be able to return to the South of France where his physician advised him to take as much exercise as possible. But throughout his life, walking had been bound up for him with the pursuit of a little white golf ball, and now that he rarely played the game he found walking for its own sake rather a bore. Nor was he especially attentive to his diet schedules. After several periods in hospital caused by left ventricular failure, he again developed fever in the late summer of 1980.

This time the hospital in Grasse failed to detect viral pneumonia. Again he was airlifted to University College Hospital where he seemed to rally – but the heart was too weak. Early in the morning of 9th November 1980 Paddy was joking with a lovely young nurse and whilst she was laughing – he died.

Sometime before, we had crossed each other at London Airport, he going back to France, I returning from Morocco. I never knew in advance what he would say so I greeted him with a certain amount of caution.

'G-G-Good good article on Jammy Clinch in the *Sunday Times*,' he said.

Jammy Clinch had been a hero in his era, not mine, so I was pleased. I was about to thank him, but he had gone off down the ramp, the shine of his bald head on top of that splendid frame diminishing into the darkness.

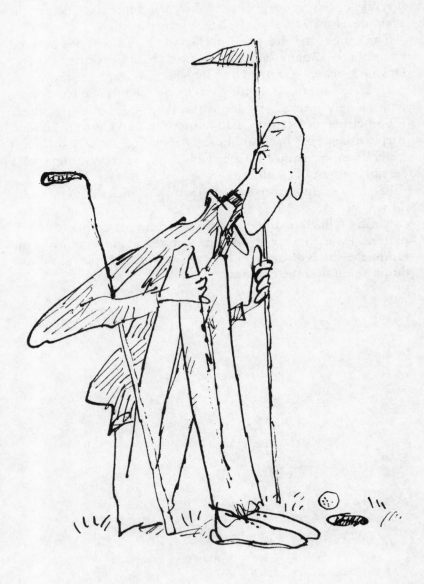

I

Noulded into a Shake

When I was a tall, sensitive boy at school I once sent up for a booklet about how to be a ventriloquist.

I was always 'sending up' for things – variable focus lamps, propelling pencils with choice of six differently-coloured leads, air-pistols discharging wooden bullets, scale model tanks with genuine caterpillar action, tricks in glass-topped boxes, and so on – anything, I suppose, to vary the monotony of straight games and education.

The booklet arrived at breakfast time one morning in a large square envelope. I told the other boys it was a new stamp album, and got on with my shredded liver poached in water. I wanted the voice-throwing to come as a real surprise.

We had twenty minutes after breakfast in which to get our things ready for first school. I had a quick run through the new book.

It was called *Ventriloquism in Three Weeks*. On the first page it explained that the word ventriloquism came from the Latin *ventriloqus* – 'a speaking from the belly'. There was also a drawing of a schoolboy smiling pleasantly at a railway porter carrying a trunk. From the trunk came hysterical cries of, 'Help! Help! Murder! Police!'

It was just the sort of thing I was aiming at. I slipped the book in with my other ones, and hurried off to first school.

In the next fortnight I put in a good deal of practice, sitting right at the back of the class, watching my lips in a small piece of mirror, and murmuring, 'Dah, dee, day, di, doy, doo.'

It was necessary, however, to be rather careful. Dr Farvox,

the author of the book, suggested that it might be as well to perform the earlier exercises 'in the privacy of one's bedroom or den'. Dr Farvox was afraid that 'chums or relatives' might laugh, particularly while one was practising the 'muffled voice in the box'.

The best way to get this going, Dr Farvox said, was to experiment 'with a continuous grunting sound in a high key, straining from the chest as if in pain'.

He was right in thinking that this exercise ought to be performed in the privacy of the bedroom. It was inclined to be noisy – so noisy, indeed, that I was caught twice straining in a high key from the chest during practical chemistry, and had to pretend that I'd been overcome by the fumes of nitric acid.

But, in the end, it was the easy, pleasant smile that terminated my study of what Dr Farvox described as 'this amusing art'.

It happened one Saturday morning in the hour before lunch, ordinarily a pleasant enough period devoted to constitutional history. Bill the Bull, who took the class, was usually fairly mellow with the prospect of the week-end before him, and there was not much need to do any work.

As was by now my invariable custom I was seated right at the back of the room with a large pile of books in front of me, and the mirror lying on the desk. I was working on the Whisper Voice, which had been giving me quite a considerable amount of difficulty.

'Lie down, Neddy, lie down,' I whispered, watching my lips closely in the glass.

'It's due in dock at nine o'clock.'

Not bad.

'Take Ted's Kodak down to Roy.'

There it was again – the old familiar twitch on 'Kodak'.

I sat back, relaxing a little, and smiled. Dr Farvox was strongly in favour of the Smile. 'What the young student,' he said, 'should aim at from the first is an easy and natural expression. He should Smile.'

I smiled. Smiling, I whispered, 'Take Ted's Kodak down to Roy.'

To my absolute horror I found myself smiling straight into the face of Bill the Bull.

He stopped dead. He was in the middle of something about the growth of common law, but my smile stopped him dead in his tracks.

'Well, well,' said Bill, after a moment. 'How charming. And good morning to you, too.'

I at once buried my face in my books, and tried to shove the mirror and *Ventriloquism in Three Weeks* on one side.

Bill rolled slowly down the passageway between the desks. He was an enormous Welshman with a bullet head, and very greasy, straight black hair. He took a subtle and delicate pleasure in driving the more impressionable amongst us half mad with fear at least five days a week.

'Such pretty teeth,' said Bill. 'How nice of you to smile at me. I have always wanted to win your admiration.'

The other boys sat back. They knew they were on to something good.

I kept my head lowered. I'd actually succeeded in opening my constitutional history somewhere near the middle, but the corner of Dr Farvox was clearly visible under a heap of exercise books.

Bill reached my desk. 'But who knows,' he said, 'perhaps you love me too. Perchance you've been sitting there all morning just dreaming of a little home – just you and I. And later, perhaps, some little ones . . . ?'

A gasp of incredulous delight came from the other boys. This was Bill at his very best.

I looked up. It was no longer possible to pretend I thought he was talking to someone else.

'I'm sorry, sir,' I said. 'I was just smiling.'

Suddenly, Bill pounced. He snatched up Dr Farvox.

'Cripes,' he said. 'What in the world have we here? Ventriloquism in three weeks?'

He turned a couple of pages.

'Scholars,' he said, 'be so good as to listen to this.'

He read aloud: 'To imitate a Fly. Close the lips tight at one corner. Fill that cheek full of wind and force it to escape through the aperture. Make the sound suddenly loud, and then softer, which will make it appear as though the insect were flying in different parts of the room. The illusion may be helped out by the performer chasing the imaginary fly, and flapping at it with his handkerchief.'

'Strewth,' said Bill. He looked round the class. 'We'd better get ourselves a little bit of this. Here am I taking up your time with the monotonies of constitutional history, while in this very room we have a trained performer who can imitate a fly.'

Suddenly, he caught me by the back of the neck. 'Come,' he said, 'my little love, and let us hear this astounding impression.'

He dragged me down to the dais.

'Begin,' said Bill. 'Be so kind as to fill your cheek with wind, and at all costs do not omit the flapping of the handkerchief.'

'Sir,' I said, 'that's animal noises. I haven't got that far yet.'

'Sir,' squeaked Bill, in a high falsetto, 'that's animal noises. I 'aven't got that far yet.'

He surveyed the convulsed class calmly.

'Come, come,' he said, 'this art is not as difficult as I had imagined it to be. Did anyone see my lips move?'

They cheered him. They banged the lids of their desks. 'Try it again, sir!' they cried. 'It's splendid!'

Bill raised his hand. 'Gentlemen,' he said, 'I thank you for your kindness. I am, however, but an amateur. Am I not right in thinking that we would like to hear something more from Professor Smallpox?'

They cheered again. Someone shouted, 'Make him sing a song, sir!'

Bill turned to me. 'Can you,' he said, 'Professor Smallpox, sing a song?'

It was the worst thing that had ever happened to me in my life. I tried to extricate myself.

'No, sir,' I said. 'I haven't mastered the labials yet.'

Bill started back. He pressed his hand to his heart.

'No labials?' he said. 'You have reached the age of fifteen without having mastered the labials. But, dear Professor Smallpox, we must look into this. Perhaps you would be so kind as to give us some outline of your difficulties?'

I picked up *Ventriloquism in Three Weeks*. There was no way out.

'There's a sentence here, sir, that goes, "A pat of butter moulded into the shape of a boat."'

Bill inclined his head. 'Is there, indeed? A most illuminating remark. You propose to put it to music?'

'No, sir,' I said. 'I'm just trying to show you how hard it is. You see, you have to call that, "A cat of gutter noulded into the shake of a goat."'

Bill fell right back into his chair.

'You have to call it *what*?' he said.

'A cat of gutter, sir, noulded into the shake of a goat.'

Bill's eyes bulged. 'Professor,' he said, 'you astound me. You bewilder me. You take my breath away. A cat of gutter –' He repeated it reverently, savouring each individual syllable.

Then he sprang up. 'But we must hear this,' he cried. 'We must have this cat of gutter delivered by someone who knows what he is at. This – this is valuable stuff.'

He caught me by the ear. 'Professor,' he said, 'why does it have to be noulded into the shake of a goat?'

'Well, sir,' I said, 'if you say it like that you don't have to move your lips. You sort of avoid the labials.'

'To be sure you do,' said Bill. 'Why didn't I think of that myself. Well, now, we will have a demonstration.'

He turned to face the class. 'Gentlemen,' he said, 'Professor Smallpox will now say, "A pat of butter moulded into the shape of a boat," *without moving the lips*! I entreat your closest attention. You have almost certainly never in your lives heard anything like this before.'

He picked up his heavy ebony ruler. His little pig-like eyes gleamed.

'And,' he went on, 'to make sure that Professor Smallpox will really give us of his best I shall make it my personal business to give Professor Smallpox a clonk on the conk with this tiny weapon should any of you see even the faintest movement of the facial muscles as he delivers his unforgettable message.'

Bill brought down the ruler with a sharp crack on my skull.

'Professor,' he said, 'it's all yours.'

I don't have to go into the next twenty-five minutes. The other boys yelled practically on every syllable. I got the meaningless words tangled up, and said, 'A cack of rutter roulded into the gake of a shote.'

45

At times Bill was so helpless with laughter that he missed me with the ruler altogether.

When the bell went for the end of the hour he insisted on being helped out into the passage, wiping his eyes with the blackboard cloth.

After that, I gave up ventriloquism, feeling no recurrence of interest even after reading Bill's observation on my end-of-term report: 'He ought to do well on the stage.'

2

Bar Sinister on an Old School Tie

I was sitting one morning outside a café on the Boulevard Saint Michel, if that's the way you spell it, wondering what to do with the rest of the day. I had already seen the Louvre, the Eiffel Tower, and the Place de la Concorde. The afternoon stretched before me limitlessly.

All at once I recognized Arthur Spencer-Watt. But Watto with a beard and a Spanish beret, and a cigarette holder several inches long! He sat down at a table near me, ordered a Dubonnet in impeccable French, opened *Le Matin*, and, apparently with full comprehension, began to read the middle page.

I examined him with interest. The last time I'd seen him had been a good ten years ago, at school, when he was a furtive, flop-eared child of fourteen. We'd had to beat him quite a lot to teach him to be a gentleman, and to wear his cap back to front in our presence. Even then it was touch and go whether he'd remember to stand to attention, and bow, before helping us to his sweets.

But now it seemed that our work had shown a profit. This new Watto was almost dapper, and there was no doubt at all about the quality of his French.

I resolved to go over and speak to him.

'Well,' I said, placing my hand on his shoulder, 'old Watto! What d'you know!'

He looked up, startled. Then recognition dawned. 'Why – hello,' he said. 'How are you? How nice to see you again.'

We beamed at one another, temporarily at a loss. To tell the truth, I was wondering if he remembered the punishment that had been handed out to him, and whether I should not make

47

some light reference to the bad old days. Things had been done to Watto that no one could be expected to forget in the space of a mere ten years.

'Well,' said Watto, 'are you living here now?'

Actually, I'd left Berlin, for Paris, in rather a hurry about a month ago. The faint possibility of commercial employment in that city had suddenly become reality, and I'd thought it best to check out before having to devote the rest of my life to the sale of copper insulators.

'I am,' I said. 'One writes a little, you know. One paints. One manages to live.'

One managed, in point of fact, to live on a small allowance from one's father, but one wasn't going to let Suspender-Pot in on *that*.

'Do you?' said Watto, impressed. 'I'm – I'm only in the travel business. A sort of guide.'

'There's nothing wrong with that,' I said. 'Come to glorious Aix-les-Bains. Shady walks, thermal baths, and sporting 9-hole links . . .'

Watto looked surprised. I was probably going too fast for him. 'Listen,' I said, 'let's meet tonight, and get ourselves a slice of pleasure. Let's see if it's true what they say about Paree. I've been working like a dog for the last three weeks, and could do with some informal relaxation.'

Watto hesitated. 'Actually,' he said, 'I'm meeting someone at the Rotonde. A friend –'

'Don't say another word,' I told him. 'Any friend of yours is a blood brother of mine. What time?'

'Well, about nine,' said Watto.

I was there on the dot, overjoyed at the prospect of an English-speaking evening with English-speaking friends. Although I'd only been in Paris for four weeks I'd already realized that the French I'd been taught bore no relation whatever to the whistling cascade that poured out of the French people themselves. At the end of the first week, in fact, I'd given up speaking French altogether, and retired into a condition of silence broken only, and that infrequently, by *Oui*, *Non*, and *Merci*.

Then I saw Watto's companion. A woman, considerably older than he was, with a dead-white face, a purple mouth, and black hair scraped back over her ears. It looked as though I was going to be struggling with *Oui, Non*, and *Merci* after all.

Watto introduced us, presenting me as – 'a friend'. To my relief I found that the lady's name was Naomi Salter, and she was a novelist, from S.W.3. A singularly silent novelist, but the few words she did speak during dinner were undoubtedly English. One of them was 'bitch'.

I was a little nervous of Miss Salter, but Watto and I, with several bottles of wine, enjoyed a number of jokes about conducted tours. I scored a special success with four lines of a poem I'd once seen in a travel brochure:

> *Where is my Motherland?*
> *The memory of thee brings ceaseless*
> *tears,*
> *It was madness to have left thee –*
> *O beautiful Andalusia.*

Even Miss Salter smiled, revealing a set of unusually powerful teeth.

After dinner I suggested that we should go on. 'Let's make the ascension,' I said, 'to old M'martre. Let's get right in among the rabble.'

The other two seemed reluctant, but in the end Watto said there was quite an amusing little place he'd heard about, if, perhaps, that would do . . . ?

They appeared to know him quite well at the door. A frightful-looking Algerian in a dinner-jacket appeared and bowed, and said, 'Sairtainly, Meestaire Spencaire-Vaat . . .'

We went into a cellar, with a number of rough-looking customers sitting round the walls. Watto gave me his coat, and Miss Salter's walking-stick – I was glad she'd abandoned *that* – and asked me to leave them in the cloakroom, while he fixed up the table.

I went through a bead curtain into a kind of large cupboard, hung up our things, and suddenly found myself face to face with a negress in the process of dressing herself in three feathers.

I backed away, alarmed. 'Pardon – *mille pardons* – I'm so sorry . . .'

The negress beamed, and said something incomprehensible.

But I did catch the word *cheri*. I returned to our table, breathing rather hard.

We watched the customers dancing for a while, and Watto bought two more bottles of wine. I let him pay, thinking it was probably on expenses. In any case, I only had a couple of hundred francs.

Then the Algerian leaped on to a chair. '*Mesdames et Messieurs!*' he cried. I lost the rest of it, but caught the last three words – '*La belle – Zigzig!*' With that the negress in the feathers burst from behind the curtain.

She posed for a moment in the spotlight, kissed her hand all round the room, and suddenly threw herself into a solo number the like of which I had never seen before. And, what is more, she seemed to be doing it specially for my benefit. Perhaps she thought she owed it to me, after our little *rencontre* in the cloaks.

I toyed modestly with the label on the bottle of wine, looking up with a lightly frozen smile whenever it seemed at all safe to do so. The technique was pretty steamy for anyone not actually born and bred in old Algiers.

The end of *la belle Zigzig*'s performance was greeted with applause. She backed, kissing her hand, through the curtain, shot out again almost immediately, pulling a red silk dress over her head, bounded across the room, and sat down on my knee!

'*Bon soir, Zigzig,*' said Arthur Spencer-Watt, '*comment ça va?*'

I supported Zigzig with difficulty. She had one arm round my neck. 'Here,' I said to Watto, 'can't we get this tulip a chair?'

A surprising thing happened then. Watto suddenly went rigid. '*What* did you say?' he snapped.

'I said – "Can't we get her a chair?"'

'No,' said Watto, abruptly. 'Tulip. You called her a tulip. By God, I remember you now!' He turned excitedly to Miss Salter. 'This is the clot,' said Watto, 'who rubbed a dead rat in my hair!'

He sat back. He shook his head wonderingly. 'I didn't know who the hell you were,' he said. 'Couldn't remember you from Adam. But I've got it now, all right. You're Campbell. You used to call the maids in the dining-hall "tulips". You, and Dixon and that frightful footballing Thorpe.' Very gently, Watto licked his upper lip. 'This,' he said, almost to himself, 'this is just the way I'd like it to be.'

Suddenly, he clapped his hands. '*Mahmoud!*' he cried. '*Champagne! Pour mon ami!*'

'Spencer-Watt,' I said slowly and carefully, 'don't play the fool.' It was difficult to be dignified with Zigzig hanging round my neck. 'That's all ancient history. You know quite well I can't pay for champagne. I want to go home.'

'*Et des petits cadeaux,*' cried Watto, '*pour la belle Zigzig!*'

He seized Miss Salter by the wrist. 'They caught me on the shooting range,' he cried excitedly, 'and rubbed a dead rat in my hair. The other two held me down, and this creature rubbed the rat in my hair. They were laughing.'

The Algerian appeared with a magnum of champagne, a large but faded box of chocolates, and a teddy-bear wearing a pair of white, frilled knickers.

'As you hev order, sair,' he said, and put the whole lot on the table in front of me.

I stood up, removing Zigzig. 'I didn't order anything,' I said. 'I have no money. I'm going home.'

The Algerian gave a slight, sideways nod of his bullet head. I saw another Algerian put his back against the door.

'I weel hev twelve Eenglish pound, sair,' said the Algerian with the presents. Zigzig snatched the chocolates and the teddy-bear and held them to her bosom, contriving an expression resembling pleasure. 'Sank you, M'sieu,' she murmured. 'You are *gentil*.'

In the extremity of terror and despair I turned to Miss Salter. 'Miss Salter,' I said, 'for Heaven's sake –'

Miss Salter looked right through me. In a deep, faraway voice, she said, 'I remember my first day at school. They painted my face with cocoa. They tied my hair on top of my head with a bootlace. Then they made me stand on a table, on one leg, and sing.'

'Did they?' said Spencer-Watt, interested. 'Tell me, darling, what did they make you sing?'

'I remember the words,' said Miss Salter, 'rather clearly. They were:

> *I'm a dirty pig,*
> *My belly is much too big.*

It was just a small thing,' said Miss Salter, 'but – *you* know . . .'

Spencer-Watt nodded sympathetically. 'Shall we,' he said, 'ask him to try it?'

'Just let him run through it once or twice,' suggested Miss Salter, 'until the orchestra gets the key.'

I made a break for the door. The largest Algerian put his foot out and said, 'Eff you please, no fighteeng.' Several waiters closed in.

I recognized an inescapable commitment.

They had no cocoa for the face painting, but they made me roll up my trousers above the knee. I climbed on to the table, and I sang Miss Salter's song. Soprano, by Miss Salter's request.

Eventually, after a number of choruses, Spencer-Watt said, 'All right, Penelope, you're initiated. Get out. And next time you can play with the bigger girls.'

I got off the table, and rolled down the legs of my trousers. 'I always knew,' I told Spencer-Watt, 'you were a dirty little swine.'

They made me sing it again, with gestures, and a rough kind of step-dance to round it off.

This time I bowed, without speaking, before walking out into the street. One of the waiters threw a grapefruit after me, but missed.

Looking back upon this incident now it seems to me to be high time that bullying was stamped out of English public-schools.

3
Three Years at the Opera

I don't know much about grand opera, but what I do know I know inside out. *The Flying Dutchman* is my forte, and even now, by thinking for a moment, I can tell you what happens in the first two acts.

I was taken to see it in the early summer of 1932 by an elderly Oriental student called Mr Maung – a resident, like myself, in the Pension Kashmir, Munich.

The treat was arranged by our landlady, the Baronin von Heckrath. The Baron had passed on some years before, leaving his lady in financial difficulties, and the Pension Kashmir, with German lessons thrown in, was her road back.

She saw us off at the door, presenting each of us with a large paper bag. 'Is blut-wurst,' she said, 'mit sauerkraut und kek.'

I was surprised. There seemed to be no need to attend the opera with a load of blood-sausage, sauerkraut, and cake. I dropped mine into the umbrella-stand on the way out.

Mr Maung, however, was delighted. He tucked his parcel away in a string bag, which already contained a vacuum flask, three or four apples, and a number of books.

Mr Maung's string bag did not surprise me. He wore chamois leather gloves, spats, and a large wing collar. A string bag full of apples was nothing.

Our seats were high up in the gallery, in the middle of a row. It took us some time to reach them, because everyone round us – like Mr Maung – seemed to be burdened with a considerable amount of luggage. To get to my seat I had to climb over an elderly man wrapped in a rug, with a picnic basket on his knee.

No sooner were we settled than Mr Maung produced the largest of his books.

'Sssoo,' he said, 'playssee of plot for lesson.'

I asked him what he was talking about. Did he want me to write something down?

'Tomollow mauling,' said Mr Maung, 'flaum Flau Balonin.'

When I'd unravelled this I felt a stab of fear. We'd come to the opera, not as I had imagined, for pleasure, but for a practical purpose! There would be questions in the morning from the Frau Baronin, at a time when her nerves were usually at their worst!

With my three words of German I'd already fallen foul of her on several previous occasions. Once, she'd even burst into tears, sobbing that she was high-born, and not accustomed to work, and that it made life unendurable unless her pupils tried their best. I'd been alarmed by her tears, seeing that she was a powerfully built woman with a marked moustache.

'Here,' I said to Mr Maung, 'let me have a look at that book.' I looked. Every word was in German, and not only in German, but in German type as well, rendering any attempt at comprehension impossible. I realized that from now on I was linked to *The Flying Dutchman* only by that slenderest of bridges, Mr Maung.

I gave it back. 'Start talking,' I said.

Mr Maung began. 'Flying Dutchum,' he said, 'sssailing Kep of Godd Ope in fuliouss wind-gale –'

At that moment the orchestra crashed out into the overture. There were several hundred of them, and they blew as hard as they could.

I leant closer to Mr Maung. '– Daland,' he was saying, 'wissh to mek sssoo lich ssailo with all tleasure blidegloom to daughter . . .'

Blidegloom? Lich ssailo? And was it Daland or *Darand*?

I cursed Mr Maung for his whistling and his fantastic trick of turning r's into l's.

'Sssoo,' said Mr Maung, 'ssecon Act iss Ssspin Cholusss. All maidensss ssspin, ssspin . . .'

'All right,' I said. 'Thank you very much. I'll pick it up when the thing begins.'

'Moossic,' said Mr Maung, 'iss now of piccolo, flute, clalio-net, basssoo, tlumpetss –'

'Shut up,' I said. 'I want to listen.'

About an hour later the curtain rose. A full-rigged ship, with a crew of three thousand, in a howling gale!

'Sssailoss cholusss!' shouted Mr Maung. 'Yo-ho-hey! Hal-lo-yo!'

I endured this pandemonium for some twenty minutes, and then Daland – Darand? – gave tongue.

Mr Maung plucked my sleeve. 'He ssay sship all lite,' squeaked Mr Maung. 'Ancho sstick fass in ssand-wyke!'

Sand-wyke? What could it possibly be? It was just the kind of question that Frau Baronin would ask. 'In Act Vun, plizz, in vat is anchored szchip of Daland?'

My head was ringing with grotesque distortions of the English language.

'What's sand-wyke?' I asked Mr Maung.

'Moment,' he said. He reached into his bag and brought out an English dictionary.

'Iss ssand of Winchester College,' he reported.

I looked at him briefly. I was sure he hadn't been able to find sand-wyke, and had invented this monstrous lie rather than admit defeat.

'Thank you,' I said. 'You may continue.'

He did. Hisses. Clicks. Yo-ho-hey and hal-lo-yo. And, then, unusually difficult passages like 'Dutchum lush blind on ssshap lockss,' which defeated me altogether.

At the end of Act I Mr Maung consumed his blood-sausage. I watched him with a certain amount of envy, regretting that my own should be in the Frau Baronin's umbrella-stand. We already seemed to have been in the opera house for several hours.

The curtain went up on Act II.

'Maidens ssspin cholusss!' cried Mr Maung, and off we went again.

By this time I was tuned in to him, and could obtain a fairly clear grasp of the situation. I might even have enjoyed the Spin Chorus if it hadn't been for my increasing appetite. Lunch had been my last meal, and it was now nearly nine o'clock.

Mr Maung produced an apple.

'Now,' he said, 'maidens mek feasst for ssailors,' and snapped his teeth into what looked like a particularly juicy pippin.

I watched him with a tight smile. I had to keep it tight, or the water would have run out of my mouth.

As the curtain went down on Act II, Mr Maung opened his sauerkraut and cake. I saw that the Frau Baronin had included a fork for ease of service.

'Look,' I said, 'you couldn't spare me some of that, could you? I seem to have left my supper behind.'

Mr Maung shook his head. 'Iss mine,' he said. He opened his vacuum flask, and poured out a steaming cup of coffee.

I stood up and with difficulty struggled out to the aisle. All round me people were digging into Frankfurters, chocolate, rolls of bread. If *I'd* known that *The Flying Dutchman* was going to last for ever I'd have brought a turkey.

Ten minutes later I was back again, minutely watching Mr Maung brushing the crumbs off his suit.

In my search for food I'd got mixed up in the queue for the men's room – an accident that I should have regarded on another occasion as a joke – and found the buffet just in time to have it closed in my face.

The commissionaire explained that Act III had already begun. It seemed that no refreshments could be served while the curtain was up.

'It is, you understand,' he said, 'respect for the performers.'

He was a large man who looked as if he'd had five or six meals already.

For a moment I thought of going home, rescuing my parcel from the umbrella-stand, and tucking in. Then I remembered the morning lesson, and my total ignorance of what was likely to happen in the last Act. I returned to my seat.

Mr Maung, having tidied himself, got to work once more.

'Now again,' he said, 'iss ssailo choluss – hal-lo-ho-hey – yo-lo-ho-ha!'

'If we could, for a moment,' I said, 'leave that on one side – have you finished your cake?'

'Yiss,' said Mr Maung.

'And your apples?' I asked him.

'I eat him now,' said Mr Maung. He did, right down to the core.

We sat it out to the end. Hours later the curtain came down, on ship-wreck, thunder, lightning, and a series of roars from the performers surpassing anything they had as yet achieved.

I scarcely heard them. I tottered out, weak as a kitten, and had to stand in the tram all the way home.

The Frau Baronin was waiting up for us. She asked us if we'd had a nice time, and then sent us off to bed.

I crept downstairs in my bare feet twenty minutes later. The umbrella-stand was empty! My blood-sausage, with sauerkraut and cake, had disappeared.

I found out why the following morning. The Frau Baronin was unusually severe. She said that while tidying up she'd found my food parcel in the umbrella-stand. She wanted to know why I'd taken it to the opera, only to bring it home again, uneaten. She also wanted to know why I'd chosen the umbrella-stand as a storage place, rather than somewhere reasonable, like the kitchen.

I couldn't answer that one.

As a matter of fact, at the morning lesson, I didn't seem to know very much about *The Flying Dutchman*, either.

4

The Dicking Bird

I'd gone down to this place to write an article about their hunt, and passed a tiring afternoon showing enthusiasm in the back of a small car driven by Mrs Milligan, wife of the Master. In the back of the car with me were two sodden dogs, a shovel and an old man called Casey, smelling strongly of ferrets.

That night was even worse. The Milligans, who'd been in charge of the hunt for two hundred years, produced endless cuttings from local newspapers about the Ballybrackens finding in Flynn's Bottom, and killing in Kelly's Drain, and seemed surprised when I didn't write it all down.

'You've got a note-book, haven't you?' said the Master, a short but powerfully built man with a quick temper, and a stiffness of intellect that made him unapproachable by anything save the simplest of words.

I made the mistake, then, of trying to tell him that I was just going for atmosphere. 'Sort of background and personality stuff,' I said.

This was received with surprise by the Milligans and by their guests – half a dozen hard-faced men and women in tweed suits and canary waistcoats.

I heard someone called Captain Fawcus say, 'How's your background and personality, Mildred?' – and Mildred replying, 'Just atmospheric, Jack.'

From then on, in a ham-handed way, they imitated everything I said. I suppose they thought it was good fun, on a level with their final gesture – a bale of hay in my bed.

Next morning, we all came down to breakfast. I sat beside

Major Darcey, Mrs Milligan's father, an old man of about ninety, who had so far lost his physical powers, or grip upon the conventions, that he ate all his meals with a spoon.

My new friends seemed quite prepared to begin again where they had left off the previous evening. I had to assure several of them that I had written no poetry during the night; Captain Fawcus pretended to cry when I refused to give him my autograph, and once I caught Major Darcey trying to dip his spoon into my porridge. It was a thoroughly uncomfortable meal.

Then, the door opened and the maid, Bridie, put one foot and a bright red face round the edge of it.

'There's a man,' she said, 'to see him.'

From the beginning she had regarded me as a visitor from Mars.

I pushed back my chair, and at that moment a figure walked into the breakfast-room carrying three cameras, a collapsible tripod, a collection of lamps, and a black velvet muffler round his neck. He stopped inside the door, bowed, clicked his heels, and said, 'Goot morning! Schraub!'

We looked at him with our mouths open. He wore a beret with a pimple on top, a black suit, and sandals.

He raised his hand. 'Do not disturb,' he said. 'I look for my lord editor. I am Schraub. I make picture of all great Irish authors for Chicago paper.'

Roderick Milligan, the Master, rose to his feet.

'What,' he said, simply, 'is that?'

'Just a minute,' I said. 'I think he wants to take a photograph of me. He's working for an American paper.'

Roderick turned his head very slowly. He seemed to be having trouble with the muscles of his neck.

'Why, then,' he said, 'is he here?'

Schraub suddenly dumped all his paraphernalia on the sideboard.

'Not to say more!' he cried. 'I am seeing my writing man!'

He bustled forward. He caught me by the hand.

'So glad to meet,' he beamed. 'I am hearing you are here in your so beautiful house. I fly back Chicago tonight. Now I make picture.' He wrung my hand several times.

At this moment old Major Darcey said, very clearly and distinctly, 'Take off your hat, you blackguard.'

Schraub jumped. Then he laughed. 'The old one is mad, yes?' he said. 'I am seeing so many of your aristos.'

Schraub looked confidently round the table. 'But most times, is it not, they are lock upstairs in rooms?'

He shrugged. 'Ah, well,' he said, 'is to work. Where must we go?'

Suddenly, I saw that the Master was about to burst. His face was working uncontrollably. He was crushing a piece of toast in his massive, purple hand.

'Wait a minute,' I said. 'Mr Milligan – sir – would you be kind enough to lend us your study for just a few minutes? I honestly didn't know Mr Schraub was coming here. I'm – I'm awfully sorry . . .'

Roderick fixed me with a bulging eye. 'I'll give him,' he said, 'twenty minutes. Then, I'll set the dogs on 'im.'

'Thanks awfully,' I said. 'Mr Schraub, come with me.'

I bustled the unbelievable Schraub into the passage, down the hall, and into the Master's study. The whole house-party followed, including Major Darcey, with a napkin round his neck.

I tried to stop them. 'I think Mr Schraub,' I said, 'would probably like to work alone.'

Captain Fawcus intervened. 'My dear chap,' he said, 'I'd rather watch this than a point-to-point.'

We crowded into the study. Immediately, Schraub began plugging in his lamps. He shifted the furniture, he strewed the books about.

'Now,' said Schraub, 'my writing man at his desk.'

I sat down. I was bathed in a blinding glare of light. I could just see the house-party in the background, peering over one another's shoulders.

Schraub stood back, half closed his eyes, and said, 'Our hair. We romple our hair like when we write.'

He leant over and did it for me. There was a gasp all round the room. I heard the voice of Captain Fawcus – 'Stap me, it's Betty Grable!' And then Schraub shot underneath his hood.

'So,' came his muffled voice, 'now we make as when we are writing. Soft face. Is dreamy, please.'

The eye of the camera stared at me unwinkingly. The lights glared down, white-hot. I tried to make soft face, dreamy please.

It nearly finished them. Major Darcey gave a whoop, and dissolved in a paroxysm of coughing. Captain Fawcus beat him on the back, neighing with laughter. And I heard the thick voice of Roderick himself.

'Damme!' shouted Roderick – 'the fella's the spittin' image of a horse!'

It was probably the first joke he'd ever made in his life, and he loved it. 'Look at 'im!' shouted Roderick – 'the spittin' image of a horse!'

Schraub reappeared from beneath his hood. He seemed to be oblivious to the noise. He advanced upon me, his eyes half closed, one hand extended before him.

'Is too formal,' said Schraub. 'Our lord editor is not enough easy. So, we make like this.'

I found he was loosening my tie. For a moment I thought of biting his wrist, and then I fell back, spent. Schraub spread my collar wide, and stepped back to his camera. Again he disappeared beneath the hood.

'Is aixcellent,' he said. 'Is litrachury. Now, hold, please. And watch – for the dicking bird!'

The door leading to the hall opened slowly, and a very old hound called Banger tottered in. Banger had long since been pensioned off, and mooned around the house all day in a dream, presumably remembering happier days in Kelly's Drain.

I watched Banger out of the corner of my eye. He staggered right across the room, halted, and with great care – he often fell down – leant his weight against one of the legs of Schraub's tripod.

Schraub threw out a hand. 'Oops!' he cried. 'Steady, I must ask! Is not to push!'

Banger gave a low wheezy sigh. I think he found comfort in the warmth of the lamps, and the presence of so many people.

Schraub popped out from beneath the hood, bringing it with him. The black velvet hung round his face, making him look like something left over after they'd cleaned out the harem.

'A wow-wow!' cried Schraub. 'A pretty wow-wow!' He fell upon Banger's neck. Banger, horrified, backed away, but

Schraub caught him expertly by the collar.

'My lord editor,' he exclaimed, 'and his wow-wow! What is making better?' A moment later I found myself lined up behind the desk with Banger.

'Holding!' cried Schraub. 'Is holding for perfect picture. Now – the dicking bird!'

He took about twenty more. Once, he tried to leave out Banger, but Captain Fawcus protested. He said it wouldn't be the same without the wow-wow, so Banger was dragged back. In between shots I had to hold my handkerchief to my nose.

Just before lunch Major Darcey had a kind of stroke, and had to be led away, but all the others stuck it out to the end. They brought chairs from the hall, and provided themselves with drinks. They begged Schraub not to hurry.

'Damme!' cried Roderick, 'the fella's a horse!'

We knocked off at one o'clock, and went in to lunch. Schraub asked for a glass of milk and some plain lettuce. He said he never ate anything else.

'What?' roared Captain Fawcus – 'no nut cutlets?' I couldn't wait for Schraub to go.

He left eventually, at half-past two, packing himself and his paraphernalia into the back of a hired car.

That afternoon they decided not to go shooting, as they had originally intended. Instead, they invented a kind of charade. Roderick Milligan took the part of Schraub, his conception of a foreign accent limiting itself to 'Donner Wetter – look at the dicking bird!' Major Darcey, revived, pretended to be me.

The others thrust the poor old man into this role. I don't believe he had the least idea what he was supposed to be doing, but he certainly played it for laughs all the way.

5
Unaccustomed As I Am

From my earliest days I have enjoyed an attractive impediment in my speech. I have never permitted the use of the word 'stammer'. I can't say it myself.

This surprising phenomenon has assumed, in its time, a wide variety of different forms, and the ability to change its nature without warning.

For instance, I used to have for several weeks at a time what I came to call the 'muted gibbon' cry. It used to go, 'May I – awah awah – awash my – ahah ahah ahah ahah ahands please?'

Then, suddenly, I would awake one morning to find that I was back again in the happy inhalation days. All at once I would begin to speak while breathing *in*, having found it impossible to produce a word even as structurally simple as 'Oh' while breathing out. This sounded like wind blowing under a door, and it was a sharp man who made anything of it.

Soon the inhalation method gave way to the impassive. Upon finding myself held up I would abandon all further effort to produce anything at all, fold the hands neatly in the lap, allow the face to become expressionless, and wait for the next word to arrive, possibly out of the air.

The snag to this device was that the audience never really knew if the show was over. Once, I got into one of these quiet times in a railway carriage, while talking to an elderly stranger about bicycles. I had been remarking upon the difficulty of riding bicycles into the wind, and was preparing to reach even more deeply into the subject when everything shut down. It was my intention to say, 'One feels so like turning round and going the other way,' but I got locked on 'one'.

Under the new system I blew the boilers down at once, and sat back looking absolutely impassively at the floor. The elderly stranger, having had one or two previous examples of the same thing in the earlier part of our discussion, sat back to wait. But after, I suppose, nearly a minute, he became uneasy. He leant forward. 'Excuse me,' he said earnestly, 'I don't want to embarrass you, but could you – er – possibly tell me if you've finished?'

I made no attempt to speak. I shook my head very slowly from side to side, without altering by an iota the blankness of my expression. Unfortunately, he had to get out at the next station, before I could come through to him again. He did so with the most abject, stumbling apologies, knowing that I was still working away. The incident may have given him some incurable complex. For me, it was just another chore in the daily grind.

Several cures were tried. Once, I spent two months lying on a psychoanalyst's sofa in Harley Street, pouring out the story of my life in a loud, clear, and absolutely uninterrupted voice. At the end of the hour I would rise to my feet and try to bid the doctor good afternoon. Nothing happened. No word emerged.

We abandoned the course by mutual consent. We parted, as a matter of fact, by gesture. I wanted to say, 'Well, good-bye, doctor – don't let this upset you,' but the shut-down was complete. By some curious kind of transference he too became afflicted, and turned rigid in the middle of the sentence, 'You will probably find things easier soon.' The word 'find' very nearly choked him. In the end we waved at one another reassuringly, with the veins standing out on our foreheads, and then parted for good.

In its time this trick has involved me in a number of unusual situations – the most unusual of them undoubtedly being Mrs Gilbert's lunch party. (It is necessary to create fictitious names. Some people are more sensitive about this matter than others.)

Mrs Gilbert rang up one morning and said, 'I hate doing this. I'm one short. You've got to come to lunch; but you're to make absolutely no attempt to speak. Even if someone asks you a direct question you are to remain silent, and pass it off with a shrug, or something – *you* know.'

'It's all right,' I said, 'there's no need to panic.'

There was a pause, and then she said, rather seriously, 'I *can* trust you, can't I? It's most important. The First Secretary of the Legation is coming, with his wife, and I don't want them to think we're mad. What makes it rather worse is that Theo is coming, too. He practically asked himself, although why *he* wants to go out at all I can't imagine.'

'Oh,' I said. 'I see it now. Theo's coming along – Theo the Whistle.'

'Don't *laugh* about it,' said Mrs Gilbert. 'I'd die of shame if by some impossible chance you both began together.' (Theo was rather worse than I was. He filled in the gaps, or built himself up for further effort, with a short melodious whistle.)

'You can trust me,' I told Mrs Gilbert. 'Not one single word will emerge.'

'I know *that*,' said Mrs Gilbert, 'but are you going to *try* to say anything?'

'Not a word,' I reassured her. 'Trust me – no chat.'

'Very well, then,' she said. 'A quarter past one for half past. And – *be careful*.'

The other guests, including Theo and the First Secretary, were there when I arrived. I kept a mile clear of Theo, and bowed, without speaking, upon being introduced to the diplomat. Mrs Gilbert looked quite cheerful as we went in to lunch.

I found myself seated beside the diplomat's wife on my left, and a rather brisk matron in a large flowered hat on my right. Theo was immediately opposite. It was clear that he had had his orders too. His eyes were on his plate. From time to time he put his hand across his mouth, as if to remind himself of his duties.

I discovered almost at once that the diplomat's wife could only say, 'Yiss, pleece', in English, and that all the rest of her remarks had to be presented in her native dialect. That seemed to look after her. There was no chance of *her* starting anything. But the matron in the large hat was another matter altogether. First crack out of the box, even before the soup had appeared, she turned to me, centred me squarely with her eyes for a moment, and then said, 'What do *you* do for a living?' I found out afterwards she prided herself upon her lack of self-consciousness.

I shrugged my shoulders, and made a vague gesture with both hands. What I wanted to say was, 'In all probability, a damn sight more than you do,' but I was under sealed orders.

'H'mm,' she said – 'nothing? Well, well, that must be very agreeable for you. And quite delightful for your poor father.'

With that, to my relief, she abandoned me, and applied herself to a retired soldier on her right.

The lunch continued upon its placid, meaningless way, Mrs Gilbert established herself powerfully with the First Secretary, and the rest of them aggravating themselves with some stuff about bridge and pedigree dogs.

And then, suddenly, it happened – out of a clear blue sky. At one moment they were all chattering away – Mrs Gilbert, the First Secretary, the brisk matron, the retired major – and at the next there was complete silence. The whole lot of them dried up, practically together. They sat there, looking at their plates, and it was obvious that none of them would ever speak again.

I got going at once. I had no moment of hesitation. I had been sitting there for nearly an hour, contributing nothing, and now that the emergency was upon us it was clearly up to me to save the day. I had no memory whatever of Mrs Gilbert's orders.

At this time I was having the muted gibbon call, with rotation. That is, my head turned ponderously from right to left, and then back again, with the effort of speech. It humped the muscles on the back of my neck like a bison, and in fact rendered any attempt at articulation completely out of the question.

But I threw myself into it. I set myself to say, 'I went bathing yesterday, and the water was as warm as toast.' I became locked at once. My head turned slowly to the left, the rich blood already pounding into my face. I met the terrified gaze of the diplomat's wife, tried to smile at her, emitted three 'ahah ahah ahah's' instead, and then found myself centred upon Theodore, immediately opposite me. To my absolute consternation I saw that he was busy, too. The fool had thrown himself into speech as well, and was now whistling away in short, piercing trills, with his eyes clamped firmly shut. My head ground round to the right. 'I awah awah awent . . .' I said to the brisk matron, and then my head started its journey back again. I caught a glimpse of Mrs Gilbert out of the corner of my eye. Her lips were moving in prayer. I had time to think that she was lucky to have them moving *at all*, when I became based upon Theodore once more. He must have played the whole of 'The Bluebells of Scotland' by this time, but he was as far away as ever from saying anything.

It went on through all eternity – some of the guests leaning forward with bright smiles, and the perspiration running down their faces, others suddenly exhibiting nervous mannerisms of their own, twitching or plucking at their clothing, or coughing loudly, but all waiting to hear what either Theo or I might have to add to the fund of human knowledge.

Mrs Gilbert broke it down in the end. Her voice, when she found it, came out in a scream, but she managed to speak. The guests leaped in their seats as if shot, but she'd done it. In another moment the whole lot of them were chattering away again – high-pitched, nervous stuff – but at least it was coming out. Theodore and I let ourselves unwind slowly, and the rest of the lunch played itself out without incident.

To this day I have no knowledge of what Theodore was trying to say. For all I know he may have been bathing too, and, like myself, found the water warm as toast. But that is Theodore's secret, and as far as I am concerned he can keep it.

6
Animal Farm

Now, here is an ugly situation. I am sitting on a sofa in the heart of mysterious Chelsea. The room is full of people, and on the table in front of me there is a glass of rum. But I also have one hand half-way down the throat of a dog called Ursula, and another dog called Roger begins barking madly every time I open my mouth.

I never thought that anything like this was going to happen when I first arrived. 'It's just a quiet evening,' they said – 'we've hardly any rum, but some writers are coming in.' I didn't see how the first situation could be improved by its juxtaposition to the second, but I decided to go along.

It was a green door set in a high wall, surmounted by a wrought-iron lantern containing, surprisingly enough, an empty cigarette packet. I rang the bell. Someone inside shouted, 'God, I *told* the fool to push the door.'

'This is it, all right,' I said to the taximan, and leant against the door. I fell into a foaming sea of dogs. There seemed to be hundreds of them, leaping, barking, and snarling in the darkness.

I was going to spring out through the door again, when my hostess appeared. Trousers, of course.

'Down, Roger!' she cried – 'Stop it, Ursula!' Then I saw there were only two dogs – fat, low, white dogs, gleaming like young pigs.

We crossed the courtyard and went into the house. It was one of those cosy mews houses where a portrait of the owner falls off the escritoire every time anyone opens the door.

The room was full of people. 'This is Miss Indecipherable,' said my hostess – 'our local sculptress. And Mr Inaudible. You know his books. And Mr and Mrs –'

I couldn't hear a thing. Roger and Ursula were barking hysterically. I shooed them a bit with my foot. Ursula caught hold of my trouser-leg in her teeth.

'There's a seat over there,' said my hostess. 'Do snatch it.' I snatched it by the laborious process of dragging Ursula clean across the room. Her eyes were closed. She seemed to be enjoying herself.

I sat down on the end of a sofa. Someone put a drink on a small table in front of me. I sat back, letting my right hand hang down. It was at once seized by something hot and wet and soft. I tried to snatch it away. Two rows of teeth sank into my wrist. It was Ursula – Ursula with my hand half-way down her throat.

'Good dog,' I said – 'good dog, Ursula. Please let go.' I pulled. Ursula growled gently, and renewed the pressure. I tried again, but it was hopeless. I turned back to the party, hoping no one had noticed. The inside of Ursula's throat felt awful.

Mr Inaudible was sitting on a stool nearby. 'Well,' I said, 'how are things going with . . .?'

Roger began to bark. He'd been sitting in front of me for some time, waiting – as it turned out now – for me to speak.

I tried again. 'How are things with . . . ?'

Roger nearly lifted the roof. Several people looked round.

After a short pause I drew a cautious breath. Roger gave a single warning growl. I breathed out. Roger relaxed. He had made the situation clear.

So here I am now in a strange house, with one hand imprisoned by a strange dog and another strange dog ready to scream the place down if I so much as open my mouth.

It's queer, but up till now I've always regarded dogs as useful allies in conversational blockages. I've often been caught at the lunch-table beside someone's uncle – the one who never wears a collar and is only allowed down to meals – and have been on the verge of inventing some mental derangement of my own to set the ball rolling, when a dog comes bounding in. At once, all kinds of subjects present themselves. . .

'What a lovely Sealyham! And he's only a puppy, too! What,

not a Sealyham? An Airedale! And *she's* nearly seven . . . ? Well, well, I never imagined . . .'

There's so much good stuff on the agenda that the only difficulty is to decide which matter to take on next.

But this is something entirely different. Here we have anti-social dogs – dogs determined that no pleasure of any kind will take place – no talk, no gesture, and, now that I come to regard Ursula's end of it more closely, no smoking.

But here's Mr Inaudible. He thinks I'm being left out.

'Having a good time?' he says. For a moment I consider shouting Roger down. But I've got to have something pretty good to shout Roger down with. I'm not going to be caught roaring, 'Yes, very nice, thank you,' at the top of my voice, in case Roger decides to let me carry on with it alone.

I content myself with pointing at Roger and then pointing at my mouth. There is, of course, no reason why Mr Inaudible should understand the significance of this, and he doesn't. He says, 'Dog's hungry, eh?' and hands me a plate of sandwiches.

I haven't got time to tell him about Ursula. I haven't got time to tell him about anything. Roger makes one spring, and rips through the sandwiches like a prairie fire.

I struggle wildly to free my hand from Ursula. I try to put the sandwiches behind my back. There is a crash, and the small table goes over, carrying my drink with it.

There is a sudden silence and then the hostess appears, distraught. It's apparently one of her Italian wine glasses. Casually – rather too casually for me – she kicks Roger and Ursula into a corner. Five minutes later I'm saying goodnight. I show myself out.

In case any of you, Dear Readers, were at the party unrecognized, please do not think of me now as a one-armed mute – a rough fellow who breaks glasses and feeds plates of sandwiches to dogs.

I was just having a little bit of trouble, that was all.

7

Mr Smyllie, Sir

When, in these trying times, it's possible to work on the lower slopes of a national newspaper for several weeks without discovering which of the scurrying executives is the editor, I count myself fortunate to have served under one who wore a green sombrero, weighed twenty-two stone, sang parts of his leading articles in operatic recitative, and grew the nail on his little finger into the shape of a pen nib, like Keats.

Even the disordered band of unemployed cooks, squabbling like crows over the Situations Vacant columns in the front office files, knew that he was Robert Maire Smyllie, Editor of the *Irish Times*, and fell silent as he made his swift rush up the stairs.

He was a classical scholar, at home among the Greek philosophers. He was the incorruptible champion of the fading Protestant cause in holy Ireland. His political and humanitarian views won international respect, and he spent most of his time on the run from the importunities of such characters as Chloral O'Kelly and Twitchy Doyle.

They lay in wait for him every evening in their chosen lairs in the front office and threw themselves in his path, as though to halt a rushing locomotive, as soon as he appeared at the door.

Chloral O'Kelly was a deeply melancholic youth who drank disinfectant, and was in constant need of 3s. 9d. for another bottle. Twitchy Doyle was a little old man with a straggly, jumping moustache who lived by reviewing reprints of Zane Grey. The moment the Editor burst through the front door they closed on him with urgent appeals, battling for position with Deirdre of the Sorrows, an elderly woman who believed for twelve years that she was being underpaid for her contributions to the Woman's Page. The Editor shot through them, weaving and jinking, crying: 'No – not tonight – tomorrow – goodbye' – and put on an extra burst of speed which carried him up the stairs to the safety of his own room, there to deliver his unforgettable cry: 'Pismires! Warlocks! Stand aside!'

I looked up 'pismire' once in the dictionary and found it meant an ant. It pictured, vividly, the unrelenting tenacity of his hangers-on.

For four years, six nights a week, I worked beside this enormous, shy, aggressive, musical, childlike, cultured and entirely unpredictable human being, separated from him by only a wooden partition, in a monastic life cut off almost completely from the world.

We worked in a high, dusty room topped by an opaque glass dome. There were no outside windows, so that the lights burned day and night. Alec Newman, the Assistant Editor, and Bill Fleming, the theatre critic, shared the outside part. Then came the Editor's office, partitioned off by battered wooden panelling. I had a tiny box jammed between him and the wall, with a sliding hatch between us for the purposes of communication. When it was open I got a portrait view of the great head, hair brushed smoothly back, brick-red face, snub nose supporting glasses and a ginger moustache enclosing the stem of a curved pipe the size of a flower-pot. 'Mr Campbell, we do not wish to be observed,' was the signal for the hatch to be closed.

Alec, Bill and I got in about nine-thirty every night and started to scratch around for leader subjects in the English papers. At ten o'clock the Editor burst in like a charging rhino, denounced pismires and warlocks, and went to ground in his own room.

At ten-thirty came the inevitable inquiry: 'Well, gentlemen – ?'

Alec assumed the responsibility of answering for all of us. 'Nothing, Mr Smyllie, sir. All is sterility and inertia.'

The reply was automatic. 'Ten-thirty, and not a strumpet in the house painted! Art is long, gentlemen, but life is shuddering shorter than you think.' 'Shuddering' and 'shudder' were favourite words of complaint.

Alec made his set protest. 'You're hard, Mr Smyllie, sir. Hard!'

'Mr Newman?'

'Sir?'

'Take your King Charles's head outside and suck it.'

I never discovered the origin of this extraordinary injunction, but it meant that some disagreement had taken place between them during the afternoon and that Alec had better be careful from now on. My own orders came floating over the partition.

'Mr Campbell?'

'Sir?'

'Prehensilize some Bosnian peasants.'

'Immediately, sir.'

The cryptic order had a simple origin. The Editor, seeking once to commend a piece of writing that clung closely, without irrelevant deviation, to its theme, had hit upon the word prehensile, which passed immediately into the language of our private, nocturnal life. Somerset Maugham, for instance, was a prehensile writer, Henry James unprehensile in the extreme. From here it was a short step to prehensilizing an untidily written contribution. Reprehensilization covered a second re-write. We didn't even notice we were saying it after a week or two.

The Bosnian peasant came from a discovery of mine on the back page of the *Manchester Guardian* – an exceedingly improbable story about a Balkan shepherd who'd tripped over a railway line and derailed a train with his wooden leg. The shepherd, in addition, had only one eye, and was carrying a live salmon in his arms. I cannot imagine, now, how even a short fourth leader could have been written on such a theme, but for months I was dependent on the *Guardian*'s Balkan correspondent for my ideas. Acceptance of this *argot* led me once to frighten the life out of the Bishop – I think – of Meath.

I'd come in very late and burst straight into the Editor's room. 'I'm sorry I got held up, Mr Smyllie, sir!' I cried. 'I can always reprehensilize some one-eyed Bosnian bastards!' It was only then that I saw the Bishop sitting in the visitors' chair with his top-hat on his knee. I've never seen a man so profoundly affected by a sentence containing only eight words.

If pursuing his personal, King Charles's head war with Alec, the Editor would suddenly give him the first, interminable leader to write on some political theme, while doing the second and shorter one himself.

Silence settled in for about an hour, with the four typewriters rattling away. Sometimes, then, we got: 'Cold – cold – cold –'

Almost anything could start it off, from the mere weather conditions to some philosophic reflection that had entered the Editor's mind. His typewriter stopped. The rest of us paused, too, expectant in our boxes. The voice rose, high and ghostly, from the Editor's compartment:

'Cold – cold – cold –'

We echoed it, still higher and thinner:

'Cold – cold – cold –'

The Editor's voice took on a deeper, tragically declamatory note:

> 'Cold as a frog in an ice-bound pool,
> Cold as a slew of gooseberry fool,
> Colder than charity –'

There was a long pause, while we stuffed our handkerchiefs into our mouths, struggling to remain silent. The next line came out with rasping cynicism:

'And that's pretty chilly –'

He allowed this to sink in, then returned to the dramatic narrative form:

'But it isn't as cold as poor Brother Billy –'

We all joined in, vying with one another to achieve the maximum in greasy self-satisfaction, on the last line:

'Cause *he's DAID!*'

There was another pause, while we savoured the dying echoes. 'Get on with it, gentlemen,' said the Editor, and the four typewriters started again. But now that his appetite for music had been aroused – and he was a profoundly musical man, with a fine baritone voice – he would give us an encore, singing the words of his leader in a long recitative, like a chant:

> 'O, the Dublin Corporation has decided
> In its wis-*dum* –'

We joined in, like a Greek chorus, in the background:

'In its wis-*dum* . . . its wis-*dum* . . .'
'To sign the death warrant
'Of the traam-*ways* –'
'Traam-*ways* . . . traam-ways . . .'
'A measure with which we find ourselves
'In agree-ment –'
'In agree-ment . . . agree-ment . . .'

There'd be a sudden break in the mood. The voice came out with a snap. 'Thank you, gentlemen, and give my regards to your poor father, too.'

When he was writing the words poured out of him in a flood, without correction, and at times, indeed, without much thought. He'd been doing it too long. But there were occasions when he bent the whole of his courageous and intelligent mind to denouncing the rising tide of parochial Irish republicanism – notably on the death of George V.

This long-drawn-out decline was being charted much more thoroughly by the *Irish Times*, with its Unionist sympathies, than by the other newspapers. Night after night Smyllie put a new touch to his obituary leader, after the routine inquiry, 'Has the poor old shudderer passed on?' Finally, the King died and the leader was sent out for setting. We were all in the Editor's room when the first edition came off the machines. He tore open the leader page to see how it looked, and gave a scream like a wounded bull when he saw that the second half of it, possibly inadvertently, had been printed upside down. Pismires and warlocks that morning were relegated to the ends of hell.

This concern for the English King got us into scattered forays with the IRA, leading once to the windows of the office in Cork being broken by a shower of stones. When the news reached the Editor he made, taking as his framework, 'They cannot intimidate me by shooting my lieutenants,' one of the most carefully formulated battle-cries I've ever heard in my life.

We were in the office at the time. He instructed me to give him the noggin of brandy, filed under B in his correspondence cabinet, and took a steady pull. 'These shudderers,' said Robert Maire Smyllie, 'cannot intimidate me by throwing half-bricks through the windows of the branch office while my lieutenants are taking a posset of stout in the shebeen next door.'

When we left, round about two o'clock the following morning, however, he was in a noticeable hurry to mount his bicycle. As he swung his massive weight into the saddle one of the pedals snapped off clean. He fell off, sprang up again, shouted, 'Mr Campbell, as your superior officer I order you to give me your velocipede!' – snatched it out of my hand, leaped aboard and sped off into the darkness. I limped after him on the broken one. When we got back to his house we drank Slivovitz until breakfast, in further defiance of 'the porter-slopping shudderers from Ballydehob.'

In the office there was indeed at this time the feeling of a beleaguered garrison, one which prompted all of us to remain in the place until daylight, rather than face the dark streets on our bicycles. Those were the great nights of the domino games that kept us locked in combat over the Editor's desk until the charwomen came in in the morning.

'A little pimping, Mr Smyllie, sir?' Alec would suggest, after the paper had gone to bed.

'A little pimping, Mr Newman, would be acceptable.'

No one could ever remember how it came to be called pimping, with the additional refinement of 'hooring', to describe the act of blocking the game with a blank at both ends, but because of Smyllie's complete purity of mind these technicalities added a notable spice to the game.

I can see him now, his green, wide-brimmed hat set square on his head, the great pipe fuming and a glass of brandy by his side, delicately picking up his tiles with the pen-nib fingernail raised in the air.

The unspoken purpose of the three of us was to do him down by a concerted onslaught, all playing into one another's hands to present him with a blank, when his turn came to play, on both ends.

'Pimp, Mr Newman, pimp,' I would urge Alec, sitting on my right. We always used these formal titles when in play.

Alec would close one end. 'Hoor, Mr Campbell, hoor!'

If, happily, I had a suitable blank I would lose no time in playing it, then we all burst into a triumphant cry:

'Hoored, Mr Smyllie, sir – hoored! Take a little snatch from the bucket!'

With an expressionless face, and the dainty finger-nail raised in the air, the great man would draw some more tiles from the middle, on occasion being lucky enough to find a natural seven, and then play it with an elegant flick of the wrist, like an eighteenth-century gallant. 'That, gentlemen,' he would say, 'should wipe the shuddering grins off your kissers. *Nemo me impune lacessit* – and best wishes to all at home.'

I left the *Irish Times* under rather dubious circumstances, intending, in fact, only to take a week's holiday in London, but I was also writing a column for the Irish edition of the *Sunday Dispatch* at this time, and thought it might be interesting to call in at head-quarters. As a result of this I wrote a piece about the English scene which they used in all the editions, and paid me a little more than five times what I was getting for a whole week's work at home. I sent Smyllie a telegram, saying I'd been held up, and hoped to be back soon. He countered with a letter saying he would be delighted to see the last of me if I'd send him a year's salary, in lieu of notice. I replied that I'd see my bank manager about it. I remained on in London, and the correspondence came to an end.

In the next three years I returned fairly frequently to Dublin, without daring to go and call on him, until one day, coming back in an aeroplane, I opened the *Irish Times* and saw a paragraph in his Saturday diary column, which he wrote under the name of Nichevo.

It was very short. 'My spies tell me,' it read, 'that Paddy Campbell is back again in Dublin, after a long safari looking for tsetse fly in the bush. He is now preparing a definitive biography of Schopenhauer, and is doing a lot of field research on the subject in the back bar of Jammet's, and the Dolphin Hotel.'

It was an intimation that peace had been declared. But he was dead before I could say, 'Good evening, Mr Smyllie, sir,' again.

8

Prince Harry Hotspur

In the afternoon we entered the Royal Shakespeare Theatre in the company of several hundred school children of both sexes and saw the first part of *Henry IV*.

Tremendously exciting theatre, heavy, brooding scenery, sombre costumes weighing a ton – the real flavour of a fearful age.

Then we had a short break and went back in again for the second part. Savage double-crossing, magnificent battle scenes and a superb Falstaff. After that we gave the Lord Chief Justice and the Earl of Worcester time to change, and took them to supper in the restaurant.

During the supper an interesting discussion began about the character of Harry Hotspur. We were agreed that he and Falstaff both represented Vanity though, Falstaff, naturally, to a much more vicious degree.

'It must have been this failing in himself that drew Harry to Falstaff in the first place,' I said. 'I mean, it must have been something more than a mere desire to get away from the frigid atmosphere of the court.'

No one said anything. They seemed to be mulling it over. In the end Worcester asked, rather cautiously, 'How do you mean?'

'Well,' I said, 'anyone who has read the programme notes knows that Harry Hotspur was a magnificent wild animal. He'd naturally be drawn to the wildness in Falstaff.'

There was another longish silence. Then the Lord Chief Justice said, 'Surely you're talking about Prince Hal?'

'That's right,' I said. 'Prince Hal or Harry – call him what you like.'

The Lord Chief Justice and Worcester exchanged what I thought was a look of some anxiety.

'Prince Hal,' I explained, 'was always called Harry on the field of battle. You remember that great cry of his in *Henry V*, just before Agincourt? "For England, Harry and St George!"'

'Good God!' exclaimed Worcester. He seemed profoundly shocked.

'My dear fellow,' said the Lord Chief Justice in measured, legal tones, 'Prince Hal and Harry Hotspur are two different people.'

'That's what you think,' I said, but in fact I was bluffing. I'd just realized I'd made a serious error or, rather, had contained a serious error in my mind for nearly forty years.

The truth of the matter was that ever since my school days I'd believed that Prince Hal's nickname was Harry Hotspur, and that nothing in my somewhat inattentive reading of *Henry IV* had led me to think differently. It was the line about 'For England, Harry and St George' that had led me astray.

I had to make another admission, to myself. During the evening, while watching *Henry IV* for the first time on the stage, I did have to allow that there did seem, in a way, to be two different characters in the drama – one called Prince Hal and the other Harry Hotspur – but having nurtured the belief for forty years that they were one and the same man I hadn't been able entirely to abandon it, despite a good deal of physical evidence to the contrary.

'You've been misled,' I told them, 'by one of Shakespeare's most ingenious theatrical devices. Harry Hotspur is Prince Hal's alter ego. Harry represents the venal side of Prince Hal's nature.'

'He doesn't!' cried the Earl of Worcester passionately. 'He's got nothing whatever to do with Prince Hal. He's a different man altogether.'

'Sorry,' I said. 'You've missed it.'

'Look,' said the Lord Chief Justice, 'look at the programme. There's Prince Hal, played by Ian Holm, and Harry Hotspur by Roy Dotrice. They're two different people.'

'Harry Hotspur,' said the Earl of Worcester between clenched teeth, 'has red hair. You can't possibly think he's the same person as Prince Hal.'

'Of course he is,' I told them. 'I tell you, he represents the unworthy side of Prince Hal's nature. It's one of Shakespeare's cleverest theatrical devices. He was always fascinated by the struggle between good and evil in his characters. Here, in *Henry IV*, you see the physical image of these conflicting characteristics – the good side is called Prince Hal and the evil one –'

'I don't want you to say it again,' said the Earl of Worcester in a low, trembling voice.

'Did you not notice,' said the Lord Chief Justice, 'towards the end of Part I that Prince Hal slays Harry Hotspur in battle? Two different men, fighting one another.'

'One man,' I said, 'overcoming the evil in himself.'

The two actors left us very soon after that.

'I wonder,' said my companion, after a thoughtful pause, 'if you could give me your analysis of the character of Othelliago?'

'Ah, get knotted,' I said, sick of the Bard and all his works.

9

Back-Seat Drivers

I now know that when a married woman says, 'Do come along –
he certainly won't mind,' it's time for third parties to take to the
woods.

This is knowledge, however, to be gained only in the hard
school of life. It had not yet come my way when Suzanne Talbot
suggested that they should put me up for the night.

There was no denying that some small emotional feeling had
arisen between us during the dance, warmed, no doubt, on
Suzanne's part by the fact that her husband, Herbert, had spent
the whole evening cementing a deal in cattle with three heavy
men from Ballinasloe.

'But what,' I said, 'will the dashing rancher feel about it?'

'He,' said Suzanne, with the faintest, contemptuous emphasis,
'certainly won't mind.'

I guessed she was telling me that Herbert's life was bounded on
all sides by cows, leaving him no time to consider the fact that his
wife was only thirty-seven.

'It would save me,' I admitted, 'a long drive home.' She was a
pretty little thing, somewhat crushed by the rigours of Irish
country life. 'We might,' I said, 'have some further conversation
about art, music, and letters.'

'You don't know what it's like,' she said with sudden passion,
'not to have to talk about hairball, footrot, and hookworm.'
She dropped my hand. Herbert was on his way across the
room.

'You ready, Annie?' he said. He nodded uncomfortably
towards me. 'Hello, Mick –' he said. Herbert was certainly short

81

on social graces. We had already been introduced. He might have tried to get a little closer to it than Mick.

'I'll get my things,' Suzanne said. 'I'll meet you in the hall.'

Herbert and I looked at the floor. I thought it would be unwise to tell him I was coming back for the night. Suzanne could do that in the car.

'Well, cheers,' said Herbert – 'look after yourself.' He slouched away.

I followed them home at a safe distance. Herbert, rigid in a boiled shirt, looked to me like a man who was ready for bed, but nonetheless I wanted to give him plenty of time to get tucked away.

He was waiting for me at the front door as I drove up. It was raining, but he came out on to the avenue in his shirt sleeves. 'Here,' he said, 'what sort of a game is this? Annie says you're staying the night.' His powerful face was knotted. A proposition had been made to him which passed his comprehension. 'You're a Dublin fella, aren't you?' said Herbert. 'What's stopping you going home?'

'Herbie!' cried Suzanne, 'whatever will Mr Campbell think of our manners?' She opened the door of my car. 'Do come in,' she said – 'have a drink – it's not so late –'

'Well,' I said – 'I'll just have one –'

Herbert crowded me enough to make it embarrassing to get out of the car. 'Here –' he said, protestingly, and then followed me, right on my heels, into the house.

There was no doubt that the situation had undergone a change. As a man who didn't mind Herbert was under false colours. And it no longer seemed important for me to brighten the life of his wife.

Suzanne threw open the sitting-room door. 'You have your friends,' she told Herbert angrily, 'I don't see why I shouldn't have mine. Sit down and have a drink – darling,' she added, 'and I'll get your bed ready.'

She was merely being defiant. It was probably the first time in her life she had turned on him. But Herbert, a simple man, took the words at their face value.

'By God,' said Herbert, 'there'll be none of that!' Resolutely, he walked across the room and picked up a shotgun, which was leaning, surprisingly enough, against the desk.

I felt for the handle of the door. 'There is no need for us to behave like savages,' I said.

Herbert pulled out the top drawer of the desk, and broke open the gun. I knew he couldn't possibly be going to shoot, but still – if he loaded the thing – it might go off in his hand –

'Good night all,' I said, 'and thank you for a wonderful time.' I was in the car a moment later, driving hard down the avenue, waiting for the shots to crash round my ears.

What did crash round my ears, three miles farther on, was a soft little sigh, followed by a sort of plopping noise. I swung round in sudden terror. The back seat was occupied in its entirety by a large black dog – a Labrador, by the look of it, waking from a deep sleep!

I stopped the car. I opened the back door. The dog looked at me heavily. It was not yet fully conscious. I examined the label round its neck.

ROGO
c/o HERBERT TALBOT
Grange House
Westmeath

My first instinct was to put Rogo out into the night, and leave him to find his own way home. But Rogo looked much too large to walk three miles, even if he did happen to know the way. I decided to take him back to Herbert's gate, and leave the rest to his own good sense.

I coasted up to the gate, with the engine switched off, and left the car a little beyond it, under the shelter of a tree. I didn't know if the Talbots had gone to bed, but I did know that I had no further desire to meet them personally.

I lifted Rogo out of the back seat. He felt exactly like a fat woman in a fur coat. 'Good boy,' I said, 'go home.' It was still raining. Rogo shivered and slowly climbed back into the car again. I tried to stop him, seizing him round his large waist, but he snarled so fiercely I had to let him go.

I got the starting-handle from the boot and tried to prod him out on to the road. The handle sank horribly into his large and yielding flank, but Rogo refused to move.

I started to bark softly, waving my hands about in the dim light of the dashboard lamp. I thought the disturbance might cause the dog to rise to his feet, and then I could suddenly push him out while he was off-balance.

I was absolutely astonished to see the face of the policeman looking in through the open door.

'Well, hello,' I said, after a moment, 'I was trying to get this damn dog out of the car.' Then, I said, 'You're out very late. Are you looking for murderers?' I wanted to remind him that he probably had some more important job to do.

He came round to my side, a young policeman like a bullock, probably a native Irish speaker if given a chance to gather his wits.

He looked at me cautiously. 'It's not in me powers,' he said, 'to acquaint the civilian population with the nature of me duties. Is this your dog?'

'Well, no,' I said, 'it belongs to Mr Talbot, up at the house. I'm trying to get him to go home.'

'And what,' he said, 'is the animal doin' out of the owner's jurisdiction at this hour of the night?'

'I drove it away, by mistake,' I said. 'It got into the back of the car by itself and now I can't get it out.'

There was a long, baffled silence.

'I'll have to ask you,' said the young policeman, 'to proceed up to the premises. You'll be drivin' the vehicle,' he added. He was not going to take the risk of being shot in the back.

We drove slowly up the avenue. The policeman seemed to occupy three-quarters of the front seat. Rogo took up the whole of the back. I had fled lightly from the Talbots. I was returning to them laden down to the scuppers.

The policeman got out. 'As a matter of a precaution,' he said to me, 'I'll have to ask you to dismount.' I joined him on the doorstep. He seized the knocker. A thunderous sound rang through the darkened house.

'Bad old class of a night,' said the policeman, in a conversational tone. I told him I'd never known worse. Then the door opened and Herbert, in a dressing-gown, stood on the threshold.

The policeman must have been accustomed to rousing people from their beds. He paid no attention to Herbert's suffused face.

'It's me duty, sir,' he said, 'to make official enquiries into the ownership of an animal found in this gintleman's motor vehicle. The gintleman is making allegations that the animal belongs to you.'

Herbert saw me for the first time. He took a pace forward. 'You've taken my *dog*!' he exclaimed. He meant that I'd settled for his dog, having failed to take his wife.

'It got into the back of the car,' I snapped. 'I didn't want any part of it.'

Herbert looked. 'Where is it?' he said.

The back seat was empty. Rogo had gone back to bed, no doubt sensing that he was home again, after an inexplicable interruption.

'Holy fly,' said the policeman, 'an' wasn't it only lookin' at me a minit ago.'

'A black overgrown thing,' I said crossly. The policeman seemed to think a miracle had happened. 'It was called Rogo. It was there all right.'

'That's my dog,' said Herbert. 'I wouldn't lose that dog for a fortune.' Suddenly, he wanted to get hold of one concrete fact. 'I'm going to see if that dog's in his kennel,' he announced, 'and if he isn't –' He made a wild gesture. He didn't know what would happen after that.

We followed him round to the yard. Rogo was at home, fast asleep in a kennel the size of a block of flats.

'Well,' I said, 'are you satisfied now?'

Herbert looked round heavily. 'With what?' he said.

I'd had enough. 'Officer,' I said, 'we're going home. You can issue the summonses in the morning.' It really didn't matter what anyone was talking about any more.

I drove him into the village and left him outside the police station. He seemed surprised I wouldn't come in. 'I've all me reports to do about the occurrence,' he complained. 'The sergeant is the divil an' all for writin' . . .'

I drove off abruptly, without saying good-bye. I must have gone less than a mile when a voice said, 'Guess who's here.' It was a subdued and wary voice, and it came from the back seat.

I had no difficulty in identifying it as the voice of Suzanne, the lovely wife of Herbert Talbot, cattle dealer, of Grange House, Westmeath.

I stopped the car. With a weary sense of repetition I went round to get the starting-handle out of the boot.

10

A Cool Figure in White

I was making, being unemployed at the time, a tour of the English shires, carrying all my possessions in a cabin trunk, and had put in a fortnight of adequate eating with a harmless young couple called Gossett. Paul and Primula their names were, and you had to talk to them slowly even about the weather.

The three of us lived a quiet life, because Primula, in about a month's time, was going to have a baby.

The Gossetts existed in a sort of daze; while I filled in the long spring evenings with old copies of the *Sporting and Dramatic*.

But, suddenly, one night, Primula put down her knitting.

'Paul,' she said, 'I think – I'm . . .' She fell back in her chair, her face white.

Gossett shot up from the sofa.

'No!' he cried – 'you're not! You can't . . . !'

I looked at Primula with some concern. If she really was going to have the child now it was me for the open road. But I had thirty shillings and a cabin trunk. Any move would have to be cautiously organized, with motor transport, and a certain destination at the other end.

'Perhaps,' I said, 'it's only indigestion.'

Paul swung round. Even in this extremity he was polite.

'It may be,' he said. 'It's quite possible. But we must be careful. Do you mind ringing the nurse?'

This had been arranged for some time. A maternity nurse lived in the town. She was to move in at once as soon as the crisis began.

I rang her up. An indifferent and apparently idiot voice replied that Nurse Fletcher was down with the shingles.

For a moment I thought the Shingles must be some family nearby.

'Get her back,' I cried. 'Tell her to come here at once!'

'It's spots,' said the voice. 'She carn.'

There was a pause.

'You could 'ave Nurse Foley,' said the voice. 'She's 'olidayin'.'

I couldn't make out what Nurse Foley was doing.

'Send her along immediately,' I said. 'Tell her to take a taxi.'

'Ar,' said the voice, and the line went dead.

An hour later there was a knock on the door. I'd been tramping up and down the sitting-room, waiting anxiously for any sound from upstairs. I rushed out into the hall.

A large woman stood on the door-step, wearing horn-rimmed glasses, a pot hat and a green tweed suit. She carried a suitcase, and there was a stub of a cigarette in the corner of her mouth.

She stepped over the threshold.

'Well,' she said, 'talk about luck. Here's me takin' a week off from me labours, and lo and behold doesn't Fletcher go an' get herself stretched, an' before I can turn round an' ask meself the time isn't there another young one yellin' to be brought into the world, an' here's me at your service day an' night, never in the mornin'.'

I took a pace back.

'Are you,' I said, 'Nurse Foley?'

She stubbed out the remnants of her cigarette in a flower pot.

'That's me,' she said. 'Foley, from Tralee. I've all me certy-fikates, so don't you be botherin' your barney. Sure, we'll have the young one before mornin', an' be pourin' out the flowin' bowl with the best of them.'

I looked at Nurse Foley. I tried to picture the effect she was going to have on the Gossetts.

'I'm not,' I said, 'actually the father. Mr Gossett is upstairs with his wife. Perhaps you'd better go up and see them.'

'Ye gods an' little fishes,' said Nurse Foley, 'look at me puttin' me big feet in it again.'

She leant forward confidentially. 'Tell us,' she said, 'what class of a pair are they? To tell you the truth I was sweatin' comin' up the drive. I'm not used to this class of a place at all. Done all me

work in Tralee. Are they havin' anny of them specialist fellas in?
Sure, it'd put the heart across me if there was one of them Hartley
Street fellas lookin' over me an' me doin' me work . . .'

Paul Gossett appeared at the head of the stairs.

'Paul,' I said, 'this is Nurse Foley. Nurse Fletcher is ill . . .'

Foley put down her bag.

'Come on down owa that, you,' she said, 'an' get yourself a
drink. Me an' McNab'll have a bit of a chat, an' sure your
troubles is only little ones.'

Paul's hand went up to his small moustache.

'McNab . . . ?' he said, faintly.

'I think she means Primula,' I said.

'Primula!' exclaimed Nurse Foley. 'There's a name for you –
up the banks and down the braes!'

She stumped up the stairs, pushed past Paul, and vanished into
Primula's room.

Paul and I went into the sitting-room.

After a moment he said, 'Do you – er – think she's all right?'

I didn't see why I had to accept responsibility for Foley, even if
we did share the same nationality.

'I'm sure she knows what she's doing,' I said. 'And, in any
case, you can always get someone else tomorrow.'

Nurse Foley walked into the room.

'Be the look of it,' she said, 'we're here for the duration. If that
one comes off before the new moon I'm a Dutchman.'

Paul, polite as ever, stood up. 'The new moon?' he said
anxiously.

'A fortnight,' replied Nurse Foley. 'But, sure, what's the harm
in waitin'? All the better when he comes. Put a bit of hair on his
chest.'

Paul winced.

Nurse Foley looked round vaguely. 'Any chance,' she said, 'of
unpackin' me traps? I've a few bits I'd like to wash before me
dinner.'

When I went into the bathroom some time later three pairs of
grey woollen stockings were hanging on the pipes. There was
also a sky-blue thing, with elastic, from which I quickly looked
away.

Primula came down to lunch the following day. It was a

difficult meal, because Nurse Foley was clearly unaccustomed even to the modest succession of dishes provided by the Gossett home. She toyed suspiciously with a leg of chicken, and said she always was partial to a bit of steamed fish. When lunch was over she asked for a cup of tea.

This was provided – the Gossetts always had coffee – and then the four of us settled down for the afternoon. It was raining. There didn't seem to be anything else to do.

By 4.30 p.m. Nurse Foley had been talking for two hours and twenty minutes. She sat squarely in the middle of the sofa in her tight tweed skirt, making it abundantly clear that she had completed the laundering of the sky-blue part, at least, of her traps, and she talked and talked and talked.

She told us of her early days in Ireland. She told us of the discussion she'd had with Nurse Fletcher about whether she should have come here at all – ' "Fletcher," says I, "I'd never have the nerve" – "Foley," says she, "are you a man or a mouse?" – "Fletcher," says I, "I'll do it" – "Foley," says she . . .'

By tea-time the Gossetts and I were nearly mad. Nurse Foley smoked incessantly – 'Fletcher says they're nails in me coffin, but sure what harm is it? – a short life and a merry one an' the divil take the hindmost . . .' She gave us the most appalling details about her previous cases, and included a long anecdote about two people who'd had twins, a certain Mr and Mrs Donald Norman.

'Donnie and Duckie they called each other,' said Nurse Foley. 'Upstairs and downstairs. Donnie this and Duckie that. I declare to God you'd think it was Clark Garrymore on the pictures.'

I took a quick look at the Gossetts. I'd heard them, privately, address one another as Primmy and Polly, but hoped they would be so confused by Clark Garrymore that they wouldn't take Donnie and Duckie to heart.

They got it at once, and it didn't make it any better when Nurse Foley told us that Donnie had walked out three weeks after Duckie had been delivered. 'An uncertain class of a man,' said Nurse Foley, 'with an eye swivellin' round all the time for the mots.'

Primula looked so distressed that I broke in to explain that 'mots' was an Irish word for a girl. A rather common sort of girl, I tried to explain, making it clear to Primula that there was no danger of her losing Paul to this sort of competition.

'Common,' said Nurse Foley, 'as mud, but sure the fellas is all the same. I'd a butcher once in Ţralee was thinkin' serious of puttin' a ring to me finger, but I up an' sent him off with a flea in his ear. Mind you,' said Nurse Foley, 'a fella's all right as a friend, but I'd never put up with that other class of caper.'

Primula, looking faint, said she thought she'd go to bed.

'D'you know what I'm goin' to tell you?' said Nurse Foley, after Primula had gone, 'that young one's not too hearty. We'll want to keep an eye on her, or the Lord knows what larks we'll be upta.'

Paul jumped up.

Nurse Foley laughed. 'God love you,' she said, 'you'd think you were the first ever brought one into the world. Go on up, now, an' give her a bit of kissin' and cuddlin'.'

Paul, bright red in the face, walked out of the room.

Nurse Foley lit another cigarette. 'That's a weedy lookin' little fella,' she said indifferently. 'We'll have him on the flat of his back the next.'

That night, Paul and Primula had something on a tray in their room. Nurse Foley and I dined downstairs. She had a couple of glasses of sherry and – in the absence of the Gossetts – let herself go on the subject of complications.

I tried not to listen, but there was no way out of it. At regular intervals she would say, 'Misther Campbell, d'you know what I'm goin' to tell you?' – and wait for an answer.

The only answer was, 'No,' but Nurse Foley insisted upon being presented with it every time.

By midnight I was ready to kill her, or to tell the Gossetts that I'd caught her taking drugs. And worst of all was the thought that this was going to go on day after day. I knew that she was probably right, in some awful psychic way, in believing that Primula would not come off – I was even *talking* like Nurse Foley now – before the full moon. I was in for Duckie, Donnie, and all the rest of it, for another fourteen days!

I wasn't. That night, just as I was about to go to bed, Paul Gossett came into my room. He was fully dressed, and his small dog-like face was grim.

'Look here, Campbell,' he said, 'I want to speak to you.'

He'd never called me Campbell before. I didn't like the sound of it.

'I must ask you *and* Nurse Foley,' said Paul Gossett, 'to leave this house tomorrow morning. You're turning the place into a – a shillelagh.'

I looked at him without comprehension.

Gossett made an impatient gesture.

'A bear-garden,' he said. 'A shambles, or whatever you call it in Ireland. It's very bad for Primula. A car will be here at nine o'clock.'

He turned on his heel and walked out of the room.

Nurse Foley and I left immediately after breakfast. I was almost speechless with rage at being lumped in and expelled with Nurse Foley and her certyfikates.

We'd almost reached the outskirts of the town before Nurse Foley spoke.

'Ah, well,' she said, 'come day, go day, God send pay day. Sure, wasn't I only tryin' to do me best.'

She turned to me suddenly.

'Do you know what I'm goin' to tell you?'

After a moment I shook my head.

'When the fella told us to hop it,' said Nurse Foley, 'didn't I go an' have a good blub in the lav.'

At the station I left her without saying good-bye.

11

A Goss on the Potted Meat

There was no doubt that Mr Jotuni Jaakkala's English was outrageously good.

He seemed to be a lecturer in his native Finnish at Cambridge. 'An unhurried existence,' as he put it, 'seeing that the number of those *in statu pupillari* who wish to study our language and culture is sharply limited by the widespread, but nevertheless groundless, suspicion that we are domiciled in igloos, and live on boiled reindeer's feet.'

You could hear the commas tinkling as he shovelled it out.

In the general laughter which followed this ornate revelation, someone, complimenting Mr Jaakkala on his English, said that he must have lived in England all his life. He looked about thirty.

'I have lived in England since 1947,' said Mr Jaakkala, with charming modesty, 'but from the pleasure it has given me you might well say that it has been all my life.'

Excited protests followed to the effect that Mr Jaakkala could not possibly have contrived so perfect an accent, so rich and flexible a vocabulary, in a mere five years.

Mr Jaakkala smiled with even greater modesty than before, and lit a straight-grain pipe.

I felt compelled to intervene. I didn't like the look of his tweed suit either. For a youthful, *English* don it was exactly right.

'Oh, I don't know,' I said, 'if you've any ear for music, and it's necessary to learn a language to earn a living, it should be a matter of two or –'

Mr Jaakkala opened his mouth.

'It should be a matter *only* of two or three years,' I said quickly, 'before one becomes entirely fluent.'

Me Jaakkala smiled again. He knew he'd nearly nipped me. 'I believe,' he said, 'you worked with a German electrical firm in Berlin for some time.'

It was a direct invitation to reveal my ear for music.

'Have another glass of sherry before supper?' I said.

Mr Jaakkala gracefully and confidently declined.

During supper he skimmed up and down and round about the English language with such mastery that gradually everyone else fell silent. To join with him in discussion would have been like accompanying Caruso on a jew's-harp.

After supper it looked as though we might settle down to listen to Mr Jaakkala for the rest of the night. He had reached Sibelius, and was carving him up with swift, dexterous strokes. I intervened on, 'the egregious dramaturgy of the avalanche, translated into terms of the contrabassoon.'

'What about a game of croquet,' I said. 'Let's go roll those balls.'

Mr Jaakkala, flexible as ever, showed immediate delight.

'Croquet?' he exclaimed. 'But indeed yes.'

'Don't tell me you play croquet in Finland,' I said, surprised. 'Surely the reindeer would get in the way?'

'They do,' said Mr Jaakkala generously. 'But not on the immemorial Cambridge sward.'

As we walked down to the court, I came to the conclusion that it was even better if he knew something about croquet. The shock, when it came, would be all the greater.

It was decided that I should play with Mr Jaakkala, against my father, and an elderly economist called Lowther. We seemed to be equally matched, in view of the fact that Lowther, while a fast man with a fiduciary issue, was incapable of getting his back leg out of the way of the mallet, and had never been known to hit the ball more than a few feet.

'It's golf croquet,' I told Mr Jaakkala briefly. 'First through the loop wins it for his side, and then all on to the next.'

'You mean the hoop?' suggested Mr Jaakkala.

'No, I don't,' I said. I looked at him, puzzled, not getting his meaning. He gripped his mallet uneasily, and looked away. Fractionally, I'd already got him on the run.

'You start,' I said, 'with the blue. Far side of the loop, coming up.'

He played quite a reasonable shot, but hit it too hard. It rolled over the edge of the grass. He stood back.

'Well,' I said, after a pause. 'The courtesy *remplacement*.'

Mr Jaakkala's brow furrowed. 'The put in,' my father said. '*Pour la politesse.*' I was glad to see that he was abiding by the traditions of the game.

Mr Jaakkala seemed to get it. He walked after his ball, picked it up, and placed it on the boundary.

As was usual with the first hoop no one succeeded in hitting another ball, and by the end of the first turn we were all lined up at varying intervals along the boundary line. It was Mr Jaakkala's shot.

I examined the position. 'It seems to me,' I said, 'that after a little Roedeanery off the yellow you should be able to *faire* direct *pénétration*.'

Mr Jaakkala shaped up to his ball, and then a slight cloud came over his face. 'How –' he said – 'exactly, do you mean? Could you, perhaps, explain –'

'Explain what?' I asked him.

My father intervened. 'He means play a gentle shot off the yellow, which will leave you in posish. Then penetrate the loop.'

'Excuse me,' said Mr Jaakkala. 'I should like to understand the terms your son has used. This Roedeanery –'

'A lady-like shot off the yellow,' I explained. 'Followed by position. *Et la loopage.*'

Mr Jaakkala looked at me malevolently. His shoulders hunched. He surveyed the other balls without hope, and suddenly lashed out in the direction of the hoop. He missed it by several feet.

'Which robs,' my father said. Mr Jaakkala walked after his ball, saying something, probably in Finnish, to himself.

Lowther, under my father's direction – two Roedeans, a bumble-over, followed by *pénétration* with a Kurdistan oblique – astonishingly enough made the first hoop, and we all surged down to join Mr Jaakkala, waiting in silence by the second.

'Well, now,' I said, 'let's see how she shapes up. We're one down. We don't want to fruddle.'

'I do not intend,' said Mr Jaakkala, 'to fruddle.' He smiled, in a ghastly way. 'I presume fruddle to be an onomatopoeic derivative, with the sense of making a mistake.'

'It's near enough,' I said. 'How are you on the Kurdistan oblique?'

'Kindly tell me, please – what is it I am to do?' said Mr Jaakkala. I knew then that I'd got him, because there, very faintly, like, perhaps, the opening bars of *Finlandia*, was the first sign of the lilting Finnish accent.

'My wife,' I said, 'born in India, finds it easier to *faire loopage* from an angle of 45 degrees. The Kurdistan oblique. Perhaps we'd better centralize. Take a Roedean on the black.'

With the utmost care, Mr Jaakkala rolled his ball along to hit the black. 'Which strikes!' I cried. 'Now – stac on the yellow!'

'Pleece?' begged Mr Jaakkala.

I felt almost sorry for him. 'Staccato blow on the yellow,' I explained. 'It's an in case.'

Mr Jaakkala peered about him like a man who'd lost his glasses.

'*Fair removage* of the yellow!' I cried, urging him on, 'in case you fail on *pénétration* of the loop!'

I let him get his mallet about half-way back when I flung my own on the ground in front of him. I shouted, 'STOP!' Mr Jaakkala started convulsively and then shot me a glance in which fear and rebellion were mixed in equal parts.

'Total change of plan!' I cried. 'Do a goss on the potted meat!'

This time it was Mr Jaakkala who flung his mallet on the ground. 'Aie goss!' he cried wildly. 'How do I know what is aie goss – ?'

Lowther intervened. He probably thought that violence was going to be done. 'A gossamer, or glancing blow,' he said hurriedly – 'on the potted meat.'

'Vaat iss potted mitt?' roared Mr Jaakkala.

Lowther seemed stunned. We'd been calling it the potted meat so long that he was incapable of providing a translation.

'The red,' said my father.

'The paint's coming off it,' I explained. 'It looks like potted meat. Chicken and ham.'

'Awwwh!' said Mr Jaakkala. It was a kind of groan. He took a pace back, and then with a low, sideways sweep he flogged out at the blue. It struck the yellow about half-way up, and crushed it into the jaws of the hoop. The blue ball sped on and disappeared, at the height of several feet, through the back netting.

'That's done it,' I said. 'You've gone and played an onomatopoeic derivative.'

'The total fruddle,' my father said.

'You've gone and yawssed the jellow ball.'

'What? Pleece? I do not know – ?' Mr Jaakkala was miles out at sea.

'You've jawsed the yellow,' I said. 'A former Swedish Consul in Dublin, a regular player here, always referred to it as a yawssing of the jellow. His accent,' I added, 'was not impeccable.'

'I yawss the jellow,' said Jaakkala wonderingly. 'I yawss the jellow.' He tried it again. 'Is it good, yes?' He was like a small child with a new toy.

I clapped him bravely on the back. 'It's a beezer, boy,' I said. '*Faire remplacement!* Take your goss on the potted meat!'

He did as he was told. He finished up with as fine a Kurdistan bouncer as we had ever seen, the blue ball leaping over the jellow in the yawss, to *faire* a tremendous *loopage*.

After the game, which we won easily, was over, Mr Jaakkala drank a pint of whisky with echoing cries of 'Skoal!' Before he left he delivered an address in Finnish, and then had to be helped down the steps.

I only hope he pulled himself together before his lectures began again next term.

12

How to Become a Scratch Golfer

I played a lot with Major M— when I was new to the game, at the age of eighteen, for the reason that he was the only member of the club who had nothing to do from Monday to Friday either.

Being at that time a novice, I believed that anyone's play could be improved by a careful study of a book of instructions, and was working on this particular day on the full arc of the back-swing, paying special attention to the need for a firm grip with the left hand at the top. I decided to pass on the message to the Major, who seemed to be in as urgent need of it as any man I'd ever met.

His method of striking was to bounce the shaft of the club on his right shoulder so that the down swing was initiated by a ricochet over which he had no control whatever, so that the ball could travel in any direction but never more than two feet above the ground.

The show-down came when he'd been bouncing the shaft with extra ferocity in an effort to hack a ball called a Goblin out of the pervading mud.

We played on a 9-hole course which consisted of three flat fields put together and divided by threadbare hedges, a venue offering little of interest to the power player except that it was downhill on a bicycle from where I lived. On this Tuesday afternoon, with an autumnal fog already settling in, the Major and I were naturally the only ones out.

It was at the short eighth that I asked him bluntly about the bouncing, an idiosyncrasy which had been weighing on my mind for some weeks.

It seemed a good time to deal with it, in view of the small, disused quarry on the right of the tee – the only feature of interest on the whole course.

We'd spent many hours in there already, poking about in nettles, brambles and long wet grass for the Major's tee-shots and not infrequently, I had to allow, for my own as well, and though we'd inevitably uprooted or flattened a good deal of this undergrowth plenty of holding stuff still remained. Furthermore, I knew the Major was down to his last Goblin, and I had no desire to lend him one of mine.

'Excuse me, sir,' I said, 'it's only a suggestion, but have you ever tried getting your hands a little higher at the top of the swing?'

Up till then I'd only criticized the style of my contemporaries and so was not prepared for the reaction of an older man. The Major glared at me with a malevolence which was surprising, in view of my innocent desire to help. 'You play it your way, sonnie,' he snapped, 'and I'll play it mine.'

He bent down, to tee up his Goblin. He was, in fact, three-up, owing to a stiff-wristed putting method I was trying out for the first time.

The foliage in the quarry looked, however, particularly dank and uninviting, so I tried again. 'But,' I said, 'you let your grip go altogether at the top of the swing so that the shaft bounces off your shoulder and ruins your arc.'

'Arc?' said the Major. 'Arc? Let me tell you something,' he said. 'Jimmy Braid always slackened his grip at the top of the swing and he'd have seen any of you young artichokes off any day of the week, wet or fine.'

In later years I learnt, of course, that anyone over the age of fifty cannot be shaken in defence of his own swing, despite the fact that he's never played a medal round in less than ninety-three. At eighteen, however, I still believed that even the mature player would be interested in advice. 'I know, sir,' I said, 'but I'm sure if you tried holding the club just a little more firmly at the top it would give you a lot more length off the tee.'

'Ha!' the Major said, dismissing this sound principle out of hand. He squared up to his Goblin. He started his back-swing or, rather, initiated the jerk that normally lifted his mashie into the air, and all at once something looked different. His knuckles were shining white, indicating a grip on the club liable to squeeze the plug out of the shaft, if he were able to maintain it.

It was a phenomenon which was later to become only too familiar – that of the player who contemptuously rejects all advice on the grounds that it's drivel and then furtively tries to apply it, in case it might work – but I was too alarmed for the Major to consider it now.

He had reached the top of his swing – or whatever it was – and was standing on tip-toe with his left arm across his eyes and the club raised vertically in the air, presenting the appearance of a monk in plus-fours and a check cap about to haul down on the bell-rope for the opening chimes of the Angelus. Under the circumstances, it seemed improbable that he intended to continue with the stroke.

I was about to step forward and break the deadlock by taking the club away from him when he slashed suddenly and viciously downwards, making an attempt at the same time to turn his hips to the left, trying to deflect the clubhead from the vertical into the horizontal plane.

The result was something I'd never witnessed before, and have never been privileged to see again.

The head of the club buried itself in the mud nearly a yard behind the ball and remained there, leaving the shaft standing upright like a flagstick. It was not attended by the Major. The force of the impact had torn it from his hands. With nothing to hold on to he swung round, staggered forward and trod fairly and squarely on his Goblin, obliterating it from view. He stood there, facing the hole, vibrating a little and peering about to see where the ball had gone. Behind him, the mashie slowly keeled over and fell to the ground.

I picked it up, wiped some of the deposits off the head, and held it out to him. 'That was bad luck, sir,' I said, for the sake of saying something. 'I think your foot slipped a little. Have it again.'

He took the club from me, with a set face. He examined it briefly, as though to make sure it was his own. 'All right, then,' he said, 'where's the ball?'

I had to hack it out of the ground with my own club. I teed it up for him again.

'If you wouldn't mind minding your own dam' business,' the Major said, waggled once, bounced the shaft on his shoulder and slashed the ball straight into the quarry. I followed him immediately afterwards, out of nervousness. After poking about unsuccessfully for some time we walked in, the Major having run out of ammunition.

On the steps of the clubhouse he spoke for the first time since the quarry. 'Interfering with a chap's game,' he said, 'is dam' nearly cheating, and I don't like it.' He allowed the door to swing back in my face.

The inexpert player regards his own game as being, in fact, sacrosanct. He buys golf books not with the intention of remodelling his swing but merely to find the one simple hint or tip which will enable him to produce his normal game from his existing, paralytic method.

The inexpert player regards his normal game as being two shots below the par for the course, after his handicap has been removed, despite the fact that at no time has he ever broken 90.

13
Dong Says It's the End

It seemed inconceivable that she was, in fact, going to give a solo rendition of 'Michael Finnegan'.

'You mean,' I said, 'you're going to sing it all by yourself, out in front, without Guy or Mister Phanie or anyone? It's bee-tend, isn't it? Not *real*.'

She stamped her foot violently, and cried 'Oh!' in an exasperated voice. 'Listen to me for one minute, will you?' she said. '*Real* – not bee-tend.'

By mutual agreement the question of something being real or bee-tend demands an unequivocally truthful answer. Both of us realize, I think, that without this safeguard we might well become lost for ever in fantasy.

'If it's real,' I said, 'you'd better sing it for me now. I've never heard it before.'

We were engaged upon breakfast, in the infinite labour of causing her to eat half the yolk of a boiled egg. She got down off the chair, and stood to attention beside it. Looking angrily straight ahead of her she shouted in a loud voice, 'There was an old man called –' She stopped abruptly. 'Oh, blow *me*,' she said with infinite contempt. 'You don't stand to attention for Michael Finnegan. That's God Save the Queen.'

We smiled at one another in a worldly way, amused by so elementary an error.

She assumed a relaxed stance, with one foot behind the other, and began again.

'There was an old man called Michael Finnegan –' She raised her finger-tips to her chin, and scrabbled at it. 'He had whiskers on his chinnegan –' She filled her cheeks with air and blew out a light spray of egg. 'The wind came up and blew them in again, poor old Michael Finnegan dong end.' She sat down again and picked up her egg-spoon.

After a moment I asked her, 'What's "dong-end"?'

'Oh, listen to me for one minute will you,' she said. 'Dong says it's the end.' She looked round the kitchen, almost carelessly. 'Can you smell glue?' she said. 'Dong.'

I accepted the glue business to be an indication that the subject of Michael Finnegan was closed.

I told my wife about the solo just as we were leaving for the fête. She took it badly. 'She's going to sing it all by herself!' she cried. 'But she can't! She's only four!' I gave her a warning look. The performer was in the back of the car, eating a bag of nuts. 'I'll handle it,' I said, 'just in a casual way. It'll be all right.' I turned round. 'Sing Michael Finnegan,' I said.

She put down the bag of nuts with extreme care, altering its position once or twice. Then she stood up. 'There was an old man called Macdollan Finnegan. Oh blow me will you listen to me for one minute that's old Macdollan had a farm with a gobble gobble here dong end.' She gave a short, terse laugh. 'Silly old Brigid,' she said.

My wife looked so alarmed I had to reassure her. 'It's all right, honestly,' I said. 'I heard her sing it. She's only fooling about.' My wife said, 'I won't be able to look. I'll die. I'll have to go and have tea while it's happening.'

That's how I got closeted in the bushes with Miss Whitney and the other four children when it turned out that Brigid would not sing Michael Finnegan, or, indeed, take any part in the concert whatever. It happened quite suddenly. An elderly gentleman in a Panama hat announced through the loudspeaker that 'Miss Whitney's nursery school children will now give a short concert.' Miss Whitney, with the other four in tow, took Brigid's hand. Brigid screamed once, and seized me so tightly by the trouser leg that it almost stopped my circulation.

'I think,' I said, 'you'd better leave her out.' I knew how I would have felt if I'd had to go up on the platform with Miss Whitney.

Miss Whitney's nostrils flared. 'I can't do that,' she snapped.

'I'm short-handed already. As it is *I've* got to do the loopy lay with Guy.' Mister Phanie – Stephanie to her parents – seized Guy round the neck. 'Here we go loopy loo!' she cried, dragging him round in a circle. 'Here we go loopy lay!' Both of them fell down. Brigid, still clutching my trouser leg, watched them with cold hostility.

'What's the matter?' I asked her. 'Why won't you sing?'

The answer was almost inaudible. 'I don't want to sin those lon sons not the little white duck,' she said. I was absolutely with her. We'd had the Little White Duck before, at another fête.

'She doesn't want to sin – to *sing* the Little White Duck,' I told Miss Whitney. '*Or* Macdollan Finnegan,' I added, hoping to confuse her to a point whereat she might abandon us. 'She doesn't like the lon sons.'

Miss Whitney looked at us as though we were behind with our homework. 'Will you sing if Daddy comes up on the platform, too?' she asked Brigid. Before I could stop her Brigid nodded, a fine reward after all I'd tried to do for her. 'Come along then,' said Miss Whitney firmly, 'we're late already.'

I found a chair at the back of the platform while Miss Whitney lined up the five children. Brigid immediately turned to face me. Mister Phanie, untroubled by self-consciousness, whirled round holding out her skirt, gaining a round of laughter from the somewhat anxious audience.

They did the Little White Duck first. I imagine it was malice on Miss Whitney's part. Brigid took a limited part in it, confining herself to the gestures, which she performed with the creaking care of an arthritis patient. She looked at me all the time with no trace of expression on her face.

The Loopy Loo, however, brightened the whole thing up. Brigid and Mister Phanie, partnered together, fell down several times in what appeared to be the traditional way, and I enjoyed seeing Miss Whitney dancing with Guy, whose white hat had fallen over his eyes.

'And now,' Miss Whitney announced, 'Brigid, by herself, will sing Michael Finnegan.' Suddenly I realized my daughter was standing directly in front of me, with her back to the audience. Miss Whitney moved towards her. Brigid buried her face in my lap. I motioned Miss Whitney away. 'Get it over quickly,' I told my daughter.

I sat back in full view of nearly a hundred people, while Brigid ran through her piece. The words 'Dong end' were the sweetest I'd ever heard. 'She's finished,' I told Miss Whitney. There was a scattered round of applause as Miss Whitney led her charges into God Save the Queen.

On the way home my wife said to me, 'I thought you looked just like Michael Finnegan during the solo.'

Without looking round I said, 'Dong!'

'What do you mean?' my wife said.

'Oh, listen to me one minute, will you?' cried the soloist. 'Dong says it's the end.'

I couldn't have put it better myself.

14
Sudden Death

'Smash' Kleingeld, stripped for action, was far and away the healthiest girl I'd ever seen.

Her arms and legs were the colour of old gold. The whites of her eyes had the unmistakable bluish tint of a life-time teetotaller. Her short, bronze hair seemed to crackle, and she moved with the compact and inexhaustible energy of a tigress just emerging from adolescence.

She carried three white racquets and a red cardigan slung round her shoulders, and since her arrival had been heard to speak four times. 'Hully gee!' had been Miss Kleingeld's contribution on each occasion.

We left it at that. There was a general feeling she might be shy, particularly in view of the performance that Oliver put on during lunch. He was a novelist, who came frequently to our house on Sundays. He weighed eighteen stone, and wore a tangled orange moustache, contrasting fearfully with a deep magenta complexion.

His subject had been a fellow writer, a woman – 'excavating an empty mind with the hopeless pertinacity of an elderly White Wyandotte scratching for worms on an infinite arterial road.'

Miss Kleingeld watched him narrowly, clearly wishing she was back at Wimbledon, discussing backhands with Tex and Rex, and her other single-minded compatriots.

After lunch we sat outside for a while, and, during a fortunate interval when Oliver fell asleep, Paul and I engaged Miss Kleingeld in some talk about tennis. Paul did most of the talking, unwisely, I thought, in view of the nature of his own game. He was a pale, spare youth who played an oboe in an orchestra, and during the weekends devoted himself passionately to tennis in the belief that it improved his wind. He held his racquet in a penholder, or possibly an oboe, grip, and counted it an attacking shot if he hit the ball over the net.

Miss Kleingeld listened to him politely – so politely, in fact, that it occurred to me that she didn't think he was talking about tennis at all.

It was in desperation that I suggested we might play. Miss Kleingeld disappeared at once, with misplaced eagerness, to change, and I roused Oliver from his sleep.

I should have waited for the two able tennis players, whom I'd invited, to arrive, but Miss Kleingeld's silence was on my conscience. She'd been a great deal more animated the previous evening, when I'd met her at the dance.

I was fixing the net as the three of them emerged from the house. They presented a startling contrast. Miss Kleingeld was exactly right, with her three racquets, her red cardigan, and her long golden legs. But Paul wore a pale-blue shirt of some shiny material, with a zipper up the front, and grey flannels. And Oliver –

I looked at him again. He'd put on his wide-brimmed, green sombrero, and a short, white vest which failed by inches of magenta stomach to reach the top of his trousers. He was smoking a large, curved pipe, and carried a whisky and soda in either hand.

Miss Kleingeld watched him with plain fear, as he put the glasses down on the bench. Then he picked up one of her racquets. 'Mind if I have a swish with this?' he said.

Miss Kleingeld started. 'No,' she said. 'Sure, go ahead.' It was the first time she'd ever lent a racquet to anyone. It was clear she didn't know they could be borrowed.

'Well,' I said, 'I suppose I'd better play with Paul, and Oliver – you play with Miss Kleingeld.'

It was the only possible arrangement. I could only hope that Oliver would get in her way sufficiently often to make some kind of game of it.

Oliver took a long draught from one of his glasses and marched round to the other side of the net, swishing his racquet.

107

Miss Kleingeld joined him, making a series of terrifying over-head smashes, loosening up. She danced about a little on her toes.

To launch the knock-up, and to give him confidence, I lobbed the first ball to Oliver, standing in his usual position on the service line. It passed perhaps two feet to his left. He made no attempt to return it. 'Not ready,' he said, indifferently. Then I saw, with one hand cupped round a match, he was lighting his pipe.

I sent the next one to Miss Kleingeld pretty hard. There was a brief flash of a golden arm, a sound like 'thunk', and the next moment Paul was sucking his fingers, with his racquet lying at his feet. The ball must have rebounded to Miss Kleingeld, perhaps off Paul's thumb, for I just had time to duck as it tore through my hair and crashed against the back netting. I looked up to see Miss Kleingeld, unnecessarily dissatisfied, take a practice swing.

Oliver blew out a cloud of smoke. 'Chuck up one of those things,' he said.

I gave it to him backhand, and half-volley. He put out his racquet, stopped it, picked it up off the ground, and with a sudden grunt slashed at it overarm, apparently practising his serve. It struck Paul, who was bending forward to retrieve his racquet, on top of the head. Paul fell back silently, and sat there, looking at the ground.

Oliver said, 'I'm ready – any time you are.'

Paul rose shakily to his feet.

'Okay-ee!' cried Miss Kleingeld. 'Let's go!' She leaped back towards the baseline, playing several imaginary smashes. From the first I instinctively sheered away, until I realized that all the ammunition was at our end.

Paul placed a ball carefully in the middle of my racquet. 'You serve,' he said. His eyes looked crossed. I wondered if he'd been concussed.

I was playing, at this time, an extremely elaborate, if slow, high-kicking service. It involved hitting the ball, with an upward flick, from a position about level with the left ear. If it got over the net it was accepted without equivocation to be untakable, by everyone who played with us on Sunday afternoons.

I let Miss Kleingeld have one of the untakables. She pounced on it and drilled it down the tramlines on Paul's side. As it passed him Paul, intentionally, was running in the other direction.

'Love fifteen,' said Oliver broadly, and walked across to the bench. He finished his glass of whisky, and strode back to receive the service, tapping the racquet in a businesslike way against his leg. 'Keep it up,' he told Miss Kleingeld, and turned to face me.

To reduce his confidence I let loose a cannon-ball with the flat face of the bat. Oliver, expecting the slow untakable, never saw it at all. It struck him full-pitch below the breastbone with a sound like a stick hitting a cabin-trunk. Oliver said, 'Whoosh!' and buckled slightly at the knees. He straightened, and glared at me beneath the brim of the green sombrero.

'Faalt!' snapped Miss Kleingeld, and moved in.

She must have guessed that my second service would be milder than the first. It bounced harmlessly, waist high, in front of Oliver.

Normally, he was a man who played a scythe-like shot at everything, hoping to make up in spin what he lacked in speed, but now, to my sudden alarm, I saw him sweep the racquet back with the intention of slashing the service at me as hard as he could. It was revenge, pure and simple. I flung up my racquet in front of my face, and stood ramrod straight, trying to narrow myself in.

I heard a click, and opened my eyes to see Miss Kleingeld, with her head laid back, staring incredulously at the sky. Oliver, baffled, was searching our half of the court for his return. It was, in fact, thirty feet above his head, and on the way down. He must have caught it on the very rim of his racquet.

Miss Kleingeld, the seasoned tactician, overcame her surprise. 'Back up!' she cried. Oliver threw out an arm defensively, and ducked. He had no idea what she meant, or what was happening. I saw Paul running quickly and lightly towards the net, holding out his racquet like a spoon. I was certain that he had no idea what was going on either, and was merely presenting an appearance of interest.

'Leave it!' I shouted. 'It's mine!'

I could see that the ball was going to drop on our side of the net, and in that moment decided to give it all I had. I got well underneath it, and then shot a glance across the net, looking for a place to put it away. I saw the broad back of Oliver, running hard for the baseline. I screwed round a little, leaped into the air, and smashed.

The first thing I knew was I'd lost my racquet. It flew over the side netting. Then I heard a shout from Paul.

I realized I'd missed, and that the ball was still on the way down. I flung myself on one side, on to the grass, as Paul rushed forward on tiptoe. Trembling with excitement, he waited for the ball to bounce, and then with infinite delicacy scooped it back into the other court. It was like a waiter serving mayonnaise.

I got to my knees, in terror of Miss Kleingeld's return, and saw that she'd been taken by surprise. She and Oliver, in fact, were transfixed on the baseline. Then both started to run.

I sprang up, to cut off their return at the net, and suddenly found I hadn't got a racquet. 'Stop!' I cried, and threw up my hand.

Miss Kleingeld, in the brief interval since they had started to run, had left Oliver yards behind. I don't think she heard me. Her concentration was such that her whole mind was focused on reaching the ball. But Oliver heard me, all right. 'Stop!' in fact, was the first coherent message he'd received for some time.

He stopped. It was like an eight-wheeled lorry slamming on its brakes on a greasy road. He fought to get a grip. Then he went down. With his feet flung out in front of him he shot across the grass, letting out a single, astonished cry.

Miss Kleingeld heard it, but she was too late. She'd only half-turned by the time he collected her. They were locked together as they crashed into the net. There was a sharp crack as the wire broke, and then they brought me down. Miss Kleingeld spoke.

After she'd gone, and we were talking it over, Paul said he'd never realized that American tennis players used that particular word.

15

The Hot Box

Once upon a time I was given an assignment to write an article about a load of archaeological remains, dug up by some fool on the outskirts of Waterford.

This was in the days when the newsprint situation allowed us to devote whole columns to fossils, brass rubbings, or even the Franciscan method of illuminating manuscripts.

Caught by the Waterford job, I made a demur. No knowledge of archaeological remains – very busy at the moment with an article about badminton. . .

'Round about 1,200 words,' said the news editor. 'Riordan, in the public library, knows all about it.'

He measured me for a moment. 'You two ought to get on,' he said, 'like a house on fire. Or an ammunition dump exploding,' he added.

I asked him what he meant.

'You mind your own business,' he said.

I went along to the library, already rehearsing 'Riordan', and 'archaeological remains'. It had, of course, to be Riordan and archaeological remains just at a time when my intermittent stammer was passing through a cycle which left me incapable of dealing with these initial letters.

There were two elderly gentlemen in subdued suits at the desk, both reading.

I chose the one on the right.

'Excuse me,' I said, 'are you Mr M'Reer – M'Reer – M'Reer. . .'

I was full of air, and putting in the intrusive 'm' – a stratagem which often worked – but this time nothing happened.

The librarian looked up. He wore half-moon, gold-rimmed glasses, and a black woollen cardigan. He nodded towards his colleague. He also put down his book and prepared to listen – with what seemed to be a disproportionate measure of interest.

I saw why a moment later.

'I'm A'Rah – A'Rah – A'Rah . . .' began the second librarian, with his eyes tightly shut.

I'd walked into another one.

I should, of course, have given it up at once – gone back to the office, and said Riordan was on holiday.

But then the fighting instinct arose in me. My intrusive 'm' against his intrusive 'a'. I'd tried the intrusive 'a' myself, and knew that in careless hands it could bring on strangulation.

I scanned the sentence that lay before me. It contained only a number of minor obstacles.

I shot it out very quickly.

'I believe you know something abow-abow-abowbow – could you tell me what you know of the Waterford arkie-arkie-arkie – the Waterford find?'

It turned out to be rather rougher than I'd expected.

Riordan sat back. 'What was that?' he said.

I looked at him coldly. He knew perfectly well what we'd got ourselves into. It was up to him to pull his weight.

'Man found some flints in Wafa – in Wafa – in Wafa –' – Even Waterford seemed to have collapsed. I took another breath. 'Man found some flints or something down south and I was told you knew something abah-abah. . . You knew something,' I said.

The other librarian had now abandoned all interest in his book, and was leaning forward intently.

'Ah, yes,' said Riordan easily. 'The archaeological remains discovered in Waterford.' You could hear every syllable, clear as a bell.

He stood up. 'I think I can find you the reference. I have aboo-aboo-aboo-aboo . . .'

I let him have it. It was sheer joy.

He'd nearly torn his memo pad in half by the time that I released him.

'You have a book,' I said, 'which will help us.'

'Downstairs,' said Riordan. He loosened his collar. 'Come this way,' he said.

The other librarian half rose in his seat, watching us right to the door. He'd taken his glasses off, and his mouth was open.

We went down into the basement, and along a passage lined with pipes.

'By the way,' I said, 'what's your first name? I think I know a friend of yours.'

I'd seen the card on his desk, in a brass slot: BRIAN RIORDAN. The chances were if he couldn't say book he couldn't say Brian either.

He stopped, as if shot. Convulsively, he gripped the handle of a low, barred door which had appeared in front of us. His neck began to swell. He drew a couple of long, shuddering breaths.

I watched him with interest. One foot came off the ground, and writhed about.

Suddenly, he got it. It came out like a tyre bursting.

'Jack!' said Brian Riordan.

'Can't be the same person,' I said easily. 'The Riordan I was thinking of is –' Everything shut down. I fought it blindly for a second. 'Someone else,' I said.

We went into the cellar with honours approximately even. It was a tiny room, brilliantly whitewashed, about six feet by six. A bare electric light bulb hung from the ceiling at eye level. It was very hot. Pipes ran all round the walls.

Riordan turned round. The light hung between us, very bright and dazzling.

'Where was this find made?' he said.

The stuff had been dug up in a place called Rathally. But as far as I was concerned, what with the heat, and the glare, and the congestion, it might well just have been Czrcbrno, a hamlet in the Balkans.

I tried everything – the finger tapping, the coughing, the intrusive 'm', even a short whistle. Nothing happened. The light, agitated by some truant blast, swayed gently backwards and forwards. Riordan waited, leaning forward politely – exultant.

I thought I was going to faint. I had ceased to breathe. I half-turned my head – intending, perhaps, to jump upon Rathally from the rear – and then I saw Theodore Blake. He was peering through the bars, and from the look of deep peace upon his face, I knew that he, too, was engaged with the priceless gift of speech.

Theodore – of all people!

Riordan opened the gate. 'Well,' he said, 'Mr Bla – Mr Bla – Bla . . .' He gave it up. Theodore came in. We moved back a little to give him room.

Theodore had lately been using an old method of my own. No sound emerged. No hint of expression ever crossed his face. He seemed to be lost in meditation. But it was then you knew that he was really on the griddle.

The three of us, tightly pressed together, the bulb hanging between us, stood there, waiting.

A full minute later Theo said, 'Hello.'

I'd better luck than Riordan. I said, 'What are *you* doing here?'

Riordan tried to say, 'What can I do for you, Mr Blake?' and nearly made it, until the 'b', as usual, beat him all ends up. He actually struck his head against the books behind him.

All this time Theodore was quietly at work. Suddenly, he got it out. 'Can I have that book on Roman coins?' he said, so careful and expressionlessly that it sounded like Roger, the talking Robot.

'Certainly,' said Riordan, and turned to the bookshelves.

It was certainly unfair. He must have known quite well where the book was, but he began fiddling about, pretending he couldn't find it.

Theo and I looked at one another. It was up to someone to say something. We got down to it together.

Theo won. 'What are *you* doing here?' he said.

I lowered my voice an octave. 'I'm gathering material on the arkie-arkie –' I couldn't go on. I simply couldn't face 'archaeological' again.

'On coins,' I said. 'M'Roh – M'Roh – the same kind of coins as yourself.'

Riordan swung round from the book-case. I'd forgotten about him.

'You said you wanted the Waterford archaeological remains!' he exclaimed.

'You've got it wrong,' I said. 'I'm doing a story abah – a story on coins.' I was going to add – 'through the ages' – and then abandoned it. 'Just coins,' I said.

The awful look of unearthly peace came over Theo's face. I knew what he was going to say. He was going to say that he'd been commissioned to write an article about coins and couldn't understand why I was doing one, too.

We waited for Theodore. It was difficult not to look at him, because we were jammed cheek to cheek, but we did our best.

Theodore looked straight ahead, motionless, carved out of stone.

'But,' he said, three minutes later, 'I'm doing an article about coins. Why are you doing one, too?'

Riordan opened his mouth.

'Ubu-ubu-ubu –' he began, harping on my commitment to archaeological remains.

'It doesn't matter,' I said. 'There has been some confusion. I can easily switch over to the arkie-arkie-arkie –'

'Ubu-ubu –' gasped Riordan, 'you asked me for that boo – boo-boo – that in the first pip-pip –'

It was absolutely indescribable. And suddenly Theodore joined in. On the very first word he slipped right back into his old habit – the wurr-wurr-wurr. God alone knows what he was trying to say. He simply wurred.

I don't know how long it went on for – me busy with arkie-arkie, Riordan pip-pipping, and Theo lost in the throes of wurr.

Steam seemed to be running down the walls. Once the electric light bulb bounced off my forehead with a sharp 'Ponk!'

Something snapped. 'Here,' I said, 'let me –' I couldn't say 'out'. I let it go. I pushed past them, fled along the passage, and a moment later was in the open air.

In my hand was Theo's book about coins.

I sent it back next day, by registered post.

16

Sean Tar Joins Up

While the back-stage secrets of the war which ended fifteen years ago continue to be preferred reading for ninety per cent of the population of the British Isles, on the grounds that those were the chummy old days in which everyone mucked in together, I should like to take the opportunity to correct some widespread misconceptions about the part played in the global struggle by the Irish Navy – a force with whom no one, except the patriots who kept it afloat, mucked in at all.

The Irish Navy came into being through a clause in the Hague Convention, which demands that a neutral country must control its ports if it's to remain neutral in time of war – control in this case meaning surveillance over all incoming vessels, to ensure that their purpose was a peaceful one.

In the beginning this meant that detachments of the Irish Army, in tin hats, green uniforms and red ammunition boots, were sent to sit in motor-launches outside the approaches to the ports of Dublin, Cork and Galway, with orders to refuse entry to any craft of a war-like nature. Their weapons were 1914 Lee-Enfield rifles.

Before British readers, rocked in the cradle of their great naval tradition, start to make derisive remarks about Ruritania or Fred Karno's Army, I should like to point out that there was nothing else to be done – except to form a new Service which at least wouldn't be seasick, while defending Kathleen na Houlihan's virginity with five rounds in the magazine.

The call went out, therefore, to Irish yachtsmen, and any others accustomed to the sea, to take over from the storm-tossed infantry, who were openly protesting that an extra 2s. 6d. a day danger-money was no compensation for being so far out of their element.

The call came to me in a public-house in Carrick-on-Shannon, through a message broadcast by Mr de Valera to the able-bodied men of Eire who were still in residence within her borders.

The outbreak of the Emergency had caused a mass exodus of a large number of these elements to England. Some went in support of their political principles, the majority because the money was better and it gave them a clean reason for getting away from their sweethearts and wives – one of the few benefits conferred upon mankind by war.

This new flight of the wild geese left me behind in the reeds that border the banks of the River Shannon, decaying in a cabin-cruiser built by a carpenter in Athlone, and powered by a Morris-Cowley car engine. My original intention had been to withdraw from a troubled world and write a novel. In the first week of this solitary pilgrimage, however, it became plain that I wasn't going to be able to think of a plot. Furthermore, the bicycle chain on the home-made water pump kept jumping off its sprockets, and the whole engine had to be lifted out of its bed to put it on again. Allowing an hour for cooling, an hour for repairs and two more for recovery I saw there would be little free time left for writing and abandoned the novel, without a backward glance, in favour of the steadier creative pleasures of light engineering, frying onions on a Primus stove, fishing for bream with a worm and growing a curled Assyrian beard, parted in the middle.

I wandered up and down the Shannon for three months, going graciously to seed, as one can do on a river better than anywhere else. The sunlit, moribund days seemed scarcely long enough in which to do enough of nothing. The only trouble was the regimen created a state of teetotal health too strong to be confined to a thirty-foot cabin-cruiser. I used to go ashore about once every ten days, wherever I might be, looking around, with the clear eye of a child, for adult pleasure. I was, as a matter of fact, in my fourteenth hour in a public-house in Carrick-on-Shannon and more than half way back to debility, when someone turned on the radio to listen to the news, revealing a unique interest in external affairs for that remote stout-laden town. After 700 years of oppression, we heard Mr de Valera say, we'd won our freedom from the foreign tyrant. Would we now betray the cause for which so many Irishmen had fought and died?

I thought I wouldn't, but for more personal reasons. If the blow fell I calculated that a man living alone in a boat, and doing nothing more in the time of Armageddon than growing a beard, would prove a source of strong provocation to any invading army. I'd certainly be shot out of hand for spying, or plain decadence, while more solid fellow nationals merely suffered forced labour, or internment at the Curragh.

The matter of the Miracle, too, had given me a poor reputation around the shores of Lough Ree. It came about in a simple fashion. I was speeding down the lake one evening, once again in search of adult pleasures in the town of Athlone, when without any warning at all I hit a rock. The impact left me in a heap in the cockpit, partly stunned from striking the rudder with my head. When I got to my feet I found the stern of the boat high in the air, but with no apparent damage done. I climbed over the side into six inches of water and pushed her off. In so doing, I fell in. When I got back on to the rock again, still concussed and now half-drowned, the boat was some distance away, drifting off on the evening breeze.

It was a moment or two before I took in the unusual nature of the situation. I was, in fact, standing in water up to my ankles in the middle of one of the largest lakes in Ireland, and the only other thing I could do was to sit down.

I contemplated swimming after the boat, and remembered I couldn't climb over the side. Hysteria was beginning to take a slow hold when I saw the turf barge coming round the headland, about half a mile away. There were two small figures in the stern. I started shouting and waving my arms.

When he first noticed me, one of the figures was making his way for'ard, carrying a coil of rope. He seemed to freeze. He dropped the rope. He gave a hoarse cry to his mate. Then both of them dropped to their knees and raised their clasped hands in the attitude of prayer.

All at once, I realized that they were not to blame. Viewed from their angle, the spectacle could have only one terrible interpretation. They saw a bearded figure, all in white, advancing towards them across the water, arms outstretched in passionate supplication. They continued to pray.

There was, I saw, only one method of indicating to them that they were in the presence not of the sacred but of the profane. With every expletive at my command I urged them to come to my aid.

The effect was bad, at first. They writhed under this new shock, with its implications of how different Paradise was going to be, as compared with earlier expectations. It was the younger and probably less devout one who came to first. He raised his head and stared at me with mounting hatred, across the smooth brown water. When, eventually, they came alongside my rock they were two of the most bitterly angry men I'd ever seen. The younger one couldn't bring himself to speak. The older one muttered over and over again, 'actin' the jackass, that's what – actin' the jackass . . .'

Acting the jackass did seem to cover my present way of life, so when the call to arms came from Mr de Valera I made up my mind at once.

I announced to the Select Lounge and Bar, amid scenes of incredulity rather than of any patriotic frenzy, that I was sailing that very night to join the Colours, whatever and wherever they might be. It took an hour or two, what with one thing and another, to get back to my boat, and then the engine wouldn't start, but less than a week later I presented myself for enlistment with the Irish Marine Service at Collins Barracks, Dublin – beardless, and in health somewhere round about C3.

The call, at least in the case of the Dublin Port Control Service, produced a varied bag, of about thirty men. There was a hard core of part-time dockers and longshoremen from the North Wall, with a sprinkling of cynical youths from the seaside town of Dun Laoghaire, who'd joined in the belief that even this lash-up couldn't be as bad as the Army. There was also myself, the only Protestant among the whole *élite* corps – an unavoidable disability that caused me for four years to be regarded, philosophically, by my shipmates, as an enemy agent.

We signed on at Collins Military Barracks in Dublin, and went through a short period of training on the square, dressed in blue boiler-suits. Our new uniforms had not yet been made, or possibly even designed. After three weeks our instructor, Sergeant Dooley, succeeded in getting us to move about in some kind of order, with our rifles in approximately the same position, and then dropped a bomb of stupefying proportions. From now on, in accordance with the Regular Army practice, all the commands would be in the Irish language.

We were lined up on a patch of ground behind the lorry-park at the time, deriding the Army and all its works and talking, as usual, about how it would be when we got to sea. No one believed that Sergeant Dooley was serious, until he suddenly shouted, 'Mel – arra!' It sounded like 'Mel – arra!', but no one knew what it meant. A stringy old ginger-haired, retired docker called Matches – the Dublin pronunciation of Matthews – leant over to me and whispered querulously, 'What's eatin' him?'

We all looked at Dooley for a clearer directive. No one moved. 'That's Attention, yez eejits,' said Dooley in the end. 'Come on now, or we'll be here all night.'

We came to attention, individually. Dooley then shouted, 'Shassig – arrash!' I, personally, sloped arms. Beside me, Matches did nothing. Two or three youths at the far end of the line turned smartly about. Some of the others started an indeterminate movement of their own, containing the rudiments of forming fours, lost their nerve and came to attention again, pointing in a number of different directions. I ordered arms, and stood at ease.

'Do y'know what I'm goin' to tell you,' said Dooley in the end, 'I'd rather be bastin' a bunch of heifers out of a cornfield.' 'Shassig-arrash' turned out to be 'stand at ease', but I felt no sense of triumph.

In the next four weeks most of us, like Pavlov's dogs, learnt to take appropriate action in response to a particular sound; but not Matches. We'd be marching along with Matches in the leading file when Dooley would roar, 'Iompig-thart!' The rest of us, after a hurried discussion, would decide this meant About Turn, and did so, leaving Matches shambling on in the original direction with the muzzle of his rifle pointing out sideways, and the seat of his boiler-suit drooping between his knees. Dooley had to catch him by the back of the belt to make him stop. A blistering altercation would break out between them while the rest of us came to a disorderly halt, before we marched into a wall. We'd stand around, then, furtively sucking cigarettes, until they'd finished.

The latent possibilities in this situation reached their finest flower at a kind of passing-out parade, where the Port Control, still in boiler-suits, were stationed in the rear of an infantry battalion. The officer taking the parade, being a native Irish speaker, had an accent which could only be described as Parisian, in comparison with Dooley's roughly phonetic delivery. We couldn't understand a word of it. At the height of the ceremonial the Port Control, at the slope, marched straight into the rear rank of the infantry, who were carved out of stone in the general salute.

The Army, including Sergeant Dooley, were glad to see us go to our own billet in a cargo-shed on the edge of the Alexandra Basin. 'Whatever youse lot are at,' he said, 'God help us all if yez ever havta pull a thrigger.'

We never did, but the next four years supplied privations that would certainly have driven the Wrens, if not the more senior branch of the other Service, to run up the white flag and take to the boats – including, in my case, failure to achieve commissioned rank.

'Dear Sirs,' I wrote to the British Board of Trade, 'for the past four years, twenty-four hours on and forty-eight off, I have been in command of the Irish Naval Vessel *Noray*, engaged upon Port Control duties in Dublin Bay, I would be grateful if you could accept this as four years' sea service, as I want to sit for your examination (coasting mate's ticket), which is essential for promotion to a comission in the Irish Marine Service –'

It was a difficult letter to write, for political reasons. The Battle of the Atlantic was in progress, and in pursuance of our neutrality our ports were barred to Allied convoys and their escorts. What I was doing, in fact, was asking the British Board of Trade to assist me towards promotion in the Irish Navy, the very force that was maintaining this embargo.

I wouldn't have gone near them, of course, for reasons of delicacy, if we'd had a Board of Trade of our own, but we hadn't.

They replied with commendable speed, in view of their other

commitments. 'Under no circumstances,' they said, 'can the patrol duties you mention be regarded as sea service. Accordingly, you are ineligible to sit for the examination to which you refer.'

That pulled the plug out of the dinghy, all right. The syllabus for the coasting mate's ticket demanded little more than the ability to read and write, and to distinguish between the sun and the moon and one end of a collier from the other. I could probably have swept through it with honours, to become Ensign – as opposed to Petty Officer – Campbell, with an increase in wages of nearly £5 a week. But an alien Board of Trade maintained that it was impossible to go to sea in the Irish Navy, and that was the end of that.

It was bad news for the manager of the Ulster Bank in College Green. It was also bad news for my leading-seaman, Matches. He'd been hoping that a commission would remove me to a shore job – in the Dublin Port Control the officers never went to sea – and off the back of his neck.

'Jaysus,' he said, 'don't tell us we're stuck widdya for the duration! If you carry on wid your allegations we'll all be blew owa the wather before we're finished.'

He was referring, I knew, to the matter of Captain Thomas, and to the only occasion in which a shot was fired in anger, during the whole global struggle, in Dublin Bay.

We were anchored on station at the South Bar Buoy, two miles out from the mouth of the Liffey, in the Examination Vessel *Noray*. The *Noray* was a small tug with about a foot of freeboard and a funnel on her like an ocean liner. In her former career she'd done odd jobs for the Port and Docks Board, but now that she'd joined the navy she was at least painted battleship grey, though remaining unarmed. Eighteen men, in three watches of twenty-four hours, lived in this iron box continuously for four years.

As Matches once observed, 'She's gettin' smaller inside every day with the grace –' The grace – or grease – was composed of diesel oil, coal-dust, cooking deposits and paraffin. It was dark-grey in colour and when attacked with scrapers it merely moved on to something else. I often used to think about trim young lieutenants in the other Service, sipping pink gins in tropical whites and listening to Vera Lynn on the wardroom radio, and reflect upon how soft they were getting it, even if someone did shoot at them from time to time. They had a further advantage, in that they knew what they were there for, which was to shoot back. Our own duties were much less clear-cut, as the field-gun incident showed.

It began round about three o'clock on a wet night with the wind in the east, so that seas rolled straight up to O'Connell Bridge. Something that looked like a collier, from her lights, came round the Baily Lighthouse, flashing her name in morse with a hand-torch. As usual this was illegible, so I sent back a message saying, 'Stop – coming aboard.'

An interval set in while Matches and the two ABs removed the turf from the rowing-boat (there was no coal in those days and if we took the turf aboard the *Noray* it got into everything, blending with the grace to form an abrasive mixture that put your teeth on edge).

With Matches and a youth called Dinny at the oars we pulled away into the darkness, trying to keep our rifles out of the wet. It was nearly an hour before we managed to get alongside the collier, crashing and banging against the rust-streaked side. Matches began well by handing up his rifle to someone on the deck; when my turn came to climb the rope-ladder I didn't blame him. As soon as I got on to it the ladder turned inside out, leaving me with my back pressed against the ship's side, with my head and the muzzle of my rifle sticking out between the rungs. Then the ship rolled, and I went in up to the waist.

The Captain greeted me as I fell over the rail – a low-sized Welshman in a thick jersey and a cloth cap. 'What the flaming hell are you trying to do, man?' he wanted to know. 'What are you doing on my ship?'

It turned out, then, that this was his first war-time trip to Dublin, and that his sailing orders had failed to inform him that the port was controlled. He was virgin territory. I recited my Standing Orders. 'I want to see your cargo manifest and crew-list, Captain,' I said. 'Then muster your crew on deck and take off your hatch covers. I've got to search the ship.'

This was virgin territory for me, too. Owing to the fact that our only naval training had been at Collins Military Barracks, I'd never seen a cargo manifest or a crew-list. Then the Captain put his finger on the other deficiency. 'Search my ship?' he said. 'What for?'

This had never really been explained either. Standing Orders mentioned 'unauthorized persons and cargo', without going into greater detail. What we were really looking for, I suppose, were German Q-ships, though it wasn't clear what we were to do if we found one.

'I'm just searching the ship, Captain,' I said. 'It's orders. Now get those hatch covers off.'

'But it's only coal, man!' he roared. 'Out of Port Talbot!'

He was obviously right, but I'd gone too far to turn back. 'Get those covers off,' I said, 'or you'll stay out here all night.' It was the first time I'd ever exercised authority while legally armed with a rifle. It gave me no great power-complex. Captain Thomas, with the help of Matches and Dinny, had opened up a corner of the hold. I flashed my torch into it. It was coal, all right. 'Very well, Captain,' I said. 'You can carry on now.'

We got back into the rowing-boat in a silence broken, a few moments later, by a loud, sharp bang, coming from the mouth of the river and – I suddenly guessed – from the Shore Battery, a field piece manned by a detachment of the army.

'Jaysus!' Matches exclaimed. 'You forgotta give him the lights!'

He was perfectly right. In all the business of trying to find something to do aboard the collier I'd omitted to give Captain Thomas the combination of red and white lights which would indicate to the Shore Battery that he'd been boarded and certified pure.

'Is he sunk, d'you think?' said Matches eagerly, peering through the darkness for flames. I was frightened stiff. If Captain Thomas had been killed it almost certainly meant we were at war with the British Empire all over again. And what would they do to the man who started it? Hang him?

Afterwards, I discovered what had happened. The Shore Battery, being as uncertain of their duties as we were, had let off a blank at Captain Thomas and then, honour acquitted, had given him the lights with a shout on the megaphone. There was a steaming row about it all, including a solicitor's letter from the collier owners, but it faded out with an addendum to Standing Orders. 'Incoming coasting vessels,' it said, 'need not of necessity be boarded in bad weather, but it is of first importance that they be given the correct signal of the day.'

After that my watch, at least, contented itself with boarding only vessels from foreign parts and mainly then, I had to admit, in search of tea.

The rations provided by the Army for twenty-four hours at sea were so inadequate that we supplemented them with dogfish, which abounded in the Bay. Two dog-fish, boiled in seawater, took the edge off your hunger all right at four o'clock on a black winter's morning, but they also left a raging thirst behind. Tea, at that time, was retailing in Dublin at about £1 a twist, if you could get it. Our rations for six men amounted to two teaspoonfuls for twenty-four hours, so that whenever we got a foreign vessel I always detailed one member of my boarding party to go straight to the galley and open negotiations with the cook, while the rest of us got on with the war.

It was the prospect of a real killing in tea that took us aboard the *Asama Maru*, a gigantic Japanese liner that showed up in a blaze of lights – looking like Dolphin Square – early one morning. Although Pearl Harbor had not yet happened I was nervous about going aboard her, not trusting her stated purpose of collecting seven Japanese diplomats, who still remained in Dublin, and returning them to the safety of Tokyo. I was still more nervous when we came alongside in the rowing-boat, and looked up at her towering side. Every deck was lined with inscrutable Oriental faces. The bridge was a blaze of gold braid. The rope-ladder, dangling from the boat-deck, looked fifty feet high.

I started up the ladder, with my rifle round my neck, rehearsing as usual a speech for the Captain which might frighten him into believing that our purpose was real. Matches laboured up the ladder behind me, the blue bobble on top of his white cap causing excited comment among the inscrutables along the rail.

I was with the Captain for nearly an hour. He spoke little English and produced bales of documents, some in the Japanese language, the like of which I'd never seen before. I studied them closely, while he urged me to hurry. The tide, apparently, was on the ebb and he was afraid of running aground.

When I returned to the ladder I saw Matches and Dinny already back in the rowing-boat far below, Matches' jersey bulging with what I took to be an unusually large haul of tea. I joined them, and found it wasn't tea at all. It was four bottles of saki and, judging by Matches' bemused appearance, he had about the same amount inside.

We pulled lopsidedly away from the great liner, when Matches suddenly let out a startled cry. 'Holy Mother! I've lost me gun!'

He had. It was nowhere in the rowing-boat. It could only be somewhere in the endless corridors, state-rooms and labyrinthine depths of the *Asama Maru*. Matches himself was vague. 'There was a bit of a cocktail bar,' he said, 'wid red leather on the seats –'

The great ship was going astern, trying to get into deeper water, but by roaring and shouting and waving my rifle I succeeded in getting her to stop. I climbed the long ladder again – Matches was beyond it – and gave the officers on the bridge a brief explanation of my return. With half-a-dozen of them, looking more inscrutable than ever, I searched the *Asama Maru* more thoroughly even than Captain Thomas' little coal-boat, but Matches' rifle had gone. There were three cocktail bars with red leather seats, but no gun. When the *Asama Maru* sailed away two days later Matches' Lee-Enfield went with her. I can only hope it played no part in the taking of Singapore.

The hungry, wet and aimless months went by. We went on rolling about at the South Bar Buoy, yearningly looking, on Christmas Eves, at the lights inshore, and telling ourselves that at least we were doing a bit more for Ireland than them bowsies in there. Finally, at the end of 1944, came my last naval engagement, later to be known as the Battle of the Hoors.

It centred around two battered tramp-steamers, with the identification SWITZERLAND unaccountably painted on their sides. They'd appeared in the middle of the night, without lights, and had anchored three or four miles off Dun Laoghaire. Judging by their height out of the water they were empty of cargo, but nonetheless seemed to be doing no harm. We left them alone for nearly a fortnight, as they showed no signs of wanting to come in, or to go away. Then, in the middle of the night – everything always happened in the middle of the night – I received an emergency call on the radio telephone. Unauthorized persons – those long-awaited and deeply unwanted visitors – were reported to be aboard, and were to be removed without further delay. I was to keep in close touch with headquarters, and proceed with the greatest caution. The whole situation was delicate in the extreme.

While we got up steam I advised my boarding party, for the first time in the whole war, to put five rounds in their magazines. 'But for God's sake,' I said, 'don't shoot anyone until I tell you to.'

The first ship was silent and dark as we came alongside. We shouted for a ladder but nothing happened. Then we pounded on the rusty plates with the butts of our rifles. The yellowing paint of SWITZERLAND stood out in the darkness, with the motorboat crashing against it in a short, choppy sea.

We were about to try the other ship, when a voice roared down at us from above. 'What you shoutin' de people up in de night foh?' it wanted to know. 'You go 'way!'

I swung my torch up. It revealed a jet-black, bearded and indignant face peering down at us over the rail. Whatever he was he certainly wasn't Swiss.

We got aboard and suddenly I saw my first unauthorized person. It was a woman, in a leather jacket and jeans, leaping out of sight into the black hole of the fo'c'sle. At that moment another one, in a tattered cotton dress, sprang out from behind the funnel and disappeared down the engine-room hatch. The coloured giant with the beard became agitated. 'Dey all good girls, boss,' he told me. 'You go 'way. You let us alone.'

They might – all twenty-eight of them – conceivably have been good girls before they left their mothers in Dun Laoghaire ten days, and nights, ago, but now, when I rounded them up on the foredeck, they'd lost all pretensions to ladylike behaviour. They clung to their various consorts whose nationalities, under the general description of Switzerland, ranged from Arab to Norwegian to Chinese, and let it be known that if they were going to be removed it would have to be by force, and then someone was going to get hurt. Their protectors, a number of whom appeared to be in the grip of methylated spirit, gave them loud support. A knife came out here and there.

Nothing in Standing Orders covered such an engagement. I didn't know what to do. It was Matches who saved the day, and the untarnished honour of the Dublin Port Control. 'Is that you, Josie?' he said suddenly, picking on one of the younger ones. He took a menacing pace forward. 'Go on home to your mother, y'ragamuffin, or I'll give you a ske'p over the ear that'll blind you!'

It cracked the defences. One by one – they'd probably forgotten about their mothers – the girls began to give way to tears. Two of them seized me by the hand. 'Don't be hard on us, sir, willya?' they begged. 'Sure, we wasn't doin' any harm –'

Matches was rounding up the other ones. 'Begob,' he was saying with dark satisfaction, 'Father Flanagan'll be doin' overtime at confession along of *this*!'

We got them all aboard the *Noray*, together with eleven more from the other, smaller ship, and bore them back in some kind of triumph to our headquarters in the Alexandra Basin. When, under pressure, they supplied their names and addresses every one of them gave as their profession – 'Child's nurse'.

Two weeks later I resigned, satiated with the rigours of war, and returned, with a bicycle, to civilian duties on the *Irish Times*.

17

Tooking for a Lowel

Even now, after all I have been through, the thought of being unclothed in the presence of women has the power to make me half mad with anxiety. I drum my feet on the floor, perspire, and whistle loudly to drive the memory away.

So far, I, undressed, have come rushing at women twice. One of these occasions was connected with a shaving-brush.

I was lying in the bath one morning, when I remembered that I had left my new shaving-brush in my overcoat pocket. The overcoat was hanging in the hall.

Everything else was ready and in position. Shaving-mirror and soap; new razor-blade; toothbrush and paste; hairbrush, comb and brilliantine tin; packet of ginger biscuits and a copy of *Forever Amber* on a chair beside the bath. When I wash I like to *wash*.

Everything was ready, then, except the new shaving-brush. I lay submerged for some time with just the nostrils and the whites of the eyes showing, trying to think of a substitute for a shaving-brush. Perhaps if the soap were rubbed on with the hand, and worked in? Or the toothbrush might be adapted to serve the purpose? The only difference between a toothbrush and a shaving-brush is that one is shorter and harder than the other, and the handle is fastened on in a different direction. But the toothbrush, properly employed, might be induced to work up a lather. I might even, by accident, invent a new kind of shaving-brush, with a long handle and a scrubbing motion. . .

All this time I knew I would have to get out of the bath, and fetch the shaving-brush out of my overcoat pocket.

I got out of the bath, in the end, at a quarter past eleven. At that time I had a hairy kind of dressing-gown that set my teeth on edge if I put it on next to my skin. I ran out of the bathroom, roughly knotting a shirt about my waist.

In this flat the bathroom, bedroom and sitting-room led off a passage. I ran lightly down the passage to the door, where my overcoat usually hangs. Then I remembered I had left the coat lying on a chair in the sitting-room. I ran more rapidly back along the passage, leaving footprints on the carpet. Already, I was becoming chilled and a little pimply. Passing the bathroom door I put on an extra burst of speed, and entered the sitting-room nearly all out.

It is difficult under such circumstances to make a precise estimate of the passage of time, but I think that a fifth of a second elapsed before I saw the charwoman standing by the window. She must have been dusting the bureau, but when she saw me she froze dead.

I, too, froze. Then I said 'Waah!' and tried to leap out backwards through the door.

The charwoman very nearly got there first. The thought must have flashed through her mind that she would be better off outside in the passage, convenient to the main staircase, and so with a kind of loping run she came across the room.

We arrived upon the mat inside the door simultaneously. The mat went from under us, and we came down. I fell heavily on the feather duster which she was carrying, and the bamboo handle snapped. I thought my leg had gone.

We lay together on the mat for several moments, not shouting . or anything, just trying to piece together in a blurry way exactly what had happened.

I came to my senses first. I was younger than she was, and probably more resilient.

I jumped up and made another break for the door. To my surprise I found it was shut, and not only shut but locked. I wrenched at the handle, conscious in the most alive way of my appearance from the back. The door was unyielding. I caught sight of a Spanish shawl draped across the top of the piano, and in a trice I was enveloped in it, an unexpectedly flamboyant figure.

Afterwards I remembered that the door opened *outwards*. I had gained the impression that it was locked by unthinkingly pulling it towards me.

And now the charwoman was also back on her feet. But to my horror I saw that she was taking off her housecoat – slowly and deliberately. It seemed to be her intention to disrobe. But why?

I watched her, wide-eyed. She folded the housecoat into a neat square. She placed it tidily in the centre of the table. 'That,' she said, 'is me notice – and now me husband will have to be tole.'

I fortunately never saw her again.

The other incident involving me and women took place when I was fourteen.

On this occasion I was again lying in the bath, but this time it was night, and I was reading *The Boy's Own Paper*. The rest of my family had gone out to the theatre, and I was alone in the house.

The particular edition of *The Boy's Own Paper* which I was reading must have contained a number of bumper tales, because when I came to the last page I found that the temperature of the bathwater had dropped from near-boiling to lukewarm. Checking back later I discovered that this had, in fact, been my longest sitting – ninety-seven minutes.

Taking care not to disturb the water, and set up cold currents, I reached out with one arm and dropped the *B.O.P.* over the side of the bath on to the floor. With the same hand I groped around in gingerly fashion for the towel.

There was no towel. I had placed it on the chair, but now it had gone. I sat up in the bath, chilled, and peered over the edge, hoping to find it on the floor. There was no towel. I sank back into the water again, trying, as it were, to *draw* it round me.

There was no towel in the bathroom of any kind. And slowly I was freezing to death. I stretched out my right leg and turned on the hot-water tap with my toe. Ice-cold water gushed out.

There was only one measure to be taken in this extreme emergency. I gathered my muscles, leaped out of the bath in a compact ball, wrapped the *B.O.P.* around me, wrenched open the bathroom door, and fled down the short passage leading to the linen-cupboard. The linen cupboard door was open. I shot into it, and slammed the door behind me. Absolutely instantaneously I discovered that our parlour-maid, a young girl named Alice, was in the linen-cupboard too.

What Alice and I did was to start screaming, steadily, into one another's faces. Alice, I think, believed that the Young Master had come for her at last.

In the end I got the door open again. It opened inwards, so that I was compelled to advance upon Alice in order to get round the edge of it. Alice, still screaming, welcomed this move with an attempt to climb the linen-shelves and get out of the window.

I tried some word of explanation. What I said was: 'It's all right, Alice; I'm tooking for a lowel.' This had the effect of throwing her into a frenzy. She tried to put her head into a pillow-cover.

It was obvious that there was nothing more I could do, so I ran back into the bathroom, locked the door, and listened at the keyhole until I heard her run down the passage to the hall, sobbing.

The only other thing I would like to say is that now, whenever I have a bath, I make a list of the things I am going to need, and check it carefully before entering the water.

18

Lemon Bites Boy

I was introduced the other evening at a minor social event to a couple of beefy, youngish men identifiable by their ties as being bound together by some corporate loyalty.

The ties were in stripes of chocolate, black and old gold. They were clenched with microscopic knots round hard, white collars, suggesting by their trimness, I thought gloomily, some regimental allegiance. It seemed I'd been thrown to a couple of regulars taking a night off from Pam and Daph, and prefabricated married quarters on the windy side of Aldershot.

'Well,' I said, dipping in with courage, 'what lot are you chaps with?' It sounded like Camberley chat.

I was expecting some military whimsicality like the Blues or the Buffs, so I was able to restrain my laughter when the red-haired one said, 'Armadillos'.

Luckily, I remembered almost immediately. 'You're the Rugger club! We used to play you at school.'

They expanded like large flowers. The dark one said, 'By George – *did* you?' I might have been at the battle of Inkerman. The other one said, 'What year? You ever play against old Packy Tulloch?'

Then it all came back. 'Tulloch?' I said. 'Packy Tulloch? Why, yes, I seem to recall the name.'

I was plucked out of my study, that fateful Saturday afternoon, at about two o'clock, where I was indulging a sensation of stupor brought on by a private tin of pears, with condensed milk, with which I had topped up the ordinary lunch in hall.

The message was that Beresford, the school hooker, had run a nail into his foot and that Sannine, captain of the 1st XV, wanted me to take his place.

It took a little time for this intrinsically unbelievable information to sink in, but when it did it brought me right out of my seat.

I was running, bound for a place of concealment behind the chapel, when I met Sannine at the front door.

This astonishing individual, who looked like an apprentice carpet-seller from Old Baghdad, was in fact Head of the School, spoke in the clipped accents of the Sunningdale landed gentry, and played every game, including water polo, with effortless Corinthian brilliance.

Sannine arrested my progress. 'Put a brace in it, old chap,' he said. 'Tog up. You're subbing for Berry.' He wore his 1st XV blazer, muffler, stockings and cap. The Persian face in the midst of this finery only made it look the more heroic.

Alone in the dormitory, I drew on my more threadbare 2nd XV accoutrements. We didn't have blazers or mufflers. I suspected I would feel the cold, if I was given the chance to feel anything.

We were playing the Armadillos, a London club that contrived to get a touring side together towards the end of the season, and travelled fairly widely, beating what I could only assume to be hell out of various public school teams.

I became convinced of the one-sidedness of the affair when I saw the Armadillos close up, and in particular their captain, Major Packy Tulloch. After looking at, or rather round, Packy Tulloch, hooped with chocolate, black and old gold, I made a furtive attempt to slip off my scrum-cap. It was made of crocheted string, with suède ear-flaps. It was in the wrong league.

As we made our way down to Big Field, Sannine pranced up, flapping his arms, keeping warm. He seemed actually to be looking forward to the coming pogrom. 'I'm playing you hooker,' he told me. 'I don't want to chop the pack about now. You'll have to be as nippy as hell. These chaps weigh a ton. They'll shove us to glory unless we get it back first.'

The Armadillos – after some cheerful shouting among themselves – one or two of them, almost unthinkably, seemed to be intoxicated – kicked off and thundered down upon our slender line. Thorpe, one of our forwards, caught it and with an absolute minimum of delay, disposed of it to the scrum-half. A passing movement developed towards the left wing. I trotted after the game, thinking that with a caution similar to Thorpe's I might well be able to avoid getting killed.

The passing movement ended with Bates, our wing three-quarter, being thrown feet first into touch. He landed on his back across some benches. I was surprised to see him spring up, instead of waiting for the stretcher.

Then I ceased to worry about Bates because the referee, our own Rev. R. B. Levit, was pointing to the ground, and whistling for a scrum.

I found Thorpe and Berwick, our front-row forwards. We threw our arms protectively about one another with something of the appearance of apprehensive virgins.

'Now, blokes' – roared Packy – 'all together!' They lowered their heads. We lowered ours. The two packs were joined with what I imagined must have been an audible crunch.

I found my face wedged between the bristly jowl of Packy on the one side, and of a throw-back called Jacko on the other. I knew his name was Jacko because Packy, burrowing, grunted, 'Skin you love to touch, eh, Jacko?' I had, in fact, had my weekly shave that morning.

Appreciative, wheezy laughter came from the other Armadillos, together with a rich and foreign aroma of pink gin, tobacco, and beer.

The ball shot in. I scraped at it feebly with my foot. I realized my back was going to be broken.

At this time I was six-feet-two, yet, owing perhaps to some dietary deficiency, I weighed a mere nine-stone. When the Armadillos applied the pressure I was leaning into them at an angle of 45 degrees. Then my back foot, protruding from the rear of our scrum, slipped. As the Armadillos swept through us I was bent over backwards into the shape and, I fancy, the semblance of a safety-pin. I remember being surprised that my stomach, with its burden of tinned pears, did not split across the front. By the time that I'd unbent myself, and found I was able to walk, the Armadillos had scored between the posts.

A 17-stone New Zealand doctor took the kick, and with what might have been a Maori war-cry booted it clean out of the ground. While some small boys were collecting it – it was a new ball – Sannine, cheerful as ever, asked me if I'd mind moving to wing-forward, and letting Thorpe in to hook.

For the next twenty minutes I was busy in all quarters of the field, from touchline to touchline, at all times near enough to the play to take immediate action, should emergency arise. The only injury I suffered during this period was when their fly-half – an india-rubber Welshman with legs so bowed that his feet turned inwards – unfairly slipped round the blind side of the scrum and let loose, with one of his simian swingers, a tremendous kick for touch. I was wondering where the ball had gone to at the time, and stopped it with my chest. Labouring under what felt like a cracked breast-bone I slowed down a good deal until the whistle went for half-time.

As I joined the other players – they were some distance away when the whistle blew – I was surprised to find myself commended by the Rev. Levit. 'Well, now,' he announced, 'in truth our young friend from the lower orders cannot be said to have blotted his escutcheon.'

'Thank you, sir,' I said. 'I'm just doing my best.'

This warmish exchange marked an advance in our relationship. The last time we'd met had been on a paper-chase. He, a man of some 45 summers, pounding swiftly along with white, protuberant knees and black gym shoes, had moved into my wake some two miles out, and from there had driven me home at a pace beyond my means with a swagger stick.

I took a slice of lemon and sucked it thirstily, listening to Packy congratulating Sannine on the quality of the school team. 'They're fast,' said Packy. 'They keep it moving. That's the way I like to see youngsters make a start in the game.'

'They're useful enough,' said Sannine. 'This half we'll run you off your flat feet.'

For a moment it was all right. Then I got the idea that Packy didn't like it – this juvenile Benares brass merchant being contemptuous about his flat but nonetheless British feet. I thought I ought to show Packy, for the sake of the team spirit, that our trusty, if dusky skipper had loyal, white support.

I stepped forward. 'We certainly will –' I began, and then something hit me with agonizing sharpness in the eyeball. I staggered forward, and fell.

In the sanatorium, to which I was led with difficulty, being almost stone blind, I achieved the first coherent account of what had happened, but even then the doctor had to apologize several times for laughing. It seemed that Major Tulloch, engaged in some chaff with Sannine at half-time, had flicked a slice of lemon over his shoulder. I, standing immediately behind him, received it in the eye.

'You walked right into it,' chuckled the doctor. 'Daftest thing I ever saw.'

Unfortunately, the incident was picked up by the local newspaper. It was headed, '*Schoolboy K.O.'ed by Orange Pip*' – a travesty of the facts, which led to my being deluged with unpleasant fragments of fruit at subsequent appearances on the football field that year.

19

'General Collapse: Present – Arms!'

Sometimes, now, when I am overtired, or feeling ill, or someone has been sharp with me and my defences are down, the memory comes flooding back of the afternoon when I forgot what I was doing in a guard-of-honour, watched with close attention by nearly fifteen hundred people of both sexes. There were some small children there as well, but they probably didn't clearly understand what was going on.

The occasion was the opening of the new dining-hall at my old school, a handsome building with a salmon, a pig, and a turkey embossed on the entrance doors, representing fish, flesh, and fowl.

I was glad to see the new hall reach completion. Once, in the old one, I had incautiously reached behind the hot pipes at the back of my seat in search of a fork, and run my hand into something appalling. It was something old and soft and tenacious, and it might have been a former helping of tapioca, or a small animal, like a ferret, passed to its final rest.

When I say I was glad to see the new dining-hall reach completion, it would be more accurate to say that I should have been glad to see the new dining-hall reach completion if I hadn't found out at the same time that the commanding-officer of the O.T.C. had selected me to be right-hand man in the guard-of-honour, which even then was being mobilized to greet the field-marshal whose task it was to declare the new edifice open. When I found that out I wanted the new dining-hall to catch fire, and be burnt to the ground.

As soon as this project was mooted I knew it was going to be the last battle in the war between me and the O.T.C. Up till now we had fought a lively contest, with no quarter asked or given, but as yet no conclusive engagement had been reached. No sooner did I succeed in concealing an uncleaned rifle in someone else's rack than the O.T.C. would catch me with my puttees upside-down, and both sides would retire to their lines with honours even. So it went all the time.

But this guard-of-honour business, I knew, would see the final victory go to either one side or the other. It was something too big for compromise.

When the commanding-officer picked upon me to be right-hand man he picked not upon the best, but merely the tallest soldier in the school. At this time, at the age of sixteen, I stood six feet four in my army boots – a distinction reduced in importance by my weight, which remained constant at eight stone. It is not true to say that you couldn't see me sideways, but it certainly was necessary to narrow the eyes a little.

Preparations were set in train at once. They found twenty-nine other boys around the six-foot mark – some already shaving, and with more or less permanent assignations with the maids in the sandhills – and the preliminary drilling began.

Without delay I made an implacable enemy – the Regular Army sergeant known to us off-duty as Gus.

Between Gus and me there was already but a small measure of mutual respect. During P.T. I'd corrected him once or twice in his grammar, and he'd caught me on two successive field-days shooting mud through my rifle with blank cartridges.

Now, matters came to a head. Gus, seeing me on the first parade standing in the post of honour at the end of the line, made an instant objection. He marched smartly up to Lieutenant Winter – who was, and should have remained, the games master, but was now in charge of the guard – saluted, and said: ''E carn't do it, sir. Ain't got the stuffin' in 'im.' Winter, of course, had no idea what he was talking about, and it took them several minutes to straighten it out. Eventually, however, Winter grasped what was the matter. He came up to me and: 'You think you can handle this job all right, Private Campbell?' I said, 'Yessir', meaning, 'A kind of miracle might see me through.' Winter nodded to Gus as if to say, 'I told you so.' I think he had some idea about upholding the prestige of the middle-class.

After that Gus went out of his way to confuse me – batting on a pretty easy wicket, since I sometimes attempted to form fours on receipt of the order to dismiss. He also referred to me with unvarying persistence as 'Beanpole', a masterstroke, seeing that I couldn't very well answer back, at least while I was in the ranks, and he was out in front.

'General Salute,' Gus would roar – 'and that goes fer Beanpole if 'e don't fold up in the middle – Preesent – *Hipe!*' 'Squad,' Gus would shout, 'by the right in column of fours, quick – 'old up, Beanpole, yer can run if yer warnt ter – March!' By the end of the first fortnight I was getting two hours' sleep a night.

But the worst thing of all was the fixing of the bayonets. By the nature of my position, right-hand-man, it was my duty to march out in front of the squad, turn left, and then with a variety of complex gestures, fasten the knife on to the end of my rifle. The others took what time there was from me.

Gradually, bayonet-fixing began to occupy my whole life. I practised fixing bayonets on hockey-sticks, cricket-bats, yard-brooms, fire-irons – anything comparatively long and straight and narrow that came to hand. I could fix bayonets in my sleep, and frequently did.

The great day dawned, a bright blue summer's day. I had hoped passionately for a waterspout, but it was not to be.

The guard-of-honour fell in outside the armoury. There was a good deal of surreptitious polishing of buttons and setting of caps. Then Gus struck his final blow. He inspected me carefully, front and back, and then, in a terrible travesty of a refined accent, he said, 'Pawdon meh, Lord Clawence, but why ain't you wearin' unifawm?' I fell for it. I shot one panic-stricken downward glance at my threadbare khaki, and realized I'd been had.

'I *am* wearing uniform,' I said coldly, 'to the best of my knowledge.'

Gus shook his head, a long and mournful process. 'Oh no, yer not, Lord Clawence,' he said. 'Wot you're wearin' is a crime – a ruddy, 'orrible, long-drawrn-aht crime.'

'Oh, shut up,' I said, 'and get on with your work.'

Gus was so delighted with himself that he betrayed no sign of irritation. After a short speech full of indescribable menace, he marched us on to the square via the playing fields, the patch of grass behind the chapel, and a complete circuit of the sanatorium. My puttees began to slip, and once I walked into a tree. But we made the square at last.

It was lined with parents in top-hats and flowered dresses. The staff and the field-marshal were disposed in a row of leather armchairs.

Lieutenant Winter took over from Gus – Winter looking as if he was on his way to execution. He brought us to attention.

This was the moment. Now came the fixing of the bayonets, preliminary to the General Salute. I repeated to myself very quickly everything I knew about fixing bayonets. I was word perfect. There was nothing to go wrong.

'Fix . . .' roared Lieutenant Winter. I stepped out smartly from the ranks, achieved the regulation number of paces, halted, and turned crisply to the left. 'Bayonets!' roared Lieutenant Winter.

Without a moment's hesitation I presented arms. With the precision of a guardsman I swung the rifle up to my side, across the body, a smack on the magazine, a stamp of the back leg, and there I was carved out of stone, frozen solid in the General Salute.

Perhaps half a minute later I saw Lieutenant Winter standing in front of me. His eyes were bulging out of his head. 'What,' he said in a shocked whisper, 'what do you think you're doing?'

He took me by surprise. I thought everything was going well. 'General Salute,' I said out of the side of my mouth, 'I'm presenting arms.'

I think he danced a little. 'You're not!' he hissed – 'you're supposed to be fixing your bayonet!'

And then it all came back. I stared at Lieutenant Winter in horror.

'Oh gosh, sir,' I said, 'what'll I do?'

Lieutenant Winter, in spite of being an incurable singer of 'Take a pair of sparkling eyes' and 'Two little girls in blue' at school concerts, must have been an instinctive leader of men. 'Come back to attention,' he said, 'keep your head, and I'll give you the order again.' I nodded violently. I would have died for him at that moment.

He withdrew to his previous position in advance of the guard.

As he walked away I went back to the beginning again, or, indeed, rather farther back than the beginning, because after ordering arms I stood at ease. With the rest of the guard still standing to attention it must have seemed to competent observers that there was nothing in the drill book that could ever bring us together again.

But Winter found it. 'Private Campbell,' he shouted, improvising a command unique in military history, 'Attention! Guard of honour – Bayonets!'

I went through it like the mechanical man. We stuck our knives on to the ends of our rifles with a magnificent flourish and click. Then I turned left, paused, and marched stiff as a ramrod back to the comparative safety of the ranks. As I marched back I saw Gus. He was standing like a statue in the rear of the platoon. Only the whites of his eyes were showing.

The rest of the programme passed off without incident. Two days later, however, I had an interview with the headmaster. As a result of it I took no further part in military training, but on future corps days went for a walk to the village with a boy called Humphries, who had weak ankles.

On balance, I suppose it was nearly worth it.

20
Free For All

One Saturday afternoon the sports reporter of a newspaper I used to work for got a winner at the races. He was brought home rigid in a horse-drawn cab, the victim in equal parts of surprise, and nineteen bottles of stout.

I was sent off, in his place, to cover a boxing tournament taking place that night on the football ground at Shamrock Park.

'And none of your "last analysis" or "subsequent developments",' said the sports editor. 'This is for the *reading* public.'

The ring had been built on the football field, about ten yards out from the touchline, immediately in front of the stand. It was surrounded by several rows of chairs, enclosed in their turn by a barrier of steel poles and wire netting.

The barrier was known as the Delahunty Line, and its purpose was to prevent the holders of the cheaper tickets breaking their way through into the ring-side seats.

The Line, consisting in its earlier form only of scaffolding poles, had frequently been breached at other tournaments, but it was now hoped that the addition of wire netting would prove the decisive factor.

I sat down at the Press table. Boone was already there, an old man who did casual paragraphs for the evening papers. He had once been a champion cyclist, and was regarded as an authority upon most branches of sport.

'Hello,' said Boone sourly, 'you covering this too? Not too much of your tandem quandem now, or you'll be writing us all out of a job.'

I took this to be another reference to my leading article style.

'Just a couple of lines,' I said. 'The results and a little background stuff.'

At this moment Delahunty clambered through the ropes. A plump young man in a pin-stripe suit, he was reputed to have made his money out of coffee-stalls in Belfast. But he must have had other strings to his bow, because quite often he was picked up in side streets covered with blood, the victim of mysterious assaults.

He was now wearing a bandage round his head. I asked Boone what had happened.

'Taxi-driver got him with a starting-handle,' he said indifferently, 'couple of nights ago outside the dogs.'

Delahunty cleared his throat. 'Ladies and gentlemen,' he roared into a microphone, using his familiar form of address, 'welcome to Delahunty Promotions – tonight at eight!'

'Nine! Ten! You're out!' shouted the crowd.

'As you know,' continued Delahunty unperturbed, 'it has always been my aim to provide sport lovers in this country with good, clean fighting –'

'An' yourself with a couple of good, clean quid,' said a voice from outside the wire.

Delahunty threw up a hand. 'Thank you very much, ladies and gentlemen. Well, I won't take up your time any longer –'

'You better not,' said the same voice as before, 'or you'll be gettin' the same again.'

'– but introduce you to the first pair of contestants –' As Delahunty climbed out of the ring a potato bounced on the canvas close beside him, and rocketed past his head.

The first three fights were extraordinarily dull – the boxers being either middle-aged, and prudent in the extreme, or very young, and incapable of doing more than flap their gloves.

Once, seeing Boone writing busily, I looked over his shoulder, thinking he was making more out of it than I was.

He had written: 'At a meeting of the Cooperative Ratepayers' Association this afternoon it was unanimously decided that representations should be made to the Minister for Local Government and Public Health –'

He was catching up on his homework.

At nine o'clock came the heavyweight contest.

'Between,' roared Delahunty, 'on my right – Joe Boy Scully, of Mullingar! And on my left – Kid Koko – Heavyweight Champion of the – CANARY ISLANDS!'

'This ought to be better,' I said to Boone, and the next moment I was flat on my back. I lay there half-stunned on the wet grass, and then I struggled to my feet.

I saw at once what had happened. The Delahunty Line had burst. All round the perimeter people were fighting their way through the wire, tough-looking young men with an undercurrent of yelling small boys. In one corner an unfortunate citizen had been trapped underneath the broken netting, and was struggling wildly to free himself like a ferret in a bag. Several people, noticing his predicament, changed course for the pleasure of running across him.

The Press table had now been taken over by five of the invaders, who were sitting on it, with their feet propped up on the edge of the ring.

I touched one of them on the shoulder. 'Do you mind moving?' I said – 'I've got my work to do.'

He turned round. He had a strip of plaster over one eye.

'You go and have a bark at yourself,' he said.

I decided to leave it at that. I could just see the ring over their heads. Boone had disappeared.

'Now, ladies and gentlemen,' shouted Delahunty from the ring, 'I can see we're having a little trouble here, but it'll straighten itself out in a moment. If those fight fans who have come through to the ring-side will just kneel down our good friends in the stand can get a clear view, and we will continue with our programme.'

A babel of sound arose.

'Kneel down, you – can't you hear what the man is sayin'?'

'What about the next fyut?'

'Hey, Joe Boy – are y'all right?'

'Get that eejit owa the ring!'

Delahunty was still shouting into the microphone as a new rush came from the stand. I found myself spreadeagled on the Press table, in the heart of a cheering mob.

A new figure appeared in the ring, a stocky young man in a

white sweater. He was carrying a spanner, bound with a handkerchief.

'Unless the fans move back,' roared Delahunty, 'we'll have to clear the ring-side.'

The young man suddenly pounced and brought his spanner down sharply on the head of an old man in a cap who a moment before had dispossessed the time-keeper of his bell, and was now ringing it wildly, shouting, 'Seconds out – time!'

This onslaught occasioned a momentary lull, broken by shouts of – 'Hey, Packy, easy on! Go easy wit the spanner! Jasus, he has him half killed!'

Suddenly, someone threw another potato. It was probably aimed at Delahunty, but it hit Kid Koko on the ear.

The champion of the Canary Islands went into action. He sprang from his seat with a roar of rage, and leaped across the ring. Joe Boy, seeing him coming, tried to get up, but, overcome by terror, was just a moment too late. Kid Koko caught him straight beneath the chin with an enormous uppercut which left Joe Boy hanging upside down with his back across the ropes.

There was a roar of outraged indignation – 'Gob, didja see that?' 'Here, lemme at him!' 'Mother of God, is Joe Boy done?'

Kid Koko swung round, all his teeth showing, apparently ready to assault Delahunty, when one of Joe Boy's seconds played an ace. He leant over and brought down an iron bucket with all his strength on Koko's head. The champion gave a gasp and sank to his knees.

At that moment I went out for another count myself. The legs of the Press table gave way, and I disappeared.

When I came to this time I was actually underneath the ring, in a dim canvas cave. The roof bounced under the feet of men fighting up above.

There were three other people in the cave. Boone, and two terrified youths crouched over a radio set.

'Get owa this!' cried one of the youths in a thin voice – 'if the radio's hurt Mr Milligan'll have me life!'

Boone, crouched in a corner with his coat collar up, said, 'Did you start this?' Without waiting for a reply he muttered – 'Bringing inexperienced people in – the Board of Control –' The old man was beside himself.

'Don't be a fool,' I said angrily, 'how could I possibly have started –'

The roof fell in. There was a splintering crash, a yell, and suddenly Kid Koko, Delahunty, the apparently lifeless form of Joe Boy Scully, several spectators and yards of torn canvas and twisted rope were all mixed up with me and Boone and the two boys and the loud-speaker set.

I got back to the office soon after eleven, and dashed into the sporting room. 'Quick,' I said, 'get me a typewriter – paper – !'

The sports editor looked up. 'It's you, is it,' he said. 'Where have you been?'

'Murder!' I gasped – 'desolation! The whole place torn up!'

'Keep it for your memoirs,' said the sports editor. 'We've gone to press.'

'But what about the story?' I said. 'It's terrific – practically civil war. . .'

'It's covered,' he said. 'One of the subs gave me a stick.'

I looked at the proof: 'A varied programme of boxing was enjoyed by a large crowd last night at Shamrock Park. The heavyweight contest, owing to a fault in the ring, was abandoned.'

It did, in a way, cover the evening's sport.

21

Cuckoo in the Nest

Once, while I was in the Irish Marine Service, I saw a woman going aboard a Greek freighter late at night wearing a fur coat. I got on to my bicycle at once, and hurried back to headquarters.

Coogan, the duty officer, was lying face downwards on his bed, one hand trailing on the floor. I shook him by the shoulder.

He struggled in his sleep, and opened one eye.

'Whassamatta, dear?' he said.

I gave him time to come round. 'Sir,' I said, 'a woman has just gone aboard the *Katerina* at the deep-water berth wearing a fur coat and carrying a suitcase. Do you want me to turn her off?'

He sprang up. 'What's that?' he shouted. 'What? Where?'

I tried to calm him. 'She looks respectable, sir,' I said. 'She may have a special pass. I was wondering if you happened to know anything about her.'

'Get back there at once!' he cried. He was half out of bed. 'That bag is full of bombs!'

He started pulling on his trousers. Nothing much ever happened in our part of the docks, so that when it did everyone blew up at once. We had a special fear about women going on board ships with bombs in their handbags. The possibility had been invented by the army authorities, and we paid it close attention.

Coogan had his tunic on by now. 'Are you coming too, sir?' I asked him, glad of the assistance.

'Me?' said Coogan, surprised. 'No, I'm going to get a cup of cha.'

I saluted. 'I'll report back, sir,' I said.

It was still raining. I pedalled down to the *Katerina* in my

149

oilskins, sea-boots, and sou'wester, nearly a mile along the cobblestones into a headwind.

The ship was in darkness, save for a light on the bulkhead just below the bridge. The woman in the fur coat might have been anywhere by now, and, with a crew of twenty-eight Greeks, Egyptians and Swedes, doing almost anything.

I decided to explain the situation to Captain Demetrius, hoping that for once he might make some effort to understand English.

I knocked on the door of his cabin. It was nearly four o'clock in the morning.

There was a pause of several seconds, and then suddenly the door was wrenched open from the inside. I'd been holding the handle on my side, and there was no time to let go. I was whipped right into the cabin, and right into Captain Demetrius himself.

'Ah, frand,' said Captain Demetrius. He was about nine feet high, with a heavy black moustache, and a face the colour of tomato soup.

I stepped back and pushed up my sou'wester, which had been crushed over my face. 'Excuse me, sir,' I said. 'I have information that a woman has been seen on board your ship. This is a controlled area. No unauthorized person is allowed in here without a pass.'

I had little hope that any of this would come through to the Captain, but I thought he might be impressed by its official tone.

Demetrius nodded resignedly. 'Oll right,' he said. 'You weesh sheep's peppers.' He stepped aside to let me in.

The woman in the fur coat was lying on his bunk! She'd taken off the coat, and was wearing a purple dress with a halter of sequins round the shoulders.

'Oh gosh,' I exclaimed. 'That's her!'

An enormous smile spread across the Captain's face.

'You lof her?' he asked. Then he added, with pride, 'My weef.'

The lady, feeling herself become the centre of attention, sat up and settled her hair. It was dead black, arranged in tight curls all over her head. She smiled, showing four front teeth bordered with gold.

'She's your *wife*?' I said, nonplussed. The Captain seemed to have laid me a stymie.

'We to marry up,' said the Captain. He laid a knotted, affectionate hand on the lady's thigh.

I couldn't make out if he meant they were married or were going to be married.

'Has your wife a pass?' I said, clearly and distinctly.

'Noh! Noh!' cried Captain Demetrius. 'She iss Grik! Like me – Grik!'

I waited for a moment and began again.

'Has she a pass,' I said, '– a permission – a letter saying it's all right?'

'Iss peppers?' said the Captain, peering at me closely, trying to help. He opened a drawer in the table, and pulled out a bundle of documents.

'Iss rats peppers, cargo peppers, crew-men peppers, steward smoke peppers?' he said, showing them to me one by one.

I gave them back. 'No,' I said. 'I've seen all those. It's your wife. Has she a *pass*?'

It was very hot in the cabin. There was a smell of foreign cooking and cigars.

'Pass – pass?' said Captain Demetrius. 'Wot is pass?' He shook his head ponderously. A new idea occurred to him. He threw an arm like a tree-trunk round the lady's shoulders.

'No pass,' he said. He smiled proudly. 'We are make up bebe,' he announced.

I thought I'd better get out. 'I shall have to report this matter to the duty officer, Captain,' I said. 'I may be back.'

Demetrius waved his hand. 'You come up for bebe,' he said. 'Iss vino. Drinkeng to frands.'

I had no idea what he could possibly mean. As I shut the door the lady lay down again on the bunk.

Coogan was again fast asleep when I got back to the billet. This time, when I tried to wake him, he seized my hand.

'C'm here, love,' he muttered, '– c'm over here.'

I shook him off. I was getting too much involved in other people's private lives.

Coogan sat up. 'What the hell's the matter with you?' he said. 'It's the middle of the night.'

'Sir,' I said, 'there's a very difficult situation on the *Katerina*. Captain Demetrius says the lady is his wife. I think she's going to have a baby.'

'You're a damn fool,' shouted Coogan. 'Of course he says she's his wife. *Go and get her off!* If the C/O hears about this you're for the glasshouse.'

I tried to reason with him. 'She's going to have a baby, sir. It's pouring rain . . .'

'You'll have a baby if you don't get to hell out of this,' cried Coogan. 'Get back aboard that ship and do your job.'

I got on my bicycle again. There was a faint trace of dawn in the wild black sky.

This time there was no answer when I knocked on Demetrius's door. I beat harder. Suddenly it flew open.

'What the holy Gott you want?' said Captain Demetrius. He was breathing hard and wearing a thick woollen vest.

I decided to be ruthless. 'The lady has got to go ashore, Captain,' I said.

Demetrius shook his head desperately. 'I am telleng,' he said. 'Iss not a shore. Iss weef. Iss *weef*!'

I pushed past him. 'That's quite enough of that,' I said crisply.

The lady was lying on the bunk scarcely concealed by an emerald and gold kimono.

I spun round and faced the wall. 'Tell her to get dressed, Captain,' I said. 'And be quick about it.'

Demetrius shrugged his shoulders. So far as he was concerned the world had gone mad.

He shook the lady roughly, and said something to her in Greek. I heard her expostulating, and then Demetrius trying to soothe her. There was a sudden silence. When I looked round they were clenched in a long embrace. They showed no signs of stopping. In the end I had to tap Demetrius on the shoulder, and show him my watch.

The lady got dressed. She put on her fur coat and picked up the suitcase.

Demetrius suddenly gripped me by the arm. 'Iss not damage,' he said threateningly. 'Not make up bebe. Iss now honeymorn.'

I said, 'That's quite all right, Captain. I'm sure she'll be able to find a taxi.' I couldn't make head or tail of what he was trying to say.

I escorted the lady off the ship, and as far as the dock gates. I was surprised to find her trying to hold my hand, but thought she was probably afraid of falling into the water.

I freed myself outside the gates. 'Not go back,' I told her. 'Must get pass. Comprenez?'

I pedalled away. She gave a cry of what might have been dismay, but I didn't look round. I'd done enough.

I went off duty at eight that morning. When I got back next day there was an urgent message for me to see Lieutenant Coogan.

He wasted no words. 'What the flaming hell do you think you were doing the other night?' he said.

'What other night, sir?' I asked him.

'Tuesday,' he cried. 'The *Katerina*. There's about a yard and a half of complaints here from the agents. They say you insulted Captain Demetrius's wife, and insisted on her coming with you. Demetrius seemed to think you thought you'd first claim, or something, although God knows how *that* happened. At any rate there's hell to pay all round.'

'But, sir,' I said – 'sir, I told you she was his wife.'

'I couldn't make out what you were trying to tell me,' said Coogan crossly. He bit into a pencil. 'I knew from the beginning you weren't up to this job.'

He removed a sliver of wood from his teeth, looking worried. 'God knows,' he said, 'it only needs a little tact.'

22

A Square Meal

'That's Thelma Travers,' I whispered. 'I believe she's as hot as steam.'

The Malcolmsons disentangled themselves from one another. They'd been married for six weeks, and were still enjoying the honeymoon. I'd been staying with them for a fortnight, against their will.

'She's well filled,' said Rory Malcolmson.

'Rogo,' babbled Mrs Malcolmson, 'you *said* you'd never look at another woman.'

Rory returned to his homework. I was glad I wasn't married to Mrs Malcolmson. She had piled-up ginger hair, and ginger wisps that hung down over a freckled neck. Also, not being married to Mrs Malcolmson, I was free to look at Mrs Travers.

Mrs Travers was widely known. Any number of wives, given an even money chance of a fair trial, would have pushed her over a cliff.

She was about thirty-five. She was tall and startlingly developed. She had a mane of black hair, and electric blue eyes, and a strange kind of brooding look.

'How would it be,' I asked the Malcolmsons, 'if we brought that dish home to dinner?'

It was their own fault. I was a normally healthy boy, just down from the university, and if it hadn't been for their interminable billing and cooing I should have been prepared to let Mrs Travers pass, fully rigged and all as she was, like a ship in the night.

'She probably can't come, anyway,' I said.

'I hope not,' said Toni Malcolmson, biting her husband's ear.

'It's all very well for you,' I told her, and walked straight up to Mrs Travers, at the other end of the bar.

'Good evening,' I said, 'do forgive me for butting in on you like this, but I met you at the Horse Show last year. You were with Spencer Cavanagh.' She certainly had been with Spencer Cavanagh. It had been necessary to take only one glance at *Mrs* Spencer Cavanagh to tell that.

Mrs Travers looked up. Her eyes travelled down to my feet. It was like being tattooed, very slowly, all over.

'Yes,' she said, 'of course.'

'We were wondering,' I went on, a little breathlessly, 'if you were alone – would you like to come and have dinner with us? I'm staying with the Malcolmsons. They've a house up at the top of the lake.'

Mrs Travers looked at the Malcolmsons. They smiled, rather apprehensively.

'How nice of you,' she said. 'I was going home, but Francis – as usual, of course – is up in Dublin . . .'

'If *you're* going back to Oughterard,' I said, 'I can't imagine what *he's* doing a hundred and twenty miles away.'

It bit right home. Mrs Travers gave me one of her smouldering looks.

We sat down to dinner an hour later. Mrs Travers behaved perfectly. She showed a close interest in the Malcolmsons' marriage, and asked Rory if he brought Toni her breakfast in bed.

I got hold of Toni in the kitchen at about eleven o'clock. 'Aren't you going to retire?' I said. For the last couple of hours the four of us had been chatting in a desultory way about racing. It seemed to me that everyone was wasting their time.

I was surprised by Toni's outburst. 'How can we?' she cried, 'with that beastly woman talking about beds all the time? It's awful. I can't –'

'Beds have passed on,' I said, 'it's horses now.'

'Oh, all right,' said Toni, 'but you'll have to tell Rory. I won't go in there again.'

Silence had descended on the two in the sitting-room. They leaped when I spoke. Perhaps it did come out fortissimo. 'Rory!' I shouted, 'Toni wants to speak to you in the kitchen!'

It took him nearly a minute to get out of the room. He said good night to Mrs Travers, knocked over a table laden with magazines, picked them up and then said good night again. I was bathed in perspiration by the time that he reached the door.

I lowered myself carefully on to the sofa beside Mrs Travers. I put another log on the fire.

'Care for a drink?' I said. 'It's early still.'

Mrs Travers put her hand on my arm! I looked at her, wide-eyed. 'Would you do something for me?' she said in her huskiest voice.

'There is absolutely nothing,' I said, 'in the whole world that I would not do for you.'

'Would you make me an omelette?' said Mrs Travers.

I didn't understand. Then I had a wild idea that she meant – scramble her about a bit. It might be a technical term from her tempestuous way of life.

'What kind of an omelette?' I said.

'With onions,' whispered Mrs Travers, 'and tomatoes. I'm awfully hungry.'

I jumped up at once. It was, in fact, one of the very few things I could cook. I wondered how Mrs Travers knew, and then I remembered I'd brought up the subject at dinner.

I cooked her omelette. I found a bottle of Rory's champagne, and added it to the supper. Supper, with champagne and Mrs Travers, in the firelight!

'This,' I said, bringing it in to her, 'is like something you read about in books.'

Mrs Travers, leaning forward, explored her omelette with a fork. 'What book?' she said – 'was it *Egg Cookery*?'

'No,' I replied, taken aback, 'I just – made it up myself.' In the middle of it she sent me to make some toast. 'Not too thin,' she said, 'and do snip off the crusts.'

I cleared the plates away. I came back to Mrs Travers on the sofa. She patted the cushions by her side. 'Sit down,' she said, 'you wonderful man.' Before doing so I threw off my coat. I'd once been spiked in a similar situation by a pencil in the back seat of a car in the Pine Forest.

'That,' said Mrs Travers, 'was delicious. If only,' she went on – her lids were lowered, her eyes more slumbrous than ever – 'we

could have something like that at home. But you know what
Francis is like. "Beef!" he shouts, in that voice of his, "for God's
sake give me a bit of beef, and chuck that muck in the yard."'

'He doesn't talk to you like that, does he?' I said, trying to slide
my arm along the sofa.

'But all the time!' exclaimed Mrs Travers. 'Yesterday evening
I made the most marvellous chicken casserole. Just enough oil to
cover the bottom of the pan. Fried my onions golden brown,
with half a clove of garlic – you know . . .'

I said I did know. But I was becoming uneasy. Mrs Travers
was revealing a remarkable interest in food. We didn't seem to be
getting anywhere else.

'Have some more champagne,' I said.

'Yum,' said Mrs Travers. I filled her glass. She put it on the
floor by her side, and leant forward again.

'Most people,' she said, 'leave the onions in the pot, and then
add the tomatoes, and all the rest, but I find you lose the crispness
if you do that. What I do is to take them out, drain them, and then
leave them in a small saucepan on the side. *Then* I fry my potatoes
– diced, you know, not sliced – and leave them on one side with
the onions. Then I fry my chicken –'

'Thelma,' I said, 'are you in love? I mean, are you in love with
anyone at the moment?'

'Don't be silly,' said Thelma Travers. 'I fry my chicken,' she
went on, eager to get back to the subject, 'for quite a long time.
You want to let the onion and garlic juice sink right in . . .'

I reached out for the bottle of champagne, poured myself a
glass, drank it, and poured another one. It was a quarter past
twelve by the clock on the mantelpiece. This would probably
continue for some time. I slipped down on the sofa, and half-
closed my eyes.

She went on and on. She cooked, and served, the casserole,
and then she ran up some Cornish pasties – enough for four. She
told me that she always parboiled sausages, as soon as they
arrived. She maintained, although it was not, she admitted,
everyone that agreed with her, that it preserved their flavour,
while definitely preventing them from going off.

At 1.30 a.m. we went back into the kitchen, and cooked a tin
of sardines in grated cheese. We sprinkled a little paprika on top,

157

and brought our plates back to the sitting-room.

'Aren't we awful?' said Mrs Travers, 'tucking in like savages.' She looked as beautiful as ever, and I couldn't wait for her to go.

At two o'clock she rose. As she stood by the mantelpiece I was tempted, for a single second, to make a strike, and then I saw before my eyes great platefuls of parboiled sausages, steaming mounds of liver, yards of onion-laden tripe.

'I'll show you to your car,' I said. The car wouldn't start. The battery gave out after ten minutes. I applied myself to the handle.

'Poor you,' said Mrs Travers. 'Couldn't the Malcolmsons give me a bed?'

Six or seven hours ago this would have been my dearest and clearest wish, but now all that I wanted to see of Mrs Travers was her rear light, turning swiftly and neatly out of the gate.

I took out the plugs and cleaned them. Then I took off the distributor head. I put it back again, and reset the carburettor. This time I swung the handle so fiercely that I bent one of the lamps. But the engine came to life, fitfully, on three cylinders.

I opened the door. 'Good-bye,' I said, 'and thanks for a lovely time.'

Next morning the Malcolmsons were already at breakfast when I came down. I went over to the sideboard, lifted the lid of the dish, and put it down again very quickly. Sausages!

'I'll take some of that grapefruit,' I said in a low voice.

Rory raised an eyebrow. 'The man-eating Travers,' he said, 'seems to have made another heavy meal.'

'Not off me,' I replied, without looking up from my plate. 'The whole thing was just a lot of tripe.'

23
The Big, Big Time

In 1949 the British Amateur Championship was played at Port-marnock, Eire – an interesting occasion in view of the fact that the British competitors had to submit to the rigours of passport examination and Customs inspection before being allowed to play in their own championship.

It was – making the situation slightly worse – won by an Irishman, Max Macready, from an American, Willie Turnesa, but what causes the event to linger in my memory is the fact that I got as far as the fifteenth hole in the fifth round – a 300% improvement on all previous endeavours.

Having emigrated, like 920,000 other Irishmen, to England I was drawn to return home for this particular Amateur by the enormous advantage of being able to stay with my parents while it was in progress, and not in an hotel.

Hotels are murder during a championship week if you're not a member of the regular tournament mob. Unless you know – as the English, whose spiritual home is the Armed Forces, say – the drill, you're liable to find yourself shacked up with seven old ladies in a temperance guest house ten miles away from the course on which the championship is being played.

On all these occasions there is always one hotel in which the knowledgeable boys are gathered together, and if you're not in it it promotes an emotional climate in which you're already three down.

There are no means of assessing – say from the A.A. book – which this hotel is likely to be. Choose the four-star one and you find that all the boys are staying at half the price in a charming road-house immediately opposite the course. If the four-star hotel is the right one you can only get into it by booking a month ahead, before you've seen the draw. When you do see the draw, and find you've got Joe Carr in the first round, a reservation for five days at £3. 10s. per day bed and breakfast looks like being an unnecessary expense.

The night life of hotels can draw you out very fine, too. After dinner you can sit in the lounge on the outskirts of the knowledgeable boys listening to them talking about Amateurs they have taken part in in the past. There is no limit to the scope or the accuracy of their reminiscences. They can recount, shot by shot, the details of every round they've played over the last five years, with sidelights on the exceptional good fortune, in moments of crisis, enjoyed by other distinguished players who beat them at Deal, Troon, Hoylake and everywhere else. Attempts by the non-tournament man to introduce subjects of a more general nature, like the plays of Ionesco, Picasso's ceramics or the convoluted literary style of Henry James meet with no success.

The alternative is to go to bed and get a good night's sleep, to be alert and fresh for the morrow. But before retiring it's obviously a good idea to get out the putter, and knock a few balls up and down the carpet.

There's a design of stripes on the carpet which, by a happy coincidence, clearly demonstrates whether or not the club-head is being taken back, and brought forward, square to the line of the tooth mug which has been placed on the floor in the opposite corner of the room. But, according to the stripes on the carpet, the club-head is coming back *outside* the line, while the follow-through finishes several inches to the left of the tooth mug, and must, indeed, have been doing so for years. It's still, however, only 9.15. There's ample time to work on it –

By 10 p.m. you're getting only one in six into the tooth mug, against a previous average as high as three. Also, the carpet is much faster than the greens are likely to be. You achieve the conviction that you're practising a putting stroke which will not only push it six inches to the right of the hole every time, but also leave it at least two yards short. Throw the putter back into the bag and get into bed and try to forget all about the stripes. Try, indeed, not to think about golf at all –

Five minutes later you're up, in bare feet and pyjamas, in front of the full-length mirror in the wardrobe, trying to see what it looks like if you really do pull the left hand *down* from the top of the swing, instead of shoving the right shoulder round. Suddenly, it feels right so you get the driver out of the bag and have a swish with it in front of the mirror and it demolishes an alabaster bowl concealing the light fitting in the ceiling. Clear it up and back into bed and try to think of some reasonable explanation for the chambermaid in the morning –

By midnight there's been another putting session – disastrous – and a spell of short chips into the wastepaper basket two of which, striking the door high up with an incredibly loud bang, provoked a thunderous and outraged knocking on the wall from the man next door. Back into bed – the feet are frozen – where you lie with the sheet up to the eyes wondering if the whole hotel has been roused and the manager, in his dressing-gown, will soon be in with a policeman, and they'll find you've smashed the alabaster bowl and knocked all the paint off the door and there's no explanation. None, except perhaps that you're playing in the Championship – or at it.

To sleep, perchance – except that it's an odds-on certainty – to dream. It's that very special nightmare, unhinging in its grinding frustration, of being on the first tee in the British Amateur Championship, except that the tee is enclosed by a small wooden shed and you're inside it and there's no room for your back-swing and in any case the tee-shot, supposing you could hit it, has got to emerge through a tiny window high up near the roof –

Stark, staring awake and the time is five to five. Get up and have a bath? It might be so weakening that the driver will fly out of your hand and blind Willie Turnesa. Read? The more interesting passages in *Lady Chatterley's Lover* would have the impact of *Eric, Or Little By Little*.

Perhaps the greens are as fast as – much faster than – the carpet. Has anyone, in the Amateur, ever taken four putts on each of the first nine holes?

If the quick hooking starts will six new balls be enough? Has anyone, in the Amateur, ever had to *buy* a ball off his opponent as early as the third hole? Is it allowed by the rules . . . ?

The waiters are still laying the tables when you come down to breakfast, and the papers haven't arrived. To spread the meal out – it's only 7.30 a.m. – you order grapefruit, porridge, a kipper, bacon and eggs, coffee, toast and marmalade. Each item goes to join the previous one in what feels like a hot croquet-ball, lodged at the base of the throat.

The chambermaid does want to know what happened to the alabaster light fitting.

The car, left outside all night because the hotel garage is full, won't start.

The contestant for the British Amateur title is ready to – and does – go down without a struggle to a nineteen-year old medical student from Glasgow University, pulling his own trolley, six and five.

For the 1949 Amateur, however, I not only had the comforting presence of my nearest and dearest around me after dark, to say nothing of free board and lodging, but also the benefit of the advice and counsel of Henry Longhurst, who was staying with us.

He was early in the field both with counsel and advice. Before going over to Portmarnock for the first round I had an hour loosening up at a course near my father's house, with Henry in attendance to see, even at this eleventh hour, if something couldn't be done to put things right.

At the end of the first fusillade he said, through clenched teeth, 'It's like watching a man scraping a knife against a pewter plate.'

Put out – some of them had finished on the fairway – I asked him to be more precise about his discomfort.

'You're trying to hit them round corners,' he said. 'It's agony to watch it.'

We conducted an interesting experiment. I stood up to the ball. Henry laid a club on the ground behind me, pointing in the direction which my stance suggested might be the eventual line of flight. When I came round to have a look I found to my surprise that I'd been aiming at a small shelter in the distance, perhaps fifty yards to the right of the true objective. 'Swivel the whole gun round,' said Coach, 'and try firing one straight.'

It seemed madness to tamper with the system now, and specially to try hitting one straight after years of hooking it back from the rough on the right. I tried it, however, just once.

Aiming, it seemed to me, diagonally across the fairway to the left, I hit one straight down the middle, quail-high and all, perhaps, of a quarter of a mile.

'Right,' said Coach. 'We'll leave it at that. You've probably only got four more of those left.'

It looked as though four would be enough. My section of the draw was infested with Americans, mostly from Winged Foot – a distinction which suggested that they were all probably well above Walker Cup standard. I'd drawn someone called Udo Reinach, a threatening set of syllables presenting a picture of a crew-cut, All-American tackle weighing 210 lb with a tee-shot like a naval gun. To remain with Udo for as many as twelve holes would surely see duty done.

I met him. He turned out to be Willie Turnesa's patron and protector who, as he said himself, had just come along for the ride. He was small and elderly and noticeably frail. In a ding-dong struggle, with no quarter given or asked, I beat him on the seventeenth by holding a long, up-hill putt which went off some time before I was ready for it. If we'd completed the course both would have been round in the middle eighties.

Next day I met another American, also from Winged Foot. I've never been able to remember his name, but he was a friend of Udo's. Indeed, he'd known Udo for nearly forty years, which put him in the late sixties. He confessed to me that he had no serious intentions about the Championship at all, having merely come along on the ride that Udo was on, and – owing to a latent heart condition – rather doubted his capacity to get round the whole of Portmarnock's 7,000 yards.

He very nearly had to. I beat him with a four on the seventeenth by putting a 5-iron absolutely stiff after hitting my tee-shot straight along the ground.

It was gratifying to see a line in one of the Dublin evening papers: 'In the lower half of the draw Campbell, a local player, is steadily working his way through the American menace.'

By the following evening I'd got through another round. I can't remember his name either, but I know he was a Dublin man who was about half my size and capable of playing, on the very top of his game, to a handicap in the region of nine. Coach summed up the situation at dinner that night. 'No one,' he said, 'since the inauguration of the Amateur has ever had it easier for the first three rounds. It's a pity, in a way, it's over now.'

He was referring, graciously, to the fact that I was to meet Billy O'Sullivan in the morning, in the fourth round.

Billy, who was well known to me, had been Irish Amateur Champion so often that it didn't seem possible he hadn't turned pro. With a two-handed, blacksmith's grip he hit it farther off the tee than anyone in Ireland. A Killarney man himself, he'd brought two-thirds of that fiercely partisan area with him, to assist in the laying waste to the city of Dublin which would automatically follow his almost certain victory in the final on Saturday afternoon.

I was devoid of hope. My coach – creator with Valentine Castlerosse of the Killarney Golf Club – had transferred his loyalties without equivocation to the local man, even inviting me to share his pleasure in contemplation of the beating that Billy, with his fine, free, slashing Killarney swing, would hand out to the plodding, mechanical, American methods of Willie Turnesa. 'We want him fresh,' were my coach's last words of advice, 'so don't keep him out there too long – not that you will.'

By the eleventh hole it looked as though Billy would be back in the club-house for a long and leisured lunch. He was four up, and on a loose rein. I was aiming the gun right out over the head of mid-wicket and hauling it so far back around the corner that time after time it finished up in the sandhills on the left. We were unattended by an audience. Even the camp-followers from Killarney were drinking stout in the bar, preparing themselves for the rigours of the O'Sullivan–Turnesa final.

Abruptly – and I can't remember how – Billy came to pieces. I got two holes back, so that on the fourteenth tee he was two up with five to go, a margin still sufficiently large, it seemed to me, not to leave the result in doubt.

Then something extraordinary happened. The fourteenth is a long, narrow green sloping up into the sandhills, with several cavernous bunkers in front. You couldn't play short and if you were over you'd a vile, slippery chip all down-hill on a green burnt brown and ten miles an hour faster than any hotel carpet. On the left, however, pin-high, was a patch of short rough into which I'd hooked all three previous second shots, by accident. They had remained there, however, leaving a comparatively simple scuffle up to the hole.

It would, if nothing else, be interesting to see if I could put it into the rough on purpose. For the first time – not having dared to try the innovation before – I swivelled the gun, played left of the green and it stayed there, a combination of almost unbelievable circumstances.

Billy, outside me as usual, played a beautiful iron shot which hit the middle of the green, ran up the slope and disappeared over the top edge. His chip back slid eight feet past. He missed the putt. I holed a shortish one for a four, to be only one down. Even in the white-hot glow of having played a hole with the loaf, and having seen Billy making the obvious mistake, I still regarded it merely as a postponement of the inevitable three and two defeat that was coming my way – particularly in view of the nature of the fifteenth.

It's a short hole – about 170 yards – from a raised tee on the edge of the beach to a green sunk in sandhills, with jungle country all round and a deep hollow on the left. A brisk breeze was blowing off the sea, straight across. A further assurance of disaster was provided by the presence of Laddie Lucas and, I think – my eyesight was beginning to go – Gerald Micklem, an expert audience ready to enjoy to the full a high, looping hook which would not be seen again or, alternatively, a furtive, defensive socket onto the beach.

One – or both – of them remarked that they were glad to see I'd got so far, in view of the fact that rumour had it we'd been back in the club-house for quite some time. No disarmingly modest response occurred to me. An uncontrollable but still faint trembling had started in my legs, more or less guaranteeing a shank. I struck at it quickly with a 3-iron. It travelled low and straight into the cross-wind, and finished six feet from the hole. Incredulous laughter, instantly and graciously muffled, broke from Messrs Lucas and Micklem. Billy, holding his too far up into the wind, finished on the right-hand edge. His putt was short. Playing for a certain half from six feet, I put mine into the hole, and we were all square. As we walked down to the sixteenth tee Billy, possibly echoing a thought put into his mind by Lucas and Micklem, made his first remark for some time. 'I don't know how you do it,' he said.

I couldn't have told him, even if he'd really wanted to know. I was too busy trying to think of a method, based upon past experience, which would put my tee-shot on the fairway, and at least 200 yards away.

The sixteenth is a long par-5, and grouped around the distant green were something like five hundred people, waiting for the close finishes. For reasons of personal dignity and self-respect I had no desire to intrude into their company, having already played four.

The knee-trembling was becoming more acute, very similar, in fact, to the time when as a child of ten I was menaced by armed members of the I.R.A. My only desire was that the match should be over, one way or the other. No trace of that killer instinct had established itself, although I'd won four holes in a row.

It felt like a fairly good one, though the follow-through was curtailed because long after I'd hit it I was still looking at the ground. It turned out to have been low and rather hooky, but on the hard ground it had gone quite a long way. Billy hit a rasper right down the middle.

Then, as we walked off the tee, we saw an extraordinary thing – a spectacle like an infantry regiment, charging towards us. It was the five hundred people – probably two hundred of them from Killarney – who'd been waiting round the green. Instinct seemed to have warned them that a Homeric struggle – I was thinking like a golf correspondent – was in progress, and they wanted to be in on the kill.

They engulfed us. I lost sight of Billy, over to the right. I became conscious of an excited steward, dragging a length of rope. 'Jaysus –' he cried – 'I never thought I'd be doin' this for you!' He put down the rope and I stepped over it. 'Get back there!' he bawled at the crowd. 'Back there now, an' give him room!'

The ball was lying just on the edge of the rough, but nicely cocked up. People were standing round it in a semi-circle, five deep, craning in death-like silence to see over one another's heads. Hundreds more, lining the fairway, made it look like a long, solid tunnel to the green. It had the curious effect of promoting confidence, so many people expecting to see it go straight.

I took a long, slow swing with a 3-wood, making it look right for the audience. There was a lovely whip off the shaft, but I never saw where it went. They were after it, almost before I'd hit it. All I saw was a mass of backs, running away from me. My caddy and I were left alone. He was a young and inexperienced lad, as staggered as I was that we'd got so far. 'I never seen a t'ing,' he said.

Billy and I were both short, left and right, though I only knew where he was by the crowd around him. Someone told me it was my shot, and asked me the score. I found I didn't know.

I'd a fifty yard chip, up to the hole. Again the crowd, pressing in, seemed to narrow down the possibilities of error. I left it two feet from the hole. Then the running backs hid it from me again, forming a solid, brightly coloured wall round the green. I'd quite a job to push through them, to find that Billy was about four feet away. Both of us holed our putts. Before mine dropped the gallery were running for the next tee.

It was still my honour. The ball was looking dingy and scuffed, after the hard, sandy fairways, but in a peculiar way I felt it was part of me, that it knew what we were trying to do. Nothing could have made me change it for a new one. We were both in this together, and what we were trying to do was to beat hell out of Billy O'Sullivan, for whom I'd suddenly conceived such a hatred that I could scarcely wait to bash one down the middle so far that he'd jump at his and please God leave himself with an unplayable lie in a bush.

We were both down the middle. As I walked slowly and shakily after the running backs, now seemingly multiplied by four, I was accosted by a well-spoken stranger. 'Are you all right?' he asked me. He appeared strangely concerned. 'Yeah,' I said. 'Yes.' He looked at me for a long moment. 'You look,' he said, 'as if you're going to faint.' I saw for the first time that it was my father. 'I'm all right,' I told him, and walked on.

We were both on in two. We both got our four. We walked in silence to the eighteenth tee – all square and one to go.

It took a long time before the stewards were able to clear the course. It was round about lunch time. People were pouring out of the club-house and the beer tents, running for positions of vantage. In a championship all square and one to go will cause any true golf enthusiast even to put down his bottle of stout, and come out and have a look.

The eighteenth at Portmarnock is a nasty one. A long, high mound on the left means you've got to keep your tee-shot well out on the right, to get a view of the green, and even then there's a rise in front of it which stops you seeing more than the top half of the pin.

I stood up to the ball, still having the honour. All hatred of Billy O'Sullivan had subsided, having given way to a bone-cracking weariness in which whatever mental processes were still alive were focused upon the immediate warming and soothing after-effects of two large Irish whiskeys in one glass.

I was shifting the club-head about, trying to get a grip with the left hand which would push the ball out to the right, away from the mound on the other side, when someone let out a roar that froze me solid. 'Fore –' he bawled – 'ya silly ole bitch!'

I looked up – and saw an elderly woman, her wits deranged by scores of shouted, contrary instructions, scurrying about in the middle of the fairway, like a rabbit fleeting from two thousand dogs. A friend or relative fell upon her, and dragged her away to safety. I started all over again. A moment later, playing with the greatest care and concentration, I hooked my tee-shot straight into the base of the mound.

'Bad luck,' said Billy. It seemed to me that his rugged features were irradiated by an expression of gentle, brotherly love. The swine hit a beauty, a mile long and out on the right, giving him an easy 6-iron to the green.

I was sloping after the running backs again, trying to calculate the minutes that remained between me and the two large Irish, when I found myself confronted by H. Longhurst, my patron and coach, of whom I'd seen nothing during the heat of the day. 'You're doing well,' he said pleasantly. 'Why not try winning, for a change?'

'Go,' I told him, 'and set them up inside. Plain water with mine.' Knowledgeable man that he is, he walked away.

It wasn't lying too badly but, being under the mound, I couldn't see the green. I took out a 5-iron and hit it high into the air. It felt fairly all right, but the gallery put me straight. They let out a great cry of, 'Oooh – !' on a descending scale, indicating beyond doubt that we were up to the ears in the radishes, for the first time for six holes.

I'd no idea where it was and still hadn't, when I reached the green, which was hemmed in by the largest crowd I'd ever seen. There was no trace of the ball or, indeed, of anyone who seemed to know where it might be found. I pushed through the people massed in front of me and then heard a disordered shouting away to the left. Someone over there was waving a small red flag on the end of a long pole. I was in a deep bunker so far off the line, and so little used, that it was full of scattered stones and weeds growing up through the sand.

I went in after it. It was lying all right, clear at least of the stones. It was only then that I remembered Billy, and the important part that he was playing in the proceedings. I asked someone what had happened to him. He didn't know. General conjecture and speculation broke out. Several people thought he'd put it stiff. Others believed he was out of bounds, in the garden of the clubhouse. In the middle of all this a man, carrying a ham sandwich and a cardboard glass of stout, came running over the hill, his face suffused with excitement. 'He's up to his doodlers in the pot bunker!' he bawled. 'Ye've got him cold!'

For the second time, in this last, vital hole, I was about to play a shot without being able to see the pin – a fair commentary, I had time to remark, upon the accuracy of my method under press-ure. I climbed out to have a look and saw Billy, already standing in the deep pot bunker cut into the right-hand edge of the green. The pin was only a few yards away from him. He'd have to play a miraculous one to get his four. If I could scuffle mine out and take only two putts, we'd very shortly be starting off down the first again, drawing farther and farther away from the healing malt in the bar.

I climbed down into the bunker again. The only unforgivable thing would be to leave it there. Expelling every breath of air from my lungs that might build up unwanted pressure, I swung the club-head slowly back and equally slowly forward. It nipped the ball rather sweetly. It disappeared over the brow of the hill.

When I pushed through the crowd and walked on to the green

I knew at once which was mine. It was four feet from the hole, a not impossible, dead straight putt, slightly up hill. Billy was three or four yards past it. No one could have holed it out of that pot bunker, with a burnt-up green.

He had a horrible curly one with a 6-inch borrow all down the side of the hill. He missed it.

I can remember exactly how I holed mine. I gripped the putter so tightly that it was impossible to break the wrists, and shoved it straight in. So incalculable are the workings of the human mind that I knew, even under that nerve-crinkling pressure, that I couldn't miss.

I don't remember anything at all about the next half-hour. There must have been a great deal of pleasure in assuring people in the bar that I had, in fact, beaten Billy O'Sullivan. The opportunity must have arisen for the extra pleasure of telling them, in part, how. There must also have been the extreme physical joy of the corrosive malt, slowly seeping through the system shaky and dehydrated by tension, fear and the need to discipline muscles jumpy and wayward as jelly. It's all a blur, but I do remember the thing that suddenly gave it edge and shape. It was the reminder, by someone who'd just bought me another large one, that I had, within the hour, to go out and do it again.

I would like, at this point, to make the frank admission that I knew I hadn't won the Championship by getting through four rounds but, at the same time, that I had reached a state of euphoria in which it practically seemed that I had. That is, to well deserved roars of applause, I'd got much further even than my own mother – a non-player – would ever have imagined and now, full of drink and glory, was more than ready to step off the bus. Except that I was still in the Championship, and was off at 2.15, facing the powerful, ruthless and determined Kenneth Thom.

I recall a private moment of agonizing – you can say that again – reappraisal in the convenience section of the gentlemen's locker room. I had to go out again and, stiff, sore, blurred and exhausted, beat Ken Thom. Another one into the rough on the left of the fourteenth, chip up and hole the putt. Another wind-splitter to the short fifteenth, and hole that one too. Then the three long holes home and the feeling of evening coming on and tattered newspaper blowing across the course and the fairways shiny and slippery with the battering of countless feet and cars filled with careless merrymakers driving away down the road because the main excitement of the day is over – except that, to survive, I've still got to get a four at the eighteenth and I'm in behind the mound . . .

Another thought occurred to me in the cathedral silence of the convenience section of the gentlemen's locker room. With this next round the Championship proper was only about to begin. The first four rounds, which had brought me to my knees, were in fact only a routine clearing away of the dross – a removal of the cheerful, slap-happy elements who'd merely come along for the ride. From now on we were getting down to work, opening up a little on the tee-shots, really picking the spots, far out, where we could start drilling home those iron-shots, going for our threes. One more round today – and two more tomorrow – *two more tomorrow*! – followed by the 36 hole final – 36 HOLES AT THE END OF A WEEK! – after which one of us would step up to receive the trophy, remark that the course seemed to be in excellent condition and that the runner-up had played a really wonderful game – and then, with the whites of the eyes rolling up, keel over backwards and fall stone dead. Except, of course, that the real men who win championships don't have much time to hang around afterwards, dying or making idle remarks. They've got to look slippy and get to the airport, because there are only three days for practice before exactly the same thing begins all over again.

I concluded the agonizing reappraisal, stunned by the size of the suddenly revealed gap between the real men and the lucky mice, and went to have lunch. There was only half an hour left before Ken Thom helped himself to a victory, the ease of which would pleasurably surprise him, at this comparatively late stage.

As soon as I got into the tent I saw that he must have had lunch already. Or, perhaps, a prey – wholly unjustifiably – to tournament nerves, he'd decided to leave it out altogether. The wind had increased in severity. Every time it blew back the flap of the lunch tent I could see him in the distance on the practice ground. With a whiplash crack he was drilling iron shots into the teeth of the wind under the expert instruction of the late Fred Robson, although I can't imagine what either of them were worrying about. All they had to do, if they were anxious about being beaten, was to come into the tent and watch me trying to wash down a lobster salad with alternative draughts of Guinness and John Jameson, a menu chosen more or less at random.

There was nothing left in the horse. Indeed, so little competitive spirit remained that I remember nothing whatever of the fifth and final round, except for the incident at the second hole.

Ken won the first – I think with a shaky five which wasn't, however, threatened at any point. At the next, I was miles away in the long, tenacious grass on the left. A clump with an 8-iron failed to do it very much harm, apart from improving the lie. I put the next one on the green, and left it on the lip of the hole for a five.

Ken already had his four. He knocked my ball away. 'Half,' he said. As we walked to the next tee, having rejected the undesirable solution of charity, I decided he hadn't seen the abortive bash with the 8-iron, presumed I was on in two and might even be counting himself lucky that my long putt hadn't gone in for a birdie.

Some light shadow-boxing took place with my conscience which, however, was in no shape for a major contest. I was storing the incident away in my bottom drawer, with plenty of old clothes on top of it to keep it away from the light, when I found Coach once more by my side. 'Well played,' he said, with apparently genuine admiration. 'A couple more of those and you'll beat him.'

It proved a confusing spur. I was still only one down after four more holes, though in reality, of course, it was two. On the fifth tee I had a night – or day – mare. Suppose by some inconceivable chance I had another resurrection and holed a four-footer on the eighteenth, to win one-up, would it then be possible to walk over to Ken Thom and in the presence of 5,000 people tell him that he'd got his arithmetic all trollocked up on the second and in fact we were still all-square? And how would Ken Thom, a dark, thick-set and dour young man, take it? What he'd do would be to concede the match, on the grounds that it was his own fault, and I'd have to get down on my knees in the middle of the eighteenth green and beg him to reconsider his quixotic decision. He'd turn away from this pitiful snivelling and the gallery would start throwing ham sandwiches, shooting-sticks, umbrellas . . .

The matter did not arise, nor did it ever look as if it would. Ken Thom won far out in the country, counting – probably having been tipped off by one of his supporters who'd seen the incident at the second – every one of the shower of sixes that turned out to be the best that I could do in the fifth round of the Amateur Championship, when all of us were opening the tap a bit and really starting to go for those threes.

At this late stage it seems improbable that I shall have another shot at the Amateur title.

You've got to qualify now before you're allowed in.

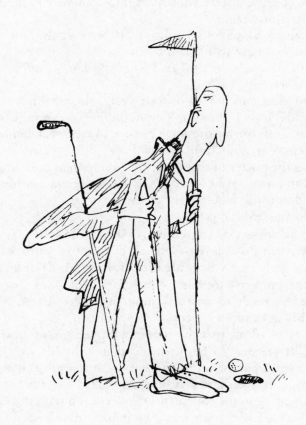

24

A Milker in the Mail

Riffling through my souvenirs in search of a prescription for vertigo, I came upon a short paragraph roughly hacked from an American magazine.

It's an extract from Ripley – 'Believe It or Not' – and it announces a new wonder of the world.

John L. Lunnon, of Well End Farm, Buckinghamshire, sent a live cow to market by post.

Even after an interval of four years, the cutting causes me a thin smile. John L. Lunnon sent it, did he? You might as well say that Enid Blyton wrote *Look Back in Anger*, that *Lolita* was the brain-child of Wilhelmina Stitch.

I was the poster of that cow, the first man in the history of the world to do so, and I want to say that there was nothing to it. It was a down-hill trot, nearly all the way.

Let's marshal the facts.

The business was started by Mr Ernest Marples, at that time the Assistant Postmaster-General, during the course of a speech to some gathering whose identity I forget. Mr Marples, always a buoyant publicist for his own department, said that the Post Office was ready to post anything anywhere. Even, he added – probably at random – a cow.

I have to admit that the report whipped me up into no great lather. It seemed to be no more than routine, after-luncheon jollity, and I passed on to some more interesting matter on the next page. It wasn't, in fact, until the following day that I saw its real potential, in the course of a conversation with my employer, Mr Charles Eade, who was then editing the *Sunday Dispatch*. I retain a clear recollection of the dialogue.

'Good morning. Got any ideas?'

'No, sir. Not yet.'

'I see that Marples says you can post a cow.'

'Yes, sir. I saw that.'

'Well, then – go and post one.'

'Good God!'

I didn't like the look of it at all. The project was beset with difficulties, not the least of which was to find a postable cow. Then I took heart. A single telephone call to any post office would surely reveal that Mr Marples, in the heat of oratory, had gone too far. I might even get a column on the familiar theme of bureaucratic confusion, with the workers struggling to keep up with the impractical boastings of the boss.

I suddenly remembered that my village post office was also called the Parade Dairy – an ideal branch in which to fail to post a cow. I called upon the sub-postmaster, a brisk young man called Browne, with whom I'd already had some amusing chats about arrears of National Health stamps (self-employed).

'Afternoon, Mr Browne. I want to post a cow.'

'To post a cow, sir?' He was polite and unsmiling, wary – I thought – of some ham-handed practical joke.

'Mr Marples says you can post cows. I just wanted to put it to the test.'

'I see, sir. Do you mind waiting a moment while I check with head office in Maidenhead?'

I followed him into the inner part of the shop, to listen to the telephone call.

'Hello – Bourne End sub-post office here. I have a gentleman who wishes to post a cow.' Short pause. 'Thank you very much.' Mr Browne put down the receiver. 'That will be perfectly all right, sir. The animal can be dispatched where and when you wish.' Not a trace of a smile. The head slightly on one side, waiting for my further pleasure.

'Thank you, Mr Browne. I'll be back. I just have to get in touch with a cow –'

I guessed what had happened. As soon as Marples shot off his neck the GPO must have got in touch with every post office in the land, warning them to stand by for cow-posters. One up – again – to the Establishment.

The position was serious. Cow-posting was on, Mr Eade desired it, but I hadn't got a cow. Then I remembered that the field over my boundary fence was infested with cows belonging to John Lunnon, with whom I'd already had some tart conversations about the injuries that might be sustained by cows struck in vital places by golf balls.

I approached him with caution.

'John, would you like to post one of your cows?'

He showed signs of restarting his tractor, to get away from the danger area.

'Marples says you can post a cow and the Parade Dairy is all for it, so I thought we might post one of yours.'

He took his foot off the clutch. The originality of the concept was nibbling at him.

'Post it – where to?'

It was an aspect of the matter I hadn't yet contemplated.

'Well, anywhere you'd like one of your cows to go.'

He thought for a moment. 'There's a market at Bracknell this week.'

'The very place. Nice and handy.'

'On the other hand, it's not a good time to sell. I'd get more later.'

It was no time for cheeseparing. 'The *Sunday Dispatch* will make up the difference.'

He considered the matter again.

'Do they actually put a stamp on them?'

I saw he was hooked. 'I'm sure they do – right on the rump.'

He suddenly rubbed his hands. 'Let's post a cow.'

Unbelievably, the whole thing had fallen sweetly into place. I rang Charles Eade.

'Sir – the cow-posting's all sewn up! I've got a cow to post and a post office to post it from! We're ready to go!'

'What are you talking about?'

It's always the same with newspaper editors. They get you into a cage of lions or about to perform a parachute drop and then they forget what it's all about, because they're busy sending someone else down a main drain. I put him back in the picture.

'Oh, that,' he said. 'Well, just make sure it doesn't get

slaughtered, wherever you're posting it to. A lot of our animal-loving readers wouldn't like to think we'd taken a cow out of a field for a stunt, and posted it to its death.'

'No, sir. Of course not.'

'Good-bye.'

In my experience a big newspaper story is always a matter of fast improvisation. All along the line objections and protests crop up. The only thing to do is to ignore them, and drive ahead towards the *fait accompli.* The lawyers can always take up the slack later on.

I didn't mention the matter of Bessie's possible fate as John and I closed in on her the following morning, in a corner of the field. I already had a clear picture – captioned – in my mind of a rubicund old farmer who, overjoyed to find himself the owner of the world's first posted cow, put her out to grass in a special paddock for the rest of her life, with a notice on the gate underlining her distinction. In any case, I felt fairly sure I could persuade the new owner to keep his mouth shut, if he had a different plan. We were in too deep to toy with scruples. We were heading for the Front Page.

The Post Office van, when it arrived to take delivery of the parcel, was a set-back. It wasn't red and it didn't carry the royal insignia. It was, in fact, just an ordinary lorry with a ramp, chartered from a private haulier. But in attendance there was a representative from the GPO – an apprehensive telegraph boy on a motor-cycle, wearing uniform, a crash helmet and goggles. He looked about thirteen. Probably the older and wiser lads at Maidenhead head office had stuck him with the job by general consent.

He regarded us warily. 'Orders,' he said in the end, 'to collect an item for delivery –'

'It's in there,' I said. 'Breathing.'

The lad gave me a look which, despite the difference in our ages, caused me to fall silent.

It was clear that Bessie didn't know she was making history, because it took the four of us to post her up the ramp and into the lorry. For the record, she was a thin, brown-and-white cow with a curiously prim disposition. When John twisted her tail she turned to look at him with every appearance of raised eyebrows and outraged virginity. I was sorry we hadn't got a cow that entered more into the spirit of the thing.

The telegraph boy didn't like her either. Post office regulations, it seemed, compelled him to accompany her from the point of dispatch to the place of delivery. He abandoned his motor-bike with obvious regret and climbed into the front seat of the lorry beside the driver, still wearing his crash helmet and goggles. When I suggested that he should, strictly speaking be in the back, with Bessie, he said, 'Do me a favour, willya?' while continuing to look straight ahead. What should have been the carnival business of posting a cow was turning into the grim performance of an unpleasant duty.

No extra sparkle was provided by our first call, at the Parade Dairy sub-post office. John and I were reversing Bessie with the intention of pushing her, for stamping, as far into the shop as she would go, when Mr Browne appeared with a small buff form. It was only necessary, it seemed, for me to sign it, and to pay the parcel post charges, and then Bessie could be on her way.

A small crowd had gathered, seeing a cow being pushed into the post office. They, too, felt deprived of drama. A lady with shopping basket was kind enough to stick a $2\frac{1}{2}d.$ stamp on Bessie's forehead, and to wish us luck, but there was no further public demonstration. We beat Bessie back into the lorry again, and started for Bracknell.

Here, things were rather livelier. Word of the enterprise had clearly preceded us, because there was quite a posse of press photographers, mostly from local newspapers. The telegraph boy and I, with Bessie in the middle, posed for a number of pictures on the ramp. The lad looked steadily at the ground, still suffering from feelings of inhibition. The photographers became pretty cool, too, when I revealed to them that the full details of the story might be discovered for the first time in next Sunday's issue of the *Dispatch*. One of them went so far as to complain that I should have told him, before he'd gone and wasted all his plates. A representative of the auctioneer appeared to say that we were holding up the business of the market, and would we kindly get the lorry out of that.

Somewhat cast down by the increasingly chilly reception being accorded to our glorious, posted cow, John and I went into the pub next door, having discovered that Bessie would come up for auction at about two o'clock.

We emerged at 1.45, to find that Bessie had already been sold, for £40, which was about right. But no one seemed to know who the purchaser had been, or, indeed, to care. They were busy with six lots of milking shorthorns, or something. Some of them didn't even know that they'd been present at an event unique in the long and colourful history of the parcel post.

We went back into the pub again, in a low state, and ran straight into Bessie's purchaser. Or, rather, he ran straight into us, and I divined immediately – with a spasm of alarm for our animal-loving readers – that Bessie had had her chips.

He wasn't a rubicund farmer with a special paddock in which Bessie could dream away the autumn of her life, remembering in tranquillity the day when Fame had struck. It didn't look likely that he'd keep his mouth shut, either, about Bessie's certain demise. 'Are you the geezers,' he said, 'what posted that cow?'

He was a short, obviously urban citizen with a black Homburg on the back of his head, and a black overcoat thrown open in the fashion familiar on racecourses. He was searching in his suit pockets with heavy concentration. ''Cos if you're the geezers,' he said, 'what posted that cow I got something here to showyah –'

I tried to get the thing back on to the carnival, cow-posting level. 'Let me congratulate you,' I said, 'as the first man ever to buy a cow sent by parcel post. What's your name?'

'Got it!' He produced a tattered square of paper from his waistcoat pocket and waved it in the air. 'See that?' he said. 'That's a gun licence. That's a licence – for a gun. And I'm telling you geezers something. There's been one of them in my family for more'n s'enty years!' He held it above his head, then put it back in his pocket. 'You gennelmen want to buy some joolry?' he said. 'The wife's got some smashin' lines –' With his thumb he indicated a lady in a musquash-type coat at the other end of the bar. She did, indeed, appear to be pressing the sale of some unnaturally shiny trinkets.

'Not just now,' I said. Everything was getting out of hand. 'Look, tell me what you're going to do with Bessie –'

The beginnings of belligerence shadowed his brow.

'The cow you bought,' I said hastily. 'I posted it here.'

'Cow?' he said. 'Be on a plate for me greyhounds tonight.' His manner hardened again. 'What's that about Bessie –?'

It was all over. As we took our leave he waved the gun licence at us again. 'More'n s'enty years!' rang out, as we closed the door behind us.

On second thoughts, now that I've marshalled the facts, I don't mind so much about Ripley giving all the credit to John L. Lunnon for posting a live cow.

Viewed in the round, it seems a pretty filthy thing to do.

25

A Blob in the Street of Ink

'You don't mean to say you *know* him?' said the young man with the two propelling pencils in his breast pocket. He'd described himself earlier as a free–lance dog-racing correspondent.

'Certainly I know him,' I said, 'or at least I'm practically certain he would recognize me if I was held up before him in a strong light.'

'Cripes,' he said, 'some people are lucky. Where did you pick him up?'

'He sent for me,' I said, 'one morning. He used to know my grandfather. I suppose he thought he would like to do something for the grandson.'

'Well, come on,' said the young man with the pencils, 'what did he do? Let me in on it.'

'He put the heart across me,' I said. 'He frightened the life out of me, and caused me to fill my mind with useless information.'

'Come on,' said the young man, '*what happened*?'

'He sent for me,' I said, 'one morning. I waited for a while in the hall, and then the butler said, "His Lordship will see you now."'

The young man sucked in his breath. 'Cripes,' he said, 'your big moment.'

'In I went,' I continued, 'and there he was. "So you want to work for us?" he said, first crack out of the box. He was surrounded by telephones, dictaphones, a large blue arm chair, and hundreds of sheets of paper lying all over the floor. At that time I would have been ready to work for anyone, except possibly a main drainage corporation. "Yes," I said, "if you have any jobs." His next question took me by surprise. "What do you read?" he said. I took about a minute over it, and replied, "All your newspapers, sir, morning and evening, and the best of the new novels." He shook his head. "Don't you," he said, "read the Bible."'

'Cripes,' said the young man.

'I said I would, from then on,' I continued. 'Then he said, "Go and write me a leader column." I thought he was joking. "What about?" I said. "The situation," he said, "bring it to me in half an hour." I went out into the hall and sat on the window-seat. I couldn't remember which political party was in power, or who was Prime Minister. Then I discovered I hadn't anything to write on, or with, even supposing that I found anything to write *about*. I knocked on the door. "Sir," I said, "could you lend me a piece of paper — and a pencil?" I don't think he'd ever been more surprised in his life. He gave me two sheets of transparent typing paper, and a heavy red pencil. I think he suddenly had an idea I might have come about the gas.'

'It was O.K., of course?' said the young man. 'I mean, he really did know who you were?'

'I think so,' I said. 'It was just that I never imagined I'd be starting work so soon. I went back into the hall with the two sheets of paper and the red pencil. I had to write on my knee. Half an hour later I'd beaten out something. The only thing I can remember now is one phrase — "Signor Mussolini's ill-timed attempt to woo the Swastika will come to naught." The red pencil went through the paper several times, but you could read it all right. I brought it back to his Lordship. He read the first page without registering anything. Half-way down Page Two he had a kind of spasm. I knew where he'd got to. He'd reached Signor Mussolini's ill-timed attempt to woo the Swastika. "What's this?" he said, reading it out. I said, "I thought that was the sort of style that you use in your daily, sir." He had an answer to that. He said, "I disagree with you." He read to the end of the page, and then, just by opening his fingers, he dropped my leader column on the floor. It joined the rest of the sheets of paper. "Go down to the office," he said, "they'll give you a desk. Good-bye." I found I couldn't open the hall-door. There was some sort of special catch on it. In the end he had to come out and do it himself. I thought he was going to burst.'

'What happened down at the office?' said the young man. 'What work did you have?'

'It was mostly answering the telephone,' I said. 'One of the reporters could imitate his Lordship's voice. He kept on ringing me up from outside, saying he was the Lord, and wanted to see me at once. I spent ten shillings a day on taxis between Fleet Street and the Lord's house before I got wise to it. I got to know the butler quite well. He thought I had hallucinations.'

'Did you ever see the Lord again?' asked the young man.

'Certainly,' I said. 'He sent for me again, and said he was thinking of buying some provincial newspapers. "Get the provincial newspapers of England, Scotland, and Wales," he said, "and write me a report on each." I was glad to be back in regular employment, until two copy-boys appeared carrying between them a bale of 312 newspapers, morning and evening. That job took me three months. The reporters used to amuse themselves by stealing forty or fifty of my newspapers, and hiding them in the washroom. Once I cried. It was like being back at school. I finished the job in three months, and brought my report to the Lord. It weighed about a pound and a half. He looked at the top page, and then he let the whole lot fall to the floor. It made quite a bump. I don't know if he bought any provincial newspapers on the strength of it.'

'Was that the end of the job?' said the young man with the pencils.

'Well, no,' I said. 'I had one more assignment. Another summons came. "Write me a series of articles, five thousand words each," said the Lord, "on 'Great Deeds that won our Crown Colonies.' How many Crown Colonies have we?" I said I didn't know. "Fourteen," said the Lord; "begin now." As a result of that commission I spent five months in the library of the British Museum. I struck up some interesting friendships there, and delivered him the stuff in a suitcase. He could hardly lift this lot. After examining the first paragraph he dropped the bundle on the table. I suppose he thought if he dropped it on the floor it might go through into the basement.'

'That about knocked the whole job?' suggested the young man.

'As a matter of fact,' I said, 'I'd no sooner given him the Crown Colonies than I thought I was in. He said, "Come with me to Victoria." I thought I was off to spend the week-end with him at his country seat. We got into the car, and the chauffeur wrapped a rug round the Lord's legs. He left me unwrapped. We drove down the street, and the Lord said, "Your grandfather was a great man." I thought he meant to say, "Your grandfather, *at least*, was a great man," and this nettled me. Without quite knowing what I meant I said, "My grandfather had no artistic appreciation." The Lord turned right round in his seat. He wanted to have a good look. "I see," he said. It was then that the car stopped. The chauffeur seemed to know about it. "Good-bye," said the Lord. I got out. I never saw him again.'

'Cripes,' said the young man. He thought for a moment. 'All the same,' he said, 'if it'd been me I bet I'd have been dog-racing editor by now. You didn't play your cards right.'

'I played them splendidly,' I said. 'The only trouble was that the Lord could see through the backs of them.'

26

Water! Water!

What had begun as a gay adventure now looked like turning into a disaster, involving considerable monetary loss.

There was no doubt that the *Pixie* had been going backwards for about half an hour. The ebb must have set in as the wind died.

'How would it be?' I suggested to Barney, 'if we dropped anchor for a bit until the fog lifts?' I didn't want to seem too definite about it. He was supposed to be the expert.

Barney looked over the side.

'There's 40 fathoma wather there,' he said morosely. 'Yeh haven't enougha chain on board to tie up a dog.'

'What are we going to do?' I said. 'The tide's going to carry us in the rocks.'

Barney removed his pipe. 'I'm ony workin' here,' he said. 'You're the fella wit' the brains.' He looked frightful, with a growth of white whiskers and the remnants of several gallons of stout around his mouth.

'You're the paid hand,' I told him. 'You're supposed to have some sort of responsibility.'

'Ah, shut up,' said Barney.

It was an unpleasant surprise. Up till now he'd gone out of his way to call me 'skipper', even if the primary purpose of it had been aimed at a tip. I began to get really anxious. Neither of the other two knew anything about boats. 'I'll just let the anchor go, anyway,' I said, giving him a chance to help.

He hunched himself up in his coat. 'Do anny dam' t'ing y'like,' he said. Visible tremors passing through him showed that the regatta refreshments were still taking their toll.

185

I went up for'ard and rather anxiously let the anchor go. I knew this was the time to assert my authority, but didn't know how to begin.

To my relief the anchor seemed to hold.

As I went back aft to the cockpit, Audrey's head came out of the lighted cabin. The head disappeared with a jerk. I heard her cry, '*Stop* it, Norman!' And then the whole of Audrey bounded out on to the deck. She wore a blue and white striped jersey and floppy blue trousers. It was probably her conception of nautical costume.

'What was all that hammering?' she said.

I explained about the anchor.

'But why aren't we going home?' said Audrey.

I laid it out for her carefully. 'There is no wind. We haven't got a dinghy. We haven't got an engine. I don't know exactly where we are because of the fog. The tide has turned and is taking us backwards. Accordingly, I have anchored.'

'But it's nearly midnight!' Audrey cried, disregarding the whole lot. 'You said we'd be home by seven.'

'Certain fellas,' said Barney with satisfaction, 'is goin' to be in throuble over this.'

'Mum will be as worried as anything,' complained Audrey. 'You never should have made me come.'

'If you recall the jollity,' I told her, 'which rounded off the yacht-club ball in the early hours of this morning, and your own insistence on joining our party – you said you wished to steer all the way . . . Why,' I said, suddenly remembering it, 'you even abandoned your gentleman friend, Fred. He tried to strike me in the car-park, but missed.'

'I never thought it was going to be anything like this,' said Audrey.

Neither, in fact, had I. We'd left Wicklow, the town still smouldering from the last night of the regatta, soon after breakfast, looking forward to the run home stimulated to know that a lady had been added to the crew.

It is true that Audrey, ashore, would have caused no very great excitement, except possibly in the heart of Fred; but Audrey afloat, almost out of sight of land in a vessel 25 feet long, was a different matter altogether. Norman, indeed, had found the situation so stimulating that Audrey passed the whole rather chilly afternoon on deck, on the grounds that she liked fresh air.

Romeo appeared in person. 'What's happened to all the water?' he said angrily. 'I'm dying of thirst.'

'There's plenty in the tank,' I told him, wondering if the anchor was still holding.

'Not any more there isn't,' said Norman. 'It's bone dry.' He made it sound exactly as if it was my fault.

I went down below and opened the filler-cap. The tank was indeed empty save for an old teaspoon that must have been in it for years.

'Who's been taking it all?' I asked them.

Audrey looked defiant. 'I had to wash up the breakfast *and* the lunch,' she said. 'And then I only rinsed out my stockings –'

'When?' said Norman, with sudden interest.

'I was going to wash my hair, too,' Audrey said, 'only you woke up.'

'Washing your hair,' I said, 'and rinsing your stockings – in fresh water – What kind of a boat do you think this is?'

Barney came down the steps, carrying a teacup, and pushed his way into the cabin. His eyes were half-closed. He shoved a blackened hand across his mouth and then turned on the tap of the water tank. Nothing happened. He opened his eyes wide. They were bright red. 'Here,' he protested, 'who's been eatin' all the wather?'

'You've had about a gallon yourself,' Norman told him.

'I only had one cup of tea for supper,' complained Audrey. 'I'm thirsty.'

'What about me?' I said. 'I've been up there at the tiller since seven o'clock.'

It struck all of us at the same moment. We were very, very thirsty indeed. The jollity at the ball had been of a singularly ferocious nature, and on top of that we'd been breathing sea air for nearly sixteen hours.

Audrey started to cry. She was a large, red-haired girl with a forthright manner. This evidence of feminine weakness on her part persuaded me that we were face to face with a genuine crisis.

'Well,' I said, 'it looks as though we're up against it. We'll have to suck a handkerchief or something until we get in.'

'Here,' said Barney, startled, 'I'm not havin' anny o' that!' He certainly hadn't got a handkerchief himself. Perhaps he thought I was going to pass mine round. He looked at us wildly. 'Me troat!' he cried. 'Help! It's shuttin' up!' He staggered back against the bunk. He was seized by a paroxysm of coughing. In the middle of it he gave a kind of small dying groan. Then he collapsed altogether. He lay, half off the bunk, with his tongue lolling out, an awful sight, his breath coming in the most alarming rusty gasps.

'What's the matter with him?' I asked Norman, suddenly remembering he must have done some hospital work.

The resolute medical student gingerly felt Barney's pulse. 'He's fainted,' he said. 'Better give him some water –' Then he realized what he'd said.

'I don't want to be here any more!' Audrey wailed. 'I want to go home!'

'Listen,' I said. 'I'll swim ashore. We're somewhere in Killiney Bay. I don't think we're too far out. I'll get a boat from someone and be back here with water in an hour. You can hold out until then.'

I waited for them to thank me.

'I'm certainly not staying here alone with *him*,' said Audrey.

'What am I going to do if he starts to die?' said Norman.

I was astonished that they seemed to be concerned only with themselves. I thought I'd welded us together into a team under my leadership. 'Well, gosh,' I said, 'what are we going to do?'

Norman applied himself to Audrey. 'Let him go and *get* the water,' he said. 'What do you think's going to happen to you?'

'I certainly won't,' snapped Audrey.

Barney heaved up on the bunk, arching his back. He looked awful. 'Jemmy – Jemmy,' he moaned. It was probably the name of some friend who had assisted him in similar difficulties in the past.

'Can you swim?'

Audrey looked at me in surprise. Her appearance had not been improved by tears. 'Yes,' she said. 'What –'

'You can swim ashore with me,' I told her, 'if you think Norman's been so maddened by your charms.'

'I didn't –' Norman began querulously.

'But I haven't got a bathing suit,' said Audrey.

I suddenly began to wonder if I could be held on a manslaughter charge if Barney passed away. 'You were the acting master of this vessel?' 'Yes, m'lud.' 'Yet you failed to take adequate precautions to see that a suitable supply of drinking water –'

'You can swim behind me,' I told Audrey. 'Anyway, it's pitch dark, and there's a dense fog.'

She stopped hesitantly half-way up the steps. 'You won't come till I call?'

'Norman and I,' I assured her, 'will get under the bunks and wrap our coats round our heads.'

When I went up on deck there was no sign of Audrey. 'I'm here,' I heard her say. I realized then that she must be in the water, probably holding on to the anchor chain. Her blue trousers were neatly folded at the foot of the mast. 'I'm quite decent really,' said Audrey, 'only I can't swim in those.'

I slipped into the water in the shorts I'd worn for the last three days. At least it would probably do *them* some good. I heard Norman's exceedingly anxious voice say, 'Hurry up, for heaven's sake,' and then I struck out into the night. A subdued splashing from behind showed that Audrey was also on the way, with the lifebelt.

Ten minutes later, just as I'd begun to think we must be approaching the Welsh coast, I felt rocks under my feet. I clambered ashore, almost exhausted, and then I heard a sudden gasp come out of the fog. 'Oh!' cried the invisible Audrey, and then there was silence. I jumped up, thinking she was drowning. 'What's the matter?' I shouted. 'Where are you? Are you all right?'

Audrey's voice came back in a kind of scream. 'Don't come near me! Go away!'

I sprang down to the water's edge in time to see Audrey in her blue and white jersey leap back into the sea again. 'I've lost – something!' she cried. 'Go away!'

It was about the last straw. You really would have thought she could have held herself together. 'What are you going to do?' I shouted. 'I've got to go and get water. Barney's probably dying.'

'I'm awfully sorry,' said Audrey, in a smaller voice than usual.

'I couldn't help it. I'll wait here until you get back.'

It was the first time that any of them had recognized my authority, or the fact that I was trying to do something to help.

'Good girl,' I told her. 'I won't be long. There's a big sort of whitish rock here. Stay round it and I'll know where to find you.'

'Thank you – very much,' said Audrey. 'Good luck.'

I started to walk back up the beach, thinking she wasn't a bad sort of girl really, and then suddenly it struck me that it wasn't going to be a very easy task to walk up to someone's house at one o'clock in the morning, in thick fog, wearing only a pair of shorts, and to ask for a glass of water. And not only a glass of water, but a bedroom jug full of water, and the loan of a boat.

I began to compose myself. I needed only to be very serious, very intent. The earnestness of my manner would persuade the householder, about to come sleepily and in trepidation to his front door, that in spite of my shorts and unusual request he was not in the presence of a madman.

I found a wicket-gate at the top of the beach and beyond it a path leading steeply upwards. It was hard going in my bare feet.

The path, after bringing me through rough grass, all at once led into a garden, and then, at the far end of it, to a small, two-storied house. It was in darkness so far as I could see through the fog.

I walked round it, guiding myself by the wall, looking for the front door. My heart was beating painfully. My mouth was drier than ever. I found myself rehearsing what I was going to say –

'Good morning, sir. Madam? Do not be alarmed. My boat is becalmed in the bay. I have come ashore to ask you for water and the loan, if you have one, of a boat, so that I may return to my comrades, one of whom is ill –'

I don't know which of us was the more astonished – myself or the dog. It had been sleeping in a basket on the porch, a reddish, rangy looking animal that might have had half an Airedale as one of its ancestors. We looked at one another, spellbound for a long moment, only the whites of our eyes showing, and then the dog took off. It leaped straight into the air from a sitting position. I knocked it sideways, turned and fled straight into the arms of Audrey! We went down together. She gave a single scream,

sprang to her feet, and after presenting me with a brief, unforgettable spectacle, vanished at full gallop into the soup.

I fled after her, looking over my shoulder for the dog. I hit the
edge of the ornamental pond in full stride and finished face
downwards in 2 feet of ornamental water. There was another
scream from Audrey, more piercing than the first, a crash as if a
heavy weight had fallen into a thicket, and then total silence
settled down upon the riven scene.

I had been half-stunned by the ornamental pond, and it took
me perhaps three or four minutes to come fully round. In that
short space of time a sudden and hideous change came over the
night. I remembered as I walked up the path feeling a breath of
wind on my bare back. Now it was blowing steadily from the
sea. The fog, writhing and swirling, was blowing away. I sat up
in the pond as all the lights suddenly flashed on in the house, and
there, standing in the front door, clearly visible across the lawn,
was an elderly man wearing a cap very straight on his head, a
topcoat over his pyjamas, and bedroom slippers. He was holding
a golf-club in his hand. On the grass the dog was tottering round
in circles, still out on its feet.

I knew it wasn't going to take the householder long to see what
was in his pond, so I decided to put him at his ease before he
became hysterical.

I cleared my throat softly and carefully. 'I'm very sorry, sir,
for disturbing your dog,' I called out in a clear voice, 'but could I
have a glass of water?'

He took it badly. He tried to get back into the hall and shut the
front door at the same time.

I knew it wasn't going to work. He went down in a heap. I ran
across the lawn and, as immediate proof that he was safe in my
hands, I helped him to his feet. I even put his cap on, and gave
him back his golf-club.

'I'm terribly sorry, sir,' I said in a low voice. 'I wouldn't have
had this happen for worlds.'

He looked at me shakily. He was a little mouse of a man who
probably counted fretwork a stark thrill.

'What –' he faltered. 'What . . . happened . . . ?'

I gave it to him straight. The comrades marooned in the bay –
the sick friend – the immediate need for water. Half-way

through I saw he wasn't listening. He was looking out into the garden, still clutching his golf-club, and very slowly his eyes were bulging out of his head.

'What –' he said. 'What's that?'

I thought he was still semi-conscious, but I turned to look. With conflicting emotions and, no doubt, conflicting degrees of appreciation, we feasted our eyes upon the only too visible form of Audrey, wrong side up, fighting silently in the grip of an overgrown rambling rose.

The old man gave tongue. 'Nellie!' he cried. 'Nellie – come and get me!' He struggled convulsively in my grasp. I shouted in his ear. 'Listen, sir, I don't know who that is – it's got nothing to do with me – a tramp – a vagrant – will you give me a glass of water for my sick friend!' At the same time I dragged him back into the hall and slammed the door. I saw a mackintosh on the hat-stand. I snatched it off the hook and put it on.

A woman about the same size as the little man stood at the head of the stairs. In her right hand she carried a china cat, raised in the air as though she were about to strike.

'Marsden,' she said. 'Marsden, what is it?'

I gave it her, as straight as I'd given it to him – the lean young lieutenant-commander, shipwrecked, near the end of his tether, yet seeming, for all that, almost dignified in a mackintosh three sizes too small.

They heard me out. Nellie lowered the china cat. 'Water?' she said. 'Yes – yes – of course. But we have no whisky, you know. My husband – doesn't – not any more –' It was almost as though I was paying a social call, but she was probably as stunned as Marsden.

'You are very kind, madam,' I said, bowing from the waist in Marsden's mackintosh. 'I only need a glass of water. Whisky, I assure you, is the very last –'

It stabbed me like a knife. 'Strewth!' I cried – 'I forgot!' I looked round quickly, saw the kitchen door, galloped in, gulped convulsively for a moment under the tap, snatched an enamel basin and filled it to the brim, sped out into the hall again, slopping the water all over the place, and a moment later was pounding down the garden path. Faint yelps came from Marsden and Nellie, but I was no longer concerned with them.

Audrey was waiting by the white rock, delicately, with her head over her shoulder, removing thorns. She gave a scream when she saw me – she seemed to have been screaming most of the night – but I had no time for her now. I heard her say, 'I followed you – I was frightened –' and then I grabbed the lifebelt and plunged into the sea. I started to swim, pushing the basin wedged into the lifebelt along in front of me. It was hard work in Marsden's mackintosh, but there was no time to take it off.

Then, a moment later, I saw that there had been all the time in the world. The *Pixie* loomed up in front of me, a dim white shape in the light of the moon. From inside it, like a chorus of all the dogs in the world, rose the voices of Norman and Barney, slow, full-charged with emotion, lingering exquisitely upon each note in turn.

'God bless you!' they sang. I heard the sob in Norman's voice. 'God bless you and keep you, Mother Machree!' They had, beyond any shadow of doubt, found the bottle of whisky I'd stored in the locker, and had entirely forgotten about until that awful moment in Marsden's hall.

I caught hold of the anchor chain. 'Norman!' I roared. 'Barney! Stop it! I've got the water! Put it away!'

There was a moment of silence, and then the sound of heavy, staggering feet on the deck. I heard Norman say, in an unrecognizably genteel voice, 'Don't tip your head on the boom, Mr Barney,' and then the two of them were looking at me over the side.

'Here,' said Barney, 'the fella – what's his name – is back.'

I held up the basin of water with one hand. 'Take it,' I said, 'quick – I'm nearly done.'

Norman took it. He looked at it for a moment in a puzzled way, and then he emptied it out over the side.

'We don't need it,' he said. 'Thanks awfully. We're taking ours as a liqueur.'

From some way behind me I heard the splashing of Audrey, labouring through the waves, and looking forward, no doubt, to a quiet end to a tiring day.

27

Defamatory Nature

I was dining quietly, at least to external appearances, with a lovely thing called Anita de Monte, paying her first visit to Dublin with a touring company extracting the last few drops of juice out of *White Horse Inn*.

Her part in the show was limited to village-belle work – sudden stampedes with tambourines, and three cheers for the Prince – but even in these routine affairs she stood out head and shoulders, and in several other departments, above the other ladies of the chorus, most of them castaways from last year's *Puss in Boots*.

It had not been easy to induce her to dine. On Sunday nights, she explained, she and the other girls liked to rest, washing their hair, perhaps, and doing some mending. 'It's the only chance we have,' she said, suddenly lifting the curtain upon her exciting private life, 'to catch up on our smalls.'

I revealed to her, then, that I wrote a column for a newspaper, and might well find the opportunity to mention her name and distinctive abilities, should we be able to find a suitable context. She seemed to warm towards the project, but remained hesitant. She asked if she could bring her two special friends, Ivy and Yvonne. I removed the two superfluous musketeers by promising Anita that their names would also appear in anything I wrote.

We had reached the coffee when Joe, the waiter, told me I was wanted on the phone. Anita had been describing to me how she'd been discovered in a pub in Nottingham by a Mr Savelli, while she was working as a shoe operative, and I was reluctant to break away. I excused myself, however, and went out to the phone box.

It was a Mr Curran. He said he was acting on behalf of his client, Mr Raymond Hunter, who, he believed, was known to me. Mr Hunter wanted to see me at once.

'I'm dining,' I said, 'with a lady. Can't it wait until tomorrow?'

'Mr Hunter insists on seeing you now,' said Curran. 'I am Mr Hunter's legal representative. We are at Mrs Hegarty's residence.'

At Mrs Hegarty's! I knew what that meant. Poker tangled up with dancing, wives sobbing in the kitchen, and the feebler guests being beaten to death on the avenue. I also suddenly guessed what might be the matter with Raymond, although I didn't quite see how it fitted in.

When I got back to the table I found that Anita had produced some press-cuttings. I looked at them dully: *A well-trained chorus line appeared to advantage in several ensembles – the song-scenes were much enhanced by a prettily dressed chorus – Anita de Monte gained plaudits for her snake-dance in the transformation scene.* I still couldn't see why Raymond should be cutting up so rough.

'Look,' I said suddenly, 'some friends of mine have asked us to a party. How about dropping in for half an hour?' I didn't want to lose touch with Anita, now that our association had advanced so far.

After some discussion she consented to come, provided that she could ring Ivy and Yvonne and let them know she would be late. 'Oh no,' I heard her say, towards the end of the call, 'nothing like that. Seems a bit soppy, really.' I began to get a feeling of persecution.

Mrs Hegarty's house was ablaze with light. There were four cars on the avenue, two of them with their bumpers locked together. 'They're a pretty brisk lot,' I told Anita, thinking it might be wise to prepare her a little. 'Racing people – jockeys – and so on.'

Anita took a firmer grip of her handbag. Mr Savelli and the public-house in Nottingham were probably as far as she'd reached into high life.

The front door was open and we walked in. Raymond, as

languid and as elegant as ever in an almost jade-green tweed suit, stood in the hall smoking a cigar, engaged in a discussion with a boiled-looking man with glasses and a fringe of ginger hair.

Raymond saw us. He put his cigar down carefully in the middle of the table, and then seized me by the coat.

'You,' he said, 'you dirty rat. Even Walter Winchell doesn't make copy out of his friends.'

I backed away. 'Don't be an ass,' I said, 'Walter Winchell doesn't ever do anything else.'

I felt it was time to introduce Anita. She was being left out of things. 'This is Miss de Monte,' I announced. 'She's appearing in *White Horse Inn*.'

Raymond didn't look at her. 'She'll have to go upstairs,' he said shortly. 'Curran and I want to see you alone.' The boiled-looking man nodded, as though it were his idea.

A tiny figure sauntered into the hall. Georgie Moon, the jockey, in a brown suit so dapper it looked as if it had been nailed on to him. 'Now *there's* a well-fleshed little mare,' said Georgie, and clamped a wiry arm around Anita's waist. His patent-leather hair came up to her shoulder. Anita looked down in terror. Not even Mr Savelli had made such a direct approach.

'Give her a drink, Georgie,' said Raymond. 'We've got something to settle with this lout here.'

'Lout!' I said. 'Why, you indolent, miserable –'

'Malice, Mr Hunter,' said Curran with satisfaction. 'I don't think we're going to have much trouble here.'

Out of the kitchen shot our hostess, Mrs Hegarty – Blossom to her friends – a solid and naturally ferocious woman, seeming to be constructed of hard, red rubber strapped into a check suit, surmounted by a crown of livid yellow curls.

'Let go that alley-cat,' said Blossom to Georgie, 'and get her out of here.'

It seemed many years since Anita and I had been chatting together about her career. I felt it was necessary to regain control of the situation.

'Don't you call her an alley-cat, you old bag,' I said.

'I suggest you watch your tongue, sir,' snapped Curran. 'You're in trouble enough already.'

'What trouble?' I said. 'What's the matter with that ass?' Anita, with no great appearance of intelligence, was staring from one to another of my friends, clearly taken aback by the speed and steam of Irish society life.

Curran produced a newspaper cutting from his wallet. 'Did you, or did you not,' he said, 'write this? *Among those most clearly visible at Baldoyle was Mr Raymond Hunter, with rich cigar and easy graces, gallantly buying champagne for the ladies in spite of an uninterrupted succession of losing investments.*'

'Yes,' I said. It seemed to present Raymond in a dashing, almost Beau Brummel light.

'All you have done by that,' said Mr Curran, 'is to ruin my client's future career. Tomorrow morning he is to be interviewed, as a preliminary to subsequent employment, by Acme Imports and Exports, Ltd. –'

'Raymond!' I exclaimed, 'going to *work*?'

'The managing director of the said firm,' went on Curran, 'is Mr Roger North, a distinguished member of the Methodist community. He has written recently a number of letters to your newspaper, adversely criticizing the prevalence of smoking, drinking, and gambling in southern Ireland.' Curran, ostentatiously, examined the cutting again. 'Rich cigar,' he quoted, 'buying champagne – succession of losing investments. I fear that my client's chances of engagement have been so seriously endangered that only substantial damages –'

'What does Raymond want to go looking for a job from a Methodist for?' I cried. 'Why can't he go on doing nothing, like he's been doing for years?'

'Immaterial and irrelevant,' said Curran, looking bored.

I found the sallow, ferret-like face of Georgie Moon underneath me. 'Here,' said Georgie, 'aren't you the chap that called me a mannequin – in the paper – at Leopardstown –'

'A manikin,' I said. 'A little man. If you'd ever been taught any more than how to pull the neck off a short-price favourite you'd know what manikin meant.'

'By God,' said Georgie, 'say that in front of the stewards –'

'No need to worry, Mr Moon, sir,' came in Curran easily. 'If you'll just take my card. I believe we have a sufficient number of witnesses to see that the affair is brought to a satisfactory conclusion.' He swaggered a little. After an unexciting career defending bicycle accidents and eviction orders, John James Curran, solicitor, was coming into his own.

Anita, finding herself free of Georgie, made her contribution to the scene. 'I want a cup of tea,' she said. 'I'm tired.'

It seemed a selfish complaint, in view of the trouble her escort was in. And *tea*! In sudden irritation I turned to her and said, 'Show-girls – yeah. Into bed by 11.30 with a nice cup of Horlicks, and Mother said not to forget me gargle. Glamour – like the annals of the Luton Wheeled Ramblers' Mixed Whist!'

'My card, Madam,' said Curran, without a moment's hesitation.

'Defamation of character, suggestion of professional incompetence.' He turned abruptly to me. 'We may find the corporate body you have also injured is outside the jurisdiction of the court,' he said quickly, 'but we can always have a try.' He was beside himself, seeing the ball large and clear, believing he had only to swing at it to bash it over the fence.

I began to wonder if he mightn't, in part, be right. I had only recently emerged from an unfortunate contretemps with the Irish Labour Party, wherein I had publicly accused them of not voting for a bill defended, at every stage, by their leader. I found out, next day, that being new to the job I had mistaken their identities and seating positions in the House, and that they had, in fact, voted for the measure to a man. It had stung my employers sharply to make good the damage in cash.

It was no time for me to be involved in another action.

'Raymond,' I said, 'what do you want me to do?'

Curran began, 'I fear the matter is no longer –'

'Wait a minute, Jack,' said Raymond. 'Look,' he told me, 'if you could just put something in the paper to say I don't – well – smoke cigars all the time, and go to race-meetings. If I don't get this job I'm done. I've had a shocking run of losers –'

'To hell with that,' said Georgie Moon decisively. 'What him calling me a mannequin!'

'An old bag!' said Blossom. 'In my own house he called me an old bag!'

'All right,' I said. 'All right, give me a piece of paper.'

That was how this paragraph, phoned through to the office,

appeared in my column the following morning:

AN UNUSUAL OCCASION

An unusual occasion took place last night at the lovely home of Mrs Maeve Hegarty, whose soirées make so important a contribution to Dublin's cultural life. Readings from the sermons of John Wesley were given by Mr Raymond Hunter, who said grace before the vegetarian supper which concluded a most uplifting evening.

We had to leave Georgie and Anita out of it. Their professions, Raymond insisted, gave them no place in so devout an affair. United by this slight, they disappeared together, not to be seen again.

Later that morning – it was just after dawn – I, holding four threes, ran head on into Curran with a straight flush.

'I'd have settled out of court for half of it,' said Curran broadly, counting with a moistened thumb the profits it had taken me half the night to wring out of the cultured Mrs Hegarty, and Raymond Hunter, John Wesley's best friend.

28

A Knowledge of the Rules

Through a mischance, on the eve of Prize Day, which disclosed our fast bowler at grips behind the gym with one of the dining-hall maids, I was once selected to represent the school in the annual cricket match against the Old Boys.

The fast bowler was confined to the sanatorium, pending an interview with the Headmaster, while I took his place in the 1st XI.

This was entirely against my wishes. I had no desire, owing to the hardness of the ball, even to be in the 2nd XI, but had been given my colours after scattering seven wickets in a house-match, and injuring two of the other four batsmen. A strong following wind had favoured my attack – a series of lightning full tosses, laced with long hops, several of which bounced right over the wicket-keeper's head.

There was, however, this much to be said for the 1st XI. The fortunate players involved got out of school at 11.15 on the Saturday morning.

I hurried back to my dormitory to change, pleased at being relieved of the tedium of practical physics. Almost immediately I discovered that someone had taken my white sweater, and had left in its place a short, yellowish thing with a large roll collar. I decided to carry it over my arm. There was a chilly wind.

I was surprised to find the pavilion deserted. I looked in the locker-room and the showers, but there was no trace of the other players. I was about to return to the school, to find out what had happened, when Higginbottom, the professional, came rolling round the corner, carrying an armful of stumps.

'Hello,' I said.

Higginbottom looked at me for some time. He was a low, squat man like a monkey, with a nut-brown face and a sweater that came well below his knees. Even while talking about cricket it took him a quarter of an hour to get a sentence out.

'Wot,' said Higginbottom, in the end, 'are you doin'?'

'I'm playing in the match,' I told him. 'I came down early.'

Higginbottom examined this explanation.

'Wot for?' he said. 'Others is 'avin' lunch.'

I remembered. The match was going to begin at 12.30. They were going to play right through till tea – an arrangement aimed at providing the parents with a full day's sport.

'Yes,' I said, 'I know. I'd a snack in my study. I'd a lot of work to do.'

'Readin'?' said Higginbottom. There was a look of interest in his small, marble-like eyes.

'That's right,' I said. 'Aristophanes.'

Higginbottom rolled away, shaking his head. He was invariably surprised by the intricacies of the school syllabus.

It was obviously impossible for me to return to the dining-hall, and break in upon the lunch. They would be well through the salmon mayonnaise by now. I began to wander round the pavilion, examining the photographs, the roll of honour, and the ball on the mantelpiece with which some terror stricken school-boy had once bowled W. G. Grace. Then, I came upon the laws of cricket. They were framed, in a glass case. I'd never noticed them before.

I started to read. I read about the implements of the game. I read about the care and maintenance of the pitch. I discovered, for the first time, that it was also a wide if you bowled a ball so *high* over the batsman's head as to place it out of his reach. That explained an incident which had puzzled me in the past. I was examining the regulations concerning wilful obstruction when Bowyer-Bond, the school captain, walked in, followed by the Old Boys, with our team bringing up the rear.

'Hello,' I said, quickly, 'I didn't feel like lunch. Too excited. I . . .'

'Thought I saw you,' said Bowyer-Bond, indifferently, and passed on. He was talking to a military-looking gentleman in gleaming white flannels, with three different permutations of stripes on his scarf, his blazer, and his cap. I guessed that this must be Major R. J. G. Monkhouse, the Old Boys' captain, and a county cricketer of note.

We won the toss, and went in. Major Monkhouse opened from the chapel end, with the wicket-keeper standing so far back as to be almost out of sight. This was a reasonable precaution, because Major Monkhouse was fast — so fast, indeed, that Bowyer-Bond and Dullis, our opening pair, seemed to have difficulty in seeing the stuff that he was sending down.

I sympathized with them. Even from the pavilion Major Monkhouse in action seemed to me to be just a blur. I waited my turn to bat with my stomach rising slowly into my mouth.

It came rather later than I expected. After an hour, Major Monkhouse removed himself — Bowyer-Bond was scoring off him frequently behind the wicket — and put on a slow bowler, a stout man wearing glasses, who might have been a stockbroker by profession.

Bowyer-Bond slashed him all over the field, until he was caught, at 83, on the leg boundary.

I met him at the pavilion door. The rest of the school team had got together no more than 30 runs. I was the last man in.

'Shove up the two hundred,' said Bowyer-Bond cheerfully. He was well pleased with himself.

'I'll do my best,' I said, and walked down the steps.

'Better put a sweater on,' said Bowyer-Bond. 'You'll find it chilly until you warm up.'

'O.K.,' I said. 'Thanks awfully.' I was pleased with this consideration, particularly in view of the indifference with which he had treated the matter of my lunch.

I turned back. Then I remembered the child's jersey with the roll collar. But it was too late.

I discovered that someone had tied the sleeves together very tightly with string. I wrestled with them, silently, while Bowyer-Bond looked on.

After a moment, he said, 'Look here, don't lark about. They're waiting for you at the wicket.'

'I'm sorry,' I said. 'Some ass has been playing a joke.'

Bowyer-Bond snatched the jersey from me. 'Never mind about it,' he snapped. 'Get out there, and do something.'

As I arrived at the wicket, Major Monkhouse took the ball. He'd been resting for some time. I imagined that he must once again be in the pink of condition.

He was. I never saw the first two balls. I thought the third one was going to cut my head off. I threw out the bat with one hand, there was a sharp click, and something hit me like a pile-driver in the eye.

I came to, in the pavilion.

'By gad, boy,' said Major Monkhouse, 'that was a horrible stroke. Never saw anything like it. Don't they teach you any better than that?'

He seemed genuinely perturbed about the state of school cricket. I turned my face to the wall.

The Old Boys went in. I could have done with a cup of tea, not having eaten since breakfast, and I couldn't help feeling that my eye needed professional attention, but I took my place – I thought with some courage – in the deep.

The Old Boys were all out an hour and a half later, for a total of 75. I had not been called upon to bowl. The probable truth of the matter was that they'd been fooling about, confident of victory in the second innings. But, until I'd witnessed this debacle, I hadn't realized that there was going to *be* a second innings. I thought I'd faced Major Monkhouse for the first and last time. This time, it seemed to be quite on the cards that he would kill me.

Bowyer-Bond and Dullis went in. To my joy and delight they knocked up 97 in just over an hour, and then Bowyer-Bond declared, leaving the Old Boys with 136 to make.

This seemed to me to be the epitome of wisdom. It was already four o'clock, and stumps were due to be drawn at six.

I had an enormous tea, and took up my position once again in the deep. I had already composed the letter I was going to write to my father about the part that I had played in the Old Boys' first defeat.

With fourteen runs wanted, twenty minutes in which to get them, and Major Monkhouse and the last Old Boy in, Bowyer-Bond threw me the ball. The match had taken one of those lightning, unexpected turns which, to some people, constitute the whole charm of cricket.

I pulled off my jersey – I'd broken the string with my teeth – and gave it to Higginbottom, umpiring at the pavilion end.

'Want any change in the field?' said Bowyer-Bond.

I looked at Major Monkhouse. He'd just turned to the wicket-keeper and said, in a surprised voice, 'They're not going to let this chap *bowl*?'

'I think,' I told Bowyer-Bond, 'everybody had better spread out a bit.'

I turned and walked back from the wicket, measuring my run. Fifteen paces. I made a small mark on the grass with the heel of my boot.

I faced Major Monkhouse. I could hardly see him, with the sticking-plaster over my eye. I began my run. I gathered speed. I saw the crease out of the corner of my eye. I leaped high in the air, and flung over my arm.

Higginbottom roared – 'NO BALL!' But it was a ball. It shot out of my hand like a bullet. I thought it was going to hit first slip. So did Major Monkhouse. He stepped back. Suddenly it began to swerve. It swung in two feet. Major Monkhouse ducked at the last moment, and the ball went through his hair. The wicket-keeper made a wild leap, missed, and it was four byes.

'I say,' said Major Monkhouse, 'steady on.' He patted the crease in front of him. There was no need for this. The ball hadn't touched the ground.

. I walked back again to my mark. The next one was a wide. The one after that would have been a wide, if Major Monkhouse hadn't run out somewhere in the direction of short leg, and bashed it into the tennis courts.

For the fourth ball I took a shorter run. I thought it was time that I bounced one on the pitch. It was a perfect length. Major Monkhouse played right back, stopped it with his glove, and the ball dropped at his feet.

'That's better, boy,' he said, and tapped it back to me along the grass.

It flashed into my head without warning. I could see clearly before me, in a glass frame.

'Rule 37: *The Striker is out, "Hit the ball twice", if the ball be struck or be stopped by any part of his person, and he wilfully strike it again . . .*'

'How's that?' I cried.

Sudden, complete silence descended upon the field.

I swung round upon Higginbottom. 'No, no,' I cried – 'I didn't mean it. Cancel . . .'

Very, very slowly Higginbottom raised his right forefinger.

''Aht,' he said. The voice seemed to come from his boots.

One by one, we turned to walk back to the pavilion. As we did so Bowyer-Bond went up to Major Monkhouse.

'I'm sorry, sir,' he said. 'I can only assure you that he is not a regular member of the team.'

Major Monkhouse sniffed. 'I'm glad to hear it,' he said. 'That sort of thing leaves a nasty taste in the mouth.'

In spite of our victory the celebrations that followed were of a subdued nature. Several of the Old Boys, including Major Monkhouse, left immediately, pleading business appointments in town. No one spoke to me at supper, and, going to bed, no one spoke to me in the dorm.

It was, perhaps, a fortunate thing that I came down with scarlet fever the following day, and was removed to the hospital on a stretcher. Afterwards, I learnt that prayers had been said in the chapel, 'for the speedy recovery of our school fellow, Patrick Campbell, who is now lying dangerously ill'.

I've often wondered how many members of the congregation joined in.

29

A Boy's Best Bodyguard

When a fellow is faced by armed men it's my honest opinion that he should have his mother around, if the situation is not to descend into flurry and confusion.

Three times I have looked down the muzzle of a gun. On the first two occasions my mother was present, and an orderly conclusion was achieved. In her absence, the third time, I handled the business so maladroitly that even the police got it back to front. The lesson is plain.

My mother and I first started gun-slinging, as it were, in 1922. The Irish Civil War was in progress and one of its victims – or very likely to be if he didn't look slippy – was my father, then a member of the Cosgrave Government. He had returned once to our house outside Dublin with three perceptible bullet holes in the back door on his car, in no mood to share my mother's opinion, aimed at restoring his confidence, that the IRA had probably mistaken him for someone else. The shots had, apparently, been fired near Portobello Bridge. So sure was my father of their intended destination that he covered the three miles home in three minutes, and went straight to bed.

When, therefore, the thunderous banging came on the back door a few nights later it had the effect of freezing him to his armchair, in which he'd been reading the evening paper. It was my mother who went to the top of the kitchen stairs, to see what was afoot. I joined her almost immediately, a pale lad of nine, having been roused from my sleep by the noise. I'd been sleeping badly of recent weeks because it was nearly Christmas, and my whole soul was crying out to take possession of my first Hornby train.

'It's all right,' my mother said, taking her customarily steady view, 'it's only some men.'

We heard the bolts being shot on the back door, and then the voice of the cook raised in indignant surprise. She was a loyal retainer, who'd been with the family for some years. 'It's youse lot, is it?' she said. 'Janey, I thought yez wasn't comin' till half-eleven.' It was, in fact, only ten-fifteen.

A male voice said peevishly, 'Ah, don't be shoutin' . . .' and then the first of the raiders came running up the stairs. I had a brief glimpse of a gun, then a face masked with a cap and a handkerchief. My mother stopped him dead. 'If there's going to be any murder,' she said. 'You can get back out of that and go home.'

More masked faces and caps appeared at the bottom of the stairs. Querulous voices arose. 'What's the matther, Mick?' 'Get on with it, can't ya?' But Mick was explaining the matter to my mother.

'Nobody's gettin' shot, mum. You needn't take on. We've orders to burn down the house, that's all.' He sounded injured by the false impression.

'You're sure of that?' my mother asked him, wishing to have the matter absolutely clear for the benefit of my father, in the event that he was still able to receive messages, in the next room.

'There'll be nobody shot,' said another raider impatiently. 'Now will you stand back owa that an' let's get on with it. We haven't all night.'

My mother remained firm. With the first matter on the agenda settled to her satisfaction, she passed to others, now of equal importance. 'What about all my lovely books?' she said. 'First editions, signed by Lawrence and Katherine Mansfield and Middleton Murry. And the pictures – Orpens, Gertlers, the little drawings by John . . .'

The raiders, jammed on the stairs, were getting hot and angry. An exposed youth, still stuck in the passage, was being berated by the cook. He appeared to be a cousin of hers, and was refusing to carry her trunk out into the garden.

'All right, all *right* . . .' said the first raider. The protracted conversation was causing the handkerchief to slip off his face. 'Take out annything you want, but for God's love hurry up about it.' He turned to the men behind. 'Who's got the pethrol an' the matches?' he wanted to know.

At this point my father appeared in the hall, unobtrusively, and still unsure of his welcome. The raiders appealed to him. 'Ask your missus to give us a chance, sir, will ya? Sure, we're only actin' under ordhers . . .'

He took command, in a voice slightly higher than normal, advising me to wake my sister, still peacefully asleep, and to put on some warm clothes. He then suggested to my mother that they should both try to save a few personal mementoes before we all withdrew to safety in the garden.

'And leave,' my mother cried passionately, 'all the children's Christmas toys behind? Certainly not!'

The possible outcome of the night struck home to me for the first time. 'Me train!' I cried. 'Don't let them burn me train!'

'Of course they won't,' said my mother. She rounded on two of the men. 'You,' she said, 'go to the cupboard in the bedroom and bring out all the parcels you can find. And look out for the doll's house. It's fragile.'

They shuffled their feet, deeply embarrassed. Several other men were throwing petrol around the hall. 'Well, go on!' my mother shouted at them. 'And leave your silly guns on the table. Nobody'll touch them.'

By the time the first whoose of petrol flame poured out of the windows she had five of the men working for her, running out with armfuls of books and pictures, ornaments, and our Christmas toys. They'd become so deeply concerned on her behalf that they frequently paused to ask what should be salvaged next. 'Is the bit of a picture in the passage anny good, mum?' 'Is there ere a chance of gettin' the legs offa the pianna, the way we could dhrag it out . . . ?'

When they disappeared into the night they left my mother, bathed in the light of the flames, standing guard over a great heap of treasures in the middle of the lawn, with Orpen's picture under one arm and the little drawings by John under the other – a clear winner on points.

Next time it was the IRA again. My unfortunate father was

now officially on the run – an appalling situation for a peaceful and dignified man – while the rest of us, being homeless, were staying with my mother's parents in Foxrock, a base that at first sight could not have been more neutral. But then, in the middle of the night, the caps and the handkerchiefs appeared again, and it turned out that we were sitting on a miniature arsenal, not, admittedly, of the first calibre, but undoubtedly containing weapons of war.

Once again it was probably the domestic staff who provided the link between the beleaguered fortress and its attackers, but – as is common in the uncertain art of espionage – they'd considerably exaggerated their report, in the interests of making it seem worth while.

After twenty minutes in the house the IRA were dissatisfied to find themselves in possession of two assegais, a knobkerry, a Gurkha knife, a 1914 bayonet and a pith helmet from the Boer War, trophies brought home from foreign service by my mother's numerous brothers. All these warriors, however, were now somewhere else, so that the depleted garrison put up no great struggle as the IRA ranged through the house, throwing open cupboards and peering under beds in search of the machine-guns and Mills bombs promised them by the cook.

While all this was going on I was standing on the rug beside my bed with a pillow between my knees, placed there by my mother. The burning of our house, followed by close proximity to my grandmother, who was a fast hand with a ruler, had brought my nerves to a low state. From the first crash on the back door my knees had been knocking together so rapidly that they were now severely bruised on the inside, making each new percussion an agony. The pillow, however, eased things considerably. I was holding it in position, fore and aft, when the raider burst into the room, waving a huge Service revolver, but I dropped it immediately when he shouted, 'Hands up!' The knees started rattling again, like castanets.

My mother went into immediate action. 'How can he put his hands up?' she shouted at the raider. 'Look at his little knees!' She slotted the pillow home again into position and returned to the attack.

'How dare you frighten the life out of a little child!' she cried.

At the age of nine I was nearly six feet tall, but the principle was right. 'Give him your gun! Let him see it isn't loaded!'

As usual, the speed and directness of her assault bouleversed the enemy. He was a lumpish youth in the regulation cap and trench-coat, with a handkerchief over his face which looked as if it had recently been used for cleaning floors. He became placatory. 'I wouldn't frighten the little fella, mum. A'course it's not loaded. Amn't I only afther findin' it down below . . . ?'

My mother pounced upon this new intelligence. 'That's Malcolm's revolver,' she cried. 'Put it back where you found it! Didn't he risk his life with it, defending you and all the other hooligans like you from the Germans?'

'Put it back, mum?' The proposition staggered him. 'I can't do that, mum. Sure, the commandant'll kill me . . .'

At this point my mother snatched the gun out of his hand. 'Let him hold it, anyway,' she cried. 'I'm not going to have any child of mine having nightmares over a filthy, silly revolver.' She thrust it into my hand.

I didn't want it at all. I only wanted to hold on to my pillow. I dropped it on the floor, with the pillow on top of it, and tried to put my hands between my knees.

In the midst of this confusion there was a hoarse shout from downstairs: 'Christy, come on owa that, willya! There's nothin' more here . . .'

Christy made a move towards the gun. My mother put her foot on it. They faced one another for a moment, with a thin, obbligato sobbing from myself. 'You'll be hearin' more of this,' said Christy unconvincingly. Then he turned and ran.

My mother put me back to bed, then she picked up the revolver by the muzzle and threw it into the bottom of the cupboard. 'I'll put it in the bank in the morning,' she said. 'Filthy, silly things. Don't you ever have anything to do with them.'

It was a piece of advice which I had no difficulty in following over the next thirty years, until I suddenly found myself staring down the barrel of a Mauser in a public house in Wapping, with no mother to guide me on a night of impenetrable fog.

I'd gone down to 'The Prospect of Whitby' to write a story about one of its familiars, a character known as Prospect Jock, who allowed customers to sign their names on his white suit. After an indeterminate interview with Jock, who could analyse his curious activities no more deeply than 'a bit o' sport', I fell into such a lengthy conversation with the landlord, Mr Broadbent, that I was still there at midnight when the man in the black hat, with the red muffler over his face, came rushing up the stairs, waving the gun.

Mr Broadbent had been talking for some time about the murky, early history of Wapping, and the glamour it certainly lent to the bright, present charms of his pub, so that when the figure in the red muffler appeared I immediately presumed that he'd been hired by Mr Broadbent, in the interests of publicity, to present some sort of masquerade of the bad old days.

It seemed to me to be an unnecessary elaboration, seeing that I was going to write about Prospect Jock anyway, and I rose to my feet to say so.

If, of course, my mother had been there she would have cut the proceedings short by telling the gunman to do the washing up, or get us another round of drinks, but I was on my own.

It was my intention to say, 'Come off it, cock – who do you think you're . . .' but before a word of this stricture could be delivered the man in the muffler seized me by the front of the coat, hit me on the back of the head with his gun and threw me down a whole flight of stairs into the public bar. It was the swiftest transition from one state to another I'd ever known.

I should think I became unconscious, while passing down the stairs, though more from fear than the actual blow, because when I came to I found the floor of the bar littered with the bodies of a number of people whom I'd last seen upstairs in the restaurant. They included Captain Cunningham, the Mayfair oyster bar proprietor, and his guests, who'd been dining at another table. They weren't dead, but acting under the orders of three men who were stamping about with coshes, telling them to keep their heads down.

I found an empty space, and another one for my wife, and then, with some regard for the family tradition, I asked one of the gangsters if we could sit, rather than lie, as we were wearing our best clothes, and the floor was rather dirty. He replied by holding his cosh directly beneath my nose. We assumed a semi-recumbent position.

They worked swiftly. The junior representatives smashed the glass-fronted cash registers with their coshes, and filled straw fish baskets with the loose change. At the other end of the bar the man in the red muffler threatened Mr Broadbent with death if he didn't open the safe. Mr Broadbent obliged. The guests on the floor were invited to unload whatever valuables might be on their persons. We obliged, too. Ten minutes later the men were gone, leaving a deeply stricken silence behind.

Even at this late stage I wish it had been my mother who'd taken charge of the investigation, instead of Scotland Yard. With her steady record in matters of violence she would certainly have been able to prevent me identifying the wrong man, putting him in gaol for three weeks, and subsequently having to make a public apology from the witness box.

She might also have been able to prevent my wife from saying, in her evidence, that the bracelet of which she'd been robbed 'couldn't have cost more than £2 because my husband gave it to me for Christmas'.

She could also have induced me to put my personal loss higher than five shillings which, while it was true, stood up badly in a list beginning: 'Wm. Broadbent, £2,500; Captain Cunningham, £75,' etc.

She could also have been there to put another pillow between my knees when I discovered that the man in the red muffler, who'd hit me with his gun, was no less a villain than Scarface Nobby Saunders, on the run from Parkhurst Gaol, who, ten days after dealing with me, shot a policeman in the eye during a warehouse raid, and got a life sentence in Dartmoor from the Lord Chief Justice himself.

If I'd known, that night in 'The Prospect of Whitby', that it was Scarface Saunders who was rushing up the stairs at me, I would not have risen to my feet, to ask him to come off it. I'd have jumped straight backwards out of the window into the river.

But there, it's what I always say. When the old equalizers come out every boy needs his mother around, if the situation is not to descend into shame, flurry and confusion.

30
Vive le Soccair

They came prancing along the beach with a ball, flicking it backwards and forwards to one another with the dramatic concentration of Frenchmen practising *le Soccair*. Two rotund, commercial gentlemen from, perhaps, Lyons, both wearing indelicately abbreviated swimming trunks, and both with the natural ball-sense and general athleticism of a couple of middle-aged women.

Hercule, in shovelling it back to Georges, lofted the ball into the air. Georges, seeing himself as some French Stanley Matthews, sprang perhaps three inches into the air, to head it back, and the resultant ricochet, at right angles to Georges's intention, crushed my hat over my eyes and dislodged my sunglasses.

Up till now, lying prone in the marvellous, incandescent sunshine on the burning sand, with the head, guarded by its protective accoutrements, comfortably propped against a pillow, I had been remotely entertained by Georges and Hercule, merely two more ciphers in the teeming world of the beach. Now, however, the situation had become different. Now I was sharply critical of the activities of Georges and Hercule, and was desirous of them making a series of apologies, culminating in their complete and absolute departure.

They should, I felt, apologize for regarding themselves as the French equivalent of Stanley Matthews. While they were at it, they should also apologize for wearing swimming trunks which would scarcely be acceptable on the lean limbs of an Australian lifeguard. From there, it seemed to me, they could advance into really serious apologies covering the threat to my eyesight occasioned by the buffet on my sunglasses, the visible damage to my hat and the equally visible damage to my nervous system, brought about by being struck in the face by a ball which Georges had been endeavouring to propel in an altogether different direction.

Instead of any of these things happening Georges danced up like a fifteen-stone goat, made the detached announcement '*Pardon*', attempted to back-heel the ball to Hercule, missed it and filled my glass of Pernod with sand. Not even this enormity, however, gave him pause. Spinning heavily on his heel and putting the other foot on my cigarettes, he succeeded this time in kicking the ball in the general direction of Hercule, calling coincidentally – an absolutely monstrous addition to a series of crimes, soberly speaking, beyond belief – '*Hopla!*' He pranced away, then, churning more sand into my face.

I lay, in the shattered remnants of bliss, waiting for some outside agency to strike Georges – and Hercule, too – down. A giant wave, perhaps, that would enfold them, carry them swiftly out to sea and bury them a hundred fathoms deep.

Instead of anything like this happening, Hercule, on the edge of the sea that should have claimed him, let loose a fly-kick on the half volley which I managed to duck only by burying my face in the sand.

Once again Georges did his enormous goat act up the beach, passing me by without a glance, and did something to the ball which caused it to strike me in the middle of the back on its return journey. This time Georges was good enough to make his '*Pardon*' contribution as he lumbered past in pursuit of it, standing on my cigarettes once again.

Yet even this was not all. Having blitzed and razed and blasted me into the ground and having filled my drink with sand and trampled my cigarettes and knocked off my hat and glasses, they might have been presumed to be satisfied, to be ready to call it a day and to go away and to execute the same fearful destruction upon someone else. But not *Hercule et Georges*. They liked it where they were. This piece of beach, with me serving as a back-stop, suited them down to the ground. They continued to flick and kick and miss and stand on the ball and spray sand around and call '*Hopla!*', and one out of about six of their deliveries either bounced off my person or caused me to take evasive action, to prevent it so doing. This remote, detached '*Pardon*' was all that I received in exchange.

Rolling, dodging, weaving and waiting tensely in the brief intervals when some idiocy on the part of Georges propelled the ball into the sea, I tried to formulate a French sentence which would, by its severity, cause these monsters to fling themselves into the water and drown.

'*Est ce que que cette place est la seule place où vous pouvez jouer?*' They would be fully entitled, upon receipt of that lot, to disbelieve that I was speaking French. Something like '*Saluds!*' or '*Va t'en*'. But perhaps in France something of this kind, spoken to strangers, might be so offensive that it would result in my being challenged to a duel.

Georges and Hercule suddenly resolved the problem by going away. Their place was taken instantly by a French child of villainous aspect who started digging a hole and spraying me with sand between his legs.

I let the nipper have it, *en Anglais*. All the venom generated by the activities of Georges and Hercule poured out. It stopped the lad dead. He stood up, turned round and pointed his little spade at me.

'Mummy, Mummy,' he screamed in the impeccable accents of Ascot, Berks, 'horrible man hurting Timmie!'

Down the beach came Mummy, much more of a man than Georges or Hercule.

31
A Dirty Big Policeman

I was in the river, trying to wrench out a post which had gone in crooked, when the three children, in their formal order of precedence, Christine, Brigid, and Guy, came wandering round the corner of the house.

Christine wore her jersey on her head, so that the sleeves hung down like ears, Brigid carried a cat, Guy was stark naked save for a pair of pink rubber boots.

I watched the procession, astonished, as ever, by the infinite eccentricity of their behaviour. They go backwards and forwards all day long between my house and Christine's, invariably in this extended line ahead.

Although I've watched them closely, I've never been able to guess at the impulse that suddenly moves them to migrate. They may be playing happily in our sandpit. Then slowly, aimlessly, Christine gets up and wanders to the gate. In a moment or two, but altogether unhurried, Brigid follows. Then Guy rises to his feet and totters after them, and there is peace for five minutes, or an hour.

I succeeded in getting a half-turn on the post, and then heaved. It came out so quickly that I sat down on the bank behind me, on the prongs of the rake. The handle whipped up with unbelievable malevolence, and struck me on the back of the head.

The children, startled by the suddenness of it, looked blank, and then Christine burst out laughing. 'He's killed himself with the rake!' she cried.

Brigid clapped her hands. 'My daddy's made himself all bleeding!' she shouted.

Guy, seeing the others laughing, joined in, a special breathless, honking sound of his own. The three of them leaped up and down, each trying to laugh more loudly than the other.

I had been in the river for more than an hour, engaged in the skilled and difficult business of shoring up the banks. It used to be just a ditch, a tangle of nettles, duckweed, and small willow trees, but gradually I'm turning it into a sort of Serpentine. It is, however, dangerous work, involving a 7 lb hammer and a pick-axe, and the possibility of stepping in bare feet, while carrying a tree trunk, on a stone buried in the mud.

'Go away and play in Christine's garden,' I told them. 'If you stay here you'll get hurt.'

Brigid spread out her hands, palms upward, in a familiar gesture. 'But how shall I go and play in Christine's garden,' she said, 'if you don't watch me off?'

'I'll watch you off from here,' I said.

Immediately, she flung herself face downwards on the grass. She writhed convulsively, then sat up and shouted, 'If you say that I won't play with Zinnia and Sandra any more!'

Zinnia and Sandra are two children who appeared for one day about six months ago. We have not seen them since, but the refusal to play with them still remains a heavy gun in my daughter's armoury.

Guy began to recite monotonously, 'Cry baby – cry baby – cry baby –' I was about to ask him what had happened to his clothes, when Brigid sat up and shouted, 'Big bully – big bully – big bully –'

After a moment they got mixed up and screamed at one another, 'Cry bully – big baby – baby bully – cry crully – big lady –'

'I called Guy a big lady!' Brigid exclaimed, delighted by the discovery. 'But how shall I call him a big lady if he's a dirty big policeman!'

'You a dirlty dig paloosman,' said Guy. He is an almost square child of two, and it's often difficult for me to understand what he says, but this time there was no mistaking it.

Brigid flung herself to the ground again. 'How shall I be a dirty big policeman –' she screamed '– if I have my nice shoes on?'

'All the hens took off Guy's clothes,' said Christine, up till now a disinterested observer of the scene.

I was standing in the river, wearing only a pair of shorts, holding a sledge-hammer in one hand and a post about six feet long in the other. My watch, removed for safety, was hanging from an arch of rambling roses above my head.

And now the hens had taken off Guy's clothes, lifting his jersey over his head with their wings, watching him closely with their beady, fussy, old eyes. Perhaps they wanted to put his jersey and trousers in the nesting-box, and lay eggs on them.

Not for the first time, in the presence of these children, but more especially now because of my own situation with the shorts, the sledge-hammer, and the suspended watch, I began to feel my grip upon reality fading away. How, indeed, shall I not be a dirty big policeman if my watch is in the roses over my head?

I put down the sledge-hammer and the post, and took a grip upon myself.

'Christine,' I said, 'how did the hens take off Guy's clothes?'

She seized the sleeves of her jersey and pulled them tight beneath her chin. 'Because they did,' she said.

For a moment I thought this was an answer. Then I realized that Christine, with the hen business, had merely been making a bid for attention, and now regretted it. 'Don't be so silly,' I told her, 'and you're stretching the sleeves of your jersey.'

'Why are you smashing in the water?' said Christine, quickly regaining the initiative.

There was no reason why I should feel it necessary to justify myself in the eyes of a four-year-old child. But I didn't want them to think I was playing with mud for fun.

'I'm making you a lovely river to play in,' I said. The idea came to me for the first time. 'You could even have a rubber dinghy and sail up and down in it.'

They examined the proposal in silence.

'Do you know,' said Brigid – it was as though she were bridging an awkward pause – 'the little ones Axie and Condie sail out from this place and then they sail out from this place and then they sail into the rain.'

A feathery sensation took hold of my mind.

'Who, for heaven's sake, are Axie and Condie?' I said.

218

'Condie has two rubber gingies each to each with a green star,' said Christine.

'And Condie is small like this,' said Brigid. She put her open palm an inch above the grass. 'And she's a telltit and she will scrub you and then she will go up and down on her feet like this.'

I watched my daughter, with close attention, marking time.

'Look,' I said, 'you're all getting over-excited. Go away and play in the tent.'

They decided to play fathers and mothers. I had time to hear them arrange for Guy to be the mother, before they crawled into the tent from the back. The front was open.

I turned back to the river again. I waded upstream for a few yards and then stuck my post into the mud to make a new revetment. I knocked it down lightly with the sledge-hammer until it came to the clay. They I began to drive it in in earnest.

It's a job which requires a good deal of concentration. A false blow with the sledge-hammer could break not only the post but also my leg. But as I bashed away at it a whole swarm of irritating little questions nibbled, like mice, at my mind.

Axie and Condie, for instance. It is a commonplace thing for children to invent imaginary companions, and they nearly always have curious names, but why should Axie and Condie sail out from this place, and then out from this place, and *then* sail into the rain?

Had the rain suddenly begun? Or, when they were sailing out of this place and out of this place were they under shelter, like in a boathouse, and only got wet when they emerged?

One side of the post began to split. I waded ashore to get a block of wood to put on top of it, and then all at once I wanted to know, passionately, why someone couldn't be a dirty big policeman, if he, or she, had nice shoes on.

The utter and complete lack of reason maddened me. No one ever talks about *dirty* big policemen. However big policemen are they are always clean. They have to be. It's part of the discipline. But even if you had a dirty big policeman I felt sure that his appearance would not be redeemed, or, indeed, his whole personality altered, simply because he was wearing a pair of nice shoes.

And tell-tale-tits. They *scrub* you, and then they go up and down on their feet!

I determined that however long it took me I would work it all back to the very beginning, and find out how these unimaginable fantasies had possessed their minds.

I lay down on the grass and put my head and shoulders through the opening of the tent.

They were sitting in a tight circle, cross-legged like natives. Christine still wore her jersey on her head, with the sleeves hanging down like ears. Guy was still naked, save for his rubber boots. It was stiflingly hot in the tent, but they were busy. They were rubbing my daughter's leg with a piece of stick.

'You will be a bit better tomorrow morning you see, Missus,' said Christine, 'after I am giving you the plaster.'

'What's the matter with Brigid?' I said. I didn't really want to know, because I knew it would sidetrack me, but I could not resist the temptation.

'The pussy put her leg on Brigid's slipper,' said Christine. 'She's all bleeding, and Guy has a rubber gingie in his stomach –'

'Stop it!' I shouted. 'Shut up! Listen,' I said. 'Don't say one single thing until you've answered this question.'

The three of them, as one child, put their thumbs in their mouths, and clamped their fingers round their noses. They looked at me intently through heavy-lidded eyes.

'How can a pair of nice shoes,' I asked them, 'stop someone being a dirlty big paloosman?' In putting it this way I think I had some idea of making it easier for Guy.

There was a short silence. Then Brigid said politely, 'Doesn't my daddy talk funny?' In a moment the three of them were convulsed with laughter.

Then Brigid said, 'Silly clot – silly clot –' Guy joined in, 'Cry baby – cry bully –' Christine, by accident, I think, said 'Silly bully –' and then they were off in a kind of chant, with bullies and babies and clots mixed in an inextricable mess.

I left them to it. I didn't want to drive them mad altogether.

32

How to Become a Scratch Golfer

I used to play in a regular Sunday morning fourball with David F., a man who took golf books like cocaine in an effort to rid himself of a hook so virulent that the ball, on leaving the club-head, became almost visibly egg-shaped in its efforts to get round the corner, causing David to have to take a step back with his left foot in order to keep it in sight while it passed over the road.

When the toss of a coin condemned us to partnership I tried with everything I had ever heard about the game to bring about a cure, particularly at the second hole, a short one, where the tee was set back deeply in an avenue of trees, making it impossible for David's tee-shot to emerge into the open.

On one such Sunday morning I applied myself to his grip, it being the only physical feature of his game over which it looked as if he might have some control.

We had, frankly, become involved in a small game of cards – half a dollar ante and five bob jackpots – at his house the previous evening which had been interrupted – only, it seemed, a bare couple of hours later – by the arrival of his wife with breakfast, an intrusion for which she apologized. But then, she said, she couldn't have borne it if we'd been late for our morning round, particularly as there was so little to do about the house now that she'd got the children off to sleep again after the singing, or whatever it was, which had broken out round about dawn. Unless, she went on, we cared to stay to tidy up the sitting-room and in particular to shift the crates of stout which, even though empty, might prove too much for her strength, undermined as it had been by a somewhat sleepless night –

I could tell on the first tee that David, unfortunately my partner, had been more adversely affected than the rest of us, because he asked me if it was raining. It was, in fact, a hot still morning in July.

We lost the first hole to a 6. I was unable to take much part in it myself, suffering from the vertiginous feeling that my clubs had been shortened or the whole course lowered several inches by some outside agency during the night, so that even by striking sharply downwards I could reach only the top half of the ball.

David, of course, was in the car-park on the left with his tee-shot and picked up, after hitting the side of the pro's shop twice.

To stop the rot, before the opposition ran right away from us, I had a word with him on the second tee, the one buried in the trees.

'I can't help you much,' I said, 'until my clubs get longer or the course comes up a bit, so that if we're going to get anything like a six here and a possible win you'll have to hit yours straight, or at least straight until it gets out of these trees. Try gripping very tight with your left hand and forget about the right altogether. I'll watch it for you, if I can see it. It's only thirty yards out into the clear.'

He replied, as so many players do to helpful advice, by trying to defend his own method, one which, he said, he'd just picked up from a book by Henry Cotton. 'I'm piccolo-ing my hands,' he said. 'It helps me to snap the wrists through.'

'However the hell you piccolo,' I said, 'it snapped your opening blow into the car-park, from which you failed to emerge after two more.'

He made a conversational detour, then, to tell me that my back swing off the first tee had put him in mind of an elderly woman of dubious morals trying to struggle out of a dress too tight around the shoulders. He was interrupted by the other two players, who said that they were both on the green and did we feel it was worth playing on?

I took, I have to admit, rather a quick swish at mine, jarring myself badly with a punchy little 5-iron which buried itself, after a very short, low flight, in the back slope of the ladies' tee.

It was David's turn. 'Never mind the piccolo,' I told him. 'Just have a good bash with your left hand. If we're two down after this we can walk in.'

He shaped up to it quite well, very relaxed, but leaning a little too far over the ball to promise complete control. Whatever he meant by piccolo-ing, I guessed it hadn't started yet. I was, in fact, just about to remind him that golf clubs had no connection with musical instruments when he suddenly played a stroke with a long, flowing arm action reminiscent of one of the supernumeraries in *Les Sylphides*. The ball passed harmlessly between his legs, but it was the other development that the rest of us found hard to credit. We turned back to look at the striker.

He was standing there with his hands held high in a good finish. After a moment, however, the suspicion seemed to enter his mind that all was not well. He lowered his hands slowly and looked at them. He examined the ground in front, and then behind. 'Where,' he said, after a short interval, 'is my driver?'

The rest of us remained silent, looking at him with concern.

'My driver?' David said. 'Where's it gone?'

'Why?' I asked him in the end. 'How do you mean?'

He tried to put everything together, working on the available data. 'My driver,' he said. 'I had it a minute ago, and now it's gone.'

We turned to look at one another with mute enquiry. One of the other men said, 'I certainly saw it in his hand just now. Perhaps,' he said to David, 'it slipped down the leg of your trousers.'

'No, no,' said the third man indignantly, 'it's not there.' He turned to David, speaking in a low voice. 'If I were you,' he said, 'I'd move a shade to your left or it might easily fall on your head.'

David acted fast, for a man in his physical shape. He sprang back silently, clutching both hands around his head. It was several seconds before he came to the conclusion that the danger, whatever it might be, had passed. He looked up cautiously, and it was then that we made the position clear.

'The hands,' I said, 'piccolo-ed through beautifully, but the club seemed to go on. That's it up there, near the top of that silver birch.'

We sat down on the grass and lit cigarettes and for the next few minutes derived a lot of amusement from watching him throwing the rest of his clubs at his driver. Some of them got temporarily stuck, and came down at odd angles. Each time we gave him sharp cries of warning, to which he responded automatically, getting madder and madder. Someone suggested that it might be more economical of effort if he were to replace all the clubs in the bag and throw that.

David was in a bad mood when he eventually knocked the driver down, collected his scattered clubs and strode off towards the green.

We let him get to the end of the trees before we asked him where he was going.

When he came back we were sincere in our sympathy. His ball was lying in unplayably long grass behind, rather than in front of, the tee-box.

Afterwards I asked him what he thought he meant by piccoloing his grip. He demonstrated what he thought he meant. It looked interesting, the wrists cocked underneath the club – very similar, indeed, to the action of a man playing a piccolo. I tried it, got two screamers in a row and put the third one off the snout of the driver into a pond.

Try anything once. It may enable you to play, for two consecutive shots, your normal game.

33
No More the Double Muffler

They used to be old, pipe-smoking gentlemen wearing two mufflers, a topcoat, a mackintosh over it, a peaked cap and a walrus moustache.

They'd sit up there in front, pushing their groaning machinery through the traffic and they knew every nook and cranny of the city because they'd been in all of them a hundred times before. The good old London cabbie, and they always called you 'Guv'.

This one we've got now, however, has just addressed me as 'Paathrick', and as of now he's certainly taking us in the wrong direction altogether.

After dining in the trackless swamps of St John's Wood our host was kind enough to ring for a mini-cab, and after an interval of rather more than half an hour this youth appeared.

There was something odd about him from the start. The moment we came out of the house he sprang out of the front seat, fell over the rear bumper and finished up in a rudimentary position of attention, holding open the back door of his limousine. It was dark, so I couldn't see him properly, but there seemed to be something wrong with his hat. Chauffeur-style, but a size too small and the peak pointing crookedly over one eye. Evidently something of a novice in the hackney car trade. And also suffering, apparently, from some trouble with his neck. At all events, as he drove off in the wrong direction, he kept his face turned almost in profile to us – a hazardous tic in a driver.

After turning into a cul-de-sac and backing out at speed he removed his cap, when we were safely going in the wrong direction again, and said, 'I see y'didn't recognize me, Paathrick, wit th'ole hat on.'

Negotiating a corner he turned almost the whole way round to look at us full-face. I'd never seen him before. 'Y'know who I am now, a'course,' he said. 'I was thinkin' youse wasn't goin' to spot me in the dark an' all.'

Madame and I sat silently in the back, actually clasping hands for protection. A part-time Irish actor, and he had us at his mercy.

For ten minutes, then, he spoke of his close friendship with Eamonn Andrews, with copious quotes of what Mr Andrews had said to him on a number of occasions, and the replies that he himself had made. It was a struggle to believe in either side of this reported dialogue. Then he turned to more personal matters. 'A while back there,' he said, 'there was a mob of telly producers afther me for the sinisther parts.' He turned the profile again, revealing something of the appearance of a dachshund. 'I'd come on very sthrong as a villain, y'see. In fac', that was the throuble. The telly fellas said I was too powerful for th'other actors, and I'd have to wait a bit till they come upta me. Thass why I'm dhrivin' th'ole car, y'see, Paathrick . . .'

When he got us home hours later at first he refused payment, and then said he'd better take 'tree quid' for the boss. Madame and I went to bed without speaking. Enough had been said already.

Next day, in pouring rain, we were trying to pick up a taxi when a large black car stopped beside us, an astonishingly beautiful girl got out, paid the driver and ran into a shop. I said, 'If you're a mini-cab, please come to our rescue.' The young man looked cautiously up and down the street. 'Not supposed to, you know, but – hop in.'

After a moment he said, 'That dolly bird's married to . . .' He mentioned the name of an actor. Madame said, in astonishment, 'He's *married*?' She tried it again. '*He's* married?' It did seem unlikely, on the actor's record. 'Surprised me too,' said our driver. 'Hang on. I'll just check.' He picked up the radio telephone, and said, 'Fred – how long has this geezer —— been married? Three weeks. Thanks.' He put back the phone. 'Fred doesn't think it'll stick,' he told us sagely.

That evening we got another mini-cab. It had a left-hand drive – and Italian number plates. And the driver spoke only Italian. We found he'd arrived in London a year ago on holiday, by car, and had been doing mini-cab work, with the same car, ever since. When we left him he said, with a big wide smile, 'Chiaou-chiaou, bambini.'

A lot of things have changed, but the good old two-mufflered London cabbie has changed a great deal more than others.

34

Doing the Cobblers' Trot

An absolutely dreadful thing happened last week to me and Nellie.

We were having this cycling holiday, you see, combined with adding to our collection of wild flowers, and to begin with it was most enjoyable.

Although we've been engaged for seven years we haven't had much opportunity to be alone together, because Nellie lives in Birmingham and I've got this job in Southend, so you can imagine it was quite a thrill for both of us as we set off awheel, side by side. Nothing 'naughty', of course, because we'd promised our parents we'd put up at separate lodgings at nightfall, and a promise is a promise, but all the same I won't be betraying any very big secret if I let it slip that a little 'light dalliance' might have taken place during our lunch breaks. Yum yum.

It was on the fourth day of our holiday that this dreadful thing happened. We were wheeling along near a little village called Patching, near Worthing in Sussex, when we turned a corner and ran into a lot of people who were queueing to get into a field.

Nellie – she's very keen on all kinds of outdoor sport – said, 'Oh, goody – it must be a cricket match. Do let's go in and have a look. Perhaps Prince Philip is playing.'

I demurred. The people who were trying to get into the field didn't look like cricket lovers to me. In fact, they looked pretty rum. Young fellows with long hair and musical instruments and nearly all the young ladies wearing dresses down to the ground. More like folk dancers, really. That kind of thing.

I pointed this out to Nellie, but she said she'd always been keen on folk dancing and if they did the Cobblers' Trot she'd like to join in. We were arguing a little about what to do when suddenly these dreadful-looking youths simply snatched our bicycles from us and threw them into a pond. We didn't know *what* they were. They were wearing German helmets and leather jackets and they had iron bars and screwdrivers and one of them had taken the chain off Nellie's bicycle, before throwing it away, and he was swinging it round in a most disturbing manner.

I said, 'You may perhaps be German soldiers but even if you are that does not give you the right to throw our bicycles away.'

The leader – he had enormous caps on his boots – said, 'Bikes is offensive weapons, mate. Not allowed at the Phun City Festival. Now split.'

He actually pushed me, so that I pushed Nellie, and all at once we were being hurried along in the middle of all these folk dancers towards a kind of stage thing in the middle of the field. There was a big sign above it: 'THE PHUN CITY FESTIVAL'. A band was playing on the stage but whatever they were playing it certainly wasn't the Cobblers' Trot. More like just yowling and banging, really.

When we couldn't go any further we sat down, like everybody else, and then we jumped to our feet again at once, because the most disgusting things were going on all round us. I mean, a lot of the young couples were actually – I mean, right in the middle of this English field, as if it was Paris, or somewhere like that. I put my coat over Nellie's head and we tried to fight our way back to the gate but it was hopeless, so we just sat down again and tried to keep our eyes on the ground, both of us under my coat.

About a minute later the coat was torn off us and it was the German-looking people again. 'Bad trip, cats?' the leader said. It sounded like a question, so I said as sternly as I could, 'We were enjoying our little outing to the full until you took away our bicycles. I shall inform the police.'

'No coppers here, mate,' he said. 'Us Hell's Angels is the law. Now cool it.' Suddenly he lashed out with his whip at a young woman who, we saw to our horror, had taken off all her clothes. 'You too, chick,' he said. She didn't even seem to feel the lash, being busy trying to do a kind of very slow dance, perhaps the Merry Harvesters' Hoe-Down, except that she kept on moaning, 'Harry Krishner – Harry Krishner . . .' She seemed to have been hypnotized by him, whoever he was.

It was too much. Stumbling over prostrate bodies, we battled our way to the exit, where we were arrested by six uniformed police, waiting outside the gate. The Sergeant said, 'Any pot, grass, or L.S.D.?' When I said we had £1.16 between us for some reason or other they let us go.

Afterwards, Nellie said, 'You'd never expect that kind of thing to happen in an English field.'

'No, dear,' I said. 'And they couldn't even spell "fun".'

35
Ne Touchez pas Maman dans le Vent

During the night the wind had been going slowly mad, and now, in the morning, it had reached a crisis of hallucination.

It shrieked out of a crystal-clear blue sky, with not a cloud in sight anywhere.

It seemed to be coming, in the main, from the north-west, yet there was no shelter from it even in the lee of a south-facing wall. It whistled over our heads and then doubled back on itself, a living thing intent upon sweeping everything off the face of the earth.

The extraordinary thing was that if it hadn't been for this demented wind it would have been a beautiful morning with the sun blazing from this cloudless sky, already hot at nine o'clock.

We decided it was an ideal day for the beach, that it was only in the mountains that there was no shelter from the shrieking mistral – except that it still seemed to be operating in the big square in Antibes.

A thirty-foot banner, announcing sombrely enough that this was the day of blood – for blood-donors – had come adrift at one end above the flower-beds in the centre of the square and was lashing itself like a huge whip. An old woman, made deaf and blind by this fearful wind, walked straight into the banner and was knocked off her feet. It was a moment or two before anyone went to help her. The mistral had turned everyone in on themselves.

The beach was infinitely worse than the mountains. Sunbathers, huddled behind umbrellas and deck-chairs, were being lashed by flying sand. It stuck to their sun-tan lotions and got into their drinks. Every time one of them stood up the others buried their heads in towels and flapping newspapers. Yet the sea was sapphire-green and unruffled. One could see twenty miles across the bay to Cap Ferrat and in the further distance the line of the snowy Alpes was as sharp as the edge of a razor. Absolute hell in blazing sunshine.

We endured the beach for a couple of hours, with the wind tearing over us and then doing this impossible trick of doubling on its tracks and howling back in again at sea-level, and then decided to have lunch on the terrace of the restaurant. Inside, French families in Sunday clothes ate decorously in the still gloom, but we had lunch outside because the sun was there, and it was changing our English pallor.

Lunch on the terrace was considerably worse than sunbathing on the beach. We weighted down the table-cloth with rocks, but it still flapped with pistol-like reports. Fish soup blew out of our spoons into one another's faces. Pieces of bread took off like snipe from the basket. One of us, recklessly venturing upon a green salad, had to hold it down on his plate with the flat of his hand.

It was notable that the two waiters – one to hold the door open and the other to sprint in and out with plates – betrayed no apparent interest in the extraordinariness of our situation. They were merely tight-lipped, turned in on themselves by the mistral. To brighten their lot one of us ordered four cheese soufflés. 'There's no need to serve them,' he explained. 'Just stand at the door and we'll catch them in our mouths as they fly past.' The waiter only said that cheese soufflé was off.

Round about three o'clock we decided that the only thing to do was to go home and stuff newspapers under the doors and pull the curtains and ride out the gale. The others went off to the showers to try to clean the fish soup and the sandy sun-tan lotion out of their hair. I was waiting for them in the car-park when a large, dominant lady drove up and sprang out of a small saloon, leaving two frail little old people in the back. She disappeared into the restaurant.

A couple of minutes later the frail little old lady, after struggling with it for some time, succeeded in opening her door, only to have it smashed shut again by the fury of the mistral. Then the frail little old gentleman had a go at opening his, with the same result.

They held a despairing consultation and then both of them tried to open the door on his side. The mistral allowed them to get it about half way, and then showed them who was master again.

I thought, in the blazing sunshine, they were probably going to die of heat-stroke. I went over to the small saloon, prized open the door on the old lady's side, put my back against it and helped her out. She very, very nearly blew away. I only just caught her arm in time and then the door slammed, almost amputating the foot of the old gentleman.

Gripping the little old lady with one hand I opened the door again and helped the little old gentleman out. He nearly blew away, too, so that I found myself, in the shrieking wind, standing there with my arms round two tiny little strangers, whose heads came up to my waist.

I was wondering where to put them when the large dominant lady suddenly materialized, and went mad. It had, it seemed, taken her nearly half an hour to get her father and mother into the car outside their residence in Vallauris and now I, a person altogether unknown to her and for reasons which she couldn't possibly guess at, had let them out.

I gave her back her father and mother, making sure she had a firm grip on both of them, and retired to my own car, regretting that the mistral hadn't turned me in on myself, as it had done everyone else.

36
Sign the Shopping Bags Here

'The best we ever did,' he said, even the far-off memory of this great event bringing a gleam to his eye, 'was Douglas Bader. Seven hundred copies, and he had to take a couple of hundred home with him. No time to sign.'

'Oh, yes?'

I uncapped my fountain-pen and as usual it had overflowed. Although I was prepared for it, and had proceeded cautiously with the uncapping, I still got a lot of ink on the palm of my right hand.

'And now,' he said, 'we're hoping to get Sir Francis Chichester. That's really going to be something.'

I tried to remove some of the ink on the underside of my right trouser-leg. One good thing had happened, at least. I was wearing a dark suit.

The manager fingered one of my own books. 'Of course,' he said, 'this is a little bit slender for thirty bob.'

Two ladies in hats, looking well-heeled, had paused in the middle distance, both of them looking at me with a kind of indignant curiosity. One of them whispered something to the other, seeming to shed a brief ray of light into a singularly dark and noisome corner. At any rate, the second one nodded curtly, registering the unpleasant news. Their indignant curiosity became an unmistakable glare of outrage, but at least they were still there.

I found a smile, and presented it to them with a courteous inclination of the head. It had an instantaneous effect. Apparent

235

terror replaced the look of outrage. They hurried away without a backward glance.

'I think,' said my publisher, standing behind me, 'it might be better if you didn't meet their eye.'

For the next five minutes or so both of us looked steadily at the top of the desk. It had been imported from the furniture department of the store, and still carried its price tag: £59 16s. 6d. I worked it out that I would have to autograph, and sell, rather more than 4,500 copies before I could buy the desk, on which perhaps to write another one. About 3,800 more than Douglas Bader. A considerable target at which to aim. To say nothing of Sir Francis Chichester, still to come.

After another couple of minutes of looking at the top of the desk I came to the conclusion that there was nothing whatever I could do in the way of aiming at anything, sitting there in the middle of this West End store, surrounded by hundreds of books, every one of them bearing no less than two photographs of my face on the jacket, and another one on the back. With the addition of my own face, live, looking at the top of the desk, it all added up to an army of me sufficiently intimidating to put the whole Israeli Air Force to flight.

I said to my publisher, 'Perhaps if we went away for a bit. Give them a chance to handle the goods without us here, ravenous for our thirty bobs.'

He advised me to stick it out. 'We'll get the lunch-time rush soon,' he said.

We got one young man with a brown paper parcel. He unwrapped it carefully. 'I bought it in Hatchards,' he said, 'but I should be very much obliged if you could sign it for me.'

I did so. The manager of the book department watched this performance with comparative indifference. As the young man went away, reparcelling his book, the manager said, 'It happens sometimes.' It was just another minor irritation in an autographing session which, unless it was Bader or Chichester, was bound to be alive with them.

Then we did get quite a little rush, though a modest one. It was halted by a volatile lady with a small child, who cried, 'I'm not going to buy your book, but I've always wanted to meet you.' She introduced me to the child, who didn't speak, but the damage had been done. Half-a-dozen people, who'd been hanging round the outskirts, came forward and asked for autographs, offering paper-bags containing their shopping, for me to sign.

Just before the end of the session an assistant-manager had a word of cheer. 'You haven't done *too* badly,' he said. 'I believe Rebecca West once went all the way to Glasgow, and signed one.'

My final score was 25 more than Miss West, and 675 less than Douglas Bader: leaving an open field for Sir Francis.

Bon voyage, mon vieux matelot.

37
Voila – le Golf!

A few holes back I was standing in the cellar of this house in France, moistening the still shining heads of my thirty-seven-year-old Pinsplitters with a nostalgic tear, and was about to stuff them back behind the cupboard when the telephone rang. Tony and Bobby, visitors from England, wondering if I would like to play golf!

We had come to live in France three years ago. Since then the only activity taking place around my golf-bag was that conducted, as already indicated, by the jersey-munching moths. Three years. Did I even remember which hand went on top? How far away the ground was liable to be? What would happen when I launched that immensely long driver at the digestive tablet? A clean miss? One that shot straight up into the air, decapitating an elderly Contessa standing by? I said I'd play – tomorrow. Far too busy today. But of course I really wanted the interval in which to think myself back into playing golf again. Even to find out what would happen if I were to agitate a golf-ball with the putter on the rug in the hall.

What would it feel like? Would there be a clank – or a thud – as the club-face met the pellet? It had become entirely unfamiliar. I might as well have been shaping up to play polo with you-know-who, without being able to ride a horse.

But the muscles were beginning to remember, on their own. I could almost feel the slow-motion swing with the wedge, the hands coming through first, the little nip of turf and the club-head going right through the ball as it floated lazily through the air, whizzing with back-spin, to pitch just beyond the stick and roll back again, uphill.

I took the wedge and half a dozen balls out on to the grass behind the house. Not ideal golfing country. The place was covered with immense olive trees, rather close together. But still room enough to lob a wedge shot or two up to the hedge of cypress trees that guard us from the road.

I laid out the balls in a line, had a waggle with the wedge, felt all right, so I shaped up to the first ball, began the old slow-motion back-swing and suddenly everything went mad. I thought I wasn't going to hit it at all. The club was too short. The ball too small. I took a quick little lurch and caught it with the very edge of the sole. The ball took off as though struck by a full 2-iron, a foot above the ground and going like a bullet. It snored between three olive trees and disappeared through the cypress hedge. A split second later there was a tremendous, metallic crash. I had struck either the front or the rear door of a large white car, which had been passing slowly down the road. Seen indistinctly through the hedge, it looked like a Peugeot 504.

It stopped. Four people – elderly, I thought – got out. Two men and two women. At first their voices were muted, by surprise. I heard the beginning of querulous questions.

'What is it that it is?'

'But what, M'sieu Thierry, has passed itself?'

Then fear – and fury – started to take over.

'One has shot at us!'

'Some imbecile has discharged his fowling-piece.'

'We will carry plaint to the police – to the town hall!'

'One must search for the assassin –'

The assassin stood very still, very thin and upright, squeezing himself into the shape of a ruler behind the sheltering trunk of an olive tree. They went on and on.

'But, see, M'sieu Ferracci, one has almost penetrated your door.'

'It is quite possible that all of us might have lost our lives.'

'Madame Thierry, you have the mien of being very pale.'

'What to do? What to do?'

In the end, after scratching about all round the car, looking for shell cases and irrelevant nonsense like that, they all got in again and the car drove slowly away. Voices floated back. 'To the Préfecture . . . a little wine for Madame Thierry . . . disgusting . . . formidable . . .'

I let them get around the corner. Then I picked up the remaining five balls and went back into the house, practice being over for the day.

That evening, I recovered sufficient enthusiasm for golf to ring up the club, to book three caddies and a starting time for 9.30 a.m. The reverberations of the bang on the side of the Peugeot were beginning to subside, but forming in their place was a clear, mental picture of myself attacking a new ball on the first tee with, alternately, every club in the bag, and with the ground around it becoming ever more hacked and scarred, the ball remaining entirely untouched, perched there insolently on its little red peg.

When we arrived at the club the following morning the car-park looked like a Rolls-Royce *concourse d'élégance*. There were seven of the brutes there, with the ultimate insult to Rolls of French number plates. Three Cadillacs, one with Florida plates, a Mustang and a Lamborghini.

I left my little Simca in the middle of them. It had suffered rather a lot of buffeting even before I bought it, third-hand, and had undergone a number of further modifications under my leadership. Once, indeed, when I left it outside the Carleton Hotel in Cannes the commissionaire – the sniffy one with the dark glasses – actually turned away and raised a white-gloved hand to his nostrils, as though in the presence of something physically offensive.

It didn't look much better here.

. We went into the Secretary's office, to pay our green fees, and came out 28 francs lighter, each. About £2 – a mildly discouraging start to the day. We changed our shoes – we were all extremely nervous. So much so that I suggested a little coffee and brandy to get us going. It was 9.10 a.m. The other men thought it would be unwise. We might miss our starting time.

Far from having three beautiful girl caddies, only to be expected in French golf, we were placed in the care of two Algerian youths, one with a cast in his left eye so pronounced that it made my head swim to look at him. It took them a long, long time to strap one bag on to one trolley, and two on to the other. It looked as if neither of them had ever seen a golf-bag, or, indeed, a trolley, before. They were entirely silent.

We walked out to the first tee and into the middle of what looked like a fashion show for *la vie sportive*. There must have been twenty or more people there, nearly all elderly, and every single one of them dressed to the nines for the game of golf. There were cartridge belts studded with tees, Robin Hood hats, black and white shoes, cashmere cardigans, one outbreak of plus-fours, two Bermuda shorts and golfing jackets and golfing slacks and red and white gloves and God knows what else. *Tout*, in fact, *pour le golf.*

There was also a man shaping up to drive off. About fifty years of age, wearing a Sam Snead straw hat very square on his head, red turtle-necked jersey, red corduroy trousers, yellow gloves and black and white shoes. He was engaged upon some private exercise which, though he was standing up to a golf-ball, seemed to me to have no connection with the game.

Slowly and fairly rhythmically he raised his shoulders up round his ears, and lowered them. Up – down. Up – down. Perhaps six times. The other players watched him intently, trying to learn something from his technique.

He got tired of the shoulder work or, perhaps, had completed that portion of the stroke, for now he became absolutely motion-less, glaring at the ball as though it had savaged him in some way in the past and he was daring it to do it to him again.

At the end of another minute he began to move. He lifted the club very, very slowly into the air until it was approximately vertical, paused for another couple of seconds and then brought it down right on top of the ball with a little cry that sounded like, 'Mimp!' The ball, responding to this pressure like an orange pip squeezed between the fingers, sprang forward perhaps twenty feet, but rather to the left.

The man watched it intently – until it came to rest. Then he walked over to his trolley and put the driver back into the bag, covering the head of it with a little sack that appeared to be made of sealskin or some other furry substance. Two miniature poodles were tied to the bag with tartan leashes. It took him some time to disentangle them, but in the end he got all his affairs in order. He seized the trolley by the handle and started to walk after his ball, twenty feet away and well to the left, rather slowly, as though lost in some private reverie. Beyond all doubt or cavil he was playing by himself. And none of the other golfeurs and golfeuses thought it in the least out of the ordinary!

Tony, Bobby and I just failed to avoid catching one another's eye. We looked away, deeply embarrassed and more nervous than ever.

'Looks,' Bobby said – the strain was evident in his voice – 'as if it's going to be a bit slow today.'

We got off in the end some time after 10.30 a.m., having been standing on the first tee, swishing at bits of grass, for more than an hour, and watching golf the quality of which would not have occurred even in nightmare. The French had obviously taken to the game with enthusiasm, and a profound and ferociously hopeless ignorance of how it should be played.

Neither were the three of us very much better off. It was difficult, in fact, after the contortions, the tribal dancings and the rigid acrobatics we had been watching, to suppose we were on a golf-course at all.

The first hole here is a short one, about 150 yards. A sunken stream runs across the fairway and there is a hedge behind the green. No trouble, really, anywhere, except for a shallow bunker on the right.

I took out my 5-iron, for the first time for three years, and for the first time for three years balanced a new golf-ball on a new peg. I stood up, then, above the ball, and could find no relation of any kind between it and the club in my hand. I simply didn't know what to do with or to either of them.

The thing was to get it over. Rather too quickly back, swing too short, falling forward, slash at it while still time – and off she went, with exactly the same trajectory as the one that had pierced the cypress hedge and caused Madame Thierry to turn so pale. A rasping big iron that whined through the air, passed non-stop six feet above the green and crashed into the hedge with the sound of a giant redwood being felled.

'Good shot,' Tony said in a low voice. 'Just a bit big.' He and Bobby, with extreme care, struck their tee-shots all of fifty yards straight into the sunken stream.

It turned out to be heavily populated, up to and including the shoulder-heaving man with the two poodles, who had been in there for more than an hour. There was a ladies' fourball in there, a male octogenarian foursome, and a couple of mixed singles, all flicking and scratching away with wedges and sandblasters, trying to scoop their ammunition out of the water.

Tony and Bobby joined them. I walked on, up over the green and started rootling in the hedge for my own missile. A moment later something crashed into the foliage immediately beside my head. I heard an accented cry of 'Forrrh!' and turned to see a thick-set man wearing a tartan cap with a woolly bobble on top standing on the other side of the green. He'd obviously succeeded in scooping his pellet out of the water, and now had just had another go at it.

He strode forward briskly, pulling his trolley straight across the putting surface, and came to a halt beside me. '*Bonjour, M'sieu*,' he said, with the greatest amiability, '*vous êtes aussi débutant?*' A beginner? Me? The lad that flattened Billy O'Sullivan in that roaring, thrill-packed finish at Portmarnock in 1949? A debutant. A be*ginner*!'

'*Mais, non*,' I replied shortly. '*J'étais professionel.*'

'*Ah, bon*,' he said. He put out his hand. '*Enchanté de faire votre connaissance.*' We shook hands, standing partly in the hedge. An absolutely absurd way to begin a round of golf, specially when one hasn't played for three years.

We waited for twenty minutes on the next tee until two terribly old ladies got far enough ahead up the fairway, striking tiny little shots with complete concentration. They were accompanied by a female wrestler of about sixty, doing caddying work on the side. Among her other equipment she carried a long pole with a wire basket on the end of it, a device for defeating the stream.

I took out my immensely long driver and had an utterly disordered flash with it and got that supremely revolting shot that almost strikes the left shoe, off the very back of the stick, and rolls at right-angles into the ditch behind you.

The man in the tartan cap said, judicially, to the two ladies he appeared to be playing with, '*Il était anciennement professionel.*'

Both the ladies, with equal appreciation, said '*Ah, bon.*'

And so the long day wore on. The stream, we found, bisected, bitched and bedevilled almost every hole. We were hardly ever out of it. After the ninth hole the cross-eyed Algerian lad took off his shoes and socks and hung them round his neck, to be ready for the next emergency. 'Hulla hulla hulla,' he said, with a fanged grin. It must have been months since he'd had such an amusing day.

We forged our way through the two little bird-like ladies, after borrowing Ghengis Kate's scooper to retrieve our second shots at the eleventh, and for the first time found ourselves with an open course ahead of us.

It all began to come back. A couple of longish clouts off the tee, an iron shot or two that actually drifted rather sweetly from left to right, instead of howling round in the usual semi-circle. The lovely game of golf, all coming back again.

Off the eighteenth tee I got a real, old-fashioned beezer. Nice and late with the hands, a sort of nudge with the right knee and off she whistled, a really big one. Struck the downward slope of the hill and galloped on to hell and gone, up in the region of 300 yards.

When I reached it, right in the middle of the fairway and further than I'd believed possible, the scene was rendered even more pleasant by the sight of two practically edible portions of French crumpet – early twenties, long yellow hair, silk trousers painted on, and animated with it. They were chatting brightly together as they walked across the course towards the club-house. Spectators, by the look of them, and very possibly the soft furnishings of the Lamborghini in the car-park.

I took a 7-iron out of the bag and then looked back to where Tony and Bobby were searching for their rather lesser tee-shots in the bushes on the right. I judged that the girls, if they had any knowledge of the game at all, would be able to see that I'd hit a genuine steamer and was now shaping to crowd a crisp seven up against the flag-stick.

They stopped, a few yards away, and fell silent. I imagined they'd never seen such a giant tee-shot in all their lives, and must now be waiting with keen expectation for this superb athlete's next production.

It was a beauty, fading gently and coming back out of the pitch mark to finish five or six feet from the hole.

I got together rather a good type of modest grin and let them have it. They didn't even look at it. They walked straight past, chatting together again as brightly as before.

One of them said to the other, clasping her lovely hands, '*Mais, Jean-Claude – lui, il est chic chic chic.*'

Her friend agreed. '*Rrrravissant,*' she said, with a tiger-like purr that would have had Jean-Claude, whoever the hell he was, clutching at his collar.

In the end I holed the putt and got this fabulous three in solitude, unapplauded by anyone, as the other two gents had abandoned the hole and walked into the club-house.

I think I'll probably put the clubs back behind the cupboard and leave it at that, going out in this private blaze of glory.

There's an amateur quality about golf in France that rather gets on the wick of us old (nearly) professionals.

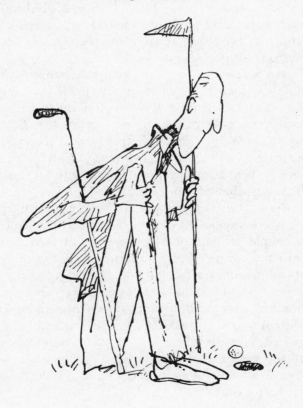

38

Gullible and the Baedeker Kid

As we heard the clunk which indicates either fatal fracture of the wing roots or the safe folding in of the under-carriage the man sitting next to me clicked a stopwatch.

'Eighteen point five secs,' he said, in an official tone, 'with a seventy-two per cent payload.' He relaxed, allowing himself a small chuckle. 'Not bad,' he said. 'But then Doggy Moorehouse is always one for pressing on.'

He spent a few moments polishing the stopwatch with his handkerchief, then lowered it into a small, maroon coloured pouch which he subsequently returned to his waistcoat pocket.

Out of the whole 72% payload – if by that he meant the passengers – it seemed probable that he was the only one who was wearing a waistcoat. A waistcoat, with its slightly old-fashioned ambience, suited him. It went with his thin, National Health glasses, the red, button nose and the gingery, tufty hair.

I'd noticed him briefly before take-off, when the hostess was handing round the boiled sweets, because he'd filled his pockets with a couple of handfuls. He was one of those men, in the middle forties, who preserve both the nature and the looks of an earnest and inventive schoolboy of about eleven.

'Oh, yes,' he said. 'Old Doggy presses on, all right. Clocked two thousand four hundred and twenty-three flying hours. I've been with him to Montreal, Rio, Philadelphia and Caracas. He's not married, you know.'

I had the feeling that quite a lot of indigestible, not to say unrequired, information was being handed out. 'Obviously,' I said, 'he hasn't time.'

My companion turned towards me, efficiently pushing the glasses up on his nose. 'Ah,' he said warmly, 'but that's where you're wrong. There,' he said, nailing it down, 'you're very very wrong indeed. Doggy just doesn't go in for that sort of thing.'

'Even in Caracas?'

For a moment he looked shocked. 'Surely,' he said, 'you must be joking. The stop-over in Caracas is only fifty-eight minutes, and he's only there once every fourth week.'

'I'm sorry.'

'That's all right,' he said comfortably, sitting back. 'It's easy to make a mistake if you're not in possession of all the facts. Would you like to see my log-book?'

I thought I'd been dismissed as someone too light-minded to support even the passive end of a conversation, so that I was fatally taken aback by this unexpected enquiry.

'What sort of log-book?'

It was his turn to be surprised. 'Flight log, of course,' he said. He reached into a livid-yellow airline bag, of a kind I'd never seen before, and brought out a thick, chunky volume bound in grey serviceable linen. 'It's all in here, you know.'

Plain curiosity caused me to reach out my hand. He almost snatched the book away. 'Just a sec, old chap,' he said reprovingly. 'I've got to fill in m'details, don't I, before I forget?'

He selected a Biro pen from a battery of six in one of the pockets of his waistcoat. For the next couple of minutes he filled in various columns with extreme concentration. He put the pen back again. 'There,' he said, 'that's all ticketyboo.' He looked at me suddenly over the top of his glasses. 'Would you like a sweetie?' he said. The idea had just come to him.

'No, thank you.'

He produced a handful and made a careful selection. 'Barley shug,' he said. 'Yum.' He worked on the barley sugar, moistening it and distributing it sufficiently widely in his mouth to permit him to speak. 'Now,' he said. 'Here we go.'

He put the thick book on his lap and opened it at the first page. He began to read, surprisingly loudly, 'May tenth, nineteen hundred and thirty-two, Croydon Airport, destination Paris, advertised time of departure ten-fifteen, actual time of departure

ten–twenty-one, Captain B. Smith, weather fair, ceiling eight
thousand feet, wind nor–nor-west.'

It seemed to go on for ever, but we reached Paris in the end. He
finished his barley sugar at the same time and slotted in another
one. 'That,' he said, around it, 'was Flight Number One. Now,
Flight Number Two. May fourteenth, nineteen hundred and
thirty-two, Paris Le Bourget –'

I had to stop it. 'You mean you've kept a record of every flight
you've ever made?'

'Of course!'

'Are you in the airline business, then?'

'No, no,' he said. 'I'm a journalist. Travel writer. You may
have seen some of my stuff.' Rapidly, he reeled off the names of
seven provincial newspapers, and three technical magazines.

'I'm afraid,' I said, 'I don't often get to read too many of those.'

'No?' he said, interested in the revelation. 'Well, I've got quite
a lot of them here.' He reached into the yellow bag again and
produced a thick bundle of cuttings, of column length. 'This one
might interest you,' he said.

It was headed, 'Colombia's Capital – Booming Bogota.'

'You mean you've been there already!' I exclaimed.

'A couple of months ago.'

'And now you're going to write about it all over again?'

He popped in another sweetie. 'Well,' he said, not in the least
defensively, 'it's a free trip, isn't it?' He chewed in the same
preparatory fashion as before. 'Now,' he said, passing a finger
down the column, 'there are some figures here about Colombian
State Railways that will probably interest you –'

'I'm frightfully sorry,' I said, 'but I've simply got to go to the
lavatory. I'll be back in a tick – a sec – I'll be back.'

I stood in the lavatory for some time, in a state almost of
shock. 'Jesus Christ,' I said to myself. 'I don't believe it.'

The proposition was indeed unbelievable. Here was a marvellous free trip to South America, to Bogota, one of the highest
cities in the world. Tropical heat, Inca remnants, bandits and the
week-end in Cartagena, on the Caribbean, and this man with his
flight log-book and National Health glasses and his limitless
stream of corroding information would be right beside me,
every inch of the way. It simply wasn't fair.

On the way back to my seat I stopped to have a word with Joe. 'Who's this character I've drawn?' I asked him. 'The one who's sitting beside me. The world–wide mine of information.'

'You,' he said, 'have got Mrs Baedeker's Little Boy, and all of us here wish you the very very best of luck.'

Some of the other newspapermen raised their glasses, in solemn toast.

'I'm going to sit here,' I said.

Joe said, very earnestly, 'He'll come and lean against your seat and you'll get it all down the back of your neck. If I were you I'd just face it bravely.'

Mrs Baedeker's Little Boy was glad to see me back. He was even concerned for my welfare. 'If you've got a touch of gyppy tumtum,' he said, 'I've got the very thing for it here. Two per cent opium extract, two and a half per cent magnesium sulphate –'

'I'm all right,' I said. 'I – I've just got rather a lot of reading to do.'

In fact, it was a paperback lump of Harold Robbins, which I'd bought in a hurry at London Airport. To stop Mrs B's L.B. opening his mouth I said, 'Trying to turn it into a film script. Wants a lot of concentration.'

He nodded understandingly. He seemed to be impressed. Perhaps writing for the screen was the only thing in the whole world he didn't know everything about.

Later that evening we prepared to land at Madrid. He took an unusual amount of care with his seat-belt. 'Doggy,' he volunteered, 'doesn't much like this one. You've got your mountains all round the airfield perimeter, you see, rising in places to anything up to – oh – two thousand feet. No, wait. I'll just check that.' He was still audibly checking it, from his log-book, when we made a slightly bumpy landing.

He looked at me, humourously, over the top of his awful glasses. 'See?' he said.

It was a long night, as we flew across the Atlantic to Puerto Rica. During it, I learnt everything I wanted to know about the railway system of Colombia. At one point my companion broke off to ask if he was boring me. 'You see,' he admitted with rueful honesty, 'I'm really a railway man, myself. In fact, I'm hoping

I can get out of flying down to Cartagena. Much rather go by train –'

I had a vision of a rickety old Victorian railway carriage enveloped in sheets of red flame, while bandits poured thousands of rounds of machine-gun fire into the ruins, but it didn't work. It was too good to be true.

In the morning, at Puerto Rica Airport, there was a calypso band and a lot of lovely mulattos and octoroons around, but I got the figures for American aid plus those for Puerto Rican emigration during the past fiscal year.

During the flight over the sparkling Caribbean I had to endure the agony, being the lesser one, of reading Harold Robbins for the second time. The airfield at Caracas, on the coast of Venezuela, seemed to be alive with wild and rapacious dogs, so that unlike everyone else Mrs Baedeker's Little Boy and I sat in the plane, while we digested recent figures for the incidence of rabies in South America, coupled with those for foot and mouth disease.

It was very hot indeed. I sat there beside my companion, listening, screaming silently but with diminishing vitality, 'SHUT UP! GO AWAY! Burst. Explode . . .' He had changed into a shirt covered with brightly coloured bananas purchased not – as one might have supposed – in the tropics, but in Sauchiehall Street, Glasgow. He wanted my assurance – in a sudden parenthesis – that it wasn't a bit too swish. I gave it to him, with all the earnestness at my command. He was relieved. At heart, he explained, he was really a bit of a buccaneer, inclined – in hot countries – to cut a bit of a dash. Sometimes he went just a little too far, but – thank goodness – he realized this fault.

'Know thyself, eh?' he said.

I nodded in sombre agreement. Then we went back to rabies and foot and mouth.

The first two days in Bogota were marvellous. An extraordinary city of concrete skyscrapers, with bulldozers in the rutted streets, and the empty ground floors of the office blocks occupied by whole families of Indians, cooking on camp fires. A city nine thousand feet in the air, with gangs of ferocious bandits alleged to be in the very suburbs. And the best of it was that Mrs Baedeker's Little Boy seemed to be extremely busy with something else. I saw him only in the evenings, dining at a small table by himself, surrounded by piles of books of reference. Once, I caught his eye and he rather gaily raised a thumb in the air. I couldn't imagine what he meant.

When I found out, it was like being sentenced to death. What he'd been doing, for the last two days, was working out the most interesting and varied method of getting from Bogota to Cartagena by train. It hadn't been easy, because the Station Master spoke only Spanish, and all the time-tables were naturally in the same language, but he'd done it in the end.

'The only snag is,' he said, 'we'll have to leave fairly early tomorrow morning – o-five-thirty-four, in fact.' Then he added a reassuring detail. 'But it only takes twenty-four hours.'

I said, slowly and carefully, 'I am not going with you in the train. I am going in the aeroplane.'

He couldn't believe it. 'But you *said*,' he cried repeatedly, 'you *said* you were a railway chap too!' He was outraged, unable to credit such duplicity.

I shouted at him hysterically, 'I hate railways! I can't stand the bloody things. I'm going in the plane, d'you understand? *I'm going in the plane!*'

Without warning of any kind he suddenly said, almost humbly, 'Have you got a sweetie?'

'Of course I haven't got a sweetie!' I bawled. 'Jesus Christ, I've only been here for a couple of days and I don't speak a sodding word of Spanish. How the hell do you think I could have got myself a sweetie?'

'I meant a barley shug,' he said in small voice.

It was a peace offering. He'd capitulated. He was prepared to go in the plane.

I felt sorry for him. 'You didn't pay for those train tickets, I hope?'

'Goodness me, no,' he said, 'I wangled them out of the airline.' Hope surged back again. 'You're sure you won't come in the train?' he said. 'It won't cost you anything and I'm sure you'll find it most interesting. They've got a 1923 Series 2B loco with a four-o-four bogie on the –'

'Stuff it up your jumper!' I shouted at him, almost out of my mind.

A roasting hot trade wind thundered through the open balconies of the hotel in Cartagena. The sea-water pool was bliss. The old city itself was like a film-set, a maze of Moorish alleyways, stately French Empire buildings and everywhere people of every imaginable colour lounging in the heat, chatting in half a dozen languages – the very essence of the Caribbean. Morgan and his pirates were just around the corner – unlike Mrs Baedeker's Little Boy.

Him I saw only once, in the first three days. The buccaneering side of his nature had taken hold, irresistibly in these surroundings. To the banana shirt he had now added a truly enormous, high-crowned, floppy hat, of red and black woven straw. His face was scarcely visible beneath it but as he passed me in the hotel corridor I caught a flash, in the National Health glasses, of the coolest imaginable disdain.

On the last day we went on a conducted tour, with a Spanish interpreter, of the old fortress that guards the harbour. As our guide, in broken English, told us something of its history Mrs Baedeker's Little Boy – a figure of fantasy in his straw hat – lounged about on the outskirts, denying the accuracy of almost every single fact given us by the guide. His voice was no more than a low monotone, but it was interspersed from time to time with a loud and contemptuous clicking of the tongue that had a great effect.

On the topmost pinnacle of the old fort was a new-looking concrete pillbox, with a complicated radio aerial sticking out of its roof. As we came closer we could hear the rapid, metallic stuttering of the Morse Code. I was aware of Mrs Baedeker's Little Boy standing beside me. Ludicrously, he had pushed his vast straw hat to one side, and was listening intently with his right ear.

'Yes,' he said, in his official tone. 'I thought so. The Mauretania – about 180 miles due south of us, making for – Miami.'

He returned the hat to its original position.

I seized the interpreter by the arm. 'Even if it's illegal,' I said, 'go into that hut instantly and ask what that last signal was all about.'

It was all about the Mauretania, 180 miles due south of Cartagena, making for Miami – and no mistake about it.

I rounded on Mrs Baedeker's Little Boy.

'How,' I said, 'did you know that?'

He was surprised. He pushed up his glasses. 'Well,' he said, 'a chap keeps up his Morse, doesn't he?'

Every time he spoke to me, all the way back to London, I said, 'Dit dit dit dah dah dit dot dash bash nit dit dit dah.'

He accepted it with weary resignation, obviously hoping that our paths would not cross again.

39
Fur on the Pope?

She answered the telephone, preoccupied with getting just the right tang of lemon in the osso bucco, and said, 'It's for you. Vaguely American, or something.'

I received the instrument and said, 'Hello'. Nothing much out of the way so far.

Then an imperious, bell-clear voice at the other end said, 'Calling Mr Patrick Campbell from Toronto. Is he available to take the call?'

He wasn't really. Toronto. I didn't know anyone in Toronto. I didn't know anyone in the whole of Canada. I didn't even know anyone who might have gone to Canada and felt impelled to ring me from there all the way to the south of France.

I said, 'This is he – him – speaking. I mean, this is me.' I hesitated, wondering how best to drive the point home. 'I'm him,' I said.

'Hold on,' the imperious female voice said. 'I have a call for you.'

Silence followed of some considerable duration. I had a clear mental picture of thousands of Canadian dollars clicking up, like electric clocks at airports that show only numbers.

A new voice spoke. A deep, comfortable, leisurely voice, a voice entirely at its ease, prepared to take its time.

'Hello, there,' it said, taking what felt like a minute over this simple greeting. 'Is that Mr Patrick Campbell?'

I tried to zip it out as quickly as I could. 'Yep.' I scarcely had time to articulate the 'p'. The clock was whizzing, notching up the dollars.

'My name,' the richly lazy voice said, 'is Richard Lubbock – Canadian Broadcasting Corporation. What kind of day have you had?'

'Not a lot doing. Verhotsun.'

The voice had a 150 dollar chuckle. 'We've got a blizzard here. Snowing all day. You're in luck.'

It was agony. I said, 'WhatcanIdoforyoumisterLubbock?'

Another 150 dollar laugh. 'Now, that's a good question. Would you like to talk to us about Henry Ford's side-whiskers?'

Holy God! Henry Ford's side-whiskers. All the way from Toronto! But at least I knew what it was about. I'd written a column about Henry Ford's side-whiskers the previous Sunday. It seemed to have got as far as Canada.

'IsupposeIcould.'

The leisurely Mr Lubbock helped himself to a 1,000 dollars worth of explanation. A radio show. I would be interviewed by a Mr William Ronald, by telephone. The interchange tape-recorded, for subsequent dissemination to the population of Canada. On the subject of Henry Ford's side-whiskers. Mr Lubbock had already talked to my agent in London. Another call!

I said, 'Howmuch?'

'We rich Canadians,' Mr Lubbock said, 'can let you have fifty dollars.'

'Yep.'

'Great,' said Mr Lubbock. 'I'll call you back when I've fixed the time.'

Call me back! Again!

'Ri'. Bye.'

About an hour later I had to break my vigil by the telephone to go to the convenience. Madame took the opportunity to ring a friend of hers. In a moment they were slotted into a chat that promised to have no fixed duration. I said, 'TheCanadianBroad-casting Corporationisringingbackatanymoment.' They terminated, reluctantly. Shortly afterwards the Canadian Broadcasting Corporation called again, to fix the time for the interview at 9.30 the following evening.

Next day I rose high in the air every time the telephone rang, as it did constantly. When it did so at 9.35 that night I was in a partial coma, as we tend to go to bed in this quiet countryside round about 8.30.

I have no memory of the first part of the interview, except that every time I finished speaking there was a long silence at the other end, either because they were waiting to make sure I'd finished or were stunned by the banality of my observations. I do, however, remember a question towards the end. Mr William Ronald said, 'Do you think the Pope ought to grow side-whiskers?'

Almost out of my mind I thought of saying, 'In the increasingly likely event of his marriage it might give his face a suitably secular look,' and then I remembered the Roman Catholic element in Quebec.

I said, 'I'm a Protestant, so I don't think I ought to talk about the Pope.'

That was about the end of it. Not a lot, really, for 250,000 dollars worth of telephone call.

40

A Stallion Sneeze

I had written:

'At eight o'clock on Sunday morning King's Road in Chelsea is a desolate waste of litter – old newspapers, ice cream cartons, torn shopping bags, cigarette ends by the million –'

Then I got this tremendous sneeze.

It was one of those sneezes the preliminaries of which seem to go on for ever. At one moment I was sitting there writing about litter in Chelsea and at the next I was in the grip of a cosmic force so powerful that without straining itself in any way it began to change my whole physical shape. I felt like putty being moulded by a huge glazier.

First, this giant force got to work upon my jaws and mouth, pressing out and hardening this delicate machinery until with the teeth bared and the upper lip drawn back I must have looked like Silver, the mad white stallion, about to do something unpleasant.

At the same time this frightful pressure squeezed my eyes shut and then shoved them along the Eustachian tubes into my ears, where they flung themselves against the drums, trying to get out.

This displacement of the eyes led almost immediately to a change in the shape of the top of my head. It began to rise into a point, with the subsidiary effect of drawing me right up into the top left-hand corner of my high-backed chair, so that it seemed that I retained a grip upon the floor only with a single toe.

For some time I held this pose, levitating, teeth bared, lips curled, nostrils flaring, eyes gone, ears bursting and nails dug deep into the upholstery. Then everything blew up.

The actual explosion was preceded by a wild cry of mindless terror – a long drawn out yell sounding something like 'AAAAAANGH' – and then it burst.

I was surprised by the damage, except of course that the circumstances were rather special.

Just before I'd written the words about the litter in King's Road I'd slipped half a large tomato, peppered and salted, into my mouth, where it joined a partially chumbled biscotte – one of those roasted bread slices which the French do so well. Into this mixture I then injected a mouthful – or as much of a mouthful as possible – of black coffee.

It was a tight fit but it would have been a viable proposition if it hadn't been for the sneeze.

The whole business – typing with the mouth bursting with breakfast – came from being suddenly seized with an idea, after being dazzled for too long by the glare of an empty page. I felt I needed this last mouthful of breakfast, to sustain me, while at the same time rattling out the first sentence, before it got away.

Anyway, it burst.

For a moment I thought I'd blown the front of my face off. There was this awful feeling of everything coming away. I almost got my handkerchief to the site of the explosion and then there came another one, louder, wilder, infinitely more destructive than the first.

I lay back in the chair, spent, drained of everything, waiting for the third eruption – the one which would deprive me of my backbone, shooting it out through my nose in a spray of tinkling vertebrae which would probably smash the window on the other side of the room.

It turned out that we'd finished. These two major explosions, one even bigger than the other, were to be our portion for the day.

But at what a cost.

The extremely high muzzle velocity of the breakfast had enabled it to reach and to penetrate every corner and crevice of the room. It had got to the bookshelf and to the Modigliani reproduction above it. It was on the door, the ceiling and all four walls. It was in the typewriter. It had even struck a portrait of me painted by an aunt of mine in 1954, where it had obliterated one eye. The other one stared back at me in outrage.

I sat there, huddled in my chair, tomatoed, thinking what bad luck it all was. I was thinking that if Tolstoy had got one of those we wouldn't have had *War and Peace*. A couple of those for Dickens would have meant curtains for both Dombey and his son.

I set to to clean up, sorry for the world that now would never hear about the surprising amount of litter in King's Road at eight o'clock on a Sunday morning.

41

Texture Men at Work

His entrance was very good indeed – smooth and practised, the man who knows his local and who is well-known in it.

He walked straight up to the bar and sat on the third stool from the left. I guessed that he always used this one, perhaps because it was opposite the till and he liked, purely for curiosity's sake, to keep an eye on the take.

'Usual,' he said to the landlord, 'and the same for my friend here. How's it going then, Tom?'

'Not bad, squire. The wife's gone up north with the dogs. Two nice pints.'

I didn't want a nice pint but accepted it rather than break the flow.

'While the cat's away, eh?'

The landlord chuckled, because he had to. 'That's it, squire. But not a word to Bessie –' If they'd been standing side by side they'd have nudged one another in the ribs.

'No names, eh, Tom, no pack drill?'

'You said it, squire.'

The landlord passed a cloth over the immaculate bar and moved away.

My friend let him get well away. Then he cast a derisive eye over the furnishings of the place. They weren't half bad. Simple but elegant tables and chairs, a pleasantly unobtrusive wallpaper and surprisingly attractive tweedy upholstery on the banquettes around the walls. Even the lighting was agreeable. The brewers had obviously employed someone with taste, who knew his job.

'They've absolutely ruined it, of course,' my friend said. He leant forward, confidingly. 'I only come here because it's handy. Otherwise I wouldn't touch it with a barge-pole.' He drank deeply. 'Absolutely bitched it up,' he said.

I was surprised. His geniality with the landlord was, of course, only a matter of habit, but it was strange that he thought the place had been ruined.

'You used to know it before, then?' I said.

Something in my voice caused him to be truthful. 'I never actually came in,' he said, 'but I passed it by many a time. It looked damn cosy from the outside. Just my sort of pub. Not all this modern fiddle-faddle.' He went on, with the confidence of a man who knows he's on a safe wicket, to denounce modern fiddle-faddle in the furnishing of public houses. I didn't listen, because I had known the pub before. While it did look comparatively cosy, in the old days, from the outside, inside it had been a low-grade sewer.

The first evening I went in there was a north-east wind howling down the street, carrying with it a good deal of sleet. I was cold and tired, after working all day on a television script in a house round the corner, and had suddenly thought of a large whisky with ginger wine as an antidote to the horrors of the evening.

I wrenched open the door of the saloon bar, hurrying to get in from the rain, and immediately ran into something that felt and smelled like an unusually heavy shroud. It turned out to be a dank, serge curtain, the colour of old blood, suspended from the ceiling by a thick brass rod.

After a short struggle I managed to part it, using a finger and a thumb, and walked into the dingiest bar I'd ever seen in my life.

The walls were a dirty yellow, shading into a dark dung colour lower down. The bar itself was short, but divided into a number of partitions, like loose boxes. The thick glass in these partitions had never been cleaned, and were now almost entirely opaque.

The place was lit by three bulbs hanging on long flexes from the ceiling. Two of them had pink paper shades. The other one was bare but it didn't matter, because it was out.

At first I thought I was alone in this fearful hole, until I saw at the far end of an L-shaped bit – obviously the public bar – the dim figure of an old man bowed over a bottle of brown ale.

He became aware of me at the same time, and showed a momentary animation. 'Game a darts, guv?' he said hopefully.

I said I was sorry, but I had no time.

'Wanter shaht then,' he said, and resumed his silent reverie.

I didn't feel like shouting, nor did I know what to shout, so after a moment I rapped a coin fairly loudly on the counter. Nothing happened. Another curtain the colour of old blood hung in front of what was probably a door leading to the landlord's living quarters, but there was no trace of life behind it.

Perhaps a minute went by and then the old man in the public bar raised his head. 'Shop!' he bawled hoarsely. Then he added, equally loudly and hoarsely, 'Nellie!'

'Wanter shaht,' he advised me, and fell silent again.

Some time later I became aware of a curious series of noises coming from behind the second curtain. There was the clump of a stick, but it was intermittent, irregular. There was also a spasmodic bumping sound as though a trunk were slithering slowly down the stairs of its own accord. I waited in some suspense for the curtain to be parted – by I knew not what.

The bumping and clumping came nearer, and then stopped. They were supplanted by a low groan. Then the curtain was parted and a large and stately old lady came through it, leaning heavily on a kind of crutch.

At first I thought her whole face was bright, pillar-box red – the symptom, perhaps, of some unspeakable malady – and then I saw that it was rouge, covering the whole of both cheeks.

She said nothing. With some difficulty she lowered herself on to a sawn-off stool behind the bar, settled down and then directed upon me the most unearthly smile I had ever seen. Her lips were painted a kind of purplish red, an altogether different colour to the rouge on her cheeks. Her eyes glittered, but without focus. I then saw that the lady was drunk. Probably gin, as an antidote to the agonies of arthritis.

I seemed to have been in this nightmare public-house for ever, but now there was no drawing back.

'Good evening,' I said. 'May I have a large whisky and some ginger wine? Plain water,' I added, after a moment.

It had no effect upon her of any kind. She continued to sit on the stool. The variegated red face went on beaming at me.

The old man in the public bar decided again to be helpful. 'Screws gotter,' he said, then added in a kindly way, 'Pore ole Nell.' Suddenly, he shouted, 'Fraid!' followed a moment later by, 'Shop!' He relapsed once more. He seemed to have made little impression on his glass of brown ale.

This time fully five minutes appeared to go by before the curtain was agitated again. When it did move it moved almost imperceptibly and then, almost as though he'd walked through it, a little old man with a pale bald head was standing in front of it. He wore a dark waistcoat over a tattered grey cardigan. On his face was a look of surprised apprehension, as though he'd been summoned without warning, from bed, to take charge of a fatal accident.

'Good evening,' I said. 'I'm sorry to disturb you, but could I have a large whisky with some ginger wine – and plain water?'

He looked at me in astonishment for quite a while. His expression now suggested that something outlandish, like an ostrich, had walked into his pub and had started asking, in what might be the English language, for a drink.

'Just the whisky would do,' I said, trying to break it up a bit, 'if you haven't got the ginger wine.'

The ostrich or whatever it was, had spoken again, further deepening the mystery.

He turned his astonished gaze upon poor old Nell, but she had no suggestions to offer. He decided upon action. He left me standing in the saloon bar and shuffled slowly into the public. 'Wanta nuvver, Charlie?' he asked the old man.

'Not yet, Fraid,' the old man said. He came to the conclusion that a more elaborate explanation was necessary. 'Aven't finished one wot I got,' he said, pointing to it.

Fraid (Fred?) hung around a bit longer, waiting perhaps for Charlie to finish his drink, but Charlie showed no sign of wishing even to pick it up.

Fraid, baffled and defeated, rearranged some dirty glasses on the counter, and then appeared to steel himself for the ordeal.

Looking at the ground, so that perhaps the ostrich-like thing wouldn't come at him too quickly, he came back into the saloon, stood in front of me and suddenly risked all on one single, desperate throw.

'Wotcha want, then, guv?' he said, holding on to the bar for support.

'Whisky,' I said. 'And water.'

The scarlet faced old lady suddenly came to life. 'Drop of gin for me, dear,' she said. The long period of silence preceding this request seemed to have done her good. 'Shockin' wevver for this time of year,' she observed, with quite a measure of old-world politeness.

Fraid had poured my drink – a small one – into a very small glass and was about to put it on the counter in front of me when the curtain guarding the street door was flung back so suddenly that the rings actually ran on the corroded brass rail. A short, vital young man stood in the entrance, with his hands on his hips, looking silently round the room with a pair of very, very cold grey eyes. He wore a horsey-looking whipcord suit that was almost champagne coloured, and chukka boots of the same shade.

With a certain apprehension I moved out of sight behind one of the partitions. This was a fairly dangerous youth, well known around town at the time.

At the next moment he was in the booth beside me, although I might just as well have been invisible. He greeted Fraid and Nellie with profoundly serious politeness.

'Edwin,' he said. 'And Cecilia! How sweetly pretty you look tonight, my dear.'

I was surprised by the reaction of the two old things. Instead of being terrified, as they should have been, both of them twinkled and simpered as though being called Edwin and Cecilia were the greatest compliment in the world. They murmured inarticulate but delighted little greetings and all at once then the whole saloon bar seemed to be full of rakish and indolent young men. There were a few girls with them, but they were drab and dowdy in the extreme.

This, of course, was in the days prior to Carnaby Street and the mini-skirt, so that the girls were dressed in old mackintoshes and tattered anoraks that had very probably been cast off by their escorts. Their hair was indescribably lank and uncared for and their personalities seemed to be in exactly the same shape.

The men, who were much better dressed, ignored them

altogether. With glasses in their hands they leant languidly against the greasy walls of the saloon bar, talking in loud aristocratic voices about hunt balls and polo and house parties in the country. I recognized, having seen their photographs in magazines, a young Earl and a couple of lordlets. It was impossible to imagine what they thought they were doing in these revolting surroundings yet they seemed to be well accustomed to them, almost as though this awful public house was their regular local.

It made me uneasy. Some sort of tribal rite seemed to be taking place, one that was gradually mounting in ecstasy, whatever the nature of the ecstasy might be. Certainly, they were becoming more and more polite to Edwin and Cecilia. Even Cecilia – or Nellie, as she had been in the good old days – had so far forgotten her disabilities that she was pouring an occasional drink and trying to deal with the change, while Edwin was unmistakably beside himself. The pale little bald head was flushed bright pink as he bustled about behind the bar, saying, 'There's yours, Mr Earl – and that's yours, Sir Lord –'

The young aristocrats received their drinks and these tributes with grave and perfect courtesy, playing – I became more and more certain – some deadly and derisive game.

One of the young Sir Lords, receiving a drink from Edwin, suddenly stretched out his hand and very delicately, between finger and thumb, felt the edge of the old man's second waistcoat.

'Quite fabulous, Edwin,' he said. 'How did you ever get it so – so –' He rubbed his finger and thumb together in the air, sensuously, apparently at a loss to describe sufficiently accurately the sensation presented to him by Edwin's waistcoat.

The old man shuffled his feet a bit, delighted that he'd been singled out for this special attention. 'Just an ole weskit, Your Lord,' he mumbled. 'Gotta keep aht the chill, y'know.'

'And to keep it in, too, Edwin,' said the young man gravely.

'That's it, Sir Lord,' said Edwin, and chuckled inanely.

It was the most cruel persecution of the poor old thing, I thought, and made all the more cruel by the fact that he didn't even know he was being sent up.

The young man turned his attention to Cecilia, who was

lowering her fourth or fifth gin since the beginning of the invasion.

'Damme,' he said, 'but I do swear, dear lady, that you grow more handsome by the hour.'

Cecilia goggled at him, with her sad red face and the glittering, vacant eye. Then she squirmed a little, with pleasure, and tried to nudge the young man across the bar. He, however, had withdrawn a little and was clicking an impatient finger.

'Caroline!' he called imperiously, 'my poor drab – come here.'

Caroline slouched up, wearing a dreadfully stained battledress jacket, with her thumb hooked into half a tankard of bitter.

'Regard Cecilia,' said the young man tenderly. 'Observe the subtlety of her maquillage. See what that so skilful touch of rouge does to bring up the colour of her eyes. Why cannot you, unhappy slattern, make some similar experiment upon your own unfortunate dial.'

Caroline looked at him briefly. 'Down, Rover,' she said, in the accents of Roedean, and moved away.

I'd had enough – enough of the squalor of the place, of the outrageously condescending persecution of poor old Nellie and Fred and most of all of the feeling that something horrible was going on that I didn't understand. I began to sidle out of my corner of the booth when something happened so quickly that for a moment I didn't take it in.

The curtain leading to the street had been pulled back. A young man stood there wearing round, metal-rimmed glasses and a neat blue suit. I think he even had a grey trilby hat, but suddenly the glasses and the hat were obliterated by a cascade of beer that struck him full in the face. For a second it seemed that the beer had simply come out of the air and then I saw that the tankard in the hand of the fairly dangerous young man in the whipcord suit was empty, when it had been full a moment before. Scarcely without turning round he had flung a whole pint of beer clean across the room, to catch the new arrival right between the eyes. The unfortunate young man disappeared, without saying a single word, back into the night.

The one in the whipcord suit looked at me with his expressionless cold grey eyes. 'Dreadful little chap,' he said levelly, though I could see that he was breathing quickly, excited by the action.

'That wretched, smooth suit,' he said. 'And the hat is *new*.' There was an extraordinary malevolence behind this innocent word. 'You see,' he said to me, and then paused, looking for the right name, 'You see – Marmaduke – we're texture men. That's why we come here. We like it greasy, thick, nubbly, unwholesome – like the unspeakable cardigan worn by the loathsome little landlord, like, indeed, Caroline's fabulously fusty battledress. Now, Marmaduke,' he said, 'is there anything I can do for you . . . ?'

'Not at the moment, thank you,' I said. I happened to be wearing a suit fairly smooth to the touch. 'Good-bye,' I said, and made for the door. As I left I seemed to hear a faint voice from far away. 'Game a darts, guv?' It was the old man in the public bar, quite unmoved by all that had gone before.

Outside the sleet had turned to hail. It felt delightful on my face.

'Well, as the man said – a bird never flew on one wing. Let's have the same again, Tom. My friend here will pay.'

I came to to find I was still sitting in this charming little pub, with the tasteful furnishings and the tweedy upholstery on the banquettes around the walls. It was impossible to imagine that it was the same place in which poor Edwin and Cecilia had been tormented, in which the old man had waited for ever for a game of darts and in which the unfortunate new arrival had had beer flung in his face because he was wearing a new hat.

'Absolutely ruined,' my friend said, probably for the tenth time, but now having reached a conclusion.

'Not absolutely,' I said. 'I rather like that nubbly upholstery. You see,' I told him, 'myself, I'm a kind of texture man.'

42

Little Kiss and Dr Merlin

Many of us have been manipulated in our time.

I don't mean manipulated in the sense of being taken for a ride by evil financiers, or used for their own ends by scheming women. I mean worked upon by other people's hands, so that we may be relieved – if only for the moment – of all those knots, nodules, lesions, adhesions, compactions, infractions, tensions and just plain agonies of the bones and the muscles and all the other working parts – some of them only just – that seem to afflict so many of us during the whole of our brave little lives.

Much mystery is attached to manipulation, be it massage or the one where the operative takes your head between his mighty hands and screws your neck so that you're looking over your left shoulder blade at one moment and peering dizzily over the right a second later.

The mystery lies in the fact that the manipulator or masseur who takes over from the last one is always absolutely certain that his predecessor has got it all wrong, and that instead of working upon what this dangerous incompetent considered to be an impacted fibula tibula he should have been kneading away, or wrenching at, your misplaced ursus major.

For instance, I once had a man who put me into a plaster-of-paris barrel, on the grounds that only total immobilization of the spine would save me, within weeks, from a lifetime in a bathchair. To save his good suit he put on a rubber apron that covered him from the neck to the ground, preparatory to covering me and the walls of our bedroom with plaster-of-paris. Within weeks I was not in a bathchair but in this barrel, which had become so loose that I had to hold up the lower edges of it whilst taking the shortest of promenades.

One day I stepped out of it and bent, for some medical reason, double, went to call upon the most marvellous old man around the corner who had the most wonderful hands. (Thus do we speak of our saviours.)

I told him about the barrel and he said, 'That must have kept you warm during the winter, but it wouldn't have done anything else.'

He then tied my arms together in a clove-hitch, sheepshanked my legs, bore down upon me with the weight of an elephant, grunted, wrenched, all the knots flew apart and I stood upright for the first time in a month. He advised me to play thirty-six holes of golf at once and if I found myself in pain at the end of it to play thirty-six more the following day. The treatment worked perfectly.

Some years later I bent down to pick up a pin, for luck, and felt that tiny, piercing, split-second tweaking of some nerve or other that means the back has 'gone out' again. Bent double once more, and this time driven to a borrowed walking-stick to get round to the premises of a fully qualified bone-man who had performed absolute miracles upon several friends. The previous wonderful old man had died; from over-exertion.

The new man had a lot of X-ray pictures taken, found some degenerative changes in, I think, the osteophytical apophy-sealactic vertebrae, offered to mend them with the knife, accepted my refusal with good humour and gave me a short course of massage which enabled me at least to get rid of the walking-stick.

In the following years I let my back go in and out as it liked, preferring not to clutter it with too many divergent diagnoses and treatments, until suddenly, the other day, I got it in the neck.

Back well in but the neck absolutely rigid, revealing itself to my tentative fingers to be a mass of knots and nodules and lesions and adhesions as iron-hard as the rivets in a battleship. Also, any attempt to turn it produced a sound like gravel being decanted from a lorry.

It was all I could do to get to the airport to meet our two dear friends from Bangkok, mother and daughter, both of them exquisite, tiny Thai-size. As we drove home up the hill I felt two

269

minute Thai hands on the back of my neck, exploring like feathers. I looked in the driving-mirror. It was the daughter, whose name in English means – so lovely I can barely bear to write it down – Little Kiss. Little Kiss nodded back and wriggled her super-slender fingers, seeming to promise super-massage to come.

It came, three times a day for the next five days, miniscule, probing fingers, searching out every nodule, soothing every burning knot, on and on, until I dissolved into a state of total Buddhist bliss.

On the day before they left, after swimming, Little Kiss suggested I lie face-down beside the pool. A moment later I felt tiny, searching feet squirming up and down my apophysealactic vertebrae. Little Kiss, going for a walk from coccyx to neck and back again and O Nirvana – O Arcadia – O Simple Ecstasy – as she did so she was nonchalantly nibbling at a peach. Match that against a plaster barrel!

For some time after that I – unlike Little Kiss – seemed to be walking on air, almost upright, almost dancing indeed at the relief from the grindings in the back that are built into the human frame by the convention that compels us to hobble about on our back legs rather than spring around on all-fours until the day came – the inevitable day – when everything got much worse.

It was obvious that Little Kiss's foot and finger fairy treatment could be blamed in no way for this relapse – that kind of thing can only do good – but on the other hand Little Kiss was home in Bangkok and I was in agony, with the additional and very serious symptom of a rigidity of both elbows which meant that either or both of them could be raised only by gritting the teeth, with a lot of splashing of refreshment to follow.

It was this emergency that led me to take the whole lot to Dr Merlin, who had been highly recommended by a friend. That, of course, is not his real name, but if ever there was a magic medico it is he, built like a rock at the age of eighty-five, with hands like a pair of pliers if he finds pressure of that kind to be a necessity, although as an acupuncturist he really works with short steel pins.

I told Dr Merlin first about the red-hot rocks that had taken the place of muscles in my right shoulder and neck. He gave me a touch of the pliers on the *left* hand side. I rose vertically from the chair with a cry which rattled the windows. As though kneading dough he began to work swiftly on the rocks on both sides, sticking in pins, imperceptibly, as he ground away. Within a minute or two the rocks had become as soft and supple as they must have been when I was only fwee!

'Now lie down on the couch,' said Dr Merlin. 'You've obviously got long legs.'

With my head and shoulders all lovely and light and airy I nonetheless stiffened. I thought he was going to shorten my legs so that I'd come out as a man of about five feet two.

But he had said, 'You've obviously got a longer leg,' and I had. My left leg – a malaise well known to the magician – was exactly two inches longer than the right one. Some more pummelling, pounding and pricking and, as swiftly as the rock-reduction, both my legs were the same length.

'Stand up,' said Dr Merlin. I did so. He said, 'That's nice,' and pointed out that my shoulders were now at the same level.

I told him I had been sure for thirty years that my right shoulder had dropped through a surfeit of slashing at golf balls in heavy rough, a deformity noticeable in even professional golfers. 'Your pelvis has been canted,' said Dr Merlin, 'not your shoulder. Lie down again.'

He armed himself with a small wooden bowl filled with what looked like rather dirty cottonwool. He set it alight. It smoked thinly. He passed it up and down my back, releasing muscles that had felt like wire netting for years. I asked him the name of this curious instrument. 'It's nothing,' said Dr Merlin. 'Just burning wormwood. I don't know how it works, but it does.'

He showed me another trick, holding in his right hand a gold watch on a thin chain. With his hand immovable, the watch began to swing violently backwards and forwards. In his left hand it hung dead. I tried it myself. In my right hand it did nothing. In my left it swung very gently. 'It's the electricity in you that repels the gold,' said Dr Merlin.

I had four days of this miracle treatment and came out of it standing dead straight, very nearly pain free, and feeling myself to be seven feet in height. Said Dr Merlin, 'It will take you a little time to grow into your new shape.'

The technicalities of acupuncture, involving Yin, Yang and meridians, are beyond me.

I only know that it works.

If only Little Kiss were here and she was not only a walking, peach-nibbling masseuse but also a needle-sticker into the bargain – a little kiss? – life would be a veritable pre-taste of Paradise.